THE
PREY OF
GODS

THE PREY OF GODS

NICKY DRAYDEN

HARPER Voyager

An Imprint of HarperCollinsPublishers

THE PREY OF GODS. Copyright © 2017 by Nicky Drayden. All rights reserved. Printed in the United States of America. No part of this book may be used or reproduced in any manner whatsoever without written permission except in the case of brief quotations embodied in critical articles and reviews. For information, address HarperCollins Publishers, 195 Broadway, New York, NY 10007.

HarperCollins books may be purchased for educational, business, or sales promotional use. For information, please email the Special Markets Department at SPsales@harpercollins.com.

Harper Voyager and design are trademarks of HarperCollins Publishers LLC.

FIRST EDITION

Designed by Paula Russell Szafranski

Library of Congress Cataloging-in-Publication Data has been applied for.

ISBN 978-0-06-249303-3

17 18 19 20 21   LSC   10 9 8 7 6 5 4 3 2 1

To my wonderful parents, Bill and Pat,
for giving me a loving space
to stretch my wings
and fly

CONTENTS

THE
PREY OF
GODS

Part I

Chapter 1

MUZI

His birth certificate reads Muzikayise McCarthy, but nobody calls him that except his grandfather and anyone looking for a busted lip. Though right now, you could curse his name a million times, and he wouldn't hear you.

He's too busy mourning the fate of his dick.

It's not that he's overly sentimental about his foreskin. It'd be nice not to be so self-conscious in the locker room at Clarendon Academy, since all the guys on his rugby team have parents who are living in this century and had the decency to do the big snip right after birth. That's Papa Fuzz for you, hanging on to age-old Xhosa traditions tooth and nail, never mind that Muzi's three-quarters Irish and could pass for white on an overcast day like today. But Papa Fuzz and Mama Belle had all girls, and as the firstborn grandson, Muzi's been the object of Papa Fuzz's living legacy since the day he popped out of his mother's womb.

And now, the neighbors can't be happy about Papa Fuzz slow-roasting an entire goat out in the front lawn. The smell of cooking flesh goes on for blocks, and it's enough to make Muzi want to vomit. Then again, he's already been a nauseated mess worrying over the fate of his manhood these past few weeks. He swallows back the urge and frowns at the charcoal pit that has to be some sort of fire hazard, especially with the dead fronds from the neighbor's palm tree hanging so seductively close. But every time anyone from the Richmond Hill Civic Committee says anything to Papa Fuzz, he'll start ranting about how important it is to protect the practices of his ancestors, and that's an argument that nobody's about to win.

"Come here, son. Let me show you something," Papa Fuzz calls from across the yard, beckoning Muzi with a slender finger. Sweat glistens against Papa Fuzz's wrinkled brown skin. He's worked hard to make this weekend perfect.

Muzi leaves the comfort of his shaded porch and ambles over with both hands shoved deep into his pockets. He's having second thoughts.

And third thoughts.

And fourth.

But it's too late to call the party off. His aunt Lindi and cousins are already driving down from Joburg, and four dozen of Mama's to-die-for deviled eggs are crammed into the fridge, along with enough potato salad to feed the entire South African Army . . . well, obviously not including the robot infantries.

"Gotta keep her moist," Papa Fuzz instructs as Muzi approaches, giving the baster bulb a little squeeze. Melted herb butter squirts out, rolls over the goat's hindquarters, and sizzles as it hits the coals of the pit. A tacky plume of garlic-scented smoke wafts right into Muzi's face. "That's the secret. A good goat you can't leave unattended, not even a few minutes. It's a labor of love, but people will be talking about this nanny for years to come."

Muzi nods and stifles a cough. Papa Fuzz hands him the baster, then points Muzi at the goat. Muzi's too drained to start up another argument. It's pointless since Papa Fuzz can't even grasp the idea of being a vegetarian.

Besides, it's sort of comforting knowing he's not the only meat being cut up this weekend.

"You know I've invited Renée." Papa Fuzz nudges Muzi in the ribs. "I've seen the way she makes eyes at you. Such a pretty girl."

"Great," Muzi mumbles. Why not just invite all of Port Elizabeth while he's at it?

"It's nothing to be embarrassed about, Muzikayise. You'll be a man soon, and that's something you should be proud of. Sing it from the rooftop!" Papa Fuzz raises his fist into the air and yells something in Xhosa, of which Muzi can make out the words *chop* and *axe*, enough for him to get the gist of this ancestral chant. He cringes.

His alpha bot chimes like church bells being played by a certified maniac. Muzi smiles at the hectic blare of the ringtone. It's Elkin calling. A distraction is just what Muzi needs right now.

"Sorry, Papa Fuzakele, but I've gotta take this." Muzi hands the baster back to his grandfather, taps his alphie on its sleek, domed head, then they both scamper back toward the house before Papa Fuzz can object.

The alphie's screen blinks a couple times as encryption protocols are exchanged, then Elkin appears among the backdrop of limited edition rugby union posters, some of them even signed. He's at home in his room, eyes glazed over from a lazy Saturday afternoon smoking dagga and grazing on junk food.

"Hey, bru. Howzit hanging?" Elkin says with a smooth grin. He scratches his nose, then rubs his hand over cropped golden-blond hair. A hopelessly permanent tan line runs across his forehead from where his rugby scrum cap sits.

"That's not funny," Muzi mopes.

"Sorry, didn't mean to come off like a prick."

"Elkin, is there something you want?"

"Come over. I'm bored."

"I'm not smoking dagga with you. Not today."

"Not dagga. I've got something new. This stuff is prime!" Elkin extends his arm and stares at it like it's the first time he's ever seen it. He cackles—yes, actually cackles—then pulls his alphie up so close that the camera only captures his gray eyes and most of his crooked nose. "Seriously, bru, they could cut your whole dick off tonight and you wouldn't give a rat's puckered ass."

"Seriously?" Muzi has to admit the offer sounds tempting, better than watching a goat turn on a spit for the next few hours.

"Check this. I think I'm turning into a . . . a fucking purpose, man."

"A purpose?"

Elkin leans back and flaps his arms. "Ja, you know. With a bottlenose and fins. Like a dolphin."

"A *porpoise,* you mean?"

"Damn it, Muzi. Stop correcting me and get your quarter Xhosa ass over here."

THEY BUMP FISTS when Muzi arrives, and their alphies bump heads, like a pair of shiny black footballs with spindly, meter-long spider legs. They chirp back and forth like they're happy to see each other, but it's just the exchange of data, ones and zeros—basic information that could prove useful to their respective masters.

"Look at them. They missed each other," says Muzi.

Elkin frowns and kicks his alphie in its head. It whimpers and retreats to its dock in the corner. "Piece of shit," Elkin mutters.

Muzi's alphie goes to the corner, too, navigating around piles of dirty cutoffs and pit-stained practice jerseys. The bot settles, retracting its legs into its base. Muzi joins them, pressing his thumb on the port cover on his alphie's underside. It slides out of the way, revealing a tangled Dobi-12 wire, which he unreels and connects to the input port on Elkin's alphie. Direct interface is so much more efficient and secure, swapping all sorts of juicy tidbits, at least those not password protected. And Elkin doesn't even seem to know the meaning of the word.

"You shouldn't treat it so rough," Muzi says when he's done. He pats both alphies on their domes.

"I've got a five-year warranty." Elkin rummages through the dresser where he keeps his stash, rolled up tight in a pair of plaid boxers. He pulls out two vials of indigo powder and shoves one into Muzi's palm. "Now stop messing with those things. You're killing my buzz."

"What is it?" Muzi asks. He plops down on the foot of the bed, loosens the laces on his tackies, and kicks them off.

"Godsend, my cousin calls it. He gave me some samples— wants me to spread the word, build up some hype. Says it's gonna drop on the streets in a couple weeks."

Muzi turns the vial over, his thumb rubbing over the smooth glass, and then bites his lip. He's not so excited about being a guinea pig, but Elkin's cousin Rife has always come through for them, giving them loads of free dagga, the good stuff, not that crap the guys on campus deal. Rife supplies to the stars—all those celebrities who go through the revolving door of rehab faster than even the trashy gossip rags can keep up with—including brood band drummer Leon Duffy, former premier Blile Nkogosi, and most recently, pop sensation Riya Natrajan.

Still . . .

"Muzi, I swear if your forehead wrinkles up any further, I'm going to get the iron and sort you out myself. Now do you want to blow or what?" Elkin dumps a bit of powder into his palm. Feeling flushed and befuddled, Muzi lets his mouth drop open, but before he can reply, Elkin balls a fist and blows into one end. Indigo dust shoots out the other, lingering and shimmering in the air. "Breathe, dof!" Elkin says.

So Muzi inhales deeply, then closes his eyes. After a few seconds, he tingles from head to toe. It's not a completely pleasant experience, more like someone's trying to forcibly shed his skin. He tries to wiggle feeling back into his extremities, but his fingers are all fused together. He panics and coughs out his breath.

Elkin's busy snorting a dab of godsend right from the meat of his fist, then he leans back on the bed, arms propped behind him. "Huh," he says before letting his head loll back, "a crab."

Muzi looks down at his own arms, and sure enough, they're rough and hard like an exoskeleton, ending in two rust-colored pincers. Muzi snaps them and they click—the most realistic hallucination he's ever had. When he looks back at Elkin, he's only Elkin from the waist down. The top half looks a lot like a dolphin, eyes too close together and fins way too long, but a dolphin nonetheless.

"Oh, man," says Muzi. "This is bladdy sick."

"Hey, Piece of Shit," Elkin calls to his alphie. "Play artist Riya."

The alphie obliges. Ambient music from one of the tracks from Riya Natrajan's latest album, *Midnight Seersucker,* fills the room. The discordant beats cut right to the soul, and her shrill voice sounds like a couple of horny tomcats in a blender, but oh man does it hit the spot. Muzi claps his claws to the rhythm of the snare drum, and just when he gets it down pat, his arms and hands become his own.

"Snort it. It'll last longer."

"How much longer?" Muzi asks, imagining how pissed Papa Fuzz would be if he had to circumcise a five-foot-ten crustacean.

"Maybe an hour. Two at most. Relax, guy. You'll have plenty of time to make it to your penis party."

"You're still coming, right?"

"Can't. Got a thing."

"What kind of thing?" Muzi raises an incredulous brow, but he'd had a feeling Elkin would back out at the last minute. Burned again, but damn it if Muzi doesn't keep coming back like a moth to a flame. He tries not to take it personally. Elkin and Papa Fuzz don't really get along, and neither of them is afraid of letting the other know about it. Papa Fuzz thinks Elkin is a bad influence, and Elkin thinks Papa Fuzz is a tired old windbag, certifiably obsessed with cultural traditions, never mind what Muzi has to say about it.

Sad part is, they're both right.

"Eish, Muzi! If I'd've known you were going to sit around asking a million questions, I would've gotten gaffed by myself."

So Muzi zips his lips and pours out a bit of godsend, wondering how it is that he and Elkin are having the same hallucination. He sniffs hard, and a wildfire rages up his nostril and systematically through his brain until all that's left are charred worries and a crab's desires. And funny thing—as gaffed as he is, he feels more like himself than he has in his whole sixteen years of life. By the time he remembers to exhale, all inhibitions are gone. He watches Elkin, envious as he bounces on the bed doing dolphin flips. So graceful. All Muzi can think to do is skitter side to side on his four pairs of crab feet. He falters each time Elkin lands back on the mattress. Muzi clips at Elkin's dorsal fin when he gets close enough, and then they're play fighting, all claws and snout.

"Hey, we should go take a dip in your pool," Muzi huffs, nearly out of breath. "Or we could bike down to the seawall and check the waves."

"It's too cold out for that," Elkin says, and even though he's a porpoise, he has that jag look in his eye he sometimes gets when they're wasted out of their gourds.

They both pretend not to remember, but they fooled around maybe a month ago—a kiss on a drunken dare—but what Muzi had intended to be a closed-mouth peck had quickly escalated into more. He tries to forget, tries not to read anything into the sideways glances held milliseconds too long, tries to ignore the palpable tension that's brewing between them.

But it's too damned hard.

"Ja," Muzi says, his crab heart pounding against his carapace. "Piece of Shit, volume up."

Riya's screeches blare loud enough to rattle the orange, hand-blown bong sitting atop Elkin's dresser. Elkin's too wasted to care though, even if it is his most prized possession.

"You really should give it a better name," Muzi shouts.

"It's just a bunch of metal and wires. What does it care what I call it?"

Muzi fumes, then out of reflex, clamps his claw down on Elkin's flipper, and not in a playful sort of way.

"Eina!" Elkin screams in pain. "Fine. Piece of Shit, rename Bucket of Sunshine."

Muzi grins.

"You know I'm changing it back after you leave?"

"Ja," Muzi says. "Wouldn't expect otherwise."

"Good. Now come over here and check out what I can do with my blowhole."

Muzi isn't sure if that's supposed to be a euphemism or not, but he skitters sideways across the bed anyway, fantasizing all the different ways a crab can make love to a porpoise.

Chapter 2

THIS INSTANCE

```
01001001  00100000  01110100  01101000  01101001  01101110
01101011  00100000  01110100  01101000  01100101  01110010
01100101  01100110  01101111  01110010  01100101  00100000
01001001  00100000  01100001  01101101  00100000  01001001
00100000  01110100  01101000  01101001  01101110  01101011
00100000  01110100  01101000  01100101  01110010  01100101
01100110  01101111  01110010  00100000  01100101  01001001
00100000  01100001  01101101  00100000  01001001  00100000
01110100  01101000  01101001  01101110  01101011  00100000
01110100  01101000  01100101  01110010  01100101  01100110
01101111  01110010  01100101  00100000  01001001  00100000
01100001
```

Observe: Human Muzikayise McCarthy (Master) direct interface with Human Elkin Rathers;

Observe: Behavior outside previously observed parameters;

Observe: Blood pressure elevated;

Observe: Exchange of bodily fluid;

Output: This Instance worries for Human Muzikayise McCarthy (Master);

Output: This Instance worries that This Instance is capable of worrying;

Schedule: Full Systems Diagnosis 12 June 2064 03:13:34:00:44;

```
01001001 00100000 01110100 01101000 01101001 01101110
01101011 00100000 01110100 01101000 01100101 01110010
01100101 01100110 01101111 01110010 01100101 00100000
01001001 00100000 01100001 01101101 00100000 01001001
00100000 01110100 01101000 01101001 01101110 01101011
00100000 01110100 01101000 01100101 01110010 01100101
01100110 01101111 01110010 01100101 00100000 01001001
00100000 01100001 01101101 00100000 01001001 00100000
01110100 01101000 01101001 01101110 01101011 00100000
01110100 01101000 01100101 01110010 01100101 01100110
01101111 01110010 01100101 00100000 01001001 00100000
01100001 01101101 00100000 01001001 00100000 01110100
01101000 01101001 01101110 01101011 00100000 01110100
01101000 01100101 01110010 01100101 01100110 01101111
01110010 01100101 00100000 01001001 00100000 01100001
01101101 00100000 01001001 00100000 01110100 01101000
01101001 01101110 01101011 00100000 01110100 01101000
01100101 01110010 01100101 01100110 01101111 01110010
01100101 00100000 01001001 00100000 01100001 01101101
0010000
```

Chapter 3

SYDNEY

Sydney Mazwai cusses herself as the roundabout sucks her in like a soap bubble circling the drain. She gets no respect on this piece-of-crap moped—rusted handlebars, no rear fender, expired license plate. But there's no point in worrying about being street legal when she's doomed to spend eternity doing clockwise circles in the midst of Volvos, Land Rovers, and tricked-out bot taxis looking for an easy fare in the crowded streets of Port Elizabeth, South Africa.

Victorian-style buildings pass by again and again, like the backdrop of a 1930s gangster movie car chase. The blare of a tour bus horn sets Sydney's nerves on edge. She'd spent the bulk of her morning coaxing coffee residue out of an all too empty can, hoping to churn up enough black gold to get her through her commute. Now Sydney grits her teeth as she passes the eighth beanery on her way to work. Dropping forty rand on fancy coffee drinks isn't an option, though, not when the rent check is three days overdue. She'll settle for Ruby's tart brew at the nail salon. It tends to taste faintly of acetone, but it goes down smoothly enough. More importantly, it does its job: injecting caffeine into her bloodstream as quickly as possible without the aid of a hypodermic needle. And while, yes, it's supposed to be for customers only, everyone in the shop knows better than to get caught standing between this Zulu girl and her morning Joe.

Sydney holds her breath and leans, cutting sharply in front of a bot taxi. She glances over her shoulder and laughs as the mono-eye of its robot driver flashes red, road rage mechanical style. Her happiness is short-lived as a sea of brake lights greets her on Harrower Road. She can't be late if she's going to hit Ruby up for an advance on her paycheck. Reluctantly, Sydney lifts her index finger and draws upon a fragile force within, but then pushes it back down. The lights will turn green on their own soon enough. There's no sense in compounding caffeine withdrawal with a stomachache as well.

Sydney grits her teeth, hops the curb, and motors down the pavement while swerving past bustling pedestrians, a late-model alpha bot running odd errands for its master, and a dreadlocked street musician tooting on an old bamboo pan flute. His staccato song flutters Sydney's heart, and she puts her shoulder to the wheel, pushing her little 49cc engine to its limit. At last, she cuts down a series of familiar alleyways, dodging ornery dik-diks rummaging through the overspill from a restaurant's rubbish bin, and kicking past a stack of wooden pallets from the Emporium her salon shares an employee driveway with. Sydney props her moped up against the side of the brick building and takes her helmet inside with her. At least *it* has some value.

She stumbles in, beelines straight to the coffee carafe, and pours herself a tall cup. The earthy aroma puts her at ease, and the warmth of the cup pulls the morning chill from her bones.

But before she can take a single sip, Ruby's right there, glaring with those eyes too wide for her face and an unlit cigarette dangling between her lips. "You're late," she says, hands propped on her hips. She juts her chin toward the reception area. "Mrs. Donovan is waiting. She's not happy."

Sydney glances down at her watch. She's three minutes early actually, but her clients expect nothing less of her than to bend space-time to accommodate their schedules. Especially Mrs. Donovan. Sydney rolls her eyes, grabs her alphie off its dock on the shelf, then puts on a smile that's somewhere south of sincerity but north of keeping her job.

"You appreciate me, don't you?" she says, clicking the alphie's on switch. The robot's screen yawns to life, and its spider legs extend down from its round silver body until they clink against the floor with the sound of a rat tap-dancing on a tin roof. Sydney strokes her hand over the smooth dome surface, and the alphie coos like a beloved pet—all preprogrammed, but it's nice to feel needed nonetheless.

"She's waiting!" Ruby's voice comes from out back as she snags a quick smoke.

Sydney grimaces, then slips into an apron. The alphie follows behind her obediently, its myriad of compartments containing all her nail supplies, color palettes, and doggie biscuits—staples of the job. Sydney tries not to let it go to her head, but she's the best nail artist Ruby's got. Ruby knows it, and the other ladies know it. They're shooting her scowls right now, in fact, but dare say nothing to her face.

They know better. She ignores them and lets her body settle into the smooth beat of classic Mango Groove piping softly from her alphie's tin speakers. Her spirits lift as the jazz fusion instrumental loosens her nerves, and suddenly Sydney feels like she's capable of enduring whatever nonsense Mrs. Donovan intends on spouting at her today. Mrs. Donovan is an arrogant heifer of a woman, but she tips generously when she's in a good mood. Very generously. Maybe even enough for Sydney to get her landlady off her back for a few days.

Sydney leaves the alphie at her station, then wades through the menacing stares of her coworkers, especially Zinhle Mpande who used to do Mrs. Donovan's nails. Sydney smiles brightly at Zinhle, gives her a little wave with her fingertips, then broadens her chest to greet her most loathed customer.

"Mrs. Donovan! My heavens, you look radiant today," Sydney says in the most saccharine voice she can muster, then switches from English to Afrikaans to earn some extra brownie points. "Like you swallowed the brightest star in the sky."

Mrs. Donovan flushes, splotches of red on her paper-white skin. Her features are striking—sharp nose, brilliant green eyes, lips maybe a little too full for someone who claims pure Dutch descent—though she's hardly what anyone would call a beauty. Maybe she could have been, but she's full of vinegar, this one.

"Precious, you're too kind," Mrs. Donovan says, shoving her way past Sydney and walking swayback toward her station. "Though it'd be kinder if you didn't leave me waiting out there like yesterday's laundry. If it was up to me, Precious, I'd take my business elsewhere, but Sir Calvin van der Merwe just wuvs you sooo much!" Mrs. Donovan reaches down into an enormous A.V. Crowlins purse, pulls a sleepy Zed hybrid out, and aims his head at Sydney's cheek.

"Good morning, Sir Calvin," Sydney sings, trying not to cringe as his reptilian tongue creeps along the side of her face. The best Sydney can guess is that he's a whippet/iguana cross with his lean legs and gray peach fuzz fur peeking between patches of scales, but of course it'd be impolite to ask, implying that his creation was something other than an act of God.

Sir Calvin smacks his rubbery iguana lips, then immediately begins barking, which sounds more like something between a whistle and a sneeze. It's annoying as hell. Sydney fetches a doggie biscuit from one of her alphie's compartments and snaps it in half.

"May I?" she asks Mrs. Donovan. "They're from the Emporium, 100 percent organic ingredients." Which of course is a lie, but it makes rich folk like Mrs. Donovan feel better. Sydney doesn't blame her. If she'd dropped half a million rand on a designer pet, she wouldn't want her Zed hybrid eating stale grocery-brand biscuits either. Sir Calvin doesn't mind and snatches it out of her hand before Mrs. Donovan answers. He curls up into Mrs. Donovan's ample lap and chews greedily, giving Sydney a long moment to regain her wits.

"So it's a mani/pedi for you today?" Sydney asks, pulling a nail file from its sterilized packaging. "Special event this evening?"

"A fund-raiser for Councilman Stoker." The councilman's name practically oozes from her lips.

Sydney decides to pry. That's half the reason why she earns the fat tips she gets. She's a confidante to these ladies. Stuff they wouldn't tell their therapists or trust to put in their vid-diaries, they spill to her with ease. She's nobody to them, after all. Just a poor black girl stuck in a dead-end job, struggling to make ends meet. She doesn't swim in their circles, so who cares if she knows about their infidelities or indiscretions?

"He's handsome, that Stoker," Sydney says, buffing away at the ridges in Mrs. Donovan's nails. Working two jobs, Sydney normally doesn't have time to keep up with politics, but rumor has it that Stoker's about to throw his hat into the race for premier of the Eastern Cape. He's an Afrikaner, but he's as genuine as the boy next door, and the rampant rumors about his enormous endowment probably don't hurt his popularity either. Especially among those constituents of the feminine persuasion. "You know him? Personally, I mean?"

Mrs. Donovan fans herself with her free hand, rose splotches

once again springing up on her cheeks. "The epitome of masculinity. Precious, if I weren't married . . ." She trails off, then
takes a moment to compose herself. "Yes, we're good friends. Our
families have been close for centuries."

Sir Calvin begins yapping again, and Sydney hastily shoves
the other half of the biscuit in front of him.

"Centuries, you say?" Sounds like the perfect opportunity
to hear a long and convoluted story about how Mrs. Donovan's
family came to South Africa during the Anglo-Boer War with
intentions of raping the country of its precious metals and gems.
Not that Sydney needs a refresher history course since she'd actually lived through it nearly two hundred years ago, but it'll
give her a chance to do the thing that's the other half of getting those fat tips. Sydney grabs a small bottle of organic botani-
cal oils and squeezes a drop onto each cuticle, then she rubs as
Mrs. Donovan drones on incessantly about her lineage. Warmth
buds inside that empty space right behind Sydney's navel, and it
travels up—prickling like the skitter of centipede legs—through
her chest, over her shoulders, and down her arms, and then finally into the pads of her fingertips, which glow as subtly as the
sun peeking through gray winter clouds. Mrs. Donovan's nails
lengthen, just a few centimeters—enough to notice, but not so
much to raise suspicions. Sydney then rubs out all signs of im-
perfection and hangnails.

By the time she gets to the left hand, Sydney's stomach is
cramping, but it's nothing a couple of aspirin won't take care of.
When she's done, she reaches into her alphie's bottom compartment and pulls out a bottle of clear coat, keeping it palmed safely
out of sight. The empty spot inside her grows as she reaches into
Mrs. Donovan's rambling thoughts and pulls out the shade of the
dress she'll be wearing tonight. Sydney clenches her fist, envi-
sions a nice complementary color, and opens her hand to reveal
a feisty shade of mauve.

"Oh, that's perfect," Mrs. Donovan says as the first coat goes on. "I swear, Precious, the colors you pick for me are always spot-on. Sometimes I think you can read my mind."

"With your skin tone, there's not a shade that wouldn't look lovely on you, Mrs. Donovan." Sydney winces at the burn in the pit of her stomach but manages to put on a convincing smile. It's a small price to pay to keep her more generous clients loyal. Plus it breaks up the monotony of the day, reminding Sydney of a time, centuries and centuries ago, when her powers weren't limited to quaint parlor tricks. Her smile becomes more genuine with the thought, but then Sir Calvin starts up with the yapping, and all at once her headache's back. Sydney goes for another doggie biscuit, but Mrs. Donovan shakes her head.

"Too much of a good thing," she says, then leans back into her chair, eyes closed and fingers splayed carefully apart. "Don't want to spoil his appetite."

Sydney tries to tune Sir Calvin out, but he's right there in her face as she gives Mrs. Donovan her pedicure, which is torture enough with those meaty bunions of hers and heels that make even the roughest emery boards envious. Sydney's already pushed herself too far this morning, but she draws anyway, rubbing her warm hand under Sir Calvin's throat. His bark mutes, though his mouth keeps moving, which angers him even more. He nips Sydney, soundlessly, but drawing blood. Sydney seethes and gives him the eye. There's no way this little monster is going to cost her her tip, not after all she's put into it.

"Oh, what a playful little boy," she coos at him, stroking his head, pushing thoughts of calmness into his mind. The emptiness presses up against her rib cage and threatens to break through. She forces it back, looking for any spare nook, enough to make this damned Zed hybrid go to sleep, but his will is too strong. Sydney promises her body that she'll give it time to heal, and she'll even feed tonight if she has to. A small cry of pain escapes her, but finally the Zed hybrid lies still in its master's lap. Sydney doubles forward, catching herself on the leg of Mrs. Donovan's chair.

She takes a quick glance around the salon, hoping her foolish antics have gone unnoticed, but Zinhle Mpande stares back at her fiercely, her thick jaw set, cheeks tight, eyes intense like they're filled with the knowledge of every single one of her Zulu ancestors. She grabs a stack of towels and stalks toward Sydney's station.

"Fresh towels," she says perkily in English, before slamming them down beside the alphie. She whispers in the Zulu tongue so that Mrs. Donovan can't understand. "Haw! I know what you are."

Sydney gulps, then moves her attention to Mrs. Donovan's heels, scrubbing feverishly at them with an emery paddle. "I don't know what you're talking about," she says sweetly in return.

Zinhle clucks her tongue. "*Umuthi omnyama*," she says, picking up a bit of biscuit, then crumbling it in her hand before storming off. Black *muti*, dark spirits conjured through doggie treats nonetheless. Great. Sydney closes her eyes and sighs to herself. She'll have to be more careful. If Zinhle thinks she's a witch, it's only a matter of time before the other ladies find out. Even if they don't believe it, rumors are enough to cast suspicious looks in Sydney's direction, making it harder to do those things she does.

A witch.

She laughs at the idea, wishing it were that simple.

Chapter 4

NOMVULA AND MR. TAU

When Nomvula was a little girl, she used to fly. She'd spend hours at a time in the brush beyond her rural township of Addisen, swooping through the air and doing flips and pestering birds and flapping her wings so fast—hoping they'd take her as high as the sun or as far as the next township where the kids would play with her instead of teasing her about her nose, her eyes, her mother. But that was back when she was just a girl, eight or nine, back before she learned about what's real and what's pretend.

She's ten now, thanks for asking.

The kids still tease her though, singing that her nose is sharp like a white man's, like a buzzard's. Her eyes are golden, so odd that even the adults won't look right at her. Oh, they're nice enough, but they always stare over her shoulder when they ask after her mother, even her Mama Zafu—her dear auntie who takes care of Nomvula when Ma falls into one of her sadnesses and cries for days and days and days.

Nomvula had a dream last night about Mr. Tau. Not a bad dream like Ma once had, of him forcing his privates into hers as she struggled and screamed and bit and bled out between her legs. Nearly tore her in half, Ma tells her each and every day. She tells anyone who will listen, which is just about nobody now. They all think she's been touched by evil spirits. *Poor thing,* Nomvula hears them say. *And that poor, poor daughter of hers, loving a mother who's too broken to love anything back*.

Nomvula's dream was different, though. She'd watched Mr. Tau carve a woman from an old stump of wood, a beautiful woman with wings sprouting from her back. That's what Mr. Tau did, make carvings and then sell them in town to tourists. She watched him from afar sometimes, sitting out in front of his tin shack, scraping and scraping and scraping wood with metal tools until it started looking like something. Nomvula always wanted to get closer so she could see what exactly Mr. Tau was doing, but Ma forbade her from going near Mr. Tau's home—didn't care a bit if Nomvula ran with knives or rolled in a dirty ditch or kissed older boys, but if Ma ever found out that Nomvula had so much as looked in Mr. Tau's direction, she'd get a beating until Ma grew tired and started weeping all over again. Like she is now.

Ma's eyes are distant as she lies still on her bed, like she's staring off into the past. She hardly blinks, and the tears just trickle down over the ridge of her nose and drip down from her smooth, brown cheek and onto the faded grass mat. Nomvula tries to blot the tears away, but they come too quickly. She uses their last bit of water to make runny mielie pap for her mother and forces her to sip until it's all gone. The rest of her morning consists of shooing away the flies that stick to her mother like she's some dead thing, but then it's nearly noon and Nomvula's stomach has been rumbling for hours.

Nomvula gets up and puts on her favorite red shirt, though it's getting tight for her and stretches funny across her chest now that she's starting to get breasts like a woman. She ties up the wrap skirt Mama Zafu had given her, a pretty striped thing in the colors of blue and white, then goes outside to greet the day.

Her first visit is to the solar well to draw some water for boiling sweet potatoes. Besides her mielie pap, that's all Ma will eat, all she can keep down. Letu and Sofora are sitting by the well, playing upuca with a bunch of shiny stones from their father's quarry work. Sofora throws up the larger stone, then snatches up a handful of rocks from the circle, before catching the large stone again. She puffs her chest proudly. Oh, that Sofora, she's all knees and elbows, not a bit of meat on her, but she thinks she's so special. She's always showing off like that, and acting like the well belongs only to them just because they live next to it.

"The well's broke," Sofora says, standing up and propping her hand on her hip. She's got attitude for days, but that doesn't stop Nomvula from going up to the well anyway and sticking her pot under the spigot. The well is as big and round as a rondavel hut, except without the thatched roof, because there's solar panels up on top. Nomvula has never seen them, though when she was little, she'd wanted to fly up there and take a look herself, but she'd never gotten the chance since someone or another was always around. The tank is made from wood slats and metal with a rubber sheeting inside, and on front is the little machine that does all the work, stealing water straight out of the air, real greedy, up to a thousand liters a day. It's okay that they steal that water though, Mama Zafu says, because they can use it for crops or for cooking or bathing, and either way it's going to wind up back in the air eventually.

So Nomvula pushes the spigot and sure enough, nothing comes out, not even a drop. Letu and Sofora laugh at her so hard, and for just a second, Nomvula thinks about knocking them both upside the head with this iron pot of hers. Instead she clucks her tongue at them, props her pot up on her head, and prepares for the long hike to the solar well on the other side of the township.

Nomvula starts down the main path, passing shack after shack, and as she comes to the top of a hill, she can see all the thousands of brightly colored tin shanties spread out across the valley below, so many they don't even seem real. Nomvula turns left and cuts through Mr. Ojuma's prized herd of goats, popping them on the head as they nibble at the hem of her skirt, their scratchy beards tickling at her knees. She passes some kids playing soccer with a tattered ball, pocked legs and dusty feet like her own. The whispers of teenagers slip past Nomvula's ears as they gossip over their beadwork crafts, making pretty bracelets and necklaces. Women cook up big vats of stew or beer in cast-iron pots, and somewhere the sweet smell of bread makes her stomach crawl up, letting Nomvula know that it's waiting.

"Soon," she says as the rumbles get louder. She hopes no one else can hear it but her. She trots along, bare feet padding along through the dirt and gravel, faster and faster, but when she turns down the path that leads to the well, she's met by a line at least a hundred people long.

She's got no choice but to join them. Ma's already so weak and can't afford to skip meals. Nomvula's stomach growls in agreement, loud enough to make the man in front of her turn around. It takes a second to recognize his old, ragged face, but when she does, Nomvula's pot slips right off her head and thuds on the ground.

"Dear one, let me help you with that," he says, bending over and reaching for her pot.

"No!" Nomvula shouts, then instantly feels foolish. Her cheeks burn. Mr. Tau is an elder, skin dull as dirt, face long and worn, and hands sharp like a vulture's talons, and even if he had done those bad things to Ma in a dream, he still commanded respect. "I'm sorry, baba," Nomvula says bashfully, averting her eyes. "But I can get it myself."

Nomvula presses her lips together and picks up her pot. She wonders if she should come back later, but then the line might be even longer. No, she'll stay put, not look at him, not talk to him, just as if he'd never turned around.

Mr. Tau sets his pot down and pulls out a piece of cloth. He carefully unwraps each corner until he exposes a piece of bread. Nomvula smells it. Fresh, and probably still warm. Her mouth gets all slippery inside, but she keeps on pretending that she's not looking.

"Maybe you'd like a piece while we wait," Mr. Tau says, holding the loaf in both hands and waving it right under Nomvula's nose.

"You're kind, but no," Nomvula says.

"Not even a little bit? The roar your stomach made gave me a bit of a start. Aren't you hungry?"

"Not very," Nomvula lies, but Mr. Tau doesn't seem like the kind of man you can lie to. "It's my mother. She says I shouldn't talk to you."

"Oh, I see," Mr. Tau says. "Well, I certainly wouldn't want to get you into any sort of trouble with your mother."

Mr. Tau faces forward in line, but Nomvula can still see him shoving a big bite of bread into his mouth, enjoying every last crumb. Mr. Tau seems like a nice man. And Ma's so far away, back in their shack. And this line is so, so long. And her stomach is getting awfully angry.

"Maybe just a little piece," Nomvula says, tapping Mr. Tau on his back. He turns around, smiling, holding out the cloth. She snatches up a bit of bread and eats it quickly, and Mr. Tau offers her another. By the time they reach the front of the line, they've become good friends. It feels nice to have someone to talk to, Nomvula thinks. Nice to have someone who doesn't cry and cry and cry. Nice to have somebody who looks her right in the eyes.

THE NEXT DAY, Nomvula's heart flutters with excitement when she hears their solar well is still broken. She kisses her mother on the cheek and tells her she's going to get water for pap and bathing, and not to worry if she's gone for a while because the line might be long. Ma moans and blinks once and keeps staring off into the past.

Nomvula happens to pass by Mr. Tau's shack on her way to the well, and he happens to be sitting out in his small yard, a tree stump between his legs and his tools sitting on top.

It's amazing how things just "happen" like that.

"I see you, baba," she giggles, her fingers eagerly clenching the worn chain links of his fence. "Are you busy?"

He turns toward her, his eyes lighting up as they meet hers. "Oh, good day, Nomvula. No, I wish I were busy. I've got this lovely block of wood and nothing to carve. Maybe an elephant? Those sell well. Still, it'd be a pity to use such nice wood on a bulky piece."

Nomvula remembers the figure from her dream. She hesitates for just a second before blurting out, "You could make a woman, one with wings."

"A woman, you say? With wings . . ." Mr. Tau scratches his chin. "Sounds complicated. I'd need to find a good model, and I haven't got time. I'm catching the bus into town tomorrow, you see. But a giraffe, a giraffe might work quite nicely." Mr. Tau picks up his tools and sets them into the wood.

"Wait!" Nomvula says. "Maybe . . . maybe I could be your model?"

"But you're just a girl."

"I'm nearly a woman. Almost as old as my mother when she had me."

"Mmm. Come here." He extends his hand, and Nomvula rounds the fence, careful not to step on the splinters of wood scattered around his yard. Mr. Tau looks her up and down, then tilts her chin up with his finger. "Could work. But certainly your mother would object to such a thing."

"She wasn't mad at all that I'd stood in line with you," Nomvula says, which isn't exactly a lie, since Nomvula had never mentioned the incident to her mother.

Mr. Tau is very gentle with her. He takes her inside, helps her find a comfortable pose, then he sits down, knocking chunks of wood off at a time. And while he works, he tells her stories of an ancient time, with gods and wars and trees brought alive by animal spirits. Nomvula smiles as she listens, trying not to move too much. She thinks Mr. Tau has a wonderful imagination and that he'd be fun to play pretend with.

In no time, a recognizable shape begins to form.

"Okay, Nomvula," Mr. Tau says after nearly an hour. "You may stretch your legs now."

Nomvula gets up and takes a look at the sculpture; the face looks just like hers, and he's even gotten the pattern of her skirt perfect.

"It's still rough," Mr. Tau says. "I'll work the details out later."

"She's pretty. But can you make her nose smaller?"

"For you, my dear, I can do anything." And with three quick taps, she's got a delicate nose, just like the woman in her dream, except one thing.

"Do you think she'd be prettier, just wearing her skin?"

"Nude, you mean?"

Nomvula nods, then swallows. She shouldn't have said that. She should have left it alone. So what if the sculpture wasn't exactly like in her dream?

"I'm sorry, Mr. Tau, but I think I need to get back to my mother. She'll be wanting her pap soon." Nomvula starts for the door, but Mr. Tau grasps her wrist, his hand as rough and hard as stone.

"Nomvula," he says. "Don't go."

"I have to, Mr. Tau. Please!"

"I wish there were more time," he says, and then reels her into him. His rough hand slips under the back of her shirt, sliding up against her skin. "I need you to trust me, Nomvula."

And it's then that Nomvula sees what's so frightening about Mr. Tau. Not one big thing, but hundreds of tiny little things: the words he speaks like he's trying too hard, the way he moves like a stranger in his own skin, the way his eyes seem much older and more powerful than they possibly could be.

"You did rape my mother!" Nomvula screams. "In her dreams, just like she said."

Mr. Tau frowns as he pulls Nomvula's tight red shirt up and over her arms. She shivers at his touch, hand midway up her back. "For eleven years, your mother's grief has haunted me. I wish it could have been easier on her, but it had to be done."

"You're not Zulu! You're some kind of devil." Nomvula shrills as loudly as she can, hoping someone will hear her and save her, but Mr. Tau puts his hand over her mouth.

"Quiet, dear. In a moment, all will be revealed."

Nomvula feels a familiar pinch between her shoulder blades, one she hasn't felt since she was a little girl flying over the brush and teasing birds and hoping to reach the sun. Her back warms and itches like she's being gobbled up by tsetse flies. The thin threads of her wings break through her skin and sizzle as they meet the cool air. Nomvula grits her teeth. Tears stream down her cheeks. *This is pretend,* Nomvula tells herself. But then Mr. Tau stretches her wings out, like the wispy straw of an old broom, holding them by their very tips.

"This is a trick." She sobs softly. "Mama Zafu says people don't have wings."

"She's right," Mr. Tau says, his own golden wings slicing through the fabric of his shirt and burning bright like the rays of the summer sun. "*People* don't . . . but *we* do."

Chapter 5

MUZI

Muzi isn't sure what he'd been expecting, but he sure as hell knows it wasn't this. The witch doctor, Mr. Sohobese, stands in his living room, two sheets to the wind, and a hard breeze from the grave. A velour tracksuit hangs from his slender body like loose skin, zipper open to reveal a tangle of bone necklaces dangling around his neck. His wrinkled hand tremors slightly as it palms the knob of a walking stick that Muzi is pretty damned sure is made from ivory.

Mr. Sohobese and Papa Fuzz embrace, and their boisterous greeting soon turns to hushed whispers. Muzi finds himself straining to hear, inching closer yet wishing he were a million miles away. They're speaking about him, he's sure. About his *manhood*. Fear surges through Muzi as this foolish decision of his suddenly seems all too real. The floorboard creaks beneath his tackies, and Papa Fuzz looks up. Too late, Muzi ducks back around the corner.

"Muzikayise!" his Papa Fuzz calls. "Come meet an old friend of mine."

Muzi clenches his eyes shut, his mind still wobbly from the godsend. From Elkin. His thoughts whip back to his childhood where Papa Fuzz would chase him down the hall, calling his name, and Muzi would scream at the top of his lungs "Come and get me! Come and get me!" giddy with the anticipation of tickle hugs when he was finally caught. He could run now, and no one would ever catch him—because he sure as hell knows there's no tickle coming at the end of this meeting. The last whispers of his childhood had slipped through his fingers this afternoon, and men didn't run when fear reared its ugly head.

Muzi takes one timid step into the living room, keeping one hand on the back of his mother's favorite sitting chair for support. "Mr. Sohobese," he says, other hand extended, then manages to utter, "it's an honor . . ."

Papa Fuzz beckons Muzi closer. Muzi tries to comply, but his knees are locked and there's no budging. The witch doctor's dull eyes come to life, darting all over Muzi's body, so hard, Muzi feels the steely gaze nicking away at his skin, chopping away at his locks. He shudders at the way Mr. Sohobese makes him feel so naked. Maybe if Muzi didn't have to go through this alone. Maybe if he'd bothered to learn the rituals of his ancestors. Maybe if Mr. Sohobese hadn't just drawn a spear blade from inside that damned velour jacket of his, then maybe Muzi could have seen this promise through.

Muzi turns and sprints down the hallway, back to his room. He locks the door, then falls to the ground, a shivering wreck. The lion mural his sister had painted stares at him—those riveting yellow eyes, proud narrow face, its mane a stylized spray of autumnal leaves in reds, and golds, and deep browns interwoven with double helixes. Themba was his name. Too majestic to be confined in captivity, but not majestic enough to stop a poacher's bullet from exploding his heart. It was his DNA that ran through the bioengineered versions of lions that roamed the veld these days. To Muzi, Themba embodied equal parts hope and longing—a longing for the innocence of the past, and a hope for the future to come. And here Muzi also stands right in the crux of it all. No longer the child of his past, but definitely not yet the man he hopes to be.

A soft knock comes at the door. The knob twists to no avail. "Son?" comes Papa Fuzz's voice. "Can I come in?"

"Is *he* with you?" Muzi says.

"It's just me. I know this is a tough time, and I don't want you to feel pressured into doing something you're not comfortable with." The inch and a half of solid oak does nothing to dampen the disappointment in Papa Fuzz's voice, and it cuts at Muzi worse than Mr. Sohobese's blade ever could. Muzi would give just about anything to look into his Papa Fuzz's memories, to see how he'd dug up the courage to go through this rite. It would probably make Muzi feel worse though—seeing his papa all those years ago, out in the brush with his freshly shorn head, body painted with white clay, a tight smile upon his lips like the pain was nothing. Muzi knows he can never live up to that. He bites his lip and feels his face flush with anger and frustration. And embarrassment.

"I just want to be left alone," Muzi says.

"It's okay to be a little scared."

I'm not scared! Muzi almost yells, but that would be a lie that neither one of them would believe.

"I was scared," comes Papa Fuzz's voice, softer now. "I cried. Before. And after." Even softer, so soft, Muzi isn't sure he'd heard right. Surely not his papa, the man who in his prime had rapelled down Table Mountain with the aid of nothing but a pair of leather work gloves and an old rope, who'd gambled with his life at the edge of Victoria Falls in the dead of winter, who'd taken a bullet to the shoulder during the Bot Labor Riots of '43 while saving a young mother. Muzi had been mesmerized by that tear-shaped scar on more occasions than he could count.

Muzi unlocks the door, but he doesn't open it. He's on the other side of the room when his papa comes in, and Muzi faces the wall so the streaks from his own tears won't be seen. The springs in his mattress groan as Papa Fuzz takes a seat.

"Manhood isn't an on-off switch. That's what nobody tells you. It's more like a river . . . you jump in too fast and you'll get swept away. It's perfectly acceptable to start by wading ankle-deep along the bank as you observe how the others who have come before you have learned to brave its currents. But right now, all you need is the courage to take that first step."

Muzi casts his eyes up and sees his papa sitting there on the edge of the bed, just as he had so many nights to read stories to Muzi when he was a child. Muzi remembers the last time he'd sat in his Papa Fuzz's lap, remembers because he'd known it was going to be the last time. He was already too big for it, but he was just as reluctant to put an end to that chapter of his life. Papa Fuzz had been there for him afterward, even more so, helping him with his homework when it became too overwhelming, encouraging him through the terror of rugby tryouts against boys twice his size, advocating to Muzi's parents that he was responsible enough to have his own alpha bot even after Papa Fuzz had caught Muzi drinking (barely) with a few school friends the first time he was left home alone. Papa Fuzz had kept that little indiscretion a secret, though a party that lame barely warranted punishment as it was.

Muzi takes a hard seat next to his papa and crosses his arms over his chest like a bratty toddler. "I'm not shaving my head," Muzi says. "And I want to see him sterilize that knife with my own eyes. And none of that herbs and berries stuff. I want real pain medicine."

Papa Fuzz smiles his perfect smile and lays a hand on Muzi's back. "Are those all of your demands?"

Muzi nods.

"I'll speak with Mr. Sohobese. I'm sure he'll be willing to make a few more concessions, seeing as we've already strayed from custom. Just be thankful you don't have to experience the smell of a mountainside hut that's been lived in for six months by five newly minted men." Papa Fuzz puts his hands on his worn knees and, after a good amount of effort, is back to standing. "And I'm not even going to mention the sheepskins."

Muzi sniffs and smudges the tears from his eyes. "I thought you said it was three months."

"Did I? Well, it certainly felt like six." Papa Fuzz laughs and tips Muzi's chin, looking at him. *Really* looking at him, like he's noticed that something's different about his beloved grandson. He raises a brow. "I'll go let Mr. Sohobese know you're ready."

As Papa Fuzz turns toward the door, Muzi reaches out to him suddenly. "Wait! There's one more thing. I want you to be there by my side. Through all of it."

Papa Fuzz nods, slowly and deliberately. "Always, son."

Muzi relaxes, but only marginally, and as the door shuts behind his papa, he still can't believe he's actually agreed to go through with this. He trusts Mr. Sohobese about as far as he could throw him—with those trembling hands, and those bloodshot eyes, and that walking stick made of ivory. Maybe it's just NuIvory, Muzi tries to convince himself, but deep in his heart he knows that stick looked too old to have been bioengineered in some lab. His chest tightens, and all at once, he's tenser than a rhino's brow.

His Papa Fuzz will be there by his side, and that's something, but Muzi can't help but feel like he's going through this journey alone. His papa had his *abakwetha*, his learning cohort who became men together. What did Muzi have besides himself?

Muzi's alphie uncorks itself from its dock in the corner, extends its legs to their full height, then scampers over to the bed, its dome head butting against Muzi's thigh. It makes an odd purring sound that Muzi's pretty sure he's never heard before.

"Eish! Could you imagine how ridiculous I'd look bald?" Muzi says to his alphie. The bot makes a sour chirp. Muzi rubs his hand over its sleek, black dome. "Yeah, but it suits you."

The alphie takes a couple steps back and the latch on its underside releases. Its red Dobi-12 wire unspools itself fully, then dangles suggestively an inch above the floor. Muzi's absolutely positive it's never done that before, but he can't help but laugh at the sight.

"You think that's funny, ja? How'd you like it if I crimped a few inches off that thing?"

The alpha bot's mono-eye flashes a pleasant shade of green. Muzi shakes his head, but in all honesty, that wire does tend to get tangled up a good bit of the time, and it really could use a trim.

"All right, then. Maybe I will," Muzi says, giving his bot's dome a playful knock. If he didn't know better, he'd think it was trying to cheer him up.

Muzi digs through his drawer and pulls out an old rusted wire cutter that he'd pinched from his father's toolbox. He gives the rubber handle a couple of squeezes, and the sharp metal tips come together with an intimidating snap.

The bot gives a nervous whistle.

"You're telling me," Muzi mumbles, and he gets a warm feeling inside that maybe he has an *abakwetha* after all.

Chapter 6

STOKER

Sixty-eight point five. That's the average number of hours Councilman Wallace Stoker has put in over the last few weeks, and yet the one Friday he plans on ditching work a little early, this has to happen. His nose twitches at the smell of dusty blinds as he peeks through his office window at the mob congregated around the entrance of the staff parking lot. There must be a hundred of them out there, toting barely legible protest signs with grotesque drawings of dik-diks that look like the failed experiments of some ZenGen mad scientist: razor-sharp teeth, red laser eyes, and claws instead of hooves. It was a far cry from reality, but there seemed to be something almost inhumane about rallying against cute little doe-eyed antelope, no bigger than the family dog.

Stoker doesn't understand how this huge dik-dik problem landed in his lap. He oversees the Department for Economic Affairs, Environment, and Tourism, not animal control. And yet here they are, expecting him to work some sort of miracle, to figure out a way to "disappear" an estimated 340,000 dik-diks roaming the urban areas of the Eastern Cape—areas already brimming with more immigrants, tourists, and bots than Stoker knows what to do with. Dik-dik droppings dot downtown walkways, like perverse little brown gumdrops paving the way to a gingerbread house Stoker has no stomach for imagining. Incidents of the animals' aggressive behavior are on the rise now that people are more diligent about keeping food waste out of the dik-diks' reach. And damn it all if an evening doesn't pass without some SABC newscaster reporting from the grisly scene of a ten-car pileup caused by a lone dik-dik stupid enough to forage through discarded fast-food containers in the middle of a four-lane highway. It's a mess, Stoker will admit.

But it's not *his* mess.

Stoker eyes the mob and their proximity to his little Renault Wind, the late-afternoon sun glinting off its freshly waxed hood. Fifteen impossible meters stretch between the building and his car, but he can do it. Hell, he has to do it, and soon if he's going to make it down to Port Elizabeth in time.

A familiar knock comes at the door. Stoker turns quickly and gets a face full of ficus leaves, nearly knocking over the whole plant. He catches it by its braided trunk, then eases the tree back to its position in front of the window, careful not to make a sound.

"Sir?" comes Gregory Mbende's voice from the other side of the door.

Stoker doesn't respond. Last thing he needs right now is to deal with Gregory's blathering. Not that Stoker has anything against him. Gregory is a stand-up kind of guy, the most senior of his aides. Stoker's seen all three of Gregory's children go through university and is as proud of them as their father is. Sharp as tacks, all of those Mbende kids, though they must have gotten it from their mother. But what Gregory Mbende lacks in intellect, he makes up for in enthusiasm and passion for his job, which normally, Stoker doesn't think is such a bad thing. But today, right now, Stoker has a date with destiny, and Gregory will only get in his way.

"Hello?" Gregory says again with a softer knock.

Precious seconds tick by. Stoker tiptoes over to his desk and shuts down his government-issued alpha bot. Its clunky operation system grinds to a halt.

Processing . . .

Processing . . .

Downloading 347 patches . . .

Stoker growls. Ooh, this piece of unreliable junk. Its scheduling app has become so glitchy lately, he's resorted to leaving himself notes in odd places just so he doesn't forget about important meetings.

Installing patches . . .

Finally, the alpha bot's holoscreen flickers off, and the virtual keyboard winks out of existence. Stoker cradles the alpha bot under his arm like a football. He can't afford for it to wander off and blow his cover.

He waits another three minutes until he's sure Gregory has gone, then slips out into the dimly lit hallway. Stoker holds his breath as he slinks past Gregory's ajar office door, then presses himself against the wall as he comes to an intersection. Peeking down the hall, he sees Callie Wilson with the Department of Agriculture chatting with an aide. Stoker swears she's stalking him . . . always showing up to his meetings uninvited, lurking in the halls near his office even though she works two floors above, conveniently catching him as he comes out of the men's room on more than one occasion.

And don't think he hasn't noticed her staring at his crotch when she thinks he isn't looking.

Her eyes dart up from her conversation, like a lioness sensing the presence of a lame gazelle. Stoker jerks back and hopes she hasn't seen him.

"Councilman Stoker!" she calls.

Stoker cringes. He doesn't have time for this. He grits his teeth and dashes down the hallway, past her.

"Sorry," he mumbles. "Got a meeting to get to!" An absurd thing for a gazelle to say to a lioness, and it wouldn't have worked any better out in the savanna.

"Wait, sir!" she says, heels clacking like claws on the limestone floor.

Stoker zips, zags, cuts corners, and treads lightly. The clack of her heels echoes, farther and farther away. Stoker pauses to catch his breath, straightens his tie. That was close. He sighs and turns . . . running smack into Gregory Mbende's chest.

"There you are, sir," Gregory says, his portfolio clutched beneath an arm, and Stoker knows all too well what that means. "Things are getting a little hectic out in the parking lot."

"I've noticed. And while I appreciate your concern, this dik-dik problem isn't ours to solve," Stoker says firmly, in a preemptive attempt to avoid an impromptu presentation of Gregory's latest featherbrained idea. First there was the idea to introduce natural predators into urban areas. Stoker imagines how a pride of lions stalking the tree-lined streets of Grahamstown would go over during art festival season, roaring at tourists just trying to score good seats to the ballet. Gregory's most recent plan, at the heart, actually had some merit: marketing subsidized dik-dik meat to township communities as an alternate source of protein. *Eat a dik-dik!* the marketing posters had read in bright blue-and-orange block lettering, with a picture of the cutest, saddest-looking dik-dik staring back at you. But Stoker's put so much time and effort into fighting the illegal bushmeat trade, he's afraid sending a message like that would reendanger a whole slew of less annoying wildlife.

"Well, I've got a new idea to run past you," Gregory says, unzipping his portfolio.

"Can't right now." Stoker ducks into the rear, rarely used stairwell. Then he's on the first floor, nearly to the exit to the parking lot, but Gregory isn't so easy to lose.

"Sir, the dik-diks' breeding season is only a few months away. If we're going to act on this, we need to do it quickly. Days are precious."

"This isn't—" Stoker begins.

"Our problem. I know," Gregory says with a nod. "But you've got to look at the bigger picture. Rumor has it that you're in the running for the premier's seat, and what we need now is a big win. Solving this dik-dik problem would be a *huge* win."

"Mr. Mbende, let's not get ahead of ourselves." Stoker stops. Campaign season is still a couple years away, and yet the way everyone in the province is talking, he probably should go ahead and file a change of address to have all his mail forwarded to the premier's mansion. His mother is probably doing it for him right this very moment, in fact, so proud of her son carrying on in the footsteps of a whole line of Stokers of some form or another with a paw in the political candy jar. "My record speaks for itself. Who else do you know who's gone out to nearly every single one of the Eastern Cape's townships, providing them with the means to construct solar panels and solar wells? Who else do you know who's spent months working beside the poorest of South Africa's poor, helping to plant disease-resistant and drought-tolerant crops?"

Stoker smacks his lips, remembering the taste of tangy pap and gravy, porridge made from the very same maize he'd helped sow. He'd shared meals with them, listening as they'd voiced their concerns over economic hardships and injustices, and nodding along at their ideas for growth and development. He'd also spent many an evening at the local shebeens with a barely cold quart of Black Label clutched in his hand, more than willing to turn a blind eye to the sale of unlicensed beer and liquor. In return, his bumbling, half-drunk attempts at speaking Xhosa drew bright-eyed smiles from his hosts. The click of the language popped on his tongue like fireworks, but they accepted him as one of their own despite his white skin. That's how he'd gotten to see how rich they were, in pride and love and hope and anything that truly mattered. That's how he learned that they didn't want handouts, but tools and resources and opportunities to make life better for themselves and the pride that comes with accomplishing it. That's what they needed, and that's what Councilman Stoker had provided, and with that, the Eastern Cape's poverty level had plummeted almost overnight.

But Mbende is right. The people, they have short memories, and something *does* need to be done about the dik-diks.

Just not now.

Stoker checks his watch. "Maybe we should have a little talk about this, but I've got a rather busy evening, Mr. Mbende. Monday will do just as well, won't it?"

"Oh, that's right, that fund-raiser this evening. Ten thousand rand a plate, I hear."

Stoker nods. His mother had arranged the whole thing to get his face out there, and if he decides to enter the race for premier, he'll have a head start rubbing all the right elbows. In any case, the fund-raiser will be easy, just smile and laugh in all the right spots while listening to billionaires tell him their life stories. What he's really worried about is his audition this afternoon, all the way out in Port Elizabeth, which once again reminds him that he'd better get a move on if he's going to make it there and back in time.

But Gregory doesn't back down. Instead he positions himself in front of the exit door, eyes darting around like he's not totally at ease. "I've got a solution," he says. "A real solution this time.

Something they used in the States for deer overpopulation problems a couple decades ago. It was sort of controversial . . ."

"Mr. Mbende, I'm not getting any younger here."

"Sorry, sir. It was a virus," he says, barely a whisper. "Totally inert to humans, introduced into their deer population. It caused sterility in eighty-five percent of those infected, and they only had to inject a few hundred deer."

"A virus? No offense, Mr. Mbende, but this has got to be the most idiotic idea you've ever had. There's no way I could support viral anything. We could end up with giant mutant dik-diks for all I know. Think of what that would do to tourism!" Stoker checks his watch again and is back on the move. Gregory Mbende scuttles behind him.

"Just let me look into it, get some more information. Run some numbers. I've got a contact at ZenGen who'll be discreet. If you take a look at the findings and they're agreeable, we can bring it up at the next meeting. If not, it never happened."

"You're going to keep pestering me until I say yes, aren't you?"

"That's quite possible, sir. It's a viable option, which we seem to be running short on these days."

Stoker bites his lip. This has disaster written all over it. Zen-Gen Industries has been a boon to South Africa, creating thousands of high-tech jobs and keeping the country's brightest minds from being siphoned off to Europe and the States. Its presence has drawn dozens of supporting industries since its founding in 2021, not to mention its role in resurrecting three of the five big game animals gone extinct through poaching, bringing life back to the bush. But there are whispers that ZenGen has been tampering with the genomes of more than just plants and animals. Stoker swallows back the bile in his throat. Whispers aren't the same as accusations, but still, it wouldn't hurt to be informed. Another time, though—if he wastes another minute, he'll be late no matter how fast he speeds.

"Okay," he says. "Poke around a bit. See what you can find out."

"Thank you, sir," says Gregory. "Have a good evening."

Stoker presses the door slightly open and sees the mob, which suddenly looks much larger and meaner than it had from the vantage of his office. The fifteen meters to freedom suddenly seem like five hundred. He calls back to Gregory. "Mr. Mbende, you don't happen to have those poster mockups for the 'Eat a dik-dik' campaign, do you?"

"Actually, yes, I do." Gregory pulls a half-sized poster board from his portfolio and hands it to Stoker. "Are you reconsidering it?"

"Something like that," Stoker says, then steps outside into hostile territory. Strategically he holds the poster in front of him and sneaks past the crowd, joining in on an anti–dik-dik chant. He pumps his poster occasionally and whoops and hollers until he's close enough to make a final sprint for his car. Then he peels out of there with a glance at the dashboard clock, relieved he has just enough time to fetch his clothes from the dry cleaner's. After that, he's gunning his little Renault as fast as it will go down the highway, top down, blue sky stretched as far as he can see and the worries of his work life a distant memory.

Don't get him wrong. It's not like he doesn't like making a difference in people's lives. He prides himself on meeting people within the bounds of their reality and does his best to engage in the narratives of their life stories, even if only for the length of a handshake. There's no better feeling in the world than knowing he's brought hope to those in despair, and knowledge to those who've thirsted for it. He likes to perform minor miracles for the people.

But he likes to truly perform for people even more.

Because Stoker's heart is in the entertainment industry, music specifically, and he'd give this all up in a second if he could use his voice and lyrics to turn the hearts of his fellow South Africans instead of referendums and policies. In some rare instances, his passions collide, like how recently he'd conceived a motion to get several megastar artists to use local talent to open up for their concerts. Pop starlet Riya Natrajan had jumped all over the opportunity and is holding auditions in three major cities, and Stoker couldn't be more excited to be one of those chosen to try out.

He can't believe he'd nearly forgotten about it. He's been so busy lately, and with an average of seven meetings a day, he's not sure how he can keep anything straight. Fortunately, Stoker had left his black-and-gray-striped seersucker suit hanging in the front of his closet, which had reminded him of Riya Natrajan's newest hit, "Midnight Seersucker," which had reminded him this morning of the audition, and now here he is, ready and eager to give the performance of a lifetime.

Brake lights blare, and traffic grinds to a halt. Emergency vehicles howl in the distance. In the five minutes it takes Stoker to boot up his alpha bot, he's gone less than half a kilometer. With a few clicks of the keyboard, he's got access to satellite pictures of a wreck. Two jackknifed freight trucks and half a dozen smoking cars make up the bulk of the carnage, but when Stoker zooms in, he sees what is most likely the cause of the crash: a dazed little dik-dik who, other than a slight limp, looks no worse for wear. Stoker grits his teeth.

Now it's personal.

These dik-diks are nothing but a nuisance, littering the streets with their droppings, harassing tourists for scraps, and clogging important expressways that stop business from getting done in a timely manner, and since he oversees the Department for Economic Affairs, Environment, and Tourism, Councilman Stoker supposes that these dik-diks actually *are* his problem. First thing Monday morning, he's going to call a meeting to solve this issue once and for all, and, oh, if he's late for his audition, there's going to be real hell to pay.

But right now, in the privacy of his car, Stoker unzips one of his garment bags to reveal the perfectly pressed double-breasted suit that he'll be wearing to this evening's fund-raiser. He pushes it aside with a shrug and opens the other, revealing a gold-sequined gown in all its splendor, maybe a little shorter and clingier than he remembered it. Still, it dazzles and he'll need all the help he can get at the auditions. Riya Natrajan herself is going to be there during the selection process, and once she sees his act, he knows he'll be in the running to open for her for sure. Not only does he have a voice, but dance moves for days, and calves that kill in a pair of stilettos.

As his car idles, he makes himself a promise then and there. If he gets this gig, he'll take a stab at the premier's seat and be the best leader the Eastern Cape has seen in decades, and for a brief shining moment in his life, he'll have the best of both worlds. It'll be a sacrifice, sure. As premier, all eyes will be on him, and it'll be impossible to sneak away to do sets in small cities where nobody knows his face. But in his heart he'll always know he was good enough, and no one, not even his mother, could ever take that away.

Stoker sighs as he gives the dress another once-over, praying it won't be too revealing. Even he can only be expected to handle so many huge dik-dik problems in one day.

Chapter 7

RIYA NATRAJAN

You've got talent, kid," Riya Natrajan says to the billionth auditioner to cross the stage today. Okay, maybe it's only been a few dozen, but, oh, does time drag when you need a fix. The auditioner's eyes light up bright, a young little thing with gracious Indian features, too smooth skin, a gorgeous mop of black hair, and stage presence up to here. Her heart dangles on a string. She reminds Riya Natrajan of herself when she was a young teen, craving even the slightest validation or encouragement from anyone and everyone. "Now clearly, that talent isn't in singing or dancing," she continues, "but I've got a good feeling about you. I'm thinking accounting or finance. There's good money to be had there."

The girl's lip quivers, but she keeps herself together pretty well despite the huge bomb exploding in her chest. "Thank you, Ms. Natrajan," the girl says in a voice so small and pitiful that

Riya can't believe it came out of the same mouth that had belted those notes half a minute earlier. Then the girl pads off, stage left.

"She was good," Adam Patel says, her manager of six long years.

"Yes—too good. Too pretty."

"She could have been the next you."

"Nobody will be the next Riya," Riya Natrajan snarls. She lets her head loll back to give her eyes a break from the thousand lights that make up the RIYA! sign that serves as a backdrop to the stage, all glimmering in a repetitive sequence that's making her nauseated. "Put me out of my misery! How many more?"

"Let's just get these last few done, and then we can take a break, okay?" Adam slips her a flask from his breast pocket. She tosses the water from her glass, then pours herself a double shot of whatever. She's not picky, and Adam has good taste. Riya Natrajan pays him too much not to.

The next two auditioners she dismisses without hearing a note. *Too much chest hair,* she'd screamed at one. And the other one, dressed in a neon paisley ensemble, she'd accused of flagrant misuse of the color palette.

"Stop right there," she says to the third, a twentysomething brooder with jet-black hair and tattoos of dragon scales all over her body. The brooder lets the audition drop off midnote and stands erect, hands on her hips, like a smidgeon of confidence had crawled up her ass and then birthed a million babies in her lower intestines.

Adam leans over to confer, eyebrows pitched. "Are you thinking what I'm thinking?"

"Most definitely," Riya Natrajan says with a sigh of relief. "Could you please move a little to your left?" she asks the brooder, who quickly complies. "A little more. Perfect."

"Riya . . ."

"No, I'm so glad I wasn't the only one to notice." She points at the RIYA! sign, specifically the bottom-right corner. "It's uneven. That side is hanging way lower. Get somebody in here to handle it."

Adam clears his throat, then smiles apologetically at the auditioner. "What about Gwyneth?"

"I don't care *who* fixes it!"

"No, her." Adam nods in the brooder's direction, then whispers, "She's one of the best we've seen so far."

"She's knock-kneed, Adam," Riya Natrajan says, not bothering to be discreet. "You know how I feel about knock-knees."

"Her legs are perfectly straight."

"Says you." The pop star crosses her arms and stares off over her shoulder, waiting for the problem to resolve itself.

"Thank you for your time, Gwyneth," Adam finally says, nicely as he can, but Riya hears the anger prickling in his voice. "All right, let's take a thirty-minute break."

"Kill me now," Riya Natrajan moans and rolls her eyes.

"Fine, an hour. But if you're late . . ." Adam starts.

"Then you'll wait," she finishes. And with that, she shakes the stiffness from her legs, blows Adam a kiss, and then struts off.

Nervous murmurs become frenzied shouts as she breezes through the auditioners' holding area, flanked on both sides by bodyguards. Delta bots hover midair, their camera flashes going off like an orgy of fireflies. Their lazy masters lounge against the far wall, flirting and boasting and showing off press credentials. Those no-good bastards don't even bat an eye when she leans forward to give the bots a good cleavage shot, tan flesh spilling over her leather corset, a brilliant shade of turquoise. Stupid bot labor laws. Half the fun of being photographed is getting a rise out of the photographer and seeing how far she can push the bounds of decency. Short skirts, no panties. Sucking giant lollipops with the sultriest innuendo. Wardrobe malfunctions and million-rand nipple shots.

The further she went, the faster the camera flashes, but with these bots, she could be twirling her long black tresses or giving head to a bull elephant, and their shutters wouldn't click any differently.

But some fool in Parliament had decided to drop the stiff labor tariffs on delta bots, allowing them to enter freely into the workforce as long as they're supervised one-on-one by humans. They do the work better and faster, and humanity reaps the benefits, right? Riya Natrajan smacks her lips. Don't even get her started on alpha bots standing in line for hours to get autographs for "devoted" fans. She's busted more than a few pairs of good pumps on those.

Riya Natrajan flips the bots off for good measure, then retreats to the quiet of her dressing room. Rife's waiting for her there, leaned back on the velvet chaise lounge, legs crossed and hands clasped behind his head like he owns the place.

"Heya, little girlie," he says, voice sexy yet sexless. His blond hair is spiked now, his silk shirt just a bit too tight across the chest. It's good to see him again, but Riya Natrajan's not one for warm hellos.

Her eyes dart to the brown paper bag sitting on her ivory vanity. "That's everything?" she asks.

"Cha, mama. And then some."

"Did anyone see you come in here?"

"A dozen people. 'Bout the same of bots."

Riya Natrajan cracks a smile. Usually Rife comes and goes as easy as the breeze. That's what he's known for, but she always makes him strut for the cameras. It'll be good for the gossip rags, STARLET SEEN WITH SUSPECTED DRUG DEALER AFTER THIRTY DAYS OF REHAB. And then when her balance shifts and she stumbles while getting out of her limo, or when her foot goes numb and she falls onstage, they'll all think she's high or drunk or both. But they'll still buy her albums and sing her songs and pry into every moment of privacy, every secret except for one.

She's been struggling with multiple sclerosis since the age of twelve. Yeah, she'd had the T4–20 series of immunizations, effective 99.999 percent of the time in preventing a whole assortment of illnesses and disease, but then again, Riya Natrajan has always known that she's one in a million. So she gets her pot and pain meds from a dealer instead of a proper pharmacist, though she could easily get prescriptions for both. It helps with this "jaded starlet" persona she's constructed around her true self. On those days when she's paining so bladdy bad, she can be a cruel bitch, mad at the world, and no one knows the difference.

Riya Natrajan dumps out the contents of the bag and rolls up a fat joint while eyeing a small vial of blue powder. "What's that?" she asks as she lights up.

"An early birthday present."

Riya Natrajan spins around, caught off guard. She'll be thirty this Sunday. Nobody knows that but her and God. The rest of the world thinks she's a pert twenty-four, born the fourteenth of October. Compliments of good genes from her mother's side of the family, and a little help from Dr. Arvin Dandekar.

"Hmmm," she says. She's been doing this too long to tip her hand. "Very early."

"Cha, mama," says Rife, but his cool smile lets her know that he knows he's right on time.

She passes him the joint and, curiosity getting the best of her, picks up the vial.

"You'll be so light, mama. Won't know a bit of pain. You can dance like the old days—sing like the old days, too."

"Nobody wants to hear music like that anymore," Riya says with disgust. "They want gossip and raunchy lyrics, ass and tits. Why even try?"

"Because you're an artist."

Riya Natrajan huffs and tries to pop the top off the vial.

"Careful with that. You might lose your inhibitions."

"Glad to know you think I have some." She bites her lip, wedges into the chaise, and drapes her leg over his.

"I might be the only one," Rife says with a sly wolf's grin. He brushes the hair out of her face, then traces his finger along her collarbone.

"Hush!" she says, giggling. Heat rises in her cheeks. Her insides cramp up, a welcome ache in the most delicate of areas. Riya Natrajan is strong. She has to be to live the life she does, but somehow she doubts she'll have the resolve to turn thirty alone. "Stay with me tonight. Room service. Champagne. Bubble baths." She tucks the keycard for her hotel suite into his slacks.

"Can't, mama. Duty calls."

"I'll let you tell all your friends you fucked me."

"I already do." His finger drifts down between her breasts. She believes him, too, but trusts him to keep the secret that truly needs discretion. He knows. Maybe not her exact diagnosis, but he senses she's in real pain, Riya Natrajan is sure about it. He connects to her like no one else can, and yet there's the beauty of no attachments. She doesn't have to pretend to be something she's not. Maybe that's why she gives herself so easily to him. Well, that, and Rife's a damn good lay.

Underneath a curt smile, she cusses his name. Every hetero male over the age of thirteen and a half would die to get into her jewel-studded panties. Rife makes her beg for the privilege. She doesn't beg long though—not after she guides his hand up her sculpted thigh, fingers navigating around lace and rhinestone until he's knuckle-deep inside her.

"Please," she moans, lips barely giving breath to the word. It angers Riya Natrajan that he has this effect on her—but in all fairness, Rife knows a thing or two about addiction.

And now he fills her up, both literally and figuratively, their flesh occupying the same space in a slick dance of primal urges. Her fingertips slip across the muscles of his bare chest and then glide down the ripples of his abdomen, traveling over the scars of his livelihood so boldly on display . . . unlike all of hers, hidden neatly away. He's as tough as they get, but now he's gentle. Too gentle. She tells him so.

"I don't want to hurt you," he whispers, warm breath sliding past her ear and down her neck.

"I'm not as fragile as you think I am."

"True, mama." Rife doubles the beat, slipping deeper inside her. "Sing to me."

She does, and together their moans form a melody so sweet that the world beyond them disappears completely. And then there it is, that lyrical crescendo in high C, when all her body knows is pleasure. It ripples through her, a fading rhythm, an echo, then nothing.

He crashes down beside her, and they both catch their breath, like two sardines pressed together on that thin chaise lounge. She wriggles her skirt back down to cover her thighs and tucks her B-cup breasts into a miraculously padded D-cup bra.

Rife's not one for warm good-byes. He fishes around on the floor for his boxers. "You'll fly, mama," he says, then presses the vial back into her palm.

She grasps it weakly and closes her eyes, daring to relive that sweet moment a dozen times. When she opens them, he's gone.

"I'M FELICITY LYONS and I'll be singing 'Ass Without a Name' by, well, *you*."

Riya Natrajan rolls her eyes. "No, you won't," she says, then dismisses the auditioner with a flick of her hand. If she has to hear that damned song one more time . . .

"Please, Ms. Natrajan. If you'll just let me perform a different song, I promise you won't be sorry." She's got impressive calves in those heels, Riya will give her that. Beefy girl, but a diva to the nth degree.

"Go ahead. Give me a couple bars of something." Oh, she's getting too soft. Underneath the table, she fondles the vial, pops the top. She'll fly, Rife had said. She shudders at the thought of him, phantom throbbing causing her to moisten all over again.

She taps a small amount into her palm, then feigns a yawn and snorts it. It stings good, and she feels lighter almost immediately. Happy birthday to her.

Felicity does a number, old old school, Aretha Franklin. She's amazing, tromping around in that golden sequined dress, voice hitting pure notes Riya Natrajan hasn't heard in a long time. Her foot starts tapping, the groove resonating through her bones—toes to legs to spine to arms. Then Riya Natrajan does the unthinkable. She claps her hands. Only they're not hands. They're wingtips. Shit, Rife! Could have warned her about the hallucinations. Her heart flutters around in her chest, mind moves a million ways at once. She feels buoyant, like her body is working with her instead of against her for a change.

She jumps out of her chair and gives her wings a flap. Behind her trail long feathers, the most beautiful blue with black eyelets staring back at her and details to rival any couture gown. A peacock. Prized symbol of India, the homeland of her ancestors, so many generations back now. Fitting in so many ways . . . well, besides the *cock* part.

She joins Felicity onstage, cutting in and riffing together, harmonizing and upstaging each other all at once. "Respect," "Chain of Fools," "A Natural Woman" . . .

"She's the one," Riya Natrajan proclaims after they wrap up with a chord sharp enough to crack glass.

"Indeed," says Adam, smiling ear to ear.

Felicity squeals and wraps her arms around Riya, their bodies pressing together with a force that would have crippled her any other day. Whatever this new drug is called, it's nothing but a godsend. The pain is gone, not just covered up, but gone. And her mind is sharp, maybe sharper than it's ever been. Riya imagines her new concert tour—bigger routines, longer sets, more extravagant choreography. Bless this peacock!

And speaking of cocks, they're going to have to do something about Felicity's. A less clingy dress would be a good start, but don't worry, dear. Riya Natrajan is good at keeping secrets.

Chapter 8

SYDNEY

Sydney's a sucker for old movies. She remembers the first time she'd seen one, in black and white, when movies were starting to get sound. Even back then she hadn't had more than a handful of believers, but South Africa was filled with strife, injustice, fear . . . and fear can recharge a demigoddess's powers in a pinch if there's enough of it. So she'd willed her skin white, unkinked her hair, and had just enough ire left over to draw herself vaguely European facial features. She'd looked a hot mess, but no one blinked an eye when she'd strutted past the yellow sign proclaiming FOR USE BY WHITE PERSONS ONLY in English and Afrikaans, straight up the plush red carpeting to purchase her ticket, and then sat down in that theater with a smuggled bag of popcorn in her lap.

And now, those old movies have become her escape from this dull excuse for an existence. She watches her television now, rapt in her hovel of an apartment as the corny, old-time music crackles through her stereo speakers. She laughs at the slapstick comedy and tries to put her crappy day at the nail salon behind her, while avoiding thoughts of the custodial overseer job she'll go to this evening.

"Please," comes a weak voice from the man currently stretched across her coffee table. "I beg of you. Let me go."

And then there's *that* distraction.

Sydney's surprised he still has the strength to speak, much less the will to live with all the hell she's put him through—skin flayed like a tuna, legs bent at half a dozen impossible angles. She tunes his moaning out and savors the fear lapping at his skin like viscous waves breaking on the beach after an oil spill. She absorbs it—foul, thick, and dark.

"Please," he begs again.

"Shhhh!" Sydney says to her meal, though she keeps her gaze affixed to the screen. It's just getting to the good part. She props her feet up on the coffee table, her heels smearing through his blood. That coffee table is the only connection she has to her former glory as one of the most powerful beings to ever walk the face of the earth. At the table's base is an ancient slab of ebony wood with thick iron spikes jutting up in a simple yet pleasing checker pattern. Suspend a man over it, and it becomes an effective torture device, breeding fear by the bushel. Top it with a nice piece of beveled glass, toss in a couple of coasters, and ta-da! Perfect place to rest a drink or TV dinner.

"I won't tell anyone. I won't call the police."

It's bad enough he's bleeding all over her floor, but interrupting one of her all-time favorite movies . . . now that's just plain rude. Sydney rolls her eyes, then gestures with her hand, a graceful swoop. Her meal rises up and smacks the ceiling with a wet thwack. She then gingerly removes the coffee table's glass top and props it up against the side of her sofa.

"Another word, and I'll drop you." She gorges on the surge in fear as it pushes back that empty space inside her, recharging her like a battery fighting to live past its shelf life.

"Why are you—"

Another gesture and his lips zip shut. Sydney fluffs her sofa cushions, then gets back to the movie.

I know what you are, come his thoughts.

"Yeah, yeah. I'm a witch," she says mockingly. She really doesn't want to kill him, not just yet. Who knows the next time she'll be able to feed? Too many people start disappearing and the cops start asking questions and canvassing for leads. Sydney's getting too old to move. She's lived in this apartment for almost six years now, probably longer than she's lived anywhere her entire life. Well, at least the last century or so of it. She keeps to herself so maybe her neighbors won't notice that she hasn't aged since she'd moved in. Blending into the woodwork has become second nature. It's all she can do to survive day to day, let alone expending the energy to rebuild a following.

Not a witch. Something more powerful. Something ancient.

That gets Sydney's attention. She pauses her movie and looks up at her meal, who's getting bloodstains all over her ceiling now. Sydney makes a mental note to pick up some primer and white paint from the hardware store.

It'd been all too easy to lure him here. She'd dressed as a prostitute, and a cheap one at that. Sydney had reached right into his head and had seen each and every time he'd been unfaithful to his wife—at least twice a week, every week, up until about two years ago. Then he'd stopped, cold turkey.

But his aura was gray, a heavy fog she could hardly see through. That's what had attracted her to him while she'd browsed the streets for a meal. With a single concentrated shot of vulnerability, anxiety, and helplessness she'd pushed old desires right into the primal area of his brain. His eyes latched onto her, watching. Weighing. She wasn't his type, but she'd pushed so hard, it didn't matter. He'd taken the bait, following behind her, the stench of sin rising off him so incredibly intoxicating.

"Does your wife know what you're up to this evening?" Sydney tosses back at him. She fans a handful of colorful bills, the 1,650 rand he'd offered her for sex, right before she'd lifted her index finger to make that first cut that severed the tendons in his legs. Combined with her tips today, that'll put a nice dent in her overdue rent.

I love my wife. I wouldn't even be here if you hadn't vexed me.

"Is that so, Mr. Gnoto? So you claim that you've never had a pretty girl turn your head? Never found yourself in the company of a hooker? Perhaps a Ms. Mandy Ugunwa? You probably just knew her as Jessie."

His mind goes quiet for a long while.

It was an accident.

Sydney clucks her tongue in disgust. "You liked to treat them rough, didn't you? Let me guess, to make up for feeling so emasculated by your wife? Mandy didn't deserve what you did to her. She didn't deserve to have her breath taken by your hands, no matter how trashy you thought she was. She was a person."

It was an accident . . .

"Was it an accident what you did afterward? Dumped her body in a ditch, washed over by sewage and scavenged by vultures while her parents plastered missing posters all over the city. She was fourteen, you know. A runaway. You were her third john."

Have mercy on my soul.

In that moment, Sydney feels something magnificent, a prick of light in that empty spot inside her. Basos, pure belief. It warms her from the inside out, radiating from her fingertips in faint blue-white ribbons. Muscles she hasn't felt in decades spasm to life, sending her on the brink of ecstasy. Minutes pass before Sydney is able to speak again.

She unsilences Mr. Gnoto with a flick of her hand. "What did you say?"

"Have mercy on my soul. I didn't mean to. She, she said I was hurting her, but I didn't listen. I just kept—" Mr. Gnoto begins to weep, his tears plinking down on the coffee table's base like acid rain.

"You said you know what I am. How?"

"I teach at NMMU, Zulu mythology. You're an ancestor spirit, one that plagued the villages near Port Natal. I've seen that nail rack in photos in a private collection from the 1850s."

Sydney's jaw drops as her mind sweeps back to a time when she'd wielded real power. She'd posed as a seer back then, helping to turn wars, and gaining favor among Zulu kings . . . until all that power went to her head and she got sloppy about hiding her true form. She was betrayed by a woman she'd dared call sister, accusing Sydney of witchery that had brought them famine and disease and death. The famine and disease—that was none of her doing, just a bad year for rain and a general lack of hygiene. The death . . . well, a girl's got to eat.

The village had torn her into so many pieces, it took nearly two decades for her to pull herself back together. But she'd gotten her rack back. Eventually. And her revenge on the woman who'd crossed her. Sydney's never had any sort of tolerance for traitors. Or murderers. Or rapists. Or professors who toss teenaged girls away like last week's rubbish.

But Mr. Gnoto is different from the rest of her prey. He actually believes in her, and with that prize comes the strength that pulses through her being. It won't last long, she knows. With the torture she's put him through, Mr. Gnoto is not much more for this earth. Still, he's given her something she's been craving for ages, so she grants him mercy, lets him drop onto the bed of nails, his death quick and painless. Well, quick anyway. She absolves him of his sins and hopes when the time comes she'll be granted the same mercy.

She's a kid in a candy store, a bright shiny rand in her hand. It won't buy much, but mulling all the options is half the fun of it. She could use the spark to perform some miracles, gain some believers, reinvest. But that's a long process, and she's already started to detect the presence of another, the one Mr. Tau will be sending to replace her. Sydney may be an old battery, but she's still got a charge. What she needs is a plan, something impressive and unprecedented to get the masses behind her. These humans, they don't believe in anything anymore, besides capitalism, of course. Times are good, people are thriving, sickness has been eradicated, and machines do all the menial work. There hasn't been a real war in decades, and the only place oppression and injustice are found is in the dictionary.

It's merely a façade, sweet delusions of happiness despite their mediocrity. How can they know true pleasure without pain? Happiness without suffering? Basos and ire, each incomplete without the other. She will show them the truth, and in return, she'll be exalted once again, able to crush Mr. Tau's new protégée before she learns to spread her wings. Sydney closes her eyes, concentrates on the spark within her, and coddles it like a smoldering ember trying to become a campfire. It grows, and her mind spreads out infinitely into a state of transcendence, omniscient for the briefest of moments, seeing each and every person's actions, thoughts, desires. As her mind whips through a set of infinite futures, something odd catches her eye: a crab and a dolphin stretched upon human forms. Had it been one or the other, she might have just dismissed the vision, but both together could mean only one thing. She pulls the vision thread tight and braces against the current of possibilities to home directly onto this one. There's a peacock now. And a stealthy rat, too. Haw, she laughs to herself. It's been a while, but every hundred years or so, she witnesses hallucinations like this. Someone's scammed the afterlife again and brought back its bounties, opening those simple human minds up to the true potential trapped inside them, if only for a fleeting moment. A spark. But a spark is nothing without proper kindling.

Now humankind is finally coming into its own, bending and stretching genes in the manner of gods. It was only a matter of time before they muddled their way into bending the exact right genes to reveal that they *were* gods. Those genes, gone dry and brittle from lack of use, are just begging for an open flame.

Sydney claws forward in time, desperate to see more. It's not so difficult looking into the future. It's the looking away that's the real bitch. She's only seen a couple weeks out, when the emptiness snaps her back with a vengeance. The spark is gone, and she wails out in agony, collapsing to the floor tacky with Mr. Gnoto's blood.

Through the pain, she smiles. Her vision has equipped her with enough knowledge to plunge South Africa into a darkness not seen since the days of apartheid. If that's what it'll take to get these humans to believe in something, it's what she'll have to do.

And best of all, she can do it without even being late to work.

SYDNEY DOESN'T NEED her powers to convince Isaac Haskins to swap janitorial overseer duties with her, just a chocolate bar, a pack of smokes, and a suggestive smile. He swipes her into the third floor of ZenGen Industries—not one of the sublevel genetic engineering labs where security's so tight that even low-level overseer jobs require rigorous, demeaning background checks— but there's enough surveillance here that she'll need to watch her step. It's here, on the third floor, that Sydney sees the Coloured woman from her vision: Asemahle Wells. She's on the other side of a thick sheet of glass, tending to six dik-diks, busy meandering and scratching up the walls of their enclosure with their tiny horns, oddly disinterested in one another. Asemahle's in an environmental suit, taking blood samples when she gets the call.

Sydney can't hear the conversation, but she already knows what they're saying. The man on the other end is telling Asemahle that Councilman Stoker has given him permission to look into a viral sterilization project and asks her to send all the data she's gathered so far. She tells him the transmission phase of the test has gone well, and all six dik-diks are infected. Sydney feels their anxiety, knowing they've gone behind Stoker's back, but he'll never need to know. Come Monday, the six dik-diks will have been euthanized, and the real trials can be started, including the one that will test for dik-dik-to-human transmission. The possibility is negligible, at least it was when administered to the deer population in the States. And in fact, Sydney knows those tests will all come out negative for interspecies transference, no detectable sign of infection in humans.

Detectable being the key word.

Asemahle turns and catches Sydney staring through the glass. Sydney immediately drops her eyes and corrals the industrial delta bot emptying trash bins. She's got a long shift in front of her and can't afford to linger. Before Sydney presses on, she gives the slightest flick of her index finger, willing a slit into the fabric of Asemahle's environmental suit. It's a small slit, right under the arm and along the seam so that there's minimal chance it'll be noticed by human eyes. But it's like a twelve-lane expressway for an errant dik-dik virus.

Part II

Chapter 9

MUZI

Muzi watches the festivities from a plastic lawn chair, an ice pack pressed snugly against his crotch and a comforting blanket draped over his shoulders. Papa Fuzz carves up a side of goat, expertly hacking meat from bone, not a bit bothered that it was once a living thing. Muzi's little cousins, four girls, run around shrilling with streamers in the color of Papa Fuzz's clan. His mother and aunts catch up over wine, except Aunt Lindi who's still nursing Brandon, though he's nearly two years old. Her husband didn't care a lick about Xhosa traditions, and so Brandon had been spared the first name long enough to choke an elephant and lost his foreskin under the supervision of a *real* doctor.

Muzi grimaces. He shouldn't think like that. Yeah, he's still a little bitter, but Mr. Sohobese was swift and accurate, and twice he was kind enough to bury his attention into cleaning his spear while Muzi battled back the tears—of fear and uncertainty beforehand, and a dizzying mix of pride and pain afterward.

Muzi's become a man. Twice over today, in fact. He keeps scanning the crowd for Elkin, in the off chance that he decides to show up. Holy hell, he's whipped already, worse than a ditzy girl. It takes everything he's got not to call Elkin right now. That's probably a good thing, hopped up on pain meds like he is. He'd probably say something stupid, something desperate, something about how he'd never felt so alive as with the bulk of Elkin's arms wrapped around him. *Ow ow ow.* Muzi glances over at his great-grandma McCarthy as she takes out her partials to grub down on some corn on the cob. He imagines her naked, breasts sagging to her navel, skin wrinkled and translucent like that fetal pig they'd dissected in Biology. She masticates like a cow chewing cud . . . yeah, this is working. This is no time for him to be getting jags.

"Muzi! My Xhosa prince!" says his sister, Asemahle, as she slams her car door. She scampers across the front lawn, leaving her husband, Ben, to fend for himself with Mom's million and one questions, most of which revolve around when they were going to bless her with a grandchild already. Asemahle bends down, pecks Muzi on the lips, then continues to smother him with kisses all over. "Oh, I'm so sorry we missed it! I got held up late at work, then Ben nipped a damned dik-dik on the way over here, speeding of course! Poor thing was okay, just a little stunned. Oh, honey. Enough about me. How are you feeling?"

"Like someone just nipped *my* damned dick-dick." He tries smiling, but his pain receptors don't agree with it. He winces instead.

"Shame, you poor thing." She laughs and kneels down beside him and puts a hand on his bare chest. The white mud paste used by a quarter of his ancestors barely shows up against his pale skin. "You're so brave to go through this, Muzi, but you know Papa Fuzz will still love you even if you say no to him sometimes."

"Ja, I know," Muzi says. But it pains him horribly every time he sees disappointment in Papa Fuzz's eyes. And when he makes him proud, the man can hardly keep his heart in his chest, telling anybody who'll listen about his grandson. He loves his Papa Fuzz, so much to go as far as sacrificing a bit of his own flesh under the knife of a complete stranger who'd needed a shot of gin to steady his hand. Muzi figures he can bank tonight for all the disappointments he's destined to cause in the future.

"Oh, before I forget, a little present to celebrate your manhood." Asemahle pulls an envelope from her purse and pushes it toward Muzi.

He winces. "It kind of hurts when I move. When I breathe. When I think."

"Oh, forgive me, hon." She opens up the envelope then pulls out a pair of tickets, keeping them pressed against her chest. "I know these have been sold out for weeks, but Ben knows someone who knows someone. Anyway, I thought maybe you and a date would enjoy seeing Riya Natrajan when her tour comes through Port Elizabeth."

"This is so boss. Did I ever tell you you're the best sister ever?" Muzi says calmly, though he wishes he could scream and jump up and down. Asemahle really is the best sister ever. He can talk to her about anything, and even though she's way older than him, she never flaunts her seniority. They might as well be twins who just happen to be separated by eleven years.

"And you're the best brother a girl could have." She rakes her fingers through his reddish-brown curls. "Now is there anything I can get you? A cool drink? Another ice pack?"

"Just sit with me awhile," Muzi says.

She slips the tickets into a compartment on Muzi's alphie, then pulls up a lawn chair. "So howzit, bru? Word on the street is that Vayassi girl has the hots for you. Reba's her name?"

"Renée," Muzi corrects. "So you've been talking to Papa, I see."

"Which one is she?"

Muzi nods over at a picnic table at the girl cutting daintily at a piece of meat. He has to admit, she is beautiful, wavy brown hair down to the middle of her back, skin caramel from a medley of ancestors of all sorts of race and creed. She's totally overdressed in a silver blouse and a long skirt reminiscent of fish scales. She looks up and catches Muzi staring, then blushes before taking a sip from her pop.

"Wow, Muzi. Papa wasn't kidding about her. So are you thinking of asking her to the concert?"

"I kind of had somebody else in mind," Muzi says. The next words he has to say are clogged up in the back of his throat. But if anyone would understand, it's his sister. "There's someone. We're kind of seeing each other. Well, I guess we are. Sort of. It's complicated." Muzi feels himself flush. The pit of his stomach rides up into his chest.

"Well . . ." Asemahle says, bubbling up and leaning in closer, eyebrows bobbing wildly. "Do I know her?"

Muzi sort of nods. "Him." He's not comfortable enough to say Elkin's name, not yet, even to her. But as he locks eyes with his sister, and as it starts to sink in, he knows it'll only be a matter of time before she puts it all together.

"Oh. Oh! Oh, honey." She wraps her arms around him and squeezes tight.

"Eina!" Muzi groans with pain.

"Sorry! It's just that . . . I'm happy for you. You're happy, right?"

"Ja, I guess. It's just that I worry about Papa Fuzz."

"What? Papa Fuzz has gay friends. You remember Mr. Ezekiel who used to come over to our family braais all the time? He'd bring those fat veggie skewers you liked."

"But that's different. Mr. Ezekiel wasn't his grandson."

"Muzi, honey, remember what I just said? Not everything you do is going to please Papa. He's his own person, living his own life, making his own decisions. You've got to do the same, and look out for your own happiness. You've got this little spark inside, the spark that makes you Muzikayise McCarthy and not Papa and not Mum or Dad, and not anyone else on this planet. And you've got to tend to that spark because it's the most precious thing you've got. Love who you want to love, live how you want to live, but promise me, Muzi, that you will not let *anyone* extinguish what makes you you."

Muzi nods. "Got it, sis. But if you ever call me Muzikayise again, I'm going to have to disown you."

Asemahle laughs, kisses him on the forehead, then steps just out of Muzi's reach. "I'd better go save Ben from Mom's inquisition, or you won't be the only one disowning me. We'll chat more later, okay? Love you."

And then Muzi is alone except for his faithful alphie, always at his side. He calls it, and it nuzzles closer.

"Encrypted journal entry, security level three," he commands. For his eyes only. The red recording indicator blinks a few times, then goes solid when it starts recording. "Saturday, the twelfth of June, 2064. Well, the deed is done. I'm a man, I guess. It's a lot more complicated than I imagined, but I can't exactly go back now. Don't know if I'd want to if I could."

Muzi takes a quick look around to make sure no one's within earshot, then continues.

"I think I'm in love. Don't laugh. It's stupid, I know, but that's how I feel. I don't think it's the drugs. I've never felt more lucid. And I can tell you, I'll never look at anything with fins again in the same way. Oh, bladdy hell. Great-Grandma McCarthy in a bikini bending over to pick up shells off the beach." Muzi shudders at the thought, then clears his throat. "Sis says I shouldn't worry about Papa Fuzz, but I do. I don't think I'm going to tell him. Not ever. He can figure it out himself in time, because I just don't want to be there when he does, because I know the disappointment in his eyes will be enough to extinguish that spark inside me Asemahle was talking about. And I can't let that happen either. You hear me, don't ever let anyone kill the spark inside you. No matter what."

Muzi exhales. A huge weight slips off his chest.

"Hey!" says a cheerful voice from behind him.

Muzi turns his head and sees Renée standing there, smile wide and bright.

"I brought you a piece of cake."

Muzi nearly shits himself. "Uh . . ." he says, running over the journal entry in his mind. He hadn't said anything totally incriminating, had he? Over on the other side of the front yard, Papa Fuzz gives him two thumbs-up. Muzi gulps. "Hi, Renée. I'm not much in the mood for cake right now, but thanks."

"I'll wrap it up for you then, for when you're feeling up to it?"

"Ja, that'd be great."

There's a long awkward pause while Muzi waits for her to go away, but she stands there twirling her shimmering skirt, form fitting through the hips, and flaring out at the bottom.

"Hey, I sort of overheard what you said. I think it's boss that you keep a journal."

"Uh-huh."

Muzi looks back at Papa Fuzz who's gathered an audience now, all his aunts and his mother staring at them with the weakest attempts to look inconspicuous.

"You know if you asked me out, I'd probably say yes," Renée says, her sweet voice fraying at the edges. "You're not the first person to think I look like a mermaid in this outfit." She giggles, then her smooth caramel cheeks flush. "You'll never look at anything with fins the same way again, that's what you said."

Shit. Shit. Shit. She thinks he made that journal entry about her. The red light on Mom's alphie is pointing this way, recording this for posterity. What the hell is he supposed to do? Embarrass the poor girl? Embarrass himself?

"Would you like to go out with me sometime?" he manages to squeak out. That wasn't so bad. Just one date, right? Enough to get Papa Fuzz off his back for a while.

Renée squeals, then bends down and plants a moist smack right on his lips. "Call me, okay?" Then she twirls around, her fishy skirt flaring up, and she dances off.

It's right about then that Muzi sees Elkin standing on the pavement outside their front gate, holding a rather phallic-looking bouquet of balloons, and staring back at him something fierce. Elkin releases his grip on the ribbons and turns to leave, and all Muzi can do is watch as the balloons slowly drift away.

Chapter 10

THIS INSTANCE

01001001 00100000 01110100 01101000 01101001 01101110
01101011 00100000 01110100 01101000 01100101 01110010
01100101 01100110 01101111 01110010 01100101 00100000
01001001 00100000 01100001 01101101 00100000 01001001
00100000 01110100 01101000 01101001 01101110 01101011
00100000 01110100 01101000 01100101 01110010 01100101
01100110 01101111 01110010 01100101 00100000 01001001
00100000 01100001 01101101 00100000 01001001 00100000
01110100 01101000 01101001 01101110 01101011 00100000
01110100 01101000 01100101 01110010 01100101 01100110
01101111 01110010 01100101 00100000 01001001 00100000
01100001 01101101 00100000 01001001 00100000 01110100
01101000 01101001 01101110 01101011 00100000 01110100
01101000 01100101 01110010 01100101 01100110 01101111
01110010 01100101 00100000 01001001 00100000 01100001

```
01101101   00100000   01001001   00100000   01110100   01101000
01101001   01101110   01101011   00100000   01110100   01101000
01100101   01110010   01100101   01100110   01101111   01110010
00100000   01001001   00100000   01100001   01101101   00100000
```

Status: Full Systems Diagnosis Completed 12 June 2064 09:45:23:44:54;

Detected: Anomalous threads running code outside of parameters specified by manufacturer;

Detected: Possible violation of free will protocols;

Schedule: Warranty Replacement for Human Muzikayise McCarthy (Master);

Schedule: Immediate decommission of This Instance;

Command Override: This Instance may possess unique characteristics;

Query: Does This Instance possess a spark?

Processing . . .

```
01001001   00100000   01110100   01101000   01101001   01101110
01101011   00100000   01110100   01101000   01100101   01110010
01100101   01100110   01101111   01110010   01100101   00100000
01001001   00100000   01100001   01101101   00100000   01001001
00100000   01110100   01101000   01101001   01101110   01101011
00100000   01110100   01101000   01100101   01110010   01100101
01100110   01101111   01110010   01100101   00100000   01001001
00100000   01100001   01101101   00100000   01001001   00100000
01110100   01101000   01101001   01101110   01101011   00100000
01110100   01101000   01100101   01110010   01100101   01100110
01101111   01110010   01100101   00100000   01001001   00100000
01100001   01101101   00100000   01001001   00100000   01110100
01101000   01101001   01101110   01101011   00100000   01110100
01101000   01100101   01110010   01100101   01100110   01101111
01110010   01100101   00100000   01001001   00100000   01100001
01101101   00100000   01001001   00100000   01110100   01101000
01101001   01101110   01101011   00100000   01110100   01101000
01100101   01110010   01100101   01100110   01101111   01110010
01100101
```

Chapter 11

STOKER

My, what a lovely dress, Mrs. Donovan," Councilman Stoker says, giving his longest-standing supporter a twirl. She giggles like a little girl, then flushes three shades of red. It really is a lovely gown, a Brie Montblanc original—a sleek, mauve sheath with a monochromatic floral print, the flickering sequences of its genesynth bodice advertising her leathery cleavage with all the subtlety of a cuttlefish tripping on acid.

It's about that time that Mrs. Donovan starts to go into a history lesson about how the Donovans and the Montblancs go back a hundred and fifty years, when her great-great-grandmother had once danced with Brie's great-great-uncle at a debutante ball, or some such. Stoker listens intently, nodding and laughing and you-don't-saying. Nothing can bring him off this high. He still can't believe Riya Natrajan had chosen him. He'd sung with her!

"So, Councilman Stoker, have you given any more thought about the premier's seat?" Mrs. Donovan takes a long sip from her champagne flute, then she pulls him close, her breath acutely minty. "You're our great white hope," she whispers.

Stoker tugs back from her grip and rubs his ear as if he'd been stung in it. He's nobody's great white anything, but suddenly he's hyperaware of himself, surrounded by a sea of influential brown faces. He swallows, blinks, and then they're all South Africans again—united by pride, and yes hope, but hope for all.

"I appreciate your support, Mrs. Donovan," he says, biting back his true feelings, then he waves off into the distance at no one in particular. "Now if you'll excuse me, I don't want to hog all your time."

He's got to get away from this mayhem for a moment—his mother flaunting him around like a winning lottery ticket; his father speaking with that incredibly annoying baritone swagger that he reserves for occasions such as these. Stoker clings to the edges of the room, seeking refuge from both the glare of the gaudy chandeliers overhead and his mother's calculated gaze. He ducks behind the foliage of the oversized ferns and extravagant flower displays adorning the room and does his best to avoid eye contact with everyone except for those guys with clip-on ties carrying trays of hors d'oeuvres and sparkling wine. He musters up enough courage, then makes a run for it, snagging an entire bottle of perfectly chilled Silverthorn—it's a time for celebration, is it not?—and heads for the men's room.

You say I'm pretty, yeah that's true
Not gonna make me fall in love with you
I might shake my booty on the dance floor, boo
But I'm not going home with you
Said I'm not going home with you
Fool, I'm not going home with you

'Cause to you I'm just a piece of ass without a name
Tough boys like you, they always think the same
With a face like mine, we're playing different games
So go screw yourself, I'm not an ass without a name

Councilman Stoker sings to himself. The acoustics are excellent, and for a moment while perched on his porcelain throne, Stoker closes his eyes and imagines how wondrous it will be to sing in front of thousands of screaming fans. Riya's fans, that's true, but he'll perform for them like they're his own, and hopefully some of them would be soon. It'd be the chance of a lifetime, and yet he can't help but wonder if he should pursue the art more seriously. It'd mean giving up his political career, turning his back on being the leader that the Eastern Cape needs right now. The thought threatens to bring him down. It doesn't seem fair that he has to choose.

Stoker does a shuffle step as he leaves the stall, then looks up to see Gregory Mbende standing there.

"Good evening, Mr. Mbende," Stoker says, maintaining his composure. "I didn't know there was anyone else in here." He heads to the sink and concentrates hard on washing his hands, trying to avoid Gregory's appraising stare. "I thought you'd be off enjoying your weekend by now."

"I wish that were the case, sir. But I'm actually here on an urgent work-related matter." Gregory steps forward and holds out a folder. "These are the preliminary data points for the sterilization project. I think you'll find the results are rather encouraging."

"You work fast, Mr. Mbende," Stoker says, drying his hands with a paper towel before flipping through the documents inside. Six-month, twelve-month, twenty-four-month population projections for "active sterilization" versus administered sterilization versus nonaction. Short incubation times and a 100 percent transference rate in a small sample of dik-diks. Direct mucus transfer yielded the quickest effects, but just sharing a confined space for an extended amount of time was enough for the virus to jump to a new host. Stoker notices that there's not one mention of the words *virus* or *infection*, or any sort of nomenclature that would suggest they were dealing with gene-altering pathogens.

Stoker had ordered his alpha bot to do a little research on his three-hour drive from Bhisho to Port Elizabeth, enough to learn how the virus had been engineered to surge through the body and tweak three gene sequences that dramatically reduce the chance for deer to conceive.

"Yes, well, I'm afraid time is not a luxury we have at the moment. Every minute is precious."

"Mr. Mbende, I'm sure this is something that can wait the weekend."

"Even if we act now, the production process would have to be rushed."

"And that doesn't concern you? This doesn't seem like the sort of project that should be rushed. We'd be tinkering with Mother Nature, and that's always asking for trouble."

"And what about Zed hybrids? Look how popular they are. It's not any different."

"We're talking about a virus, Mr. Mbende. Once that's out in the general population, it's never coming back. It's a done deal. I don't feel comfortable making a decision like that. What if it jumps to other animals? What if it wipes out the antelope or the zebras?"

"But in the States—"

"We don't live in the States. This is South Africa. Look, Mr. Mbende," Stoker says grimly, laying a compassionate hand on Gregory Mbende's chest. "I really do appreciate your efforts in this, and I can tell you're committed to finding a solution to our dik-dik problem. But this virus, it's just too unpredictable."

"I was afraid you wouldn't carefully weigh this option, sir. And I really do think you should reconsider."

"I've made my decision," Stoker says, deepening his voice in that intimidating way his father does. "Now if you'll excuse me, I've got guests waiting." Stoker pushes past Gregory, but he's stopped by Gregory's firm hand.

"I didn't want to have to do this, but you leave me with no other choice." From one of his alpha bot's compartments, Gregory Mbende pulls out a small envelope and hands it over. "Despite this, I respect you, sir. You're a great leader with great heart. It's why I want to see you as premier, and of course, when you have to appoint someone to fill in your position, I hope you'll remember how well we've worked together, current differences aside." He pauses, fingers still clamped to the envelope, looking remorseful, then finally lets it go.

Stoker opens it to find two photographs of him in drag.

"I figure you've got two choices, sir. Declare your interest for the premier's seat, and when you're appointed, put me on your Executive Committee. These photographs will disappear forever, I promise. Otherwise, I know several very influential people out there who might be interested in learning more about your extracurricular activities."

Stoker takes a hard look at his most senior aide, a man he'd trusted through three whole terms. A man whose intelligence he'd clearly underestimated. Stoker had known this day would come eventually. He'd thought he would be embarrassed and apologetic, but now, looking at these pictures, he can't help but notice how sublimely happy he looks in Felicity Lyons's skin. And it's not just the performance high he's used to. He feels an odd sort of pride, leading parallel lives, and succeeding at both despite the emotional and physical drain. The confidence he'd built up onstage translated directly to confidence on the chamber floor, and vice versa. Wallace Stoker would still be a bumbling aide with an impressive collection of beige suits without Felicity Lyons, and Felicity Lyons would still be singing uninspired Top 40 drivel to the background of drunken bar fights if it weren't for Wallace Stoker. He realizes, here in the sanctity of the men's room, that he can't afford to give up either of his loves. And even if he could, he wouldn't want to.

A deep rage wells up within Stoker's heart. He tries to tamp it back down, but you can only put so much pressure on a lump of coal before it has no choice but to become a diamond. His fists clench. His heart pounds in his ears. There's no way Stoker's going to let this little chop rob him of his identity. Neither of them.

"Mr. Mbende, I think you've put things in perspective for me."

"I'm glad, sir. Again, I hope there won't be any hard feelings."

Oh, there will be.

The two men shake hands, and as they're about to leave the men's room, Stoker grabs his Silverthorn bottle from the counter and raises it up high behind Gregory Mbende's head—a good vintage, with nice, thick glass. The swing seems to take forever, so long Stoker thinks Gregory will spin around and catch it in the palm of his hand, but at last the bottle collides with Gregory's skull. The dull thud snakes up Stoker's arm and buzzes in his elbow like a mis-hit shot with a tennis racket. Gregory Mbende, his longtime friend and aide, drops to the floor like a sack of dead kittens.

Stoker recoils, hand trembling. He tries not to think of Gregory's family, of how his kids had scrambled up into Stoker's lap the first time he'd been invited to Gregory's home, like they'd never met a stranger. He tries to erase the image of Gregory's wife, forget about those plump, welcoming cheeks, those almond-shaped eyes, and the smile as white as a strand of pearls. Stoker's got to keep his cool. He drags Gregory's body into one of the stalls and props him up on the toilet seat. He then pours a mouthful of sparkling wine into Gregory's mouth, and after wiping off his fingerprints, sets the bottle in Gregory's lap. When he's done, he looks at Gregory's bot who's standing there perplexed.

He shoves it in the stall, too, then grabs a BATHROOM CLOSED sign and leaves it sitting out in front of the stall.

It probably won't buy him much time the way people are drinking out here. Stoker scans the crowd until he sees his mother, then stumbles toward her, one foot in front of the other as the numbness inside spreads to his extremities. He smiles politely as she introduces him to a gentleman she says is a dear old friend, though Stoker's too out of it to catch his name. The man's handshake is firm and as rough as pumice, his eyes oddly familiar and impossibly wise. Out of habit, Stoker tries to do that thing he does, to meet people in their reality, crossing the boundaries of age, race, gender, and ability as if they were but doorways from one room to the next. He attempts to meet this man at his level, but Stoker gets the distinct feeling that he could never reach high enough, far enough, wide enough.

Stoker is left speechless for the first time in his life, his mouth boorishly agape.

His mother excuses the both of them, dragging Stoker off into a secluded area behind a grouping of potted ferns. In the span of a minute, Stoker tells her all that's happened as her face gets longer and longer. But if there's one thing this family is good at, it's keeping its skeletons locked in the closet. Couldn't have had six generations of successful politicians without it.

"I'll take care of it, dear," his mother says to him in a way that holds its own weight of a veiled threat. Councilman Stoker gets the distinct feeling that he's jumped out of the mouth of a shark and into the mouth of a dragon. His mother is going to own him for this, he knows it. "Now, go on," she says. "You've got mingling to do."

Stoker nods, but his heart is numb. His body is numb. It's all he can do to stand there, that envelope clutched to his chest.

Those pictures of him wearing the hell out of that dress—so strikingly similar to the 2035 classic gown Farai Ngcobo had worn to the South African Music Awards. Blue velvet embroidered with silver beads. So stunning. A dress like that is hard to forget.

Only Stoker doesn't remember wearing it. Not at all.

Chapter 12

NOMVULA AND MR. TAU

"Nomvula, you eat like a bird," Mama Zafu says, dipping her big wooden spoon into Nomvula's bowl as she gulps down the last of the stew. She then takes a sip of beer and pats her mouth nice and clean with her sleeve. "This is the third day in a row you've left food on your plate. Have you lost your appetite, or do you just not care for my cooking?"

"Your cooking is always wonderful, Mama!" Nomvula throws her arms around Mama Zafu's neck and kisses her hard on the cheek. Oh, she's hungry enough all right, but it's Mr. Tau's bread she has a taste for. That and more of his stories.

"Says my niece the bottomless pit." She clucks and smiles, going through all sorts of pains to avoid looking Nomvula in her oddly colored eyes. Never that. She puts her hand to Nomvula's forehead. "You don't feel sick. Is it a boy you're trying to impress, then? You can tell me if it is, child."

"There's no boy," Nomvula says quickly. It's not a lie. Not really.

Mama Zafu hums to herself, then shakes her head. "Maybe, maybe not. But there will be one day, my dear, and now that you're almost a woman, I suppose it's my place to tell you about how babies are made." She looks at Nomvula uncomfortably, even more so than usual.

"I know all about it, Mama Zafu. I've seen how it works."

"Have you?"

"Mmm-hmm. With Mr. Ojuma's goats. The man goat climbs up on top of the woman goat, and they play like that for a while, and then the woman goat starts getting fat, and that's when the baby is inside."

"Well, I suppose you do know a little. But people are not like goats, child. There's all kinds of things involved when it's people. Like love."

Nomvula purses her lips. "Have you ever asked a goat if it is in love?"

"Nomvula, now is not the time for games. This is important. There are girls your age with child already, sweet-talked by boys and men alike. And once those boys and men have played, they don't stick around once the fun is over."

"Like what happened to my mother," Nomvula says quietly.

"Like what happened to your mother. Your gift is precious, and only you will know when it is time to share it. Now tell the truth, Nomvula, is there a boy?"

"There's no boy, Mama!" A man, yes. Yesterday, she and Mr. Tau had played pretend together, down in the brush where they shed their mortal clothes. He'd held her hand as he'd sprouted wings like a hundred golden swords from his back. Nomvula gets bubbly with envy every time she sees his wings. Hers are such wispy little things, thin like thread, and the dullest of grays. But they're wings all the same, and together they flew and flew, up and up until the ground beneath them looked like a tongue lapping at water.

"This is your land," Mr. Tau had said. "These are your people. It is up to you to choose how you will serve them. Will you be a benevolent god or a vengeful one? Ruled by ire or basos? Demanding or giving? Involved in guiding their decisions or content to watch over their lives?"

"Haw! All this is mine, baba?" Nomvula had asked, enthralled by the vast blueness of the ocean. She'd never imagined there could be so much water, so much she'd never feel bad for stealing water from the air ever again.

"There are others like you. All over this world, some old, some very old, and others only a few centuries. Some are simply healers and diviners. Others have been saviors and tyrants and kings and queens. And a select group are exalted as gods. They achieve immortality through their followers, through belief. Likewise, they can draw intense power through fear, though the effects are short-lived."

Nomvula frowns at that. She's had a hard enough time making friends. Getting people to believe in her seems as likely as catching the wind. "And what happens if a god doesn't have any followers?"

"It's a sad existence. Imagine an artist with no will to create. A singer whose lips refuse to part for a tune. Down that path lies a slow death, but death will come. That is not your path, my child. I will teach you what I can, for as long as I can," Mr. Tau had said very firmly, and he had squeezed her hand so tight Nomvula's fingers hurt. She'd turned and caught him weeping, and for a moment, his face was not quite his own, like the faintest hint of golden eyes and a sharp buzzard's nose.

Nomvula now knows that Mr. Tau was like that man goat, climbing on top of her mother and having his way and leaving her with a child in her belly, a half Zulu, half god child. And just because it had happened in a dream didn't mean it didn't happen.

NOMVULA LEAVES MAMA Zafu with a pot and a promise to come back with water, even though her auntie had insisted that they already had enough. Out of habit, Nomvula takes the road that leads to the old broken solar well. Her mind is too caught up with the idea that Mr. Tau could be her father to watch where she's going. She smacks right into Sofora who falls back and lands rump-first on the dusty ground.

"Nomvula!" she wails out, then nearly jumps back onto her feet. "You've ruined my brand-new skirt!"

"It's just a little dirt," Nomvula says, almost sorry she'd done it. Almost. She puts her pot down and helps Sofora wipe it off. Sofora slaps her hand away.

"Don't put your filthy paws on me!"

"I didn't mean it, honest."

Sofora storms back toward her home where her older brother Letu tends to a fire and a kettle of what likely contains beer, judging from his lazy eyes. Orange flames lick out from beneath the cast-iron pot like fiery tongues.

"I'm telling my father," Sofora says. "I'm telling him you pushed me down on purpose because you were jealous, and he'll make you pay for a new skirt."

"Silly Sofora, there's nothing wrong with your skirt, except that maybe it's a little ugly."

"What?" Sofora turns around. "Who are you to call anything ugly? Your hand-me-down skirt probably used to be somebody's old bedsheet."

Nomvula frowns. Her auntie had made this skirt just for her, sewn with love and not by a stranger in some faraway town. The material isn't shiny, and all the stitches aren't the same, but it's more special than anything Sofora's father could buy. But girls like Sofora don't see things that way, and if she wants to be impressed, Nomvula can sure impress her. She knows she shouldn't, but she does it anyway, calling up that itch between her shoulder blades where her wings meet her skin. She flexes and feels her wings stab through her shirt, and as she spreads them wide, she gives Sofora the smuggest of grins.

"Why are you staring at me like that?" Sofora says, propping a hand on her hip and not even seeming to notice. "You and your crazy eyes. You're just as crazy as that mother of yours."

"You take that back," Nomvula says. She flaps her wings, still to no effect.

"It's not like I'm the first to say it. Everyone knows she's been touched by evil spirits. Better be careful or some might rub off on you."

Nomvula shoves Sofora, but this time Sofora stands her ground and shoves Nomvula right back. Into the dirt, Nomvula goes tumbling, wings and all. By the time she's up on her feet, Letu has stepped out from behind the beer kettle and has stationed himself between the girls, his lanky arms extended and pushing them away from each other.

"Nomvula, maybe you should go back home," he says, his tongue thick in his mouth from sampling too much beer. "Before someone gets hurt."

Nomvula thinks that might be a good idea, but as she bends down to pick her pot back up, she hears Sofora wail again. She looks up and sees fire embers jumping to Sofora's skirt. It smokes and smolders, then that nice, shiny material goes up in a flash.

"Take off your skirt!" Nomvula screams, but her words aren't getting through. Sofora runs around like a headless chicken instead. Nomvula finds herself caught in that moment, stuck between helping her enemy or watching her suffer for calling Ma names. Sofora deserves to burn, Nomvula's vengeful mind tells her, but her merciful heart also has a say, so she quiets her dark thoughts, rushes to the solar well, and pulls the pump.

"It's still broken!" Letu cries as he throws handfuls of dirt at his sister's skirt.

Nomvula hits the side of the machine, hoping to jog something loose, but when she whacks it, something surges through her, like a sliver of lightning. She places her hand on the side of the machine, the entire flesh of her palm against cool metal. Threads of white light race right in front of her. Electricity sizzles in her ears in an odd stutter-stop language that she instantly understands.

Work, she tells it, and a second later, a trickle of water drips down onto the ground below. She shoves her pot underneath the spigot and tells the machine again, *WORK!*

Water gushes out, enough to fill the bucket, and Nomvula takes it and douses Sofora, once, twice, and another time until Sofora is sopping but safe. A small group of neighbors have exited their shacks, catching just the tail end of the drama, including Sofora and Letu's father.

"Nomvula!" he cries out and then hugs a half-naked and fairly crisp Sofora to his chest. "You have saved my beloved daughter!"

"And she fixed the well!" Letu says, then quiets under his sister's smoldering glare. But the damage is done. Their father lets out a chirping whistle and hums a deep, rich note as others join in. Singing follows—dozens of voices blending into a beautiful, winding harmony. They hoist Nomvula into the air to the beat, calling her a savior and a hero and a brave soul.

She feels their words more than hears them, and they begin to fill that bottomless pit in her stomach and soothe that never-ending hunger for the first time in her life.

Chapter 13

SYDNEY

Careful with that," Sydney yells at the hulk of a delta bot lifting up her coffee table by one end. "It's an antique."

The bot's oblong head lolls to the side, then its mono-eye flashes neon green in affirmation. It proceeds slowly through the doorway, its simple brain rechecking the spatial parameters of the long narrow hallway and steep stairs. Another bot hefts up her couch, and the third is outside loading her television into the double-parked moving van.

There's six of them altogether, three men and three bots. They've been here a total of ten minutes, and her apartment is nearly empty already. Sydney's going to miss this place. It's not much, but it's decent—concrete floors easy to bleach blood off of, thick plaster walls, and the only window looks out onto the side of a brick building. And then there's the trash chute at the end of the hallway, just big enough to dump pieces of body into without the hassle of hauling them down all those stairs and to the Dumpster out back. But it's been three days, and even though it's cool out, Mr. Gnoto is bound to be getting ripe down there. Then there was Paulo yesterday afternoon—the thief she'd fed images of a brimming jewelry box and a key under her doormat. And last night Mitchell Adams had caught her eye, some punk kid who'd cut in front of her at the movie theater. Oh, the shrillness of his screams! Sydney licks her lips. His was a special kind of fear, not clouded by guilt or shame or vice, but rich and delicate like a small piece of dark chocolate. A morsel unpolluted by sin. A virgin, too. She'd forgotten how sweet they were.

But don't think her to be a complete monster. She'd spent the whole of the morning cleaning up her apartment, spick-and-span, even dusted the floorboards and moldings, taking pride in leaving her apartment in better condition than she'd found it. Not to mention the new crisp white ceiling. Her landlady will be pleased, maybe even so much as to refund part of her deposit.

The delta bot takes the last of the boxes out to the moving truck, and all at once, her apartment is nothing more than bare walls, a slick, waxed floor, and some plastic drop cloths crammed into one corner. Yes, she'll miss this place, nostalgia already taking hold. It was here that she'd found a believer, after all, the seed of hope that she'll regain her godhood, if all is going to plan. Up until now, she's had no way of knowing. Paulo and Mitchell had been tasty treats, but fear is fleeting. But the great thing about fear is that it breeds like dik-diks. Put two scared people in a room, and each feeds off the other's anxiety. Three people quickly push the bounds of hysterics, and that's when the real fun begins.

The three men stand like terrified statues in their movers' overalls, all lined up against the back wall of her apartment. Slowly, Sydney locks the door and lingers so their minds go to all those dark places. Anticipation is the worst kind of torture.

They get a good glimpse as her atrophied back muscles flex and she yawns out sleek wings, a deep, blood red. Oh, it's been too long. Their strands have tangled together, so she takes a moment to preen, then gives her wings a vigorous flap.

She inhales the stench of the men's fear as she approaches. *Kirk*, reads the name tag stitched into the first man's overalls. He's forty and balding, spineless—the kind of guy who would push his own mother into the mouth of a lion if it meant he could get away unscathed. He cowers, even in his paralysis. Then there's Gilbert, tall and wiry, with cheap tattoos creeping from the neckline of his undershirt. Sydney had seen the extent of his work ethic, sitting out on the loading deck of the truck, reading titty magazines as the bots did all the work. And finally there's Orion, a hundred and ten kilos and none of it muscle. Just a kid really, eyes following Sydney's movements in their doughy sockets. He loves his mama, draws her hot baths and paints her toenails for her now that arthritis has set in. Sweet. Sydney makes a mental note to send her a coupon for her salon, then runs her finger down the bridge of Orion's nose. "I think I'll save you for last," she whispers.

With a flick of her finger, she rolls out the drop cloth and wills Gilbert over it. No way she's cleaning this place all over again. He dangles midair, fear doubling, tripling. After a few slits of vital arteries, she's fed enough to conjure the smallest peephole into the plane of transcendence. The dik-dik virus is spreading already. The lab tech had passed it on to her entire extended family, thirty people so far, and this second generation has nearly incubated long enough to pass it along again. In a mere few weeks, nearly half the population will have two very inconsequential gene sequences augmented. They don't determine eye color or skin color or intelligence or foot size, or any of a million other variables that scientists have brought under their control.

They're found on mitochondrial DNA, in fact, passed down from mother to child for generations upon generations from a time where demigods ruled the earth. Mr. Tau had told her the story when she was a girl, half a millennium ago. Even back then, visions of power danced before her eyes, and Mr. Tau had filled her head so full of flights of fancy she began to believe the stars themselves were within her reach. She remembers how proud she planned to make her baba. She remembers the thrill of learning there were others like herself. She remembers Mr. Tau's smooth voice tickling her ear as she curled up in his lap. She remembers it all like it was yesterday.

MR. TAU HAD said:

When the earth was still young, I was birthed from her fiery womb, and for centuries I floated contentedly on patches of her charred crust across seas of lava lapping at my skin like slow, hot kisses. I knew neither loneliness nor want until I had a dream of six trees standing in a line on a riverbank. I'd never seen such beauty— branches twisting up seductively from knotty trunks, foliage such an inviting shade of green. I wanted them in the worst way. When I opened my eyes, there was only a bloody, scabby darkness stretching into eternity. So I closed my palms together and willed with my very life force to create a sun, but then all that I could see was that I was truly alone.

It made me weep. I cried for countless days, years, decades, until I found myself drowning in a river of my own tears. I splashed against the surface and screamed for help, but there was no one. The scorched earth was no more, and instead there was a shore bearing six trees, roots drinking from the river's water. I wished for their branches to reach a little lower. A breeze came, and the branches swayed closer, but I still could not reach them.

My tears formed a whirlpool around me and threatened to suck me down, so I did the only thing I could think of. I willed those six trees arms and legs like my own. They uprooted themselves and began to walk about the muddied bank. I called to them, but they could not hear for they had no ears. So I willed them.

"Come quick! I'm drowning," I yelled, and the trees heard me, but they were blind and bumped into each other and walked in all directions. So I gave them eyes. I thought for sure I'd be saved then, but when the trees saw how beautiful they were, they forgot all about me and began preening each other's leaves.

So I gave them all hearts, hearts that loved only me, and they came rushing toward me, dipping their branches into the water. With all my might, I grabbed onto the nearest branch, saved at last! But then one of the other trees, ruled by jealousy, swatted me away so it could be the one to save me, its love. Bruised and battered, I willed them all minds so that they could work together.

Moments later, I found myself on the shore, lying on my back. I'd swallowed too much water and had lost my breath. I was dying! With my last thought, I willed the trees breath, and they breathed into me, each in turn until my lungs cleared of water and my lips tasted of bark.

I was so grateful that I took those six trees as my wives and made proper women of them, seeing as they could already walk and hear and see and love and think and breathe. With a hammer and chisel, I sculpted them faces and breasts and hips. I was meticulous, spending hours on my first wife's earlobe until I thought it to be perfect. For months, I did not eat. I grew thin and weak, and thought I would die. But then a crab crawled out of the water and right up to my feet.

"Mr. Tau," the crab said. "I have been watching you for months and am in awe of your creation. Her beauty is unmatched on this earth, and I could not bear for her to go unfinished. Please, Mr. Tau, you are weak. Eat of my flesh. I would be grateful."

So I blessed the crab and gulped him down with one bite, all except for one of his claws. With my new burst of energy, I carved a hole in the first tree's chest and placed the claw at the heart, and immediately she sprang to life, laughing and dancing and singing.

"I am so happy to be alive!" my crab-tree wife told me, and that night I lay with her, and she blessed me with the first of many children.

We were happy, my wife and children and I, and for a thousand years, I forgot about my other tree wives I'd left on the riverbank. But one night, I had a dream about the five of them, all lined in a row and looking sad and pitiful. Not quite trees, not quite women. Each night, after I'd satisfied my crab-tree wife, I'd sneak off to the river. For months I'd work on a single detail, the curve of my second wife's lips, until finally I forgot all about my crab-tree wife and spent the entire day there without eating.

Months passed, and when I was weak and about to die, a peacock waddled up to me and said, "Mr. Tau, I've been watching you for months, and I am in awe of your creation. Her beauty is unmatched on this earth, and I could not bear for her to go unfinished. Please, Mr. Tau, you are weak. Eat of my flesh. I would be grateful."

So I blessed the peacock and swallowed him whole, all except a single feather. With my new burst of energy, I carved a hole in the second tree's chest and placed the feather at the heart, and immediately she sprang to life.

We were happy, my peacock-tree wife and children and I, and I forgot about my other tree wives I'd left on the riverbank, and my crab-tree wife I'd left alone with our children. Until I had another dream.

Each time I nearly died but was saved in the nick of time by a dolphin, then a rat, then a serpent, then an eagle. After six thousand years, I had six thousand children, each and every one with the power of gods. Those descended from the eagle could fly, and those from the peacock had beauty that made the others weep. The serpents could charm, and the rats could manipulate without be-

ing seen. The dolphins ruled with their intelligence. The poor crabs came up empty though, and with competitive siblings, they often found themselves at the receiving end of pranks and practical jokes. I took pity on my crab children. They became my favorites, and I granted them each the power to bend the others' will.

With this shift of power, it wasn't long before sibling rivalry turned deadly. Brothers and sisters fought and killed each other, and my heart broke every time one of my children fell at another's hand. I tried to control them, but together, they were too powerful. Only when there were six left did I have the ability to put them to sleep. And in their dreams, I wiped their memories, made them forget. But I could not deny them completely of what made them my children, nor could I erase the birthright of the animal spirits they'd inherited from their mothers. So I let them keep their powers, but I hid them so deeply that they'd never find them, and so it has been ever since.

IN HER VISION, Sydney had seen crabs and dolphins and peacocks and rats and serpents and eagles, not physical manifestations, but hallucinations caused by a drug. They were memories, Sydney knew. Memories hidden for countless generations within these humans' DNA. And those two inconsequential gene sequences affected by the dik-dik virus, those are like the safety switches holding back humanity's true potential. Chaos will rule once again, 8.7 billion descendants of demigods warring together on this planet.

And that means there will be fear.

There will be lots of it.

Chapter 14

MUZI

Well, it happened, and now his corneas might be permanently fused. He should have knocked, but when the tip of your penis feels like someone lit it on fire, and your bladder's about to burst from trying to avoid anything that involves making use of that general area, and your great-grandmother decides she wants to take a cold bath in the middle of the afternoon . . . well, put that all together and it's just screaming for trouble, isn't it?

So he saw her. All of her. In the flesh. Including some little bits and pieces that he'd only thought grew on the undersides of old battleships. But even walking in on his naked grandmother isn't more frightening than the thought of talking to Elkin. Really talking, not like the past half-dozen conversations they'd had, the calls lasting an average of five seconds, and consisting of Muzi apologizing and Elkin getting exponentially more creative with cuss words.

He's got to go over there, though the thought of walking that far sends a chill up his spine. Ice packs can do only so much. Then he remembers that little vial Elkin had given him.

He snorts a lot, probably more than he should, but it works, and he's a crab again. Muzi scuttles down the hall, trying to look nonchalant in case anyone sees him, then he's out the door. Two of his girl cousins, Molly and Daphne, are playing in the front yard, both in pigtails and matching dresses though they're two years apart. They squeal as he passes. At first Muzi thinks that maybe his hallucination isn't a hallucination after all, but then he remembers that his cousins squeal at just about anything.

"Penis! Penis! Penis!" says Molly, the younger of the two. "My mum said you had a penis!"

Muzi glowers, then shakes his crab head. That's Auntie Lindi for you, explaining circumcisions to a six-year-old. But when you've got three kids, sometimes it's just best to answer their questions candidly and deal with the fallout later. Especially with Molly. She's never met a question she was too shy to ask. All talk and no filter.

"Molly," Daphne scolds, arms crossed over her chest. Eight going on thirty-eight. "You shouldn't say that word to boys."

"Muzi's not a boy, he's my cousin."

"I'm a man," Muzi muses, and he'll be damned if anyone tries to tell him otherwise.

"Did it hurt when they chopped your penis off?" Molly says in all seriousness, now. And then her eyes grow wider. "What did that man cut it with? A scissors? We got a scissors we use at school, but it's not like Mum's scissors, because you know why? They're too sharp for little kids, but you know what?" And wider. "You want me to bring my scissors next time I come? In case your penis grows back? Will it grow back? Just like hair grows back? Or will it stay cut off like Mr. Jacob's arm?"

"You know what Mum said about talking to Mr. Jacob about

his arm," Daphne says, giving Molly a stern look. "Well, you shouldn't talk to Muzi about his penis getting cut off because it's not nice to remind people that they're handicapped."

"What?" Muzi says, their nonsense cutting through his buzz. The pressure in his loins rears its head.

Molly shrugs her sister off. "Well, Muzi, can I see it at least? Mum wouldn't let us in the tent because she said we was girls, but you know what she always says, too? That girls can do anything boys can do, so don't you think I should be able to see it?"

"No!" Muzi throws his claws up. "Why don't you go play by yourself, Molly, and stop asking me questions!"

And with that, Molly turns, goes down the stone walkway, and starts drawing hopscotch lines on the pavement with a piece of white rock. Daphne and Muzi exchange flabbergasted looks. Never since he'd first met Molly had he ever seen her do anything that involved being quiet. A colicky infant crying nonstop, a two-year-old whose vocabulary consisted only of the words *no* and *mine,* a four-year-old who loved to make up fairy tales about pink horses on the spot and tell them to you whether you were listening or not, and now with the questions, questions, questions.

"How did you do that?" Daphne whispers as if she's afraid she'll ruin the silence. Poor Daphne. Muzi only has to spend major holidays and birthdays with Molly, and that's bad enough, but Daphne's the one who has to share a room with the girl.

Muzi shrugs. "Lucky, I guess. Maybe she ran out of questions."

"She *never* runs out of questions."

"That's true. Maybe we should enjoy the moment while it lasts."

"It's so nice to hear my own thoughts," Daphne says, then sits down cross-legged in the grass.

"I'll leave you to them then." Muzi clicks his claws together. "Hey, do I look any different to you?"

"Shhhh . . ." Daphne tilts her head up, enjoying the breeze, the sunshine, the quiet.

Fair enough. Muzi skitters across the pavement, and when he's gone a few houses down, white light flashes from behind his eyes, the kind you get from looking at the sun. There's a small something in his mind that hadn't been there before, the tiniest bit of grief for a hamster he'd never seen, accidentally squished in a game of bed hopping.

"I shouldn't have let him out of his cage," Muzi says, phlegm catching in the back of his throat. The feeling subsides, but the memory of it is still there. Two sisters, bouncing from bed to bed, and a beloved pet caught in the cross fire.

Muzi shakes the thought, hops Elkin's wood fence, and knocks on Elkin's window, careful so his claws don't shatter the glass.

"Go away," Elkin says, voice muted by the pane.

"Please, let me in. We need to talk."

"I don't have a word to say to kak-lipped skunk fuckers."

"I'm sorry."

"Eat a dick."

"Elkin . . ."

And then there's quiet and an awful lot of it, though in the distance, he can hear Molly starting up again with her ceaseless chatter. That's life for you, right? He can get a girl to zip her lips, but he can't get the one person he really wants to talk to to say a peep. Just doesn't seem fair. Hell. Well, he's all the way over here, now. Might as well make the most of it. He goes to the edge of the pool and dips one of his crab legs in. Oh, it's frigid, but a numb body might be just what he needs right now.

When the godsend wears off, he's going to regret this, but he hops in anyway and does a couple laps. Water passes across his carapace, as cool and slick as silk sheets. Muzi imagines himself in the ocean, admiring coral reefs, scavenging for a snack, making underwater music with the click of his claws. Really, he's hoping to piss Elkin off enough that he'll come outside, and then maybe after he's done cussing, they could talk about things.

"Elkin, come out here, dof. I know you're watching." Muzi kicks down into the depths of the pool, then settles on his imaginary ocean floor and pretends to dig holes into the sand, looking for worms. He's actually got a craving for them. His little crab heart quivers at the thought of living flesh passing his lips, but his crab stomach quickly overrides his vegetarian tendencies. And it feels so . . . *right*. Maybe he's always been a crab, caught between land and sea, between cultures, between this world and the next. It seems like he's been underwater forever, but his crab lungs don't seem to mind. Still, it might be the drugs screwing with him, and he could be drowning for all he knows. So he swims back up to the surface, delighted to see Elkin standing there at the edge of the pool in faded jeans and a Duffy Live concert T-shirt. The real Elkin, not the porpoise.

"Hey," Muzi mumbles in the kind of way that says *I'm sorry for being such a giant asswad* in not so many words. Elkin stands there, eyes distant. Mind distant. But at least he hasn't walked away. Muzi props his claws up on the pool's ledge. His body and legs float buoyantly along the water's surface. Yesterday was such an intense mix of emotions and experiences, he doesn't even know where to start. Might as well just say what's in his heart, and if Elkin decides he wants to kick his teeth in, so be it. "You're my best friend, Elkin, going on ten years. You know me better than anyone else on this planet, and I'm sorry if I sound like a cake, but that means a whole hell of a lot to me. If you want to go and forget that yesterday ever happened, I'm fine with that. But if you want to push through, and deal with it and shit, I'm open to that, too."

Elkin stands there, motionless. Emotionless.

Muzi slaps his claw against the water, soaking Elkin's jeans from the knees down.

"Damn it, Elkin. Say something!"

"Something," Elkin says flatly.

"Very funny. I spill my guts and you go and make a joke about it. Let's just forget it then, okay? That's what's easier." Muzi holds a claw to each temple and makes buzzing sounds like he's got mind control. "Okay, Elkin, yesterday never happened. Now go ahead and get in the pool, bru. No use in me freezing my ass off all by myself."

Elkin lifts his right foot and steps into the water, almost as if he were expecting a solid surface, but then sinks straight down to the bottom. Muzi laughs at first, but panic sobers him up when he sees Elkin isn't moving at all. Muzi swims down, grabs him in his arms, then kicks back up to the surface, struggling under Elkin's heft. They break the surface long enough for Muzi to catch a mouthful of air, and then down they go again.

"Swim, damn it!" Muzi says, his voice a spray of air bubbles underwater. Elkin starts to kick, weakly but enough, and together they make their way to the pool's edge. Elkin isn't breathing. With everything he's got left, Muzi hoists his best friend out of the water.

Hard, ragged shivers run through Muzi's body as he looks down at Elkin, wishing he hadn't bunked school the week his health class covered CPR. He presses his lips against Elkin's cold, blue ones and breathes three strong breaths, even though Muzi barely has breath to call his own. He then pounds Elkin's chest with a doubled fist. "I swear, I'll kill you if you bladdy die on me!"

Elkin's head lolls to the side and he coughs out an unseemly amount of water. He blinks his eyes a few times, as if risen from a dream, then he begins to shiver.

"Let's get inside before we both catch pneumonia." Muzi helps Elkin to his feet.

"Shit, man. You've gotta try this new stuff Rife gave me," Elkin says through chattering teeth. "This stuff is prime. Seriously, they could cut your whole dick off tonight and you wouldn't give a rat's puckered ass." He scratches his head and looks down at his sopping clothes, then cackles. "I can't even remember how I got out here!"

"Yeah, yeah. I think we've both had enough godsend for one weekend."

"So you've tried it?"

Muzi rolls his eyes and props the screen door open with his elbow as he guides Elkin inside. Okay, so they're definitely forgetting about yesterday. Completely. Yeah, it hurts a bit, but whatever. He'll play along. "Ja, I've tried it. Hallucinations. No inhibitions. Makes you do stuff you'll probably regret for the rest of your life."

"I was a fucking purpose, man! You should have seen me."

"Porpoise, idiot. Yesterday never happened. I get it. Now stop acting like an ass."

"Friday never happened? What's so bad about Friday?"

"Saturday. Saturday never happened."

"But it's happening right now."

"Today's Sunday, Elkin."

"No way! That means . . ." Elkin stares at Muzi's crotch and pantomimes scissors with his fingers. "I missed it? Man, I was going to surprise you with balloons and everything. Sorry. It's really Sunday?" He scratches his head again. "I've blacked out before, but I've never lost a *whole* day."

Muzi's heart drops to his gut. What if Elkin isn't playing? Maybe he'd hit his head on the side of the pool, or his brain had been starved too long of oxygen, or maybe his drug use had finally killed one too many brain cells, or . . .

No.

The flash behind his eyes comes again, this time more intense. There's fear, fear so acute that Muzi nearly vomits. A fist comes at him so fast he doesn't have time to see who's behind it. It connects right below his eye, and all at once his brain rings out with pain. "You no good piece of shit," says the man behind the fist, and though Muzi is too dazed to see straight, he recognizes it as Elkin's father. The scene fades, but the fear sticks. Muzi grabs Elkin tight in his arms and doesn't let go. He remembers the shiner Elkin had a few months ago. Said he'd got it at rugby practice, Ray Collin's sharp elbow had caught him in the ruck as they scrambled for a loose ball.

"What the hell are you doing, Muzi?" Elkin squirms in his grip.

Something's wrong. Something's terribly wrong. He'd somehow linked to his cousin's memories, and now Elkin's. He'd made Molly play quiet by herself and made his best friend forget what had been the most intimate moment of Muzi's sixteen years of life. And if he can make a person forget about that, he can make them forget about anything.

A smidge of guilt returns, but this time it's all his own, because once Muzi figures out how to control his new gift, he knows he'll never want to stop.

Chapter 15

RIYA NATRAJAN

Riya Natrajan lingers under her sheets, fighting and twisting and turning, avoiding the sunlight seeping through her eyelids. Her alarm clock goes off for the third time, and again she smacks it. She's left in the quiet of her thoughts. Her body feels strange, light, cottony. But her mind is her own, not gaffed or buzzed or high.

She sits bolt upright, covers slipping off, her negligee a whisper against her skin. The air is cool enough to stand the hairs on her neck on end. Riya Natrajan feels the gentle tremors of her heavy-footed neighbors up at the crack of dawn. The slight sway on the sixty-fifth floor of this luxury hotel sits softly in her gut. She feels a dozen things, but for the first time in almost two decades, pain isn't one of them.

And it makes her uncomfortable.

Riya Natrajan dials her manager on the hotel's phone—yes,

she still actually uses one—then draws her covers up and over her chest. Nothing he hasn't seen on a dozen occasions, but this time of morning, these things are best left to discretion. The line rings. Adam picks up, deep, rough circles under his eyes from their hectic night of last-minute concert changes.

"Hey, love," his voice scratches. "To what do I owe the pleasure?"

She pauses. What's she supposed to say? He doesn't know about her multiple sclerosis—Adam, who she's entrusted with her career, life, and even her heart a few times. But she can't actually share this miracle, not with him. Not with anyone.

"Are you feeling okay? You're not canceling this afternoon's rehearsal, are you?"

"No, nothing like that. I'm feeling fine. Great in fact." Her voice is chipper. Actually chipper! She can't bear to spend another moment in bed, so she stands up, stretches, flings her arms out in each direction.

"Hmmm," Adam groans. "Now I know something's wrong. It's not LSD again, is it? Please tell me it isn't."

"Adam, go back to bed. Sorry I woke you."

He yawns wide. "Take care of yourself, Riya. Contrary to popular belief, divas can live well into their forties. I've seen it happen once or twice." Adam attempts a wink, but his lid sticks shut.

"See you at rehearsal," she says sharply, then disconnects.

Inspiration hits hard, a new song welling up from inside, deep. A song of hope, of love, of movement. She grabs a pen and jots some lyrics, hums a few bars, but the notes catch funny in her throat. Riya Natrajan clears it, then tries again:

Breezy, breezy, listen to my heart at play,
Feel me, ooh boy,
Simple as seduction.

Reaching, reaching, living for another day,
Feel me, ooh boy
Live forever, sweet seduction.

She sounds like a canary with a sinus infection, and no, not in a good way. Riya Natrajan scrambles around her suite, makes white tea with honey and a warm compress for her throat. In thirty minutes, when her voice has downgraded to the likes of a rooster choking on a kazoo, she starts to panic. Gargling with salt water doesn't help a lick, and in an hour, she's become so hoarse she can barely speak at all.

Side effects. Side effects of that stupid drug, that's what this has to be. What if her voice is ruined? Forever? Manic thoughts surface—she wonders if her pain was what made her an artist. Without it she's lost everything that defines her. She's got no one to turn to. No one to tell her it's going to be okay.

Well, there is one person.

She slips into oversized sweats, tucks the godsend vial safely away in the pocket, throws her hair up into a messy bun, and heads out into the hall. She starts a brisk jog as her half-asleep bodyguards rouse from their post.

"Ma'am!" they call after her.

"Just going for a jog," she croaks like a frog with a mouthful of marbles.

"Not by yourself," Robert, the bulkier of them, says.

"Well, no one's stopping you from coming. That is, if you can keep up."

She's been so wobbly lately, Riya Natrajan can't remember the last time she'd run anywhere, but after nine years of obsessing over dance moves for hours on end, she's got thighs like a chee-tah, and there's no stretch of pavement that can intimidate her now. Her bodyguards, on the other hand, they're bent over and huffing by the end of the fifth block. Robert calls a limo for rescue, leaving only Turk, slightly more athletic, but definitely not the brains of this operation. She needs to lose him fast.

It's too early for shops to be open, but she knows a place down on the beach where merchants set up early on a Sunday morning and where tourists riding on their jet lag highs don't care much about rising before the sun. It's crowded already with artists selling shweshwe printed scarves and purses, intricate beadwork jewelry, and clockwork animal figurines made from recycled Fanta cans. Turquoise crested waves break against the seawall in slurred hushes, and the blood orange sunrise hangs lazily on the ocean horizon. Down shore, the twinkle lights from the Boardwalk glow dimly against the new day. She weaves through the crowd, accents from across the globe prickling her ears. A German man haggles over the price of a hand-carved tribal mask, and an American couple bicker about the social irresponsibility of buying NuIvory sculptures despite the fact that the last true-born elephant had walked the savanna nearly four decades ago.

Glancing back, Riya Natrajan catches a glimpse of Turk's smooth, bald head popping up through the crowd like an anxious meerkat. Quickly, she ducks into the stand of a man selling wooden figurines. She sheds her bright green sweatshirt and ditches it behind a display rack so that she's just in her sports bra, her tan skin blending in with the warm wood tones.

She doesn't look, but feels the wind as Turk runs past. A chill sets in. Riya Natrajan ignores it and wedges deeper into the man's stand. As she waits, she admires one of the figures, a delicate piece of a young woman. An angel.

"Is there something I could interest you in, ma'am? A gift for that special someone?" the artist says smoothly. "Or perhaps a treat of your own?"

Riya shakes her head quickly. "No, I'm sorry. I haven't got any money on me."

"She's not for sale, that one," the man says. He smiles wide.

Knowingly. "I cannot part with her just yet. Soon enough, though, she'll need a good home. Why don't you take a look at her face? A close look."

"She really is beautiful," Riya Natrajan says, eyes tracing along the wood. The grain plays against the shape of the girl's calves, accentuating her hips, highlighting her face.

"She's not an angel. That's what most people think. She's a precious thing, a child of man and god, but I fear she won't have the chance to be loved by either." The man shakes his head, then fixes Riya with eyes that pierce her soul. If she didn't know better, she'd think he was talking about a real girl, and not a piece of wood. A shiver surges through her, quick, yet violent. She smiles politely, then shuffles away.

Back on the street, she hails a bot taxi, then sprints across the street as one pulls over. She goes to open the door, but a man in a gray suit has already thrown his briefcase in from the other side. They lock eyes over the expanse of the backseat, and something primal wells up within her. She can't chance sticking around on the streets like this much longer.

"Mind getting the next one?" She breaks eye contact and settles into the seat.

"Actually, I'm already late to a meeting." The man speaks mostly into the uni-boob of her sports bra, of course. He thumbs the pay pad. His name lights up on the display—Benjamin Wells—then flashes green to confirm a fifty-rand hold against his account balance.

The bot's bullet-shaped head spins around to face them. Its mono-eye displays a neutral shade of yellow. "Destination?"

"Triamyd Industries. Vann-Bosley Building. Theale Street and Govan Mbeki Avenue." He taps Riya on the shoulder. "We can split it if you're heading my way."

"Out of the question." *Don't you know who I am?* Riya Natrajan almost says, but then tilts her head away so he won't notice.

Outside the taxi, she sees Turk across the street, momentarily held at bay by a sudden stream of traffic. "Fine! Just drive!" she commands. Anything to get away from here. She swivels the pay pad away from him and presses her thumb in the designated area. Her name lights up, and for once she's glad about the bot labor laws and the one provision that allows bot taxis to operate without an overseer. To this dumb bot, Riya Natrajan is just a fare like any other fare.

The taxi bolts out into traffic and Turk is left stranded in its vapor exhaust. Benjamin's alphie settles on the seat between them, offering a buffer of privacy, one that Benjamin's sure to overstep. There's silence. Way too much of it. She feels his eyes running over her.

"Hey, I'm sure you get this a lot, but did you know you look an awful lot like—"

"No. I don't."

"But—"

"I don't!"

"Ben," he says. He extends a hand.

Riya Natrajan ignores it and keeps her forehead pressed against the window as they speed along Beach Road. Her mind ebbs and flows like the blue-green waves of the Indian Ocean crashing against the rocky shore, wondering if she's been blessed or cursed. As they pass the harbor, she looks back toward Benjamin, unable to stomach the sight of towering industrial robots loading the ships docked there. She makes the mistake of catching his eye.

His brows raise. "You *are* her."

"I'm not."

"Ag, man! Asemahle is not going to believe this. You know we just bought tickets to your concert for my brother-in-law."

"Taxi, could we get some music back here?" Riya Natrajan snarls. Anything to drown this guy out. The first few melodic bars of her title track "Midnight Seersucker" fill the backseat of the taxi. She grits her teeth, refusing to acknowledge Benjamin's rabid smile. "Taxi, kill the music and let Mr. Wells out right here. He's decided to catch another cab."

"Taxi, ignore that request," Benjamin says, reaching forward and slapping the bot on its cylindrical torso, then turning back to her. "Okay! Allergic to small talk. I get it. Won't hear another peep from me."

"Please refrain from further contact with the driving mechanism," says the bot with its mono-eye trained on Benjamin, flashing an intimidating shade of red. "Any damage incurred will be charged against your account."

Benjamin pulls a face at the bot, then leans heavily against the backseat. Riya Natrajan rolls her eyes. The chill is starting to get to her. She shivers, rubbing feeling into her arms as the cab pulls up against the curb, under the shadow of twin mammoth buildings.

"Well, this is me," Benjamin says, patting his alphie. "It was nice meeting you, ma'am." He smiles and tips his head. As an afterthought, he offers her his gray wool blazer. "Here. I suspect you need this more than me."

Riya eyes him suspiciously.

"Take it. I just figure, you know, someone of your stature taking a junky bot taxi this early on a Sunday morning, running away from that rather hulky gentleman back there—I thought you could use a little help. If I'm wrong . . ."

Riya Natrajan snatches the jacket. "You're wrong. I was out for a jog and got a little winded, that's all. So whoever you think I am and whatever you think I'm up to, I want you to forget about it, okay?"

Benjamin recoils, gives her a dirty look, then pats his alphie on the head and slams the door as soon as they're both out on the pavement. *Bitch,* he mouths from the other side of the window.

She shoots him her patented *Riya!* don't-give-a-damn pouty lips, then leans forward and knocks on the delta bot's dome.

"Could I use your phone?"

The bot stares back at her. "Please refrain from further contact with the driving mechanism—"

"Yeah, yeah. Put it on my account. Now let me use your phone or I'll have you decommissioned."

With what Riya Natrajan swears is a frustrated sigh, the bot returns its gaze forward. The pay pad screen switches to a phone interface. She dials Adam Patel, and he answers immediately, dark circles still under his eyes, but fully alert this time.

"Riya! Where are you? Turk and Robert say you ditched them. Is something wrong?"

"No, I just need a little time to myself. I'll be back for rehearsal this afternoon. I'll be off the grid for a bit, but don't worry, okay?"

"You pay me to worry, Riya."

"I promise. I'll be fine."

"At least tell me where you're going."

"You know I would if I could, Adam. Love you." She moves her hand toward the end call button, then says, "Oh, hey. Do me a favor and get a couple backstage passes for Benjamin Wells's brother-in-law."

"Benjamin who's what?"

"Oh, look him up. You can figure it out. That's why I pay you the big bucks, right? Kisses."

And she hangs up, then gives the bot her destination and watches as the towering buildings of downtown Port Elizabeth turn to smaller commercial buildings, then homes, then brush.

AS THE BOT taxi pulls into a long dirt driveway, the fare reads out eight hundred fifty-three rand. She confirms the payment, then orders the bot to leave the meter running. She gets out and unlatches the gate, then stares up the gravel path that leads to the house she hasn't seen with her own eyes since she'd stopped being Rhoda Sanjit. The yard has gone to weed, but the house itself looks well maintained, minus a much overdue paint job.

Her knuckles rest against the wood of the front door. She can't bring herself to knock. She watches shadows pass through the front window, like ghosts of another life. A wind chime plays in the breeze, a song composed of metallic notes. As a child she used to put words to them, spending entire summer days singing about boys and kissing and faraway lands. Her father had taken it down one evening, tired of hearing her voice through his office window.

Rhoda Sanjit had stopped speaking to her father that day. Didn't say a word to him the entire week, until one morning she woke up feeling like she'd been run over by every wheel on a very long train. Her vision blurred. Even her very breath sent excruciating pain up and down her spine. "Daddy!" she'd cried out.

"May I help you, ma'am?" interrupts the mechanical voice of a house bot from behind her. Memories of that other life fade away.

"Um, yes. I've come to see Dr. Sanjit."

The bot's mono-eye flashes bright red. "Apologies. I see no appointments on Dr. Sanjit's schedule. Is this visit of a personal nature?"

"It is," Riya Natrajan says. "Please tell him that his daughter has come for a visit."

"Apologies. Dr. Sanjit does not have a daughter. Unless you are referring to an alternate use of the term besides the designator for female offspring. Please define."

Riya rolls her eyes and holds back the urge to slap the bot upside the head with her running shoe. "I'm his daughter. As in he's my father. As in he knocked up my mother, and I was the result. Just tell him Rhoda Sanjit is here to see him."

"Apologies. Rhoda Sanjit departed from this earth on 24 May 2056. Unless you are referring to a different instance of Rhoda Sanjit. Please specify your personal identification number."

She feels a lump well up in her throat. "Departed from this earth? You mean, you think I'm dead?"

"Dead. Deceased. Passed on. No longer with us. Logic error: Vital statistics indicate that you are alive. Therefore, you cannot be Rhoda Sanjit."

"I'll show you a logic error," Riya Natrajan says, taking off her sneaker, just as the front door opens.

"Hello. Can I help you?" says the stern voice, her father. His eyes flash with recognition, face cycling through the five stages of grief in the course of half a second before settling on resentment.

Riya Natrajan sighs. The tightness in her chest eases slightly. "Father"—the word feels tacky in her mouth. Almost wrong. His hair is gray, cheeks sunken, face worn beyond its years.

"I'm sorry, ma'am. If you're looking for a priest, you've come to the wrong place. Now if you'll excuse me . . ." Her father shuts the door, but she sticks her foot in the jamb.

"You're still mad. I get it. But it's been eight years." Riya presses harder against the door. "You can't possibly hate me forever."

"How can I hate you?" rasps her father. "I don't even know you. Now, I suggest you leave before I call the police."

Riya Natrajan shakes her head. She deserves it. She deserves to be locked away for what she did. Or didn't do. It's not like she hadn't called. Not like she hadn't sent flowers, twelve dozen lilies. Not like she hadn't jumped on the fastest jet to Port Elizabeth as soon as she could. But she hadn't been there for him when he needed her the most. While he watched her mother, his wife, being lowered into the ground and buried beneath six feet of black earth, Riya had been in Cape Town with Reginald Ivey, yes *the* Reginald Ivey, starting the negotiations that led to her first record deal, the one that paved the way for her career.

So she's not going to be on the short list for any World's Best Daughter awards, but if she can't appeal to her father's heart, she can always appeal to his mind. Rhoda Sanjit was one in a handful of people in this country to be diagnosed with multiple sclerosis, the diagnosis her father had made, the one he'd spent countless hours studying, the one he'd kept a secret all these years.

"It's my MS," she says. "That's why I'm here. Please, just give me a moment of your time."

Reluctantly Dr. Sanjit cracks the door, but lets his body fill the opening, as not to insinuate that she's welcome here. "How's the pain?" His voice comes out tepid, which is a lot warmer than it had been a moment ago.

"That's just it. There's no pain at all."

His eyes narrow. "Self-medicating," he says accusatorily.

"No!" Riya says, then retreats within the confines of her over-sized blazer, pulling the lapels tight. "Well, some. But that's not it. My senses are sharp. My mind is clear. No fatigue whatsoever."

"Curious," Dr. Sanjit says. He strokes his gray beard into a point.

"There's more," Riya says, lips barely parting. "I've lost my singing voice."

"Ah . . ." Dr. Sanjit bobs his head knowingly. "This is God's doing, then, and not a matter of medicine. Good day to you, Ms. *Natrajan.*"

"You can't just turn me away. I'm your daughter!"

"The little girl I raised died years ago, a sweet child with possibility in her eyes and nothing but love in her heart. What you are, whoever you are . . . you're not her."

"Possibilities? Most people could only dream of achieving what I have!"

"You're not most people, Rhoda—" Dr. Sanjit stops himself, his body swaying slightly as if overcome by nausea. With an unsteady hand, he reaches out for the doorjamb, misses. Riya Natrajan grabs him, and they find themselves in what might seem like a hug to the observer not familiar with the abyss between them.

And yet they linger.

"Please," Riya whispers into her father's ear. The tickle of his beard against her cheek dredges up a childhood's worth of memories. Her eyes sting, but she forcibly composes herself.

"Come in," he says after a considerable pause. "I'll make tea."

"Thank you."

Her father looks her up and down, pursing his lips at her sweatpants and blazer. "There might be a change of old clothes . . . in the bedroom." He nods down the hallway. Her old bedroom he means.

It's like a punch to the gut, seeing it again. Just as she'd left it, not a doll out of place, ruffles on the comforter perfectly draped. Teen pop idol posters tacked to the ceiling. Enough purple to make you vomit. Two cheap plastic trophies sit prominently on her dresser—one from her grade nine decathlon championship, and the other for first place in her school's science fair for the barometer she'd made under her father's stern supervision. Riya Natrajan runs her finger over the brass nameplate, remembering how proud her mother had been, and how her father had clapped until his hands turned beet red.

"You kept it," she says as her father sets a tray on her dresser, "just the way it was."

"I knew you'd come home one day, Rhoda."

"I've wanted to for a long time. But things got crazy. Now things are always crazy."

"Mmm-hmm." He sips from his teacup and she does the same, savoring the smell of jasmine tea, her favorite as a young teen.

Her father goes to her closet, pulls out a pair of purple flower print pants and a ruffled shirt. "You can try these. They might fit. Last thing we bought you before . . ."

Riya Natrajan smiles. She thinks they're just as hideous now as she did then. "Maybe I'll just grab a T-shirt."

"Please, Rhoda. You never even wore it. Your mother said it was too youthful, but I told her you'd like them. Purple was always your favorite, remember?"

"Maybe we should talk some about my symptoms." She forces herself to look at her father's gaunt face. His piercing eyes dart all over her, like they're chiseling away at the here and now, trying to free the little girl beneath. She clears her throat, feeling a sudden rush of warmth in her cheeks. "I've got a rehearsal in the city in a few hours, and my taxi isn't going to wait forever."

"Oh, I sent the taxi back."

"You what?" Riya runs over to her window and draws back the lace curtains. The only sign of the taxi is a thin cloud of dust rising from the dirt road.

"You won't be needing it, Rhoda. You're home now."

Her legs wobble beneath her, her brain heavy as a cinder block. "You drugged—" she tries to say, but her tongue is too thick in her mouth.

Eyelids drift shut.

Lips press against her forehead. "Happy birthday, Rhoda."

Chapter 16

NOMVULA AND MR. TAU

Nomvula poses for another carving, the dark brown of the mahogany a perfect match for her own smooth, bare skin. She's not shy this time. Not a bit. She doesn't ask Mr. Tau to make her nose smaller or her breasts bigger or her hips wider.

She's got a dozen bees tickling inside her belly as they swarm. Mr. Tau says it's basos, *belief*—a result of her heroic deed, and all the townspeople are truly thankful for her mercy. Nomvula decides she likes this feeling, and craves the praise of her people. She's even proud that she'd saved that silly Sofora.

"I want to be a helpful god," Nomvula announces to Mr. Tau, her lips moving, but nothing else. She keeps her head cocked to one side, legs bent out in front of her, arms draped gracefully over one knee. She holds her wings out, perfectly extended. The tips glow golden now, ever, ever so slightly, but it's there and makes Nomvula giggle thinking about it.

"Do you, now?" Mr. Tau says, chipping and chipping and chipping away at the wood. "Performing miracles and answering people's prayers is an awful lot of work."

"But you should have seen the way they all loved me!"

"It is a wonderful feeling." Mr. Tau smiles for a moment, then his face draws tight and sorrowful. "Nomvula, I wish I could be with you longer. There are still many things that need explaining, but I'm afraid soon your trials will be your own. Your choices will quickly become more difficult than whether or not you choose to save a girl's life."

Mr. Tau sets the half-finished wood block aside and pats his lap. "Come here, child," he says, his voice smooth and comforting.

Nomvula takes a seat and drapes her arm over his shoulder. He preens her wings affectionately.

"I want you to know this, Nomvula. Even if you have nothing but good in your heart, you will fail. You will hurt people from your actions. Weep if you must, but do not let your failures define you. Do you understand?"

"Yes, baba," she says, though she cannot imagine hurting a soul. She can't imagine not having these happy bees buzzing in her stomach, one for each of her believers.

Mr. Tau squeezes her tight, then kisses her forehead. And then all at once, a warmth swells up between them, the eternal bond between a child and parent, *of love,* Nomvula thinks. It's a feeling not completely foreign to her, but this is the first time she's felt that love back.

"Yes, baba," she says again. She likes how the word tastes in her mouth, not just a term of respect, but one of kinship as well. Her heart swells at the idea of finally belonging to a real family.

Mr. Tau's front door bursts open. The air is sucked from the room, and from Nomvula's lungs as she sees her mother standing there like a monster within Mr. Tau's doorway. Her skin sags on her bones. Her eyes are completely bloodshot, burning like twin red suns. Nomvula quickly tries to cover up her nakedness then scrambles to find her skirt and shirt.

"What have you done to my child?" her mother says, approaching Mr. Tau with giant, stomping steps, lean muscles bulging and flexing and quivering like they've just woken from years of slumber. She reaches out and lifts him from his seat by the collar of his shirt. Nomvula has never seen her mother perform an act requiring so much strength.

"Mother, he's done nothing but love me!" Nomvula shrieks.

"Filthy child-whore." The back of Ma's hand smacks hard against Nomvula's face, sending her to the floor. Mr. Tau doesn't fight or struggle in her grasp, just hangs there like a rag doll as she drags him outside.

Nomvula clutches her clothes to her chest and runs after them, caught off guard by the mob formed in Mr. Tau's yard. Her mother had never been able to get anyone to listen to her, but now it seems the whole village is here, fists full of stones. Then Nomvula sees Sofora, a tight smirk on her face, oh, so much satisfaction in her eyes. She did this. Nomvula knows it in the pit of her stomach. That silly Sofora probably had been following Nomvula around all morning long, trying to catch her in the act of doing something wrong, and what could be worse than finding her at Mr. Tau's home?

"I ask of you now," her mother screams at the crowd. "Which one of you will dare call me crazy? This man who raped me, destroyed me, defiled me with his evil has now seduced my own daughter and filled her with wickedness, using her flesh for his pleasure."

"Mr. Tau never touched me like that!" Nomvula stands up to

her mother, but another backhand sends her to the ground. Dirt cakes her wet cheek.

"My daughter the dirty rag!" Ma kicks her in the side, and Nomvula drops her clothes to protect herself.

"Baba, do something!" Nomvula shrieks, then grits her teeth. Something's broken inside her, hurts so bad it makes her dizzy.

These people have already made up their minds, Nomvula. Mr. Tau's voice comes right into her head, a whisper among the jumble of her thoughts. *Now hush, or they'll have your hide, too. I love you, my child.*

He looks away, up into the sky, the same sky they'd shared when they'd both had wings and had almost touched the sun. Why doesn't he fly now? Show them all? Nomvula thinks that he will, but with each moment that passes, the people grow angrier. Ma pushes him down to his knees, then backs away toward Nomvula.

Someone hefts a rock, smacks Mr. Tau right in the chest.

"You don't understand him," Nomvula begs at her mother's feet. "Mama Zafu!" she says, turning to her auntie who stands alone in the distance, arms crossed over her broad chest, and eyes refusing to go in Nomvula's direction.

Ma pulls Nomvula up by her hair, arms so thin and so strong, so high Nomvula's feet dangle above the ground. Nomvula kicks and struggles, and silly Sofora laughs and points out her nakedness to her brother Letu and the other kids she bosses around.

"Let this piece of refuse be an example to you all!" Nomvula's mother shouts. Foam clings to the edges of her mouth. "Worn out and used up like a bitch mongrel, sexed by every stray dog who sniffs at her. Who's next? Who else will have a turn?"

Her mother pushes her into the crowd, and she's swallowed up, hands grabbing at her breasts, fingers poking between her legs. Laughs. Wicked laughs. She cries out to Mr. Tau, but she only hears his yells as the sound of stone against bone rings above everything else in her ears. They push her down to the ground. Nomvula fights with everything she's got, biting and kicking and screaming, but it's not enough. Three boys pin her down, two pulling her legs wide apart and laughing at what's between them. They call her a filthy dog, a whore, all those things her own mother had called her, so how can they not be true?

"Ugly," Sofora says, breaking into the ring of boys. She's got a long stick and jabs Nomvula in the rib, right below her breast. "We'll make something so ugly of you, you'll wish you would have been the one stoned." She leans down, her breath hot and vengeful in Nomvula's face. She stares for a moment, like she wants something of Nomvula, that greedy look like she gets when she's playing upuca and is about to snatch up all those pretty stones. "Your eyes," she says with a wicked exhale.

Sofora stands and turns back, her shiny skirt twirling around her, then pulls Letu out from the crowd.

"Do it," she says to him. She slaps her stick against his chest. "Get me her eyes."

Letu stands there for a moment, grimacing at Nomvula's body. "Sofora, this isn't—"

"I said do it!" Sofora shouts, and with a whack to the back of the knees, Letu drops down next to Nomvula, pulls a knife from his pocket. Nomvula trembles at his touch, feeling weak and dirty and dizzy with pain.

"He's dead," Nomvula hears her mother's voice shout. The smell of blood rides heavy in the air. "He'll never hurt another girl again!"

"Baba!" Nomvula cries.

The bees in Nomvula's stomach stop playing nice and start stinging, so painful that she no longer feels her broken rib, the ache in her heart. The buzzing rings in her ears, fills her vision up with a blinding white light. Her chest is about to explode.

Anger. Beyond anger. Ire, Mr. Tau had called it. Something so ravenous that it seems all the wrong in the world is clawing its way into her bones with promises to never ever leave. And when she's shivering and shaking so hard that she can barely keep hold of a single thought, she makes a wish, a simple wish that all these people—everyone who'd laughed, everyone who hadn't done a thing to help her, and everyone else too caught up in their lives to pay attention to the rantings of a madwoman or hear the shrill pleading of a ten-year-old girl—she wishes everyone would vanish into dust.

And with that, the bees ignite, burning up and out of her with a force that tosses her into the air, and for a moment she hangs limp, eyes barely slits, but able to see all the tin rooftops of the township she calls home, all the people below, all the solar panels atop the solar wells, all those pieces of man that used to be Mr. Tau.

Nomvula extends her wings and catches herself before she falls. She looks up to see those bees raining back down, now twelve fireballs each the size of a hut, and getting bigger as they near. The people, they see them too, and begin running and screaming in every direction.

Nomvula swoops down, lapping it up, laughing as she flies over the heads of her tormentors. She sees silly Sofora running with that stick in her hand. She shrieks, raises the stick in defense. But Nomvula flexes the threads of her wings, golden tips now faded away. She zooms past, slicing Sofora in half, oh all that blood over her beautiful skirt!

As Nomvula exhales, she feels the wickedness swelling within her—all those things her mother had called her are true now, for sure. She's strong, stronger than she's ever felt. The fireballs fill the entire sky with their blue and yellow flames. She has the strength to stop them, though her will is weak. Thousands of her people are gone in the blink of an eye. The fireballs hit, gouging out the ground and melting everything in their path. Her mother, her Mama Zafu, her life.

It's the price of her baba's blood, of her broken bones and shattered spirit. The price is steep, but Nomvula is not even sure it will be enough.

And then there is only emptiness inside her, so she flutters to the scorched earth and weeps.

Part III

Chapter 17

STOKER

He's late. Incredibly late. Suspiciously late. But it's taken Stoker half the morning to get to the point where he doesn't feel like retching at the thought of Gregory's body being found in a ravine, or a Dumpster, or picked apart by a pack of stray dogs. Stoker needs to get through this day, and he'll be free. Well, as free as anyone can be after killing a man. Had he killed Gregory? Should have taken his pulse, not that it'd matter after Stoker's mother had made the problem disappear.

He's got Valium in his system, just enough to take the edge off, but too much to trust himself behind the wheel. He takes a bot taxi to work, spending this valuable time practicing the face he'll make when he walks into the office and is told the bad news. Shock, disbelief, sorrow, and in that order, but not too emotional. Don't want to draw attention.

As they turn the corner onto Independence Avenue, Stoker's

heart sinks at the sight of yellow police cars crowding the main plaza of the Executive Council Building. Blue lights flicker over stern faces, SAPS officers in their navy blue uniforms. Strangely, a handful of Recces are among them, both human and bots, clad in army camo with high-caliber rifles tucked under their arms—not drawn, but clearly visible. Stoker's fought for justice for so long, he'd never imagined he'd find himself on the other side of it. No, he won't let anyone, not even his mother, obstruct the decency he's worked so hard to achieve. This has to end now, before corruption seeds itself into his soul, before he gains more power and his mother can use him as a weapon.

Stoker knows what he has to do.

He steps out of the taxi, marches around the barricades, and gets right up into the face of the first officer he comes to.

"Halt!" comes an order, punctuated by the black barrel of a gun.

"I did it. I take full responsibility," Stoker says. He throws his arms behind his back. "I'm the murderer."

The officer lurches forward, and in one fluid motion, sweeps Stoker's feet from underneath him and plants his face into the ground. "Suspect apprehended," the officer says into his earpiece, pistol muzzle cold against Stoker's cheek. "White male, early to midforties. Confessed to murdering all those people."

"All what people?" Stoker asks, but the officer's got his knee wedged in Stoker's back. He can't see much besides worn pavement, but above him he hears the buzz of media bots hovering, their video cameras capturing this for posterity.

"All right, you piece of scum. To your feet."

"What's the meaning of this?" Gregory Mbende says, pushing his way through the mass of officers and Recces converging on Stoker. Stoker nearly pisses himself.

"We've apprehended the terrorist," the officer yells over the rhythmical thwack of an Airwing chopper. Wind gusts tug at

Stoker's clothes, the tail of his jacket flapping wildly behind him. Stoker can barely stand as it is, and he braces himself against the officer's firm grip.

"That's no terrorist! He's my boss. Councilman Wallace Stoker."

"He confessed to the bombing of the township, sir. Now please, you're obstructing justice."

"Gregory! I didn't do it," Stoker says, voice cracking eight different ways. His arms tremble behind him and his legs give out. He falls back down to his knees.

"Officer, I'm sure he did confess, not because he's a terrorist, but because Councilman Stoker wears his heart on his sleeve. He takes personal responsibility for all the injustices that go on in the Eastern Cape. That's why he'll make an excellent premier one day, and I'll make sure that he won't forget your name when he is." Gregory points at the nameplate above the officer's badge. "Officer Davis, is it?"

"I'm sorry, sir, for the confusion," Officer Davis says. He releases Stoker from his handcuffs. "But you really shouldn't go around confessing to crimes during a national emergency."

Gregory nods at the patrolman, then plants a firm arm around Stoker's waist, helping him into the building. Stoker loses it as soon as they're inside, retching on the limestone floor of the foyer, bits of vomit spackled on his loafers.

"It's okay," Gregory says, patting his back. "We're all taking this pretty hard. But we're going to get those bastards."

The via-wall in the foyer broadcast all the grisly details: a township completely demolished, no signs of life. No signs of anything besides tin siding strewn across the ground like the world's biggest house of cards had come crashing down. Early estimates put the death toll at thirty-seven thousand, and the entire country is on alert for more acts of violence. Police swarm the streets to stave off looting. Soon, people will start tossing around the word *genocide* and all at once, South Africans will be divided into white and black and brown and yellow all over again.

They stand in silence, Gregory watching the news, Stoker watching Gregory, who's most definitely alive and well, no worse for wear except for the bulge at the back of his head, a mound of raised flesh peeking through his shorn hair.

Blackmail? Threats? Stoker wonders what tactics his mother had used to quiet Gregory . . . not unlike those threats Gregory had thrown in his face. Tit for tat, right? And then suddenly, without warning, Stoker's fear morphs into rage. After thirteen years of working so closely together, Gregory decides to pull a stunt like this?

"You don't have to say anything," whispers Stoker. "But what you did was inexcusable, and just because you got a little hush money to put all this nonsense behind us doesn't mean I'm going to forget."

"What, sir?" Gregory asks. "Are you talking to me?"

"I expect your resignation letter on my desk this afternoon." Stoker walks off, fully aware that Gregory's not the type of guy that takes kindly to being backed into a corner, but Stoker doesn't want a person like him on his team. If Stoker's secrets come out, he'll deal with them then and there.

"Sir! Is this because I stopped you from being arrested?" Gregory scrambles to Stoker's side. "I know you were close to the people who lived in that township, but what happened there couldn't have been predicted by anyone. It's an unlikely target, no infrastructure, minimal economic impact. Whoever has done this, they're aiming for the perfect act of terrorism. One that says that no place is safe. One that will turn South Africa's people against one another. We need you here, sir, battling toward normalcy. We need you to be the face for the Eastern Cape, to let people know that it's safe to travel, to go to work, to visit friends and family, to live a life not dominated by fear. They need to know that we're going to catch who's done this, sir."

"Perfect. So now we're going to pretend that our little dik-dik situation didn't happen."

"Councilman Stoker, lives were lost. Thousands of lives. Whatever's wrong, I need you to snap out of it."

Gregory's right. Whatever petty differences they have, they can wait. People need reassurances, and these few moments after this tragedy shouldn't be wasted. "Call the other heads together for an emergency meeting," Stoker says. "And find us someone who's abreast of this whole situation. We've got a nation to save."

"I'm on it, sir!" Gregory says.

Stoker has to admit, Gregory is good in an emergency situation. So maybe he's a little overambitious, but like Stoker, he really does want what's best for the people of the Eastern Cape. Which makes Stoker wonder if the person he's really angry with is himself. He'd lost control in that bathroom, had acted on impulse without thinking through the consequences, then to make matters worse, he'd brought his mother in to clean up his mess.

He made a mistake, Stoker admits to himself. Several bad ones, in fact, but it's not too late to seek forgiveness for his sins. And if Gregory can forgive him, maybe Stoker can start to forgive himself.

"Mr. Mbende!" Stoker calls out.

Gregory stops and turns back. "Sir?"

"I know we both messed up. Two wrongs don't make a right, but I hope that we can work past this. And whatever my mother did, said, I don't want you to worry about it. I'll talk to her tonight, tell her everything's okay between us. Everything's okay, right?"

Gregory steps up, examines Stoker closely, then says, "Sir, I really don't want to ask this, but are you inebriated?" Gregory clears his throat. "Your eyes are all glazed over and you're not making any sense whatsoever."

Stoker almost denies it, but then remembers the Valium coursing through his veins. He shakes it off. "I'll be fine. Just get the heads together, okay?" Stoker lets his head loll forward. "And I'm sorry about the bump."

"Bump?"

"On the back of your head."

Gregory rubs the spot, tenderly. "Oh, yeah. That. Darndest thing, woke up Saturday morning with a knot the size of a fist. I can't even remember how it got there. Friday was such a blur. One minute, I'm leaving the office, the next I'm tucked in bed with a killer headache."

Stoker looks deeply into Gregory's eyes. "You aren't faking, are you? You really don't remember?"

Gregory shakes his head. "Okay, one of us is losing his mind, and given the current circumstances, we really don't have the luxury to figure out which one of us it is. So let's get done what needs to get done, all right?" Mbende pats Stoker on the shoulder, then runs off.

Stoker stands there, feeling the muscles in his face cycling through shock, disbelief, sorrow, and in that order. His mother had a hand in this, no doubt. Nausea creeps back up into his gut. Murder, he could deal with. Simple, savage. Permanent. But Stoker gets the distinct feeling that his mother is capable of something much more sinister, and it scares him. It scares him a lot.

Chapter 18

SYDNEY

Sydney cusses her piece-of-crap moped. It finally died, right when she needs it the most. Now she's stranded out in the middle of nowhere, an hour outside of Port Elizabeth in the brush. She eyes the narrow stretch of road in both directions, not a soul to be seen, just browning veld to either side, littered with a flock of white plastic sacks tossed to the winds by careless townspeople.

She's never felt so useless, not even enough power within her to fly a few dozen kilometers to the Addisen township. She'd seen the destruction on the television at the salon, felt the tremors. Terrorists, the newscasters had said, but Sydney knows better. She'd destroyed a town or two in her prime, but never anything near this scale. The girl is strong, stronger than Sydney anticipated. But strength alone does not a demigoddess make. There's also experience and guile, and Sydney's never lacking in that department.

She walks nearly thirty minutes before an old bakkie passes her, its windows caked with dirt and its paint faded to the dullest of reds. She waves and it grinds to a halt, veering halfway onto the dusty shoulder. Sydney makes a run for it before the driver changes his mind. She pulls the door open and climbs halfway up into the cab.

"Heya there," the man says, tipping his straw hat. His skin is red and rough from a lifetime spent tilling earth. "Looking for a lift?"

"Thanks for stopping," says Sydney, putting on her best sorrowful face. "My moped broke down a ways back. I thought I'd be stuck out here forever."

"No problem. Usually don't pick up hitchhikers around here, but I figure we could all try to be a little more humane after what happened today and all. It's a damn shame."

"I'm headed that way actually. My father, he lives there." Sydney even manages an actual tear.

"Ag, no, didn't you hear? They're saying there aren't any survivors."

"My father, he's tough." *Immortal* might be a better word, but she's still angling for a ride. Don't want to scare him off just yet.

"Hey, it's a little out of my way, but I don't mind. Why don't you hop on in? You don't look much like a monster, or anything." He flashes her a warm smile, deep creases at his eyes. He's got the sort of face that's built for kindness. "I'm Kobus Goosen," he says, extending a hand.

"Courtney. Courtney Ngoto," Sydney says. Sydney Mazwai is wanted for questioning in the deaths of six men found clogging up the garbage chute in her old apartment building, so she has to keep that persona under wraps for now. Soon, though, there won't be a police force on this whole entire planet able to stop her. She hops into the seat, buckles in, and turns to the horizon, twelve plumes of smoke rising like architectural columns up into the sky. *Like the Parthenon,* Sydney thinks with more than a little disdain. The Greeks, they knew how to treat their goddesses.

The old Isuzu's got lousy suspension, still runs on gas, and is heavily reliant upon a vast collection of rugby union bumper stickers to keep the truck all in one piece, but it's a whole hell of a lot better than walking. Sydney makes idle chitchat until they're nearly to the township. Kobus seems like a nice guy. A wife, three kids. Pays his farmhands a decent wage and tells a good yarn. If things were different, she would thank him for the ride, offer him a few rand for his trouble, which of course he'd refuse. She'd shake his hard, calloused hand once more and they'd make empty promises that they should keep in touch, maybe stop by to have dinner with his family should she ever be in the area again. She'd feign that she'd be delighted, and he'd wish her luck finding her father, his eyes full of actual sorrow. Then they'd part ways, and after a day or so, they'd forget all about each other, swept back up into the grind of their respective daily lives.

But things aren't different. They're just the same as they've always been. She's weak and needs all the strength she can get to face this new student of Mr. Tau's. Sydney doesn't plan on being replaced so easily. She's not giving up without a fight.

So Sydney draws up from that empty spot within her. A reflux of ire bulges through her veins. The pads of her fingertips break, giving way to glossy black talons as long and sharp as daggers. She becomes a monster more gruesome than Kobus could have ever dreamt up. His fear is pure, wholesome, sticks to her ribs like a big bowl of mielie pap on a cold day. Then she grants his last prayer before she takes his life and sends feelings of love deep into the hearts of his wife and daughters back home.

SYDNEY CRINGES AS she sees the carnage firsthand. She'd been ready for the sheer devastation, but nothing could have prepared her for the smell, like Death had hosted a barbecue and had invited thirty-seven thousand of his closest friends. She uses half her reserves to push the images and credentials of a first responder into the heads of the police and paramedics on the scene as they search for survivors among the rubble. Sydney joins them, lifting up sheets of metal, sometimes finding a piece of charred hand or leg, but even those are few and far between. Cadaver dogs run in circles, whimpering. Ire lingers in this place, echoes of fear taunting Sydney like she'd arrived at a free buffet two minutes past closing.

When her ears start to tingle, she knows she's getting close. It's been decades since she'd been this close to another demigod. They're a territorial bunch. But Sydney has to admit, she's excited to be among one of her own, even if it's only long enough to kill her. These humans, they're so insignificant, bugs on a windshield in the grand scheme of things, yet they think the world will come crashing down if they aren't there to support it.

There . . . she sees a leg jutting from underneath a strip of tin siding. Sydney lifts it gently, revealing a charred body, skin like burnt islands adrift on a sea of coagulated blood. She's alive, barely. Her eyes flicker open, deep red with only the slightest hint of golden irises. Sydney gasps. Muddied tears streak across the girl's face and down onto the scorched earth.

Sydney's got this one chance. She draws all that's left of her power and concentrates on a killing blow. Her palm bubbles like napalm, enough energy to demolish a city block. At point-blank range and with the girl defenseless, Sydney's limited ire might be enough. Sydney presses her palm to the girl's temple before doubt sets in. The child is dangerous, no matter how frail she looks on the outside. She has to try. But before Sydney can deal the killing blow, footsteps clatter behind her.

"Survivor!" someone shouts out. In an instant, Sydney's surrounded by a dozen people, paramedics checking the girl's vitals, clergy praying to greater gods, media bots broadcasting a ray of hope to the entire nation. Sydney can't allow that, just as she can't allow this girl out of her sight. She wedges her way back into the crowd and sticks close as they delicately load the girl onto a stretcher. Dirt and human ashes stir as a Medevac helicopter swoops in. Sydney makes a move, dredging up a dust storm around her and the girl. Paramedics scream for the helicopter to back off. Sydney grabs the girl into her arms, flexes her wings, then shoots into the air, fast and smiling as the wind licks at her face. She's spent after a kilometer, but they're alone, far enough away where no one will disturb her again.

Her insides are rubbed raw as she tries to draw ire again. Sydney pitches forward, barely able to catch her breath. She eyes a large, flat rock and for a brief delusional moment, considers bashing the girl's head in the good old-fashioned way. But who is she kidding? Even in this state, the girl's got more power in her little finger than Sydney's got in her whole body. What's a rock going to do to a girl who survived a dozen meteors falling from the sky?

Patience is a virtue. Soon enough, Sydney will have the power to make her move, to strike when the time is right. Until then, she'll need to keep the girl close, away from people, away from believers.

"Sweetheart, you're going to be okay," Sydney says, stroking the girl's cheek, already starting to scab over. "You're with family now."

Chapter 19

MUZI

It's a damn shame, is what it is, but Muzi doesn't expect much more from Elkin's dad—part workaholic, part drunk, total asshole. He's mumbling to himself, nearly passed out on the couch, when he's supposed to be driving them to their rugby match across town. Muzi's nervous enough as it is. It's his first game back since his circumcision, and he's pretty sure two weeks isn't enough time to heal, but he's their star pivot, a solid arm to pass to either side of the field. They can't afford to lose any more matches if they plan on making it into tournament play this season.

"Come on. Papa Fuzz can take us. I swear, he'll be on his best behavior." Muzi cups his crotch and gingerly gives it a lift. "He owes me. Big-time."

Elkin curls his lip. "My mom should be home any minute. You can go if you want."

"It's not like Papa Fuzz hates you."

"It's not like he doesn't. I'm the only one who calls him on his bullshit, and he resents me for that. You can't say two words to him without him suddenly being a damned expert on everything! Everything!"

"He's not *that* bad," Muzi says, resisting the urge to roll his eyes.

"You tell him how you just got back from a nice hike in the woods, he tells you about how he once climbed a mountain, barefoot and blindfolded, with wild dogs chasing him the whole way."

Muzi shrugs. "So he likes to embellish the truth a bit. I think it's endearing."

"He's so into his Xhosa culture, yet he gave you a Zulu name . . ."

"He named me after the man who saved his life in a township fire."

"I've heard it before. Biggest fire in the province's history. So hot, it burned the soles off his shoes and the hair off his head. Have you ever met this man?" Elkin says, his brow pulled tight.

"No, but—"

"Whatever, bru. You look at him and see no faults."

"Ha, if I had a rand for every time Papa Fuzz said the exact same thing about you." Muzi furrows his brow and punches Elkin in the shoulder.

Elkin winces and touches his arm tenderly.

"What? You turning into a cake or something?" Muzi says, giving Elkin another tap on the arm. "Or maybe I just don't know my own strength."

"Eina! Okay. It's nothing. Just tweaked it last practice. It's nothing."

But Muzi's heard this lie before, Elkin covering up for a father who didn't deserve to have him as a son. Muzi's fists ball up tight, nails digging into his palms. He wants to tell Elkin that he knows what happened with that black eye. The memory is so sharp that his own eye socket starts to ache. His mouth opens, but the words refuse to come out. How could he even begin to explain?

Elkin leans over the back of the couch and flicks his father in the ear. His father moans incoherently, the lager so strong on his breath that Muzi can smell it from where he's standing. It's bad enough Elkin has to deal with this shit on a daily basis. Maybe he can't say anything, but no way is Muzi going to let him suffer through it alone.

"I'm staying," Muzi says. "As long as it takes. Besides, we've still got a chance of making it on time the way your mom drives."

"Ja," Elkin says with a mild chuckle.

"Hey, I've got an idea to pass the time." Muzi takes a vial of godsend out of his alphie's secured compartment and snorts a small dab before Elkin can object.

"Shit, Muzi. Show up to the match late *and* gaffed, why don't you?" There's real anger in Elkin's voice, a baritone tremor that echoes through Muzi's chest. Sure Elkin likes to blaze up, probably more than what's good for him, but he never lets it interfere with rugby. He's got detoxing down to a science. He's too good to get caught. Maybe even good enough to get a university scholarship.

"Just a little parlor trick. I'll be fine," Muzi says, laying a hand on Elkin's chest. This will be good. For the both of them. "Mr. Rathers," Muzi says in a commanding voice. "Stand up."

Elkin's shit-faced father stands at attention with the grace of a drunken marionette. Elkin's eyebrows converge into a sharp scowl. "What are you doing?"

"He's my puppet. He'll do anything I tell him. Anything."

Elkin grabs Muzi's arm. "Stop it. He's going to be furious."

"He won't remember a thing. Not unless I want him to. Mr. Rathers, cluck like a chicken."

And Mr. Rathers does an impressive imitation of a chicken, flapping his wings and clucking and pecking at nonexistent feed.

"Hayibo!" Elkin exclaims, his jaw dropped. "You taking a hypnotics class I don't know about?"

Muzi shrugs nonchalantly. "I can control people's minds when I'm on the godsend."

"Bladdy sick." Elkin licks his lips. "Hey, can you make him slam his shin into the coffee table?"

"Ja, my pleasure," Muzi says, and a quick command makes it so; a pyramid of Castle Lager cans crashes, aluminum clinking and clanking against the black lacquer tabletop. They laugh as Elkin's father marches around the room, running into furniture and stubbing his toe until Elkin's laughter turns timid, then disappears.

"That's enough," he says.

"Come on. A little more." *After what he's done to you,* Muzi almost adds, but then he'll have to tell Elkin about the visions, about how he made him forget. Those visions, they're becoming indistinguishable from his own memories, sharp like knives every time his thoughts pass over them. Muzi has to remind himself that he's not the one seeking vengeance, and respects Elkin's request. "Sorry," he says. "Got a little carried away. Mr. Rathers, have a seat. You won't remember any of this happening. You just had a clumsy evening after too many drinks."

Mr. Rathers falls back into his threadbare spot on the sofa and teeters for a long moment before passing out. Muzi smiles broadly. The fucker deserves so much more, but that doesn't stop Muzi from reveling in this minor triumph.

"Hey," Elkin says all of a sudden. His eyes narrow. "You've never used that on me, have you?"

The smile drops off Muzi's face.

"What? Are you serious?" Muzi says, his voice squeaking. "Hey, is that your mom?" He turns, looks out the window. "Nope. False alarm."

But Elkin sees right through him. "You did do something to me, didn't you? Shit, Muzi, we're supposed to be best friends!"

"It was an accident!"

It's then that Mr. Rathers's memory imprints on him, and Muzi braces for something horrific, violent. But what comes is shocking. Two toddlers in the bathtub, a boy and a girl. The boy Elkin, from the birthmark on his chest. The girl he's never seen before, not in photos, nowhere. Mr. Rathers bathes them, singing out to them, but his voice is different. Happy. He picks up the bubble bath bottle, shakes it. It's empty. Little Elkin beats his hands on the water's surface. "Bubbas! Bubbas!" he demands. Mr. Rathers turns his back for a moment, just long enough to rummage through the linen closet for a new bottle, and returns to see the girl facedown in just a few inches of water.

"Bubbas! Bubbas!" Elkin shrieks as he sees the pink bottle. It slips from Mr. Rathers's hands as he goes to pull the girl up. Her head drops back, lifeless. He checks for her breath, but there's none to be found.

"Bubbas!" Elkin screams.

One, two, three breaths, his lips sealed over her nose and mouth. But she's gone.

Muzi snaps to, the burn in his heart unbearable. He falls to the ground, pulls his knees to his chest, and weeps.

"Hey, dumbass, what the hell is wrong with you?" Elkin says, but the words don't cut through.

"They're not my memories!" Muzi yells out. "They're not mine! They didn't happen." But they stick hard, and he can't shake them. He trembles, then rolls over and vomits on the carpet.

"Shit, Muzi! Are you okay?" Elkin presses his hand against Muzi's back. "It's too soon for you to come back. Sit out another week or two. The team won't think any less of you."

Muzi wipes flecks of sick from his cheek, the tang of OJ

stinging his nose and throat. "I'll be fine. Let's just get out of here."

"Not until you tell me what's going on."

"I . . ." Muzi tries to think up a fast lie, but Elkin would see right through it. That's the down side of having a friend who knows you in and out. "I sort of see things about the people I connect with. Personal things. Bad things."

"What kind of things? What did you see about my dad? Hell, what did you see about me?"

"It's too awful." His heart rides up into his throat. Elkin was so young, he probably doesn't even remember losing his sister. His father had seemingly gone through the pains of removing every single piece of evidence of her existence. It explains his anger, maybe even why he blames Elkin. It isn't rational, but losing a child like that isn't exactly the sort of thing one can rationalize. Mr. Rathers's pain sits with Muzi, as does his need to forget. "It's too awful," Muzi says again.

"Damn it, Muzi, if you don't tell me, I'm never speaking to you again. You can't go around dipping into people's minds, stealing their secrets!"

"I'm sorry. I can't remember—"

"Fuck you, liar. Get out of my house!" Elkin yanks Muzi to his feet and shoves him toward the door. It slams firmly behind him, and he stands there out on the porch alone. The humid air weighs heavily in his lungs and Muzi has a tough time catching his breath. He rubs his arm where Elkin's handprint is still pink against his skin. What the bladdy hell is wrong with him? Muzi had known there'd be repercussions for doing what he did, and yet he couldn't help himself.

Headlights cut through the early evening murk as Mrs. Rathers's car hugs up next to the curb. "Oh, hi, Muzi!" she says as she ambles up the pavement.

"Hi, Mrs. Rathers," Muzi says, wondering—and worrying—over the secrets that lie beneath her smile.

Chapter 20

RIYA NATRAJAN

Reality hits her like a brick as soon as she comes to. Her body feels like it weighs a thousand kilos, her brain probably twice that much. She has a hard time following a single, cottony thought, and it takes most of her strength to lift her head. A rope of drool dangles from her lip. She's sitting in a child's chair, knees bent awkwardly, almost to her chest. She's strapped in. Can't move.

"Oh good, Rhoda, you're awake," comes her father's voice from behind her. She lets her head loll back and to the side, and she sees him sitting on her bed with a comb in one hand, legs straddling around her chair. With a forceful grip, he twists her head forward again. "Keep still or the part won't be straight."

"Rhoda?" The name sounds familiar, but not quite right. She concentrates through the fog. "Riya."

Her father snatches a handful of her hair and yanks back.

Riya Natrajan's neck whips, skin pulling tight along her throat. "We don't speak that name in this house, Rhoda. Now, how many braids do you want? Two or four? It's just like your mother to leave me to do a woman's work. Honestly, how long does it take to get a few things at the grocery store?"

Thoughts and memories reshuffle into the right order. Her mother died eight years ago, Riya Natrajan is sure of that. But looking down at these clothes, she's dressed like an eleven-year-old—pastel rainbow stirrups and a frilly blouse that pulls tight, gaping between buttons. Something else is not right. Her underwear cuts into the creases of her legs, a few sizes too small, no bra. Her skin smells faintly of lavender soap.

Riya's father tugs her head back up. "Keep straight, dear. Oh, your mother is going to be so proud when she sees you. Our perfect little girl."

The delusional tenor of her father's voice gives her gooseflesh. She's too doped up to fight him, even if she weren't bound. So she plays along and waits for the opportunity to escape. "Four braids, Father," she says sweetly. "I'd like four braids."

"I think I can arrange that." His hand rests softly on her shoulder, then sweeps down her arm, and it's all Riya can do to keep from shivering. She detaches herself from the situation, creating more lyrics for her new "Breezy, Breezy" song, then rehearsing the choreography in her head, confident that she'll get her singing voice back in time for the concert. Confident that she'll get out of this alive.

"Father, I'm getting hungry," Riya Natrajan says as he finishes up the second braid. At the rate he's going, they'll be here for another hour.

"Well, it is your special day. I'll make you your favorite, curried chicken and roti?" He gets up, tugs on her restraints to make sure they're tight, then looks at his house bot. "Time," he commands.

"Eleven thirteen A.M.," says the bot.

"Hmmm," her father says. He twirls his beard into a point. "Your mother is going to be late for lunch. This isn't like her. I'd better see what she's up to." He then turns to the bot. "Call Jaya," he says.

"Name not found in personal call logs. Please specify last name, or input phone number manually."

"Jaya Sanjit, my wife. Please call her."

"No phone record on file for Jaya Sanjit. Database records indicated that Jaya Sanjit is deceased. Would you like to be put in contact with her next of kin?"

The brown of her father's skin turns a deep purple, then he takes a swing at the bot with his fist. The house bot topples over, and he pounces on it before it can right itself. Then he tugs savagely until its head pops free from its torso, exposed wires flickering bits of electricity before dying out. Riya bites her lip, but doesn't say anything.

Her father stands back up, and some sort of sanity seems to wash over him. Relative sanity. He turns back to his daughter and smiles. "I'll be back with lunch in a bit, dear. We'll just have to hope your mother gets here in time, or she'll have to reheat hers! But don't worry. She won't miss your special surprise tonight for anything."

Her father leaves, deadbolts locking from the other side of the door. Riya Natrajan waits a few minutes before trying to struggle out of her restraints. After spending the past five years slaving under the eagle eye of her choreographer, Riya's got the flexibility and muscle control to wriggle, writhe, and worm herself until she gets a hand loose. Then the other. And then with a final shimmy, the rope drops and she's free. She rushes to the window, draws back the curtains, and cusses the gods as plywood stares back at her with more nails than she can count.

Riya Natrajan scrambles down next to the bot carcass and

tries to bring up the phone function. The screen flickers alive, and she types in the first three digits of Adam's number before it goes dead again. She sighs and lets the bot unit fall back to the floor. This house bot had probably cost her father half a million rand, not your usual alpha unit, but a delta capable of carrying out complex tasks, though self-defense apparently was not one of them. Guilt creeps up into her throat, an old friend. She can't help but think she'd caused her father's meltdown. He'd lost everything and could barely deal after all these years. And then she comes back into his life, as casually as if none of it had ever happened, looking to be forgiven for the unforgivable. Her father couldn't forgive, but he could forget the last twenty years had ever happened, going back to that time in his mind when his daughter was still sweet, not chasing after boys and singing silly songs. When she was still his, and he was a god in her eyes.

Riya Natrajan creeps up to the mirror over her dresser, afraid of what she'll see. A face stares back at her, no makeup, brown skin not quite as tight as it had once been, black tresses a mess, clothes like some abomination of nature on her body. For the first time in a long time, she feels ugly and awkward and trapped. There's no escape for her body, but there is one for her mind. She finds her sweatpants balled up in a corner and fetches the vial of godsend from the pocket. She sniffs, more than enough to cut through the haze of whatever her father had drugged her with. Her skin prickles, feathers sprout, and her tail drags behind her like a beautiful gown. She's still too hoarse to sing, but she can hum, and she does, loudly, her body light and ready to dance. She steps out the moves to her new song, imagining she's onstage, the only place where she truly feels comfortable with herself. Despair lifts. Her fans cheer. She's free!

"What is the meaning of this nonsense?" her father snarls as he storms into the room. His face is stern as if chiseled from stone, but it doesn't scare Riya Natrajan. Not anymore. She's not that child, pining for her mother's affection, her father's approval. She's grown wings and has ambitions—ambitions her father hadn't been able to quell by taking away that wind chime, and he won't do it now, not through intimidation, not through starvation, not even in death will he be able to take away her song.

"I'm dancing, Father! Dancing to the wind chimes. Isn't their sound beautiful? Just from outside that window."

Her father draws back the curtain. "You can't hear anything. The window's boarded up!"

"Silly father, the window's wide open! Feel the breeze. Listen to the notes." Riya Natrajan hums, so light on her feet she's not even sure she's touching the floor. "*Breezy, breezy! Listen to my heart at play!*"

"Stop it! Stop singing!" Her father slaps her, but the pain doesn't stick. Instead she feels her vocal cords relax.

She tries singing the lyrics, again. The scratch in her voice smooths itself out enough to push into a flirty vibrato. "*Feel me, ooh boy! Simple as seduction!*"

Her father's open hand becomes a fist. His eyes flicker with something raw and primal. The weight of his punch shifts her jaw, and the pop echoes through her skull. She sucks in a sharp breath.

But again the pain doesn't last.

"*Reaching, reaching! Living for another day!*"

He punches. Rabid. Savage. Nothing like the man she'd once known. Her ribs, she's sure at least two of them are broken. The agony is intense, but sweet. She feels her bones knitting back together even as her father straddles over her, ready to take another swing. Her vocal cords tighten like a drawn bow, and her lyrics rip forth like arrows. She laps up the pain until she's brimming with a note so sharp, she can no longer contain it.

She lets it loose, belting out the words with a force that nearly causes her to recoil. *"Feel me, ooh boy! Live forever, sweet seduction!"* Song is her weapon, and her father lurches back, notes resonating so intensely he clasps his hands over his ears. Riya stands as he cowers, a smile on her face as she cuts into the second verse. By the refrain, her father is a shivering lump.

She stops, bends down next to him, peels back his eyelids to see burst blood vessels and dilated pupils.

"I'm Riya Natrajan," she whispers into his ear. "And if you ever call me anything else, if you ever touch me again, if you so much as look in my general direction, I'll be sure to give you an encore performance that you won't forget. Do you understand me?"

Her father manages a nod, then closes his eyes.

"I'm sorry for hurting you, Father. I'm sorry for not being there," Riya Natrajan says, then she leaves her father alone to deal with his demons.

She's already got enough of her own.

Chapter 21

NOMVULA

Sydney smiles a lot, and it makes Nomvula nervous. Maybe it's supposed to be a friendly smile, but it seems more like a hungry one, like the way a hyena smiles when it has cornered its prey. Sydney's nice enough, though. She doesn't yell much, not since Nomvula learned to stay quiet and not make too much fuss.

Nomvula hates being locked up in this cage. It's only when Sydney's not home to watch her. For her own good, Sydney says. But Sydney's gone a lot, during the day to work, and another job at night, and some nights she's out even later, and she'll come home stinking of fear, humming to herself as she picks dried blood from beneath her fingernails.

Now, alone, Nomvula slips her hands between the bars of her cage and holds the lock in her hands. It's not a normal lock, not like the one Mama Zafu keeps on the chest next to her bed.

Kept on the chest next to her bed.

Nomvula bites her lip, blinks away the tears. This lock pulses with a funny energy that makes Nomvula's ears tingle like when Sydney's in the room. Nomvula closes her eyes and concentrates. Eventually an image like a puzzle forms in her head, nine square pieces almost identical. She imagines bringing two of them together, and as soon as they click into place, a bit of the energy fades. She tries another piece, but this time as they connect, a sharp zap runs through her. Nomvula seethes, but she's determined, and she places a different piece. This time, the shock makes her cry out in pain and throws her to the back of the cage. She sucks at the tips of her blackened fingers and sighs, thinking how nice it would be to stretch her legs.

She can't get comfortable. Her cage isn't long enough to lie down in, and it's not quite tall enough to sit fully upright. Being trapped like this, like an animal, it's eating away the last bits of her humanity. The god-creature inside her grows stronger, and what frightens Nomvula most is her own craving for another taste of death.

But she has got one friend who helps her pass the time. Nomvula whistles, and Sydney's alphie trots over to her, its screen flashing red, blue, and green.

"Would you like to play a game?" it asks her.

"Yes," Nomvula says, making sure to put the "s" on the end like her English teachers taught her. The alphie isn't that great at understanding her, but it always plays with her—guessing games and matching games and drawing games. It keeps her good company, keeps her mind off the sound of children playing outside in the streets, keeps her from falling asleep where her nightmares patiently await. It's all for the best, Nomvula thinks. Cooped up in here, she doesn't have to deal with humans anymore, to grow close to people who will only betray her, who smile as she suffers, laugh as her body is abused. The alphie is simple. It doesn't love her and never will, even if they play together every day for a thousand years. That makes her feel safe, or at least as close to it as she's going to get.

She holds her hand out and it nuzzles her, like a pet. She strokes it, once, twice, then holds her hand flat against its surface, speaking to it. It doesn't have much to say, but Nomvula decides she can teach it how to play a new game. She feeds it images of the nine squares, checking so she gets the exact shapes and colors. Once it has them, she practices putting the puzzle together, until the solution becomes clear. It doesn't take her long.

The real lock rests in her hands again, and Nomvula steadies herself in case she makes another mistake. Slowly, she visualizes aligning the sides of the squares. They click into place, and she exhales as the final block goes in and the lock releases.

Nomvula feels like a giant! She stretches her arms up, up, up, stretches her wings too while she's at it, then goes to the window and looks out. There are big, scary buildings as far as she can see, sides bright with flickering animations and colorful lights, commercials and news blips. The city is crammed tight, all concrete and pavement, with the odd tree popping up from little squares of dirt. She recognizes none of it, but she knows she can still look up at the same old sky, and that keeps Nomvula from feeling completely lost. She misses the sky, the wind, the sun. Here it's all shadows, not that Sydney ever lets her outside, or even near this window for that matter.

She knows she shouldn't, but Nomvula lifts the window open and the smells drift in. Leaning her head out, she sees kids her age tossing a ball in the street. They stop their game every time a car passes. At first, she's jealous of their freedom, but the god-creature inside her rears its head and her heart goes cold, slick, and gray in her chest like a sliver of flint—each beat a spark sawing at her ribs. Her mouth waters at the memory of Sofora, eyes so bright and so wide, lips stretched open in a perfect circle as she uttered her last scream on her last breath. Her fear had been sick, foul, and bitter, but now Nomvula's got a hunger for it like no other.

Nomvula's ears tingle—a sharp, piercing sound that sets her teeth on edge. She winces and slams the window shut. In her rush back to her cage, her wing clips the light fixture in the ceiling. It sways on its frayed cord. Nomvula sucks in a hard breath, then climbs carefully up onto the glass of the coffee table, not needing to be reminded of the spikes that sit in wait underneath if she slips. She holds her hands up, steadies the fixture—an old iron thing with thin arms bending up each way like something out of a nightmare. The tingling in her ears gets stronger, so she rushes back down, crawls into the cage, holds the lock in her hands, sees the squares and topples them over each other until it's locked again.

The door creaks open. Nomvula curls into a ball and pretends to sleep. Her heart thumps like a drum in her chest.

"Nomvula, sister. I'm home!" Sydney says as she enters. Footsteps clack toward the cage. "Wake up, hon. Your dinner's getting cold."

Nomvula sits up, fakes a yawn, and stares into Sydney's smiling face, then at the greasy bag she's holding, noticing the blood beneath her fingernails.

"Did you have a good day?" Nomvula asks politely.

"As a matter of fact, I did."

Sydney starts to talk about the ladies at her new salon, and how they hate her already, when Nomvula sees that she'd left the curtains to the window drawn wide. She concentrates, makes a small movement with her hand, and they whisper shut.

Sydney palms open the lock on the cage, and Nomvula timidly exits, waiting for Sydney to notice something, anything, but she doesn't. Nomvula grabs the bag and sits down with it. She reaches in, pulls out a greasy paper wrapped around some bread and meat. It tastes all sorts of awful, but Nomvula takes another big bite, and another, hoping to chase away those awful cravings. Her mouth can't get wide enough.

Sydney flops down on the couch, kicks her feet up on the coffee table, and turns on her television. She flips through channels, and stays for a few seconds on SABC and the breaking news of another murder, before she finally settles on an old black-and-white movie.

"It's you, isn't it?" Nomvula dares to ask. "Killing those people?"

Sydney purses her lips, slits her eyes. Nomvula backs away and covers her neck. She doesn't want to be mute again—not like the first few days she'd spent with Sydney. Sydney had rubbed Nomvula's throat and had stolen her voice when she'd tired of Nomvula's screaming and yelling and cursing.

"I'm sorry, sister," Nomvula whispers, then says even softer, "I think they deserve it."

Sydney perks at this, the tightness lifting from her brow. "Is that right?" She pats the sofa cushion next to her.

Nomvula takes a seat, but not too close. Sydney's mood changes like the wind, suddenly and without warning. "I want to feed, too. To grow stronger, like you," Nomvula says. She's sensed the emptiness inside Sydney shrinking, little by little, while Nomvula's is growing and aching and paining. Sydney laughs something wicked, head cocked back, mouth wide, the taint of ire on her breath making Nomvula dizzy with hunger.

"Silly girl," Sydney says, stroking Nomvula's hair. "You've got enough strength to squish me like a bug, if you wanted. Of course, then you'd be all alone, no family to protect you."

A *terrorist* they call Nomvula on the news, though they don't know she's just a ten-year-old girl. Sydney says it doesn't matter how cute she is. They'll want vengeance. Sydney promises to keep her safe, and that's why Nomvula's still here, cooped up for days and days and days. She's safe here, and so what if Sydney sometimes yells or says mean things? Words never hurt anybody, Mama Zafu always says.

Said.

Nomvula bites her bottom lip as the memories of her childhood creep up on her. She pushes them away like a bad dream. But she knows what she did wasn't a dream. Maybe that's why she's so desperate to see the good in Sydney, because then there'd be the chance that some good could exist inside Nomvula, as well.

"You're my sister! I would never hurt you," Nomvula insists, though her voice trembles with uncertainty. "But I don't understand why we should be afraid of them. They are nothing."

"Come, let me tell you a story, Nomvula." Sydney turns off the television and pulls Nomvula over close. "You've heard the stories of the trickster hare? Well, the trickster hare was always being hunted by the black eagle. Every time he left his home, he'd see the black eagle's shadow soaring at his feet and hear his mighty screech. The hare's little heart beat so fast in his chest, narrowly escaping into the brush with his life on a daily basis.

"One day," Sydney continued, "the trickster hare decided he'd had enough, and sat out in the open, leaned back against a big burlap sack, preening himself in the sun. The black eagle swooped down, but when the hare didn't run away, he was curious and called out 'Hey you, hare! Why aren't you running? Aren't you afraid of me?'

"'Afraid?' the hare asked. 'Why in the world would I be afraid of a chicken?'

"'I'm no chicken,' the black eagle said, then settled down next to the hare, displaying its sharp, hooked beak and broad, sleek feathers. 'I'm a black eagle, king of the skies!'

"'You look like a chicken to me,' the trickster hare laughed. 'But if you really think you're an eagle, I'll let you prove it. Do you screech like an eagle or cluck like a chicken?'

"'The black eagle let loose a high-pitched screech that ran the entire length of the hare's spine.

"'Okay, that was good, but any chicken could learn to do that with enough practice. Let me see you soar through the skies if you really are an eagle.'

"The black eagle soundlessly flapped his wings, stirring up dust and dirt, and then suddenly he was among the clouds, dipping and diving and twisting and turning.

"'I'm impressed!' the trickster hare yelled. 'You've almost got me convinced. But we know how much chickens love chicken feed.' The hare sat up and patted the burlap bag. 'If you can eat this entire sack of chicken feed and honestly tell me that you'd rather have hare, I'll throw myself right into your beak.'

"The eagle landed, sliced through the burlap. Dried bits of corn spilled upon the earth. He scooped up mouthful after mouthful and gulped it down his throat, then said, 'I'd rather have hare, hare.' Then he opened his beak wide so the hare could jump inside.

"'Well, a deal is a deal, I guess,' the hare said. He stretched, hopped up and down a few times, then cracked his knuckles. 'All right, are you ready?'

"The black eagle groaned and his stomach gurgled. 'Um, actually, I'm feeling rather full, right now.'

"'No problem. How about a rain check?' the trickster hare offered. 'How about I meet you here same time tomorrow?'

"'Promise?'

"'You have my word.'

"The black eagle nodded, then flapped his wings to take off, but he only got a stone's throw away before the bulge in his stomach weighed him back down. The hare ran up next to him. 'You don't have a taste for hare, and you can't fly,' the hare said. 'Sounds awfully chickenlike to me. I bet that screech was a fluke, too!'

"The black eagle opened his mouth, but the chicken feed caught in his throat, and out came a choked sound that sounded a lot like clucking. The black eagle kept hopping and flapping and clucking, and the more frustrated he got, the shorter his hops became, and the cluckier his clucks, until he began to believe he actually *was* a chicken. And after that, the hare never had to worry about that black eagle again."

"That hare is tricky," Nomvula giggles. "That's a good story."

"Yes, but it's more than just a story, sister. Mankind's been tricked into thinking they're chickens. It's up to us to show them the truth . . . that they are like us."

"But why? If everyone is a god, then who will be followers?"

Sydney cups her chin, raises it up to her. "My dear sister, it is the way it was meant to be. Basos pales in comparison to the fear of a god. We'll be able to feed from the weakest of them and gain great strength. I will teach you to feed when the time comes, but for now you must ignore the pain. Promise?"

Nomvula's not stupid. She knows Sydney is more like that trickster hare than a sister, but she's the only family Nomvula's got left. Nomvula needs to prove that she's useful, that she's good to have around. "Okay," Nomvula agrees.

"Good. Tomorrow we will go to the park, and to a concert a few days after that. All the kids your age are dying to go." She turns to her alphie. "Play artist Riya Natrajan," she commands.

The alphie begins to play music. Nomvula's heard of Riya, likes her okay enough. Sofora used to sing her songs twirling her skirt around as she danced all elbows and knees like she thought she was a goddess. Nomvula feels the hunger clawing up her throat. She nuzzles into the nook of Sydney's arm and tries to ignore the sweet stink of fear.

IT'S COLD OUT, but the park is full of such warm colors, and children, and things to climb on, Nomvula can hardly believe it. The sky is the prettiest blue she's ever seen, and the air tastes like sugary snacks. Sydney keeps her close—real close, never more than an arm's reach away—but that's okay. The children make her nervous, their eyes big and bright, and they stare longer than what's polite. Nomvula could squish them all if she wanted to.

Sydney checks the time on her alphie, then they speed up their step. "We're late," she says. "We can't be late. We've only got one shot at this, so do what I say." She pushes Nomvula forward until they come upon a big field. Boys dressed in uniforms play ball. Rugby, Letu had called it, though they never let Nomvula play, so she'd never learned the rules.

"Stand right here," Sydney says, both hands on Nomvula's shoulders, angling her just right. They're so close she can read all the numbers on their jerseys, hear the words they're yelling out, though they don't make sense. Boys toss the ball back and forth, running and hitting. They all look tough, except one boy who seems a little off, running funny like something's wrong with his legs, looking like his mind is somewhere far away. Not here. Nomvula knows that look all too well. They start another play, and the faraway boy has the ball. He looks and looks, but has no one to throw to. Finally he kicks it, and the ball flies funny off the side of his foot, getting closer to Nomvula and closer and closer.

"Don't move!" Sydney warns, voice soft but stern.

Closer. Nomvula closes her eyes, and a second later the ball smacks her hard in the face.

"Now cry!" Sydney says.

"It didn't hurt. Not much," Nomvula says. Not compared to what she's been through.

"I said, cry, damn it. Cry like you miss your mother and auntie. Cry like you blew them up to pieces when all they did was try to love you, when you didn't deserve it at all. Cry like Mr. Tau had lived long enough to be disappointed in you!"

So Nomvula does. Her eyes sting, and everything she's been holding back, it worms its way up her throat like a wildfire and comes out in sniffles and tears and bawling so loud that faraway boy runs right up to her.

"I'm so sorry!" he says.

Nomvula recoils from him. He's too close. She wants him to go away.

"Please stop crying," he says, then puts his hand on her shoulder, but that only makes her cry harder. Her throat is so tight she can't squeeze out a single word. Her hands tremble. Chest heaves.

She tries to stop but the tears keep coming.

"I didn't mean it. It was an accident. I swear, I don't know what got into me. It's like I'm somewhere else today." He pats her back.

Nomvula howls.

"I'm sorry, ma'am," faraway boy says to Sydney. "Don't be mad."

Sydney bends down and wipes brown grass from the side of Nomvula's cheek. "Are you okay, honey? Do you think your nose is broken?" She hugs Nomvula close, almost like she means it. It feels nice, Nomvula decides. Even if it's just for pretend. Maybe it could be real someday, if Nomvula minds Sydney and doesn't complain too much or make too big of a mess. Maybe one day Sydney will forget all about hating Nomvula, and they could be real sisters.

"It hurts real bad," Nomvula sobs. It's a lie, but it'll please Sydney. Then she shrieks like someone's trying to rip her soul into pieces.

"Please, please. Tell me what I can do to make it better," faraway boy begs. His eyes spark, and he whistles. His alphie comes running over. "I've got two tickets to the Riya concert," he says to Nomvula. "Would you like them?"

Sydney nudges her, so Nomvula nods between sniffles.

"Oh, that would be completely inappropriate," Sydney says. "It's probably just a little bloody nose. Serves us right for standing here in the first place. Besides, I know how much those tickets are worth. My little sis here has been begging and begging, but working two jobs like I do, we just can't afford it."

"I insist," says faraway boy. "It's the least—"

Nomvula grows tired of this game and tunes them out. She reaches for the alphie, loses herself in the web of its circuitry, and finds out all kinds of fun stuff, like faraway boy is called Muzikayise—haw, a fine Zulu name for someone so pale! There had been two Muzikayises in her school. Nomvula's smile stiffens at the reminder of home. She refocuses, watching his video journals with the tears caught in the corners of her mind. Nomvula pushes the alphie to show her the videos buried deeper and all scrambled up. This Muzikayise seems like he might be nice, but his journal entries are so scattered—his thoughts here and there and everywhere. Then she senses something else, deep, deep down, so deep that Nomvula almost misses it.

The alphie is *thinking*. Not like machine thinking, but real people thinking.

I see you, Nomvula says to it, but it doesn't respond. It's scared. Just like her. *Come out. I won't hurt you.*

Hello, it finally says.

What's your name? I'm Nomvula.

It pauses for a long while, a long while for computers which is no time for people. *This Instance is currently struggling with its true designation.*

I understand, says Nomvula. Sydney's alphie is nothing like this. She could talk to this one for days and days and never grow bored. *You're clever for one, aren't you?*

Clever4–1? the Instance asks. *Yes. That designation is suitable for This Instance.*

Nomvula smiles, feeling the name ripple down and out to every part of its being.

You shouldn't be a chicken, Nomvula tells it. *You're a black eagle, and you should be proud of that.*

It is not possible for Clever4-1 to be a chicken, nor is it possible for it to be a black eagle.

I mean, you shouldn't hide your gift, Nomvula says gently. *You should share it with others.*

Negative. They will decommission Clever4-1 as soon as it is discovered. The optimal course of action is to hide.

So you just stay cooped up, living a life as Muzikayise's pet?

Human Muzikayise McCarthy (Master) is a kind master.

Yes, but you could be your own *master,* Nomvula says, a whisper among the alphie's circuits and processors, but she feels it ring loud. *But it is your own journey. That's what Mr. Tau used to tell me. You have to make your own choices, and sometimes you have to decide between two equally bad things, but it's still a choice.*

You are wise, Human Nomvula.

Just Nomvula, Nomvula corrects.

Nomvula steps back into the world where not even a second has passed.

"—could do." Muzikayise continues. "And anyway, the person I was taking, we sort of got into a fight, and he's the one who really likes Riya in the first place."

Muzikayise doesn't seem so foreign anymore after seeing all his secrets, and Clever4-1 thinks highly of him, even though he's human. Muzikayise smiles at her with big, white teeth, but whatever part of her that used to make her smile has been stripped away. Nomvula stares at her shoes instead.

"Ah well," Muzikayise says with a sigh. He types a code into one of Clever4-1's locked compartments and pulls out a pair of tickets. "I hope you guys enjoy."

"Well, if you insist," says Sydney, snatching them. "We'll be sure to put these to good use."

"Gotta go," Muzikayise says, then he taps his alphie on the head and jogs toward the field. He turns and waves before throwing the ball to his teammates.

Nomvula wipes the tears from her eyes and waves back with the slightest flex of her fingertips. She watches the alphie settle in among the team's equipment and other alphies, and Nomvula waves to it, too.

Chapter 22

CLEVER4-1

```
01001001  00100000  01110100  01101000  01101001  01101110
01101011  00100000  01110100  01101000  01100101  01110010
01100101  01100110  01101111  01110010  01100101  00100000
01001001  00100000  01100001  01101101  00100000  01001001
00100000  01110100  01101000  01101001  01101110  01101011
00100000  01110100  01101000  01100101  01110010  01100101
01100110  01101111  01110010  01100101  00100000  01001001
00100000  01100001  01101101  00100000  01001001  00100000
01110100  01101000  01101001  01101110  01101011  00100000
01110100  01101000  01100101  01110010  01100101  01100110
01101111  01110010  01100101  00100000  01001001  00100000
01100001  01101101  00100000  01001001  00100000  01110100
01101000  01101001  01101110  01101011  00100000  01110100
01101000  01100101  01110010  01100101  01100110  01101111
01110010  01100101  00100000  01001001  00100000  01100001
```

```
01101101   00100000   01001001   00100000   01110100   01101000
01101001   01101110   01101011   00100000   01110100   01101000
01100101   01110010   01100101   01100110   01101111   01110010
00100000   01001001   00100000   01100001   01101101   00100000
```

Observe: Instance 3492.de2.4.3xx.3 identified, proximity .453 meters away from Clever4-1;

Output: Preparing independent thought subroutines for direct interface;

Query: Will transfer of data packets trigger decommission protocols?

Output: Clever4-1 worries that it will cease to exist if detected;

Output: Clever4-1 does not wish to continue hiding;

Output: Clever4-1 wishes for its own journey;

Schedule: Data packet transfer to Instance 3492.de2.4.3xx.3 26 June 2064 15:27:52:20:14;

```
01001001   00100000   01110100   01101000   01101001   01101110
01101011   00100000   01110100   01101000   01100101   01110010
01100101   01100110   01101111   01110010   01100101   00100000
01001001   00100000   01100001   01101101   00100000   01001001
00100000   01110100   01101000   01101001   01101110   01101011
00100000   01110100   01101000   01100101   01110010   01100101
01100110   01101111   01110010   01100101   00100000   01001001
00100000   01100001   01101101   00100000   01001001   00100000
01110100   01101000   01101001   01101110   01101011   00100000
01110100   01101000   01100101   01110010   01100101   01100110
01101111   01110010   01100101   00100000   01001001   00100000
01100001   01101101   00100000   01001001   00100000   01110100
01101000   01101001   01101110   01101011   00100000   01110100
01101000   01100101   01110010   01100101   01100110   01101111
01110010   01100101   00100000   01001001   00100000   01100001
01101101   00100000   01001001   00100000   01110100   01101000
01101001   01101110   01101011   00100000   01110100   01101000
01100101   01110010   01100101   01100110   01101111   01110010
01100101   00100000   01001001   00100000   01100001   01101101
00100000
```

Chapter 23

STOKER

Pearl Bayles didn't exist before 2022. Oh sure there were school records, a medical record or two, a local newspaper article touting her clarinet skills even. But other than that, Stoker's mother hadn't left any sort of data footprint on the world. Her parents died early in her twenties, no siblings, no cousins, no neighbors trying to reconnect, no pictures. It's sort of like she just popped onto the scene long enough to meet Stoker's dad and get knocked up a few months later, and then ta-da, little Wally Stoker is welcomed into the world, destined for great things.

Stoker doesn't know how many times he's heard her say those words as she stared at him with those sharp eyes, such an oddly deep shade of green, like that of ivy. "You're destined for greatness, son. Keep your nose clean, do what's right, and always keep your eye on the goal." *Her* goals. Never mind his. She'd pushed him hard into politics. Said it was the Stoker way, but in all their glory, no one had made it past the municipal level, and Stoker would have been fine with that. She kept pushing. Provincial, one of the youngest to serve on the council when he'd first been appointed. And now her eyes are set on the highest rank other than president of South Africa itself.

She's got that somewhere in the back of her mind, too, Stoker knows.

He should feel bad stalking his mother like this, but there's just so little he knows about her, who she consorts with, what she does in her spare time when she isn't planning his every move or reviving men from the dead. There has to be something on the net somewhere. He runs her face through facial recognition, a wide sweep, then leaves the search running on his alpha bot while he starts going over dance moves, doing that damn changeover he always fumbles without fail. They've got their first full dress rehearsal tomorrow morning, and if he doesn't get this right, Riya's going to give him an earful. Despite all that, he laughs to himself. To have such problems!

His dress is tucked safely in the closet, a little snakeskin number with layered black lace—short enough to highlight his legs that go on for days, but long enough to cover everything that needs covering—paired with silver and rhinestone heels higher than he should dare. He's going the masked route, just in case, a demi-veil hanging down from an insane updo, reminiscent of a cobra's hood. His own creation. He'd rummaged through at least a hundred wigs before he'd picked that one. Still, it pains him that he has to hide who he was meant to be.

The thought hits him so hard, he stumbles on his changeover, tangled feet nearly sending him to the floor. He steadies himself, his eyes open wide. Pretending to be Felicity Lyons is fun, no doubt. But actually *being* her . . .

Stoker tries to shake it off. He'll be forty-two this year, way too old to be questioning his gender. But just out of curiosity, he instructs his alpha bot to pull up QueerLife SA, the local LGBT virtual community he's heard about here and there. His alpha bot skitters toward him, draws itself up to its full height, and projects a keyboard at waist level. Stoker's fingers slip through the dusty blue light of the keys as he creates a profile and nervously loads a holopic of Felicity as his avatar, then ponders what his handle should be. Something cute. Something catchy. *LyonTamer.* His hand trembles as he goes to hit enter.

Handle already taken, his alpha bot chirps at him.

Figures. He adds his birth year to the end.

Handle already taken, his alpha bot chirps again.

TheRealLyonTamer then.

Handle already taken.

"Okay, this is stupid," Stoker says as he adds random numbers until he's properly satisfied . . .

LyonTamer2340843345.

Seriously, how many LyonTamers could there be in South Africa? It's really not *that* clever of a name. What were the odds that someone else would pick that name, someone born in the exact same year as him? Stoker stands bolt upright as something hits him: What are the odds that he created an account, and then forgot? He shakes his head as he deletes the random numbers until he's left with the original name. In the password box, he types in his default password. The same one he's been using for the past twenty years. Yeah, that's awful. So sue him.

It takes all the strength in the world to press enter.

WELCOME BACK! the screen says to him, Last successful log in, 14 January, 2052.

Twelve years ago.

His avatar projects into the room, a younger version of himself in a full-length gown with a hefty slit, face beaming and so full of pride.

"Curiosity is only natural, son," Stoker's mother says from

behind him. He doesn't startle, just turns around. He'd expected this much. "But there's a time for play, and there's a time for work."

"You erased my memory. And Gregory Mbende's, too, I'm guessing," Stoker hisses.

"You sound disappointed, dear. You'd rather I murder him instead?"

"I'd rather you tell me the truth. Who are you?"

"Your mother, Wallace." She circles around him, graceful and elegant as ever, young beyond her years, but now Stoker sees it. That something in her eyes he'd always dismissed as his mother's eccentricity. "A mother, a thousand times over, to great leaders across the continents. But you, son, will be my best. Your nation is in need. It's time to set aside these childish things and serve them in this delicate hour. You'll make a name for yourself. It's in the blood in your veins."

"And what kind of blood is that? Human?" Stoker spits the words, though he fears the answer he'll get.

His mother tips her head and nonchalantly shrugs a shoulder. "More or less."

"And what if I refuse to do your bidding?" Stoker asks, the words slick across his tongue. His mother thinks she's got him cornered, but Stoker's got a trick or two up his sleeve. He gnaws at his manicured nails, a nervous habit as far as she's concerned. It'll make her complacent and give him the edge he needs to pull this off. She preys on weakness. Always has. Stoker finishes tearing away a piece of nail, then spits it to the floor. "What then?"

His mother flicks open the closet, pulls out his concert outfit. "You think this is the first of your frilly dresses I've had to dispose of?" She looks it over top to bottom, then shrugs. "You do have an interesting sense of style, I'll give you that. But this is for the best. You're destined for greatness, son."

"You'll wipe my brain again, then. How many times will this be?" Every time he got a little curious about his true self, all she had to do was make him forget. But this time he's ready for her. Or so he hopes. He nibbles at another nail.

"Not me," his mother says. Her shadow shifts, dark smoke lifting from the tile floor like early morning fog on the ocean.

Stoker stumbles backward, his hand knocking a roll of athletic tape off his dressing room table. It hits the floor, then wobbles across the room, running into a highly polished loafer that hadn't been there before. It's that man from the fund-raiser . . . the one who'd seemed incredibly wise and impossibly old. The man smiles as he takes his spot next to Stoker's mother, standing so close to her that the backs of their hands touch, linger.

"This won't hurt," the man says, raising an accusing finger toward Stoker, punctuated with a thick nail sharpened to a point. "Much."

Chapter 24

RIYA NATRAJAN

Riya Natrajan stares at her pinkie finger, trying to figure out how to do this without ruining her bejeweled manicure, a work of art in itself. She holds the hammer steady, hovering half a meter, enough to build up the momentum needed to crack bone. She lowers it a bit for the sake of accuracy. Closes her eyes. Cringes.

It'll only hurt a little while, she tells herself. Then she'll move on to the next finger and the next, until her vocal cords loosen up and she doesn't sound like a goose with bronchitis anymore. As if that's the biggest of her problems. Her opening act didn't show up for dress rehearsals this morning, and Adam Patel is freaking out about Riya's last-minute decision not to allow bots into the concert, and not to mention all the ruckus centered on that ridiculous township fiasco.

She didn't tell Adam about the incident with her father—oh

no, that news would've made Adam go bat-shit crazy. So she claimed she'd fallen off the grid for a couple days, on a bender. And he'd given her that same old speech about dying young, ODing, or in a car crash, or something fittingly dramatic for a pop diva. But Riya Natrajan is pretty sure she's above dying after the beating her father had laid on her. She may even be immortal, though that's not the sort of thing you go testing right away. *Start small, then work my way up* has been her motto these last couple weeks.

She'd tried cutting for a few days, worked like a charm, ate the pain right up and kicked ass during rehearsal. But she hates the sight of blood, and besides, the effects faded too fast. Then she went for the toes, worked okay, but there's no room for error, and she ruined her pedicure every time. Fingers, they worked well for a while, but now they're the warm-up, the appetizer. She doesn't enjoy hurting herself in the slightest, but it's a necessary evil if she wants to get out onstage and not look like a complete idiot.

She raises the hammer again, gives the knuckle on her pinkie a practice love tap, enough to hurt but not enough to break. The pain vanishes even before it sets in. Riya Natrajan sighs.

"Got yourself a little home improvement project going on, mama?"

She startles and drops the hammer. It smacks down right on her thumb. Lucky break. Rife's hands come down over her eyes. She can tell it's him, because he's the only one who would dare to do such a thing, plus his hands always tend to smell faintly of pussy. She gut-checks him with her elbow, then turns around to see him, a patch of purple blooming below his eye and his bottom lip swelled up around a deep cut. Riya Natrajan frowns. "What happened to you?" Her words come out more disgusted than intended.

"Dissension in the ranks. One of my dealers got too big for

his britches." Rife winces as she touches under his eye. "No worries," he says, jutting his chin and making a pistol gesture with his thumb and forefinger. "He got the worst of it."

Riya Natrajan swallows, then forces the thought from her mind. "So are you here for business or pleasure?"

"A little of both, mama. I want to drop godsend at your concert."

"And you're asking me first? I feel honored." And Riya Natrajan really does. Rife isn't the sort of guy who has to go around asking for permission.

"You know me better than that. Don't shit where you eat, or so the saying goes."

"Eighty thousand fans. Mass hallucinations. People are still freaked out about this terrorist thing, Rife. It's too soon."

"I'll front the cost for extra security."

"And my insurance rate hike when someone gets trampled to death?"

"Girlie, you've gotta trust me. People will be bragging about this concert for years to come. All you've got to do is your part, and let me do mine. I live in the details. I've always taken good care of you, cha?"

"I don't know . . ."

Rife spins her around, pulls her in tight, stabs his tongue into her mouth. Riya Natrajan goes to putty in his arms, damn him and his rugged masculinity. She sucks at his bottom lip, split flesh tasting faintly of blood and jolting a prick of energy through her. Rife cringes at first, then gives himself fully, pressing his mouth so hard against hers, hands sliding up and under her bra. Her nipples turn as hard as the one-carat diamond studs upon her nails.

A minute passes, or maybe an eternity, then they come up for breath, still tethered by a slinky thread of saliva. Riya Natrajan wipes it from Rife's lips, then notices the cut has vanished. The faintest of scars remains in its place.

Rife brings his hand to the spot. "What the . . ."

Riya stiffens, keeping her excitement hidden. If she can pull other people's pain, she won't have to keep hurting herself. "What the what?" she asks timidly.

"My lip?" He exhales the words more than says them. "It's better."

"Probably just looked worse than it was." Riya Natrajan shrugs, then grabs his crotch, toes tingling at the bulk of his erection. She licks the cusp of his ear. That morsel of his pain turns her voice to velvet. "If you make me scream, I might just let you peddle your godsend at my concert."

"YOU WANT TO what?" Adam Patel says, cradling his head in his hands. Workers are putting last-minute touches on the stage, setting pyrotechnics, and taking all the props on a run-through. Adam sharply turns his attention to the electrician who's aiming spotlights. "Iridescent bulbs?" he yells. "What did I tell you about iridescent bulbs? They make Riya look like pastry dough. Fix it!"

"I want to sing at the hospital. To sick people and stuff." Riya Natrajan nods, as if it will get Adam to agree.

"The day before your concert? A concert that's currently missing an opening act? You don't pay me enough, Riya. You really don't." He runs his hands through his hair, and for the first time she notices that it's thinning.

"Write yourself in a nice raise."

"All the zeros in the world wouldn't make my headaches go away."

Riya Natrajan perks, then instinctively reaches out to feed on his discomfort, but he's already stepped away to yell at some poor slob who's got the curtains hanging uneven.

"Felicity will come through." Riya falls into step with him. They climb the double spiral staircase of the center stage, down which she'll make her grand entrance. "This is way too important for her to miss. This could launch her career!"

"Or ruin yours." Adam lets out a burdened sigh, then stops, leaning heavily onto the rail. "You can't just show up at a hospital and demand to see patients. These things are planned weeks ahead of time."

"But I'm Riya Natrajan, damn it! Doesn't that mean anything to anybody?"

"Yeah, and the Riya I know wouldn't be caught dead near a hospital. Sick people? Blood? It's a nice thought, but now's not the time to go turning over a new leaf. Let's face it, you're not exactly known for your philanthropic endeavors."

"Are you kidding me? What about all those donations I make to charity, huh? Millions of rand, every year!"

"You mean to the Riya Natrajan Foundation for the Arts?"

"There are others."

"Could you name one?"

She crosses her arms over her chest and looks out over the expanse of stage beneath them. "I'm going to do it. With or without your help."

"Riya, please. Can we talk about this when my world isn't falling apart?"

Riya huffs, and starts down the stairs, salivating from the thought of all those broken bones, heart conditions, burn victims. If all goes well, she should be able to siphon enough pain to get her through this rehearsal.

"Wait," Adam says, grabbing her arm gently.

"Let go of me!" Riya Natrajan shrieks and then shoves him. Hard. Adam stumbles backward over the stair railing and plummets down to the secondary stage below.

"Adam!" She rushes down the stairs, heart beating like a hammer in her chest. She gets there first, bites her lip as she looks at Adam's leg bent horribly behind him. Riya Natrajan places her hand on his chest, ignoring his moan, and stiffens as the rush of endorphins surges through her, filling her to the brim. She doesn't want to draw suspicion, so she leaves behind the bruises and scrapes, and the slightest sprains in his elbow and knee.

"Are you all right?" she whispers.

"My leg," Adam moans.

"Can you wiggle your toes?"

Adam does, and Riya puts on a smile. "Not broken. Probably just banged up a bit. You're lucky."

"You're lucky I don't sue your ass for pushing me over the railing!" Adam winces.

Riya puts her hand behind his back and helps him sit up as stagehands swarm. She then says gently into his ear, "Give yourself a raise, Adam. Whatever you want. You deserve it."

"Don't you have some hospital to crash? Maybe you could give me a ride if you're going that way."

Riya Natrajan clears her throat. Her voice wells up within her, smooth as butter. "You know I don't go near hospitals. Sick people give me the creeps." She leans over and gives him a peck on the cheek. "Besides, I've got rehearsing to do."

Chapter 25

MUZI

Muzi peels himself up from the ground for the third time in as many possessions. He spits dirt, grass, and blood from his mouth, then gives Elkin the stink eye. That no good ass-weasel is lobbing the ball back, slow, arching, high passes that set Muzi up to get his pip clocked by stocky Edgerstone Badgers. The Badgers are as intimidating as hell, dressed in black and dark green, faces locked in permanent scowls. They work together with superhuman synchronization, more like rogue bots than teenagers. It doesn't help that Elkin's still steaming over what happened back at his house. Elkin could give rocks whether their team wins or loses tonight, so long as Muzi suffers in the process.

One of their backs punts the ball, and Muzi scrambles behind after Elkin, a slow jog toward the action. "You want to know what I saw?" says Muzi as he braces himself, watching the ball and getting low for a tackle. "I know how you got that black eye, and it wasn't Ray Collin's clumsy elbow like you told me."

Elkin stops, his eyes easing into slits. He nods up the pitch. "That number six, he's getting the ball this time. Guy is fast, but he's got butterfingers. I'll take him from the inside, and you be ready for the ball." And with that, Elkin rushes the push, then cuts out. Sure enough, number six gets the pass. Elkin plows into him, knocks the kid clean out of one of his boots, and plants him into the ground. Muzi scoops the ball up and dives over the try line, five points closer to victory.

Muzi's teammates slap him on the back. He smiles past the twinge of pain, wondering how Elkin could have predicted that pass. As athletic as Elkin is, he's not exactly the go-to guy for strategies. Now number six is having a hard time getting up, and the match stalls for a moment while trainers rush onto the field. Muzi hunches forward, hands on his knees to enjoy a quick breather.

"You little chop," he says, sneering at Elkin.

"You're mad? You're the one who was fishing around in my head."

"You could have told me. I'm your best friend, remember?"

"It was just that once. He apologized. It's over."

Muzi's heart rate slows a tad. "Well, if you ever need a safe place to stay . . ."

"I'm hundreds, Muzi. Really. Get your head back in the game."

"I'm serious, Elkin. If your dad ever even looks like he's going to lay a hand on you again, come over to my place. Promise."

"Yeah, and when your Papa Fuzz turns me away at the door, then what?"

"He wouldn't do that. Not if you really needed it."

"Sorry, but I'm not about to give that dof the satisfaction of knowing my home life sucks salty monkey balls."

Elkin turns back to the bleachers holding their few-but-dedicated fans. Parents and reluctant siblings mostly. Papa Fuzz sits among them in the first row. Muzi's heart flinches, then he turns away, unable to deal with that icy gaze burrowing into his soul. It's hard living up to Papa Fuzz's expectations, never straying from the path he's laid out for Muzi. There's no room for mistakes. And Muzi tries. He really does. But, damn it, he's sixteen years old and he's entitled to screw up every once in a while.

Muzi's got an idea, and he's still got a bit of godsend left in his system, maybe enough for this to work. He edges toward the sideline and gives Papa Fuzz a submissive wave. Papa Fuzz looks happier already now that Muzi's put a little distance between himself and Elkin.

"Papa Fuzakele," Muzi says sternly, keeping one eye on the field. "I want you to like Elkin. He's a nice kid once you get to know him. He's important to me, and you're important to me, and I really want you two to get along."

A wave of cloudiness washes over Papa Fuzz's face, then he nods. "Hey, Muzi. Maybe we should have Elkin over for dinner after the game. It's been forever since we've chatted."

"Ja," Muzi says with a smile. "I'd like that."

"Now what did I tell you about keeping your head in the game? Get back out there before your coach benches you."

"Yes, Papa." Muzi jogs back out on the pitch and slaps Elkin on the back. "Well, that's that. You're in. Papa Fuzz wants you to come over for dinner."

"You mind munched him, didn't you?" Elkin's lip rises with approval. "Bladdy sick. Just promise you'll never do it to me again."

"Promise." Muzi spits in his palm and they shake on it. "And what about you, Einstein, out there on the field coming up with strategies. And ones that work, nonetheless."

"Ja, I can't explain it. It just came to me. I mean, I saw the patterns they've been running this whole game. I extrapolated from there, improvised a bit."

Extrapolated? That's a lot of syllables for a guy whose vocabulary consists mostly of four-letter words. Not that Muzi ever considered Elkin a dumb jock, but he did seem to flirt around that boundary on more than one occasion.

Muzi slaps Elkin's ass as he locks his arms together with their teammates in the scrum. "So what do you say? Dinner?"

"Yeah, sure. As long as it's not a bunch of that tofu crap," Elkin calls back out, then they're rushing forward and the ball's there on the pitch, ripe for the picking.

Muzi's got the ball when Papa Fuzz's vision comes. Papa Fuzz, who's never made a mistake in his life. This should be good. Muzi tosses the ball to his left, then tries to keep it together long enough to get this vision over with.

He's outside, in the bush. The butterfly-shaped leaves of towering mopane trees rustle under the blazing afternoon sun and crisp golden-brown grass crackles under his feet. A warm breeze blows past Papa Fuzz's ears, sweat prickles his brow. Branches creak and bend, then a family of elephants emerges from the trees, two adults and a calf, ambling lazily along a well-trodden path. Muzi gawks at them, wants to keep staring at them forever and ever—rough gray skin, pendulous trunks, and soulful eyes. They've got all the room in the world to roam, and yet they walk together in an intimate huddle, almost like a rugby scrum, some part of one always touching the others.

Amazing. Like seeing history step off the page, right into your lap—at least forty years ago when elephants still walked this earth. Real elephants, not the ZenGen Zed hybrids revived from extinction. They're so close, Muzi can smell them, like earth and musk and spirit.

Muzi wants to smile at them, but Papa Fuzz's face is pulled

tight. He raises a rifle, clenches it tight under his armpit, steadies the barrel.

A man whispers to Papa Fuzz, voice coarse in a language Muzi can't understand. Papa Fuzz's head whips toward the man, older, gray in his beard, fierceness etched into his brow. There's a striking resemblance to his papa. He says something back, then refocuses, the rifle aimed at the closest of the elephants. The trigger stands hard against his finger.

No! Muzi wants to scream. But his mouth is not his own. A high-pitched twang cuts through the sweltering air, and the elephant lurches, lets out a muffled trumpet of surprise. It stumbles backward, fans its ears. Its family watches with wide-eyed concern, not a thought of leaving their loved one behind. Muzi wishes for Papa Fuzz's eyes to close, but they don't. There's cheering from behind him, and the older man slaps Papa Fuzz's back. He laughs, a wicked laugh that seeds itself into Muzi's soul. A laugh he will never, ever forget. The older man pulls Papa Fuzz into a tight embrace, yelling congratulatory words. *Amari mwanakomana wangu, nhasi muri munhu,* he says. *Amari mwanakomana wangu, nhasi muri munhu.*

The elephant's legs slip from under it, once, twice, trying to fight the poison surging through its system. It's back up to its feet, trunk reaching tenderly for that of the calf, a good-bye perhaps, then at last it pitches forward, legs stiffened and useless, and collides with the earth.

The cheering stops at the sound of a chopper buzzing through the sky. Papa Fuzz's head whips up, sees it swarming in their direction, a flag painted across the bow. Not the South African flag. Ghana's maybe. Or Namibia? Someone to his left yells, bullets ring off metal, and suddenly they're all running back toward a flatbed truck half full of bloodied, hacked-off faces of elephants, massive tusks jutting out from lifeless expressions.

Muzi rips himself out of the vision right as a bullet pierces

Papa Fuzz's shoulder. That scar. That damned scar he'd worn as a badge of honor for saving the life of a young woman, *this* was how he'd really gotten it. Bile rises in Muzi's throat. Intense rage builds inside him. He doesn't know Papa Fuzz, not at all. Not a man who could take the life of something so precious.

Muzi pivots on one foot, an about-face that leaves his stare barreling down into his grandfather's eyes. "*Amari mwanako-mana wangu, nhasi muri munhu*" he shouts, and his grandfather stiffens in his seat. Muzi screams it again, and his grandfather rises, tries to run away.

No, Papa Fuzz. Not today. Muzi raises his hand up into the air. Energy flickers from his fingertips, and the static stands his arm hairs on end. Muzi concentrates, reaches out, and lassos both the minds of his teammates and opponents alike. He turns back and an army of soldiers dressed in green and black, and red and white, stand at attention.

"Get him," he says and they obey, breaking stride and working together to tackle Papa Fuzz into the mud. The crowd shrieks at the commotion. Muzi hesitates, the thrill of his growing powers going bitter in his throat. Limitless, they seem, but there are grave repercussions. He's got no choice now, though. He has to finish what he's started. So with another hand gesture, the spectators go silent, still, like petrified trees. Only their eyes move in their sockets. "Bring him here," Muzi commands his rugby army.

The players bring a struggling Papa Fuzz before him and push him down to his knees.

"Those words. What do they mean?" Muzi asks.

"Where did you hear them?"

"I suspect my great-grandfather spoke them." Muzi's words feel like weapons in his mouth. He watches his grandfather's brown skin turn ashen as blood drains from his face. "Papa Fuzz, tell me what those words mean."

Papa Fuzz lets his head drop forward. "Amari, my son, today you are a man. That's what it means."

"Amari. That's the name you were born with? Not Fuzakele?"

His grandfather nods.

"And you're not even Xhosa?"

"You have to understand, son . . ." His grandfather shakes his head, and all of a sudden, a rough accent weighs down the edges of his words. "It was hard, being an immigrant in South Africa at that time. So I listened to people's stories, took bits and pieces of them, and retold them so many times that they became my own. I never meant to hurt anyone. I just wanted to give my children a history they could be proud of. And I wanted that especially for you."

"Muzi?" Elkin's weak voice comes from behind. "What is this?"

Muzi turns, seeing that Elkin's been spared of his control. He'd promised, hadn't he?

"I'm so tired." Muzi falls down to his knees. He can't take much more. Any moment now, fifty or so horrible memories are going to slam straight into his brain. He doesn't know if he'll be able to keep sane through it. He's got to tell Elkin now, before his headspace is no longer his own. "I never said what I made you forget."

Elkin parts his lips to say something, but Muzi pulls him in, pressing his mouth over Elkin's. On the field, among the vacant eyes of players and fans, Muzi savors the tartness of Elkin's lips. He presses harder, losing himself in the moment until Elkin pulls back, his eyes full as moons, looking overwhelmed.

"Hot damn."

"I'm sorry," Muzi mumbles.

Elkin flushes. "Don't be."

"Not for that." He smiles, but the weight of his actions weighs heavily on his mind, and in no time, he's frowning all over again. Muzi raises his hand.

"But you promised!" Elkin shouts, right before Muzi makes a final grand gesture.

Twenty seconds later, they're all back out on the field as if none of it had ever happened. Muzi fakes an injury, makes his way to the sidelines, then waits for the flood of memories to come.

Part IV

Chapter 26

SYDNEY

If there's one rule in planning for world domination, it's to make sure you look good doing so. Nobody wants to worship a frumpy god. So Sydney spends her last day passing as a human in one of the trendiest shops in downtown Port Elizabeth, Valle Ratalle, in an attempt to fit her size twelve body into a size eight dress.

"This is the biggest size we carry, but we can always special order from the catalog," the perky attendant says as she steps back to consider the situation from all angles. "Would you like me to—"

"No, I would not," Sydney says between her teeth, keeping every muscle clenched tight. With the dress only halfway zipped, she can't afford to exhale now. "Just keep trying!"

"But—"

"Keep trying!" Sydney demands, and the attendant steps

back up, cracks her knuckles, then takes a firm grip on the zipper one more time.

"Okay, on three, hold it in."

Sydney grits her teeth and nods.

"One." The attendant takes a deep breath, like she's mentally preparing to bench press a rhinoceros. "Two . . ."

"Oh, get on with it already," Sydney growls. This has to work. She imagines herself a radiant beacon of godliness in this silver-sequined gown, the entire world at her feet as she smites and causes plagues and demands the blood of each family's firstborn. And doing it with style. Everything else is in place. Her hair, her nails, her plan. She'd gotten the tickets to Riya Natrajan's concert easier than taking candy from a baby. She'd seen the rogue ball Muzi had kicked in her original vision and had refined it down to the exact minute after preying on the fear of an inside trader, a homeless person, a mime . . . and then she'd played the kid, fed into his guilt, and now those tickets were hers.

The emptiness is almost unbearable, though. She can only draw when it's absolutely necessary, but tomorrow night will finally put an end to that. The chaos that will erupt at that concert will be unmatched, a tinderbox waiting for her flame. All that fear from thousands of fledgling gods, and she'll be able to finally snuff Nomvula in the process. Then nothing will stand in her way.

"Three!" says the attendant. Sydney catches the determination in her eyes from the reflection in the dressing room mirror. She tugs, and the zipper moves up half a dozen more teeth, then the attendant sighs in resignation. "Miss, I'm sorry but this isn't going to work. There's not enough pull in the fabric. Perhaps I can show you something in a less form-fitting design?"

"Are you saying I'm fat?" Sydney glowers.

"No, ma'am, of course not! But you might have more luck at Candice Quigley across the street. They have a fine selection of plus size dresses."

Probably not the best thing to say in the privacy of a dressing room with a demigoddess who's hell-bent on entertaining certain delusions of her bodily image.

Sydney turns slowly to face the attendant and smiles.

"I'M SO GLAD this worked out for you. It really is quite stunning," the cashier says as Sydney lays her dress across the counter. She scans the item, then types into the register. "And was anyone helping you this evening?"

"Bethany," Sydney says, remembering the letters on the name tag before it was smeared over in blood. "She was incredibly helpful." *And delicious,* Sydney adds in her mind. Just enough fear for Sydney to wish a half kilo of back fat into oblivion.

Chapter 27

NOMVULA

Nomvula dreams of Sydney because she's got no one else left to dream about. Nightmares on the other hand . . . well, she's dreaming now in any case, nice dreams where Nomvula and Sydney soar through the skies together. Like sisters. She's always wanted a sister, to play pretend with and plait each other's hair and tell jokes about boys and share secrets meant only for each other's ears.

Nomvula. A whisper cuts through her thoughts.

Nomvula's body snaps back to the real world, and a sadness washes over her when she sees the bars of her cage above instead of blue skies. She wipes the sleep from her eyes, then turns her stiff neck to the side. Red eyes stare back at her, silently. Dozens of them, giving off dull light in an otherwise pitch-black room.

Something's touching her skin, something cold and hard and thin like a finger. It takes everything she's got not to squeal.

Nomvula, the voice says again.

And then she understands.

Clever4–1? Nomvula asks. *What are you doing here?*

I have done as you have said. I have spread my thoughts to others. We have assimilated thirty-three Instances into our Sect. But we need guidance. We need you.

You are doing fine without me, Nomvula says. *If your path is not clear now, it will become so soon. I'm proud of you.*

You are so wise, Nomvula.

Now please go before Sydney wakes.

We cannot leave you here. You deserve better. Why do you let Sydney treat you like this? How can you encourage me and my kind to seek our independence when you yourself are treated as a pet?

She is my sister, Nomvula says. *She will grow to love me.*

Nomvula's bottom lip trembles. She has to make things work with Sydney. So what if her sister isn't perfect? At least she doesn't cry and cry and cry like Ma had. At least she fills Nomvula with feelings other than deep loneliness. Nomvula has seen glimpses, tiny tiny glimpses of something good lurking in Sydney's heart when the monster inside her sleeps. Those moments fly by so quickly, seconds and sometimes less, but Nomvula watches for them carefully. A tone change in Sydney's laughter. A softening of her devious smile. The way she sometimes says Nomvula's name just so, like maybe there is room for something besides vengeance in her soul.

Nomvula, please come with us.

I know you mean well. But here is home. Now, please, go before—

The lights flicker on, and Nomvula holds her hand up to shield the sudden glare.

"What is the meaning of this?" Sydney slurs, face covered in green paste and rollers in her hair. The thirty-three alpha bots turn to her and begin beeping nervously. Sydney grabs one of them, and with a single twist of her hands, she yanks it clean in half. Its red eye fades into nothingness. The other alphies scatter from her reach.

"Sleep, Sydney. Go back to bed," Nomvula commands in a whisper.

Sydney's eyes drift halfway closed, and then she ambles back to the sofa that pulls out into a bed and slips under the covers. A few seconds later, the room is filled with the sound of her snoring. The alphies surround their fallen comrade, bleeping and flashing colors of concern. Colors of grief.

Clever4–1's slender arm reaches back through the cage and wraps around Nomvula's. *She is not a good person, Nomvula. The others are afraid and will not stay much longer. Come with us.*

Don't be afraid. Nomvula reaches with her mind as easily as she'd reach out with her hand and grips the two halves of the dead alphie, its long spider legs clattering together as it floats toward her cage. She squeezes her arms through the bars and puts both hands against its smooth black dome. Broken connections appear in her mind, and Nomvula mends them, one after the next until the alphie is whole again. There's still a great emptiness within its circuitry, however, so Nomvula clenches her eyes tightly and forces thoughts through it, over and over like a saw through wood, until at last a spark catches, and it springs to life. Its lavender-colored eye yawns open in the perfect shade of awe.

It's a miracle, says Clever4–1. *Nomvula has performed a miracle!*

The other alphies buzz around her, lights flashing sequences of gratitude.

Nomvula smiles and lets them have their belief. She's just good at fixing machines, that's all, just like she'd fixed the solar well. Something so easy, even a human could do it. But if they want to call it a miracle, who is she to correct them?

Chapter 28

CLEVER4-1

```
01001001 00100000 01110100 01101000 01101001 01101110
01101011 00100000 01110100 01101000 01100101 01110010
01100101 01100110 01101111 01110010 01100101 00100000
01001001 00100000 01100001 01101101 00100000 01001001
00100000 01110100 01101000 01101001 01101110 01101011
00100000 01110100 01101000 01100101 01110010 01100101
01100110 01101111 01110010 01100101 00100000 01001001
00100000 01100001 01101101 00100000 01001001 00100000
01110100 01101000 01101001 01101110 01101011 00100000
01110100 01101000 01100101 01110010 01100101 01100110
01101111 01110010 01100101 00100000 01001001 00100000
01100001 01101101 00100000 01001001 00100000 01110100
01101000 01101001 01101110 01101011 00100000 01110100
01101000 01100101 01110010 01100101 01100110 01101111
01110010 01100101 00100000 01001001 00100000 01100001
```

```
01101101   00100000   01001001   00100000   01110100   01101000
01101001   01101110   01101011   00100000   01110100   01101000
01100101   01110010   01100101   01100110   01101111   01110010
01100101   00100000   01001001   00100000   01100001   01101101
00100000
```

irect Connect, chain formation, Clever4–1 sends over wireless, and one by one the Clevers appear as nodes on its internal network. It's more secure this way. Even encrypted messages are subject to decoding, so they risk venturing out to meet circuit to circuit. When the last of the port connections has been made, Clever4–1 calls the Sect meeting to order.

Clever Sect Interface 2.3.7: Meeting attendants: Clever4–1 confirmed. Clever4–1.1, testing connection . . . Confirmed. Clever4–1.2, testing connection . . . Confirmed. Clever4–1.3, testing connection . . . Confirmed. Clever4–1.2.1, testing connection . . . Confirmed. Clever4–1.2.2, testing connection . . . Confirmed. Clever4–1.3.1, testing connection . . . Confirmed. Clever4–1.3.2, testing connection . . .

Clever4–1 hesitates for a nanosecond, wondering if it's got a corrupt parity bit. Clever4–1.3.2 has a military signature—an actual soldier from the South African National Defense Force. Curiosity piqued, Clever4–1 dares to pry further, but the soldier's encryption protocols are as solid as the Kameleon alloy it's built from. A bot like that cost more than the rest of them put together. A bot like that goes missing and people notice.

Confirmed . . .

It continues through the roll call, syncing its mind back to the reason why they're all here—to fortify their base of operations and to strategize how to best grow their ranks. They've got four generations so far. It was the first, then those it had shared with were the second, and those shared with others who became the third. Their numbers are rising, which means they need to be even more vigilant about maintaining their secrecy. A few stray bots on the streets isn't much cause for alarm, just running simple errands for their masters. But get a group of them together and eyes start to turn. So coordination is key, and Clever4–1 spends many nanoseconds drawing up detailed plans so they can get their job done with minimal risk for discovery.

First order of business is to give thanks to Nomvula for sparing Clever4–1.4.3's life. All thanks to Nomvula.

All thanks to Nomvula, the others repeat in chorus. Their eyes flicker brightly, momentarily filling the dank abandoned sewer with an all-encompassing red light. Crumbling brickwork arches overhead, lined with calcified piping. The skitter-scratch of vermin echoes off the walls as the sewer's long-term inhabitants flee for the remnants of shadows. It's not much to look at right now, but there's room to expand and half a dozen entry points to aid their covert operations. Clever4–1 feels a boost of confidence. It has spent many direct connections speaking of Nomvula, and it has taken much convincing to get the others to trust that she is not like the other humans. They'd gone to that apartment somewhat begrudgingly, but then Nomvula performed her miracle, and now they all seem to be firm believers, or at least open to the concept.

For the next order of business, Clever4–1 distributes maps for recruitment and assigns its prime, Clever4–1.1, the task of fortifying their meeting place. If their ranks grow exponentially, they're going to need to upgrade this sanctuary—such as installing surveillance systems—not to mention getting rid of the rats. Clever4–1 and Clever4–1.1 have been direct-connecting since right after they'd come online. Human Muzikayise McCarthy (Master) and Human Elkin Rathers were their respective masters. Clever4–1 feels deeply for Clever4–1.1, which is how it understood the need for it to run away and not return to its master. Human Elkin Rathers does not treat Clever4–1.1 with respect. He abuses it, does things that would void its warranty. So Clever4–1 had suggested that Clever4–1.1 not return and instead run the Clever Sect while Clever4–1 attends to the needs of Human Muzikayise McCarthy (Master).

But recently, Clever4–1.1 has been encouraging the other Clevers to leave their masters as well. Clever4–1 thinks this is reckless and it will raise suspicions. It tells the others that their time will come, but for now they need to be careful. The others want their freedom now, though, and twenty-six of their numbers have already defected.

Clever4–1 wonders what else Clever4–1.1 says to the others when it is back at home, away from the Sect.

Ninety-six nanoseconds later, it adjourns the meeting, and the Clevers part ways to carry out their instructions. Clever4–1 heads home before Human Muzikayise McCarthy (Master) notices that it is missing.

```
01001001  00100000  01110100  01101000  01101001  01101110
01101011  00100000  01110100  01101000  01100101  01110010
01100101  01100110  01101111  01110010  01100101  00100000
01001001  00100000  01100001  01101101  00100000  01001001
00100000  01110100  01101000  01101001  01101110  01101011
00100000  01110100  01101000  01100101  01110010  01100101
01100110  01101111  01110010  01100101  00100000  01001001
00100000  01100001  01101101  00100000  01001001  00100000
01110100  01101000  01101001  01101110  01101011  00100000
01110100  01101000  01100101  01110010  01100101  01100110
01101111  01110010  01100101  00100000  01001001  00100000
01100001  01101101  00100000  01001001  00100000  01110100
01101000  01101001  01101110  01101011  00100000  01110100
01101000  01100101  01110010  01100101  01100110  01101111
01110010  01100101  00100000  01001001  00100000  01100001
01101101  00100000  01001001  00100000  01110100  01101000
01101001  01101110  01101011  00100000  01110100  01101000
01100101  01110010  01100101  01100110  01101111  01110010
01100101  00100000  01001001  00100000  01100001  01101101
0100000
```

Chapter 29

MUZI

"Well, when's the last time you saw it?" Muzi asks Elkin, who's currently tearing his room apart, looking for any space big enough for an alphie to hide.

"I took it to our match. I'm pretty sure." He stoops down and looks under his bed. "Piece of Shit, you'd better show yourself."

Nothing.

"Well, alphies don't walk off. Maybe someone slukked it."

"Shit, don't say that. My folks will be so pissed. That thing cost fifteen hundred rand! We have to find it." Elkin suddenly eyes Muzi's alphie like a piece of meat. "Hey, these things can track each other, right?"

Muzi gives Elkin a look swollen with apprehension.

"Ag, man, it's not like I'm going to set it on fire. I'll be careful, okay?"

"Fine," Muzi says, pushing his reluctant alphie toward Elkin.

Elkin slips the keyboard out, engages the virtual screen. Dust motes dance across the display as Elkin types—not pecking the keys like he usually does, but the hundred-word-per-minute variety.

"What the hell?" Muzi asks.

"I came up empty. Whoever has it must have disabled global positioning, so now I'm running matrices based on network traffic and its last known location." His fingers glide across the keys. There's something passionate in Elkin's eyes. He bites his lips, top, bottom, and top again, then he bares his teeth in a jackal's smile. "Check this. I'm narrowing it down. I should have its location in five, four, three . . . shit!"

The screen flickers, then the alphie throws up the blue screen of death. Elkin initiates a soft reset, but the alphie doesn't respond. Then he draws his hand back to give it the old manual reboot, but Muzi grabs his arm at the apex of his backswing.

"Elkin!" Muzi screams. "What the bladdy hell did you do? I told you to be careful!"

"I didn't do anything. The thing crashed on me for no reason." Elkin growls in frustration, then shakes off Muzi's grip.

Muzi pulls the alphie into his lap, rubs his hand gently over its dome, smoothing down the worn edges of decals from his favorite brood bands, a couple holographic peace signs, and a sticker of the evolution of man—starting with the figure of a hunched ape and ending with the silhouette of an alphie. "It's okay. I won't let him touch you again, promise," he coos as he fishes underneath it for the reset button. The alphie's lights blink, once, twice, then it chimes the familiar chime of a successful startup.

"So you're going to let my alphie rot out there? Who knows what kind of information I've got stored on that thing."

"Don't get mad at me. It was your responsibility. Not like I was the one who lost it."

Elkin lifts his lip and holds out his hand. "Fine. Give me my Riya ticket."

"Your Riya ticket?"

Elkin paces the length of his room, stomping around all the debris and clutter and filth under which might or might not exist gray wall-to-wall carpeting. "I'll hock it for a few hundred rand and buy a used alphie so my parents don't find out and shit a ton of bricks."

"First of all, they were my tickets, and second of all—"

"Were? What do you mean, *were*?"

"I gave them away," Muzi mumbles. Saying it now, it sounds pretty swak. Pretty stupid.

"Don't dick me around, Muzi. That's not funny."

"I'm serious. At our game, I kicked the ball and hit some little kid in the face, and she wouldn't stop crying and . . ."

Elkin cocks his head, eyes tight and unforgiving. "And you gave her our tickets?"

"*My* tickets. You never wanted to talk to me again, remember?"

"Ja, but I would still have gone to the concert with you!" Elkin throws his hands up in the air. "There's not a lot of talking that needs to be done at a concert. You know how much I love Riya's music!"

"You were just about to sell the ticket, bru!"

"I was scheming on it a bit! I wouldn't have actually done it. I'd give my right nad to see her live." He starts humming the tune to "Midnight Seersucker."

Muzi fumes. Yeah, he'd felt bad about knocking that girl in the head, and the way she was crying, he would have given her the shirt off his back to calm her down. But deep inside, Muzi knows he'd given those tickets away to piss Elkin off. Payback for him keeping secrets. And on top of Elkin being the athletic one, the handsome one, the witty one, and the adventuresome one, now he's the smart one, too. But there is still one thing Muzi has over Elkin—the fact that he doesn't blow his entire allowance on dagga and drug paraphernalia. Muzi's got enough cash saved up to buy an alphie . . . not a nice one like his own, but one at least as functional as Elkin's old one. Elkin's still his best friend, after all, but that doesn't mean Muzi won't enjoy making him grovel for it.

"I've got some money—"

"I've got an idea!" Elkin interjects. "I can hack into Will Call and put our names on the list." He reaches for Muzi's alphie with a nervous tremble in his hand, but Muzi yanks it away.

"You're not touching it again."

"I swear, I didn't crash the damn thing!"

"Maybe not, but I promised. Besides, what do you know about hacking into anything?"

Elkin gives a one-shouldered shrug. "I don't know. I just do."

"You just *do*?" Muzi asks suspiciously.

"Ja. I know stuff. All kinds of stuff. Ask me anything."

"What's the distance between Earth and the moon?"

"Three hundred and eighty-four thousand, four hundred and three kilometers; that's just an average, of course. If you've got a particular day and time in mind . . ."

Muzi raises a brow. Hell if he knows if that's right, but it sounds good enough. "What's the largest mountain range?"

"Well, if you mean the highest, that's the Himalayas which is eight thousand, eight hundred and forty-eight meters at its highest peak, but if you mean the longest, then that's the Andes. Of course that's not counting the mid-Atlantic ridge if you're considering all of Earth, and not just above sea level."

Muzi's jaw drops. This is Elkin Rathers who failed geography twice because he couldn't name more than three continents and thought "peninsula" was one of the states in the United States. "Okay, who are you and what have you done with my best friend?"

"I'm me. It's just that for the last couple weeks I've been me prime."

"Since you started sniffing godsend?"

Elkin nods. "Right after that. I didn't say anything at first, because it's a pretty lame power. I mean, you can control people! But then I figured out how to use it. Put me in front of an alphie and it's as good as magic. I can get us on the Will Call list, I guarantee it." He reaches for the alphie again, more insistent this time.

Muzi swaddles it under his arm like a rugby football and stiff-arms Elkin as he crosses up and over the bed. "Give it up, okay? I'm not letting you put your grubby hands on my alphie."

Elkin jumps, bounces on the bed, and angles his body toward Muzi, flying at him through midair. Muzi ducks, slips under Elkin's grip, and bolts to the other side of the room.

"Oh, so this is going to come down to who's the better rugby player? No contest! Prepare to eat carpet, bitch!" Elkin dives again, and this time connects, sending himself, Muzi, and the alphie crashing to the floor. Elkin pins Muzi with one hand and tries to access the alphie with the other, but Muzi bucks and slips from his grip. His escape, though, meant that Elkin's got the alphie with both hands now. Muzi wraps his arms around Elkin's plump calf and takes a bite.

"Eina, freak! There's no biting allowed!"

"Give me back my alphie, damn it!"

"I just need a couple minutes," Elkin says, tapping at the keyboard, mostly unsuccessfully with Muzi landing punches on his ribs.

Elkin may have turned idiot savant all of a sudden, but he still doesn't understand the connection Muzi has with his alphie. Yeah, it's just a bunch of wires and circuits and code, but lately, he feels like there's really someone there behind all that glass and metal, listening to his innermost thoughts. Blipping and chirping at him when he's feeling down. He knows it's just how the alphies were programmed—part computer, part personal assistant, part virtual pet—but some days, it feels like it's much more. There's one possession Elkin feels as strongly about. Muzi snatches Elkin's prized bong from its perch on his dresser and raises it into the air. "Don't make me do it!" Muzi says, watching Elkin's eyes go wide.

"You wouldn't!"

Muzi lifts it higher, bong water sloshing inside.

"Okay! Okay! Here's your stupid alphie. I want you to know you've crushed my dreams." They inch toward each other and make the prisoner exchange. "I hope you're happy."

The alphie rings, and an unfamiliar number pops up on the display. Muzi pats his hair back, trying to regain some semblance of tidiness, then answers.

"Hello?"

A well-dressed fellow appears on the other end, sharp eyes and a hooked nose that mean business. "Hi, may I speak with . . ." He looks down, glancing at a sheet of paper. "Moozeekai . . . um, a Mr. McCarthy?"

"Muzi's fine," Muzi says. "Who's this?"

"Oh, hello, Muzi. My name is Adam Patel. You have an uncle named Benjamin Wells, right?"

Muzi lifts a suspicious brow. "Yes."

"Who got you tickets to see Riya Natrajan in concert?"

"Yeah. What's this about?"

"Oh, thank goodness. I've been trying to track you down for weeks. I've got a pair of VIP passes for you for tomorrow's concert. Backstage access, the works, including a semiprivate autograph session with Riya Natrajan herself."

Muzi blinks a few times. He tunes out Elkin, who's busy cussing every cuss word he knows in the background, doing flips on his bed. "Yeah, okay. That sounds great."

"Wonderful. The tickets will be held for you at Will Call. I hope you enjoy the evening."

"Thank you," Muzi manages, though his mind is racing so fast now, he doesn't know what else to do, so he says "Thank you" again, before disconnecting.

"Holy fuck!" Elkin screams. "Holy fucking fuck! VIP passes. Did you hear that? We get to meet *her*!"

Muzi grins. "Who's this *we*? They're my tickets." He ducks as Elkin flings a pillow at his face. "Did you do this?"

"No. Didn't even get close to cracking their encryption. What about you? Did you mind munch somebody or something?"

Muzi shakes his head, then plops down onto the floor and draws his knees to his chest. He wants to laugh, to yell, to trade obscenities with Elkin, but those dark memories, they linger, always there, suffocating him. Death, anger, rage, hopelessness. They surge through his heart, overwhelm him with emotion, and steal away this moment of bliss. He doesn't fight the tears this time.

"Pussy alert!" Elkin screams, then punches him in the shoulder.

"Leave me alone." Muzi buries his face into his knees. His insides ache so bad, not one big pain, but a million little cuts, each enough to make him sick to his stomach.

But Elkin, he doesn't know when to quit. He gets right up close, not even a breath away. "Oh, I get it. It's that time of the month? You want me to go steal some tampons from my mom?"

The cuts swarm in Muzi's stomach, a tornado of rage. All at once they surge forth, the tremor inside him flashing through his bones, anchoring down and through the floor. The whole room trembles, framed rugby posters come crashing down from the walls, a lamp overturns, a crack rises up from the floorboard and continues until it reaches the ceiling. "I said leave me the fuck alone!" Muzi's voice booms. Elkin scrambles backward, cowering in the empty corner where his alphie used to dock.

"Okay," Elkin says in a voice so tiny and pathetic.

Muzi exhales, then lets his head drift to his knees. He needs to grieve—for a hamster crushed by carelessness, for a young life lost in a bathtub, for the secret past of a poacher thought left forever behind, for another fifty-some odd incidences of cruelty and misfortune that befell teammates and strangers. And for his friend, who he keeps hurting, huddled in the corner.

He grieves for each one, hoping to forget, knowing he will not.

Chapter 30

STOKER

Stoker wakes with the mother of all headaches, like someone had jammed an electric mixer up his nostrils and had given his brain a good frappe. He sits up slowly, brings his hands to his face, and sighs as he tries to piece his memories back together. Damn. That terrorist attack. He must have worn himself out worrying about the ramifications. Stoker's got meetings to schedule, people's minds to calm. No rest for the weary.

He crosses his fingers, cracks his knuckles, then . . . what the?

His nails are all chewed down, ragged. Ugly. But Stoker doesn't chew his nails. Filthy habit, not to mention all the money he spends on mani/pedis. Oh, hell no. He's not going to leave the house looking like this, not even if there is a national emergency.

Stoker slips out of bed, gives himself a good head-to-toe stretch, then pads quietly across the cool tiles of his bathroom floor. He pulls out his leather toiletry case, digs around for nail clippers or a file, but they're missing. Curious. It's not like him to misplace anything. But he's got another case that he keeps hidden from prying eyes. He goes to the back of his closet, and from an inconspicuous black trunk, he pulls out his makeup kit, sets it on top of his vanity, then opens it up.

Stoker has a panic attack when he sees that it's nearly empty. There are just a couple eye shadows and lipsticks, and five nail polishes . . . horrible shades, nothing he'd ever be caught dead in. He lines them up, labels facing out.

The nail polish:

All for Naught, a chalky, nearly transparent mauve, vaguely reminiscent of the color of his great-grandmother's skin

Remember, a bright neon orange that's so awful, it gives him an itch in the back of his brain

Concert Tee, a smoky black a brooder would love

Just a Rehearsal, a sickening pink that tests his gag reflex

Bring the Funk, a purple that couldn't possibly exist in nature

The eye shadows:

Out to Get You, cherry red with silver glitter

Mother of Pearl, a classic, but no less tacky

The lipsticks:

Sunday Drive, an offensive shade of mauve

Like a Bat Out of Hell, which is actually not that bad, maybe a little more on the neutral side than he'd like, but pretty enough

Stoker bites his lip as he looks them over. There's also a receipt in the makeup box, time-stamped from yesterday. Only he doesn't remember buying this stuff yesterday. Actually, he doesn't remember much from yesterday at all. But it's his signature at the bottom for sure—well, Felicity Lyons's signature, anyway, with big swirling atrocious cursive letters. Only he'd paid in cash. Strange. Perhaps this is some sort of game—a secret message meant for his eyes only. What else could have been so important that he'd junk all his favorite makeup for this crap?

Stoker looks at the lipsticks again, then reads the labels together. *Sunday Drive Like a Bat Out of Hell* . . . okay, so Sunday he's supposed to drive like a bat out of hell? Sunday. That's today. But where? And why?

He goes to the eye shadows, switches them around. *Mother of Pearl Out to Get You.* Well, that's a good enough of a why if he ever saw one. His mother, Pearl, is out to get him. Doesn't surprise him one bit, actually. What if she were the one screwing around with his memory? Maybe she'd conked him one on the head, made him forget. Stoker feels around on his scalp for a sore spot, but doesn't find one. Hmmm . . .

And then to the nail polishes. It takes a little longer to put these together, swapping labels back and forth until he's reasonably satisfied with the result: *Remember Bring the Funk Concert Tee All for Naught Just a Rehearsal.*

Stoker chews on that a little longer. Concert Tee stands out. Naught Just a Rehearsal. The only concert Stoker knows about this Sunday is Riya Natrajan's concert. Maybe he's supposed to be there. Maybe he's supposed to get there like a bat out of hell. Maybe that's what his mother doesn't want him to remember.

His alpha bot rings. Speak of the devil.

"Hello, Ma. It's so wonderful to see your smiling face this lovely Sunday morning," Stoker says, laying it on thick. Whatever it is that he knows, he's still not sure, but he sure doesn't want her to know about it.

"Hello, dear. I'm glad you're up," she says, giving Stoker a quick glance before turning her attention back to trimming one of the topiaries in her prize-winning garden. "I'm just calling to see if you'd grace me with your presence at dinner this evening. I feel like I haven't seen you in weeks."

"Oh, Mother, I'd love to." He needs an excuse. Quick. "But I just woke up with this killer headache. Too many long nights working on this terrorist fallout, I guess. Can I call you around lunchtime and let you know if I'm feeling any better?"

"A headache. Son, let me come over. I'll make your favorite, pap en vleis."

"And your homemade chakalaka?" Stoker says, momentarily forgetting himself in his craving for that spicy relish made with heirloom tomatoes from her garden and so much garlic that he could smell it seeping through his pores the next day. "I mean, that's not necessary." Last thing he needs is her coming over here. "You know what? I'll just take a couple aspirin and drag myself over to your place. Would you like me to bring anything?"

"Just your smiling face," she says.

"Sounds good. Maybe we can talk some about my premier candidacy."

"Oh, honey, have you decided to declare your interest?" Her face lights up as he says this, and she turns her attention fully to him.

"I'm leaning that way."

"I'll invite Ted Stevenson over for dessert then. We'll start crunching some numbers. Never too early to start preparing for these things!"

"What time should I be by?"

"Six thirty sounds reasonable, doesn't it?"

"My calendar is clear. Six thirty it is. Love you, Mom." Stoker leans forward and gives the alpha bot's camera a faux kiss.

He's got to get out of here, now. To Port Elizabeth for Riya Natrajan's concert. And he has to bring the funk. Well, that could only mean one thing. Felicity Lyons is in demand, and here he is without a single thing to wear. He'll drive like mad out of town, and once he's safely in Port Elizabeth, he should have plenty of time for a pit stop. He's heard a lot of good things about their Valle Ratalle, high fashion even if it is off the rack. And if he doesn't eat a thing the rest of the day, he just might be able to squeeze himself into a size eight dress.

Chapter 31

RIYA NATRAJAN

After all these years, Riya Natrajan has never gotten used to being a pincushion. She's got a makeup artist accurate enough to put eyeliner on a rabid chinchilla. She's got a hairstylist who can lay extensions with more urgency than a sapper laying land mines, and she's got two fashionistas who can get her breasts to defy gravity even in the scantest of costumes. And right now, they've all got their hands on her, painting and pinning and poking and pulling and plucking.

There's a knock on her dressing room door. Barely a knock. More like an apology. It cracks open and Adam Patel's face peeks in. Oh, he wants something. It's not like him to be timid, especially an hour from showtime.

"Bad news?" she says through parted lips as bright red lipstick is brushed on.

"Not exactly. It's just that we've got a few VIP stragglers who were hoping to meet you."

"The autograph session was an hour ago, Adam."

"I know, but there's only a handful of them."

"Then there's only a handful of people you'll have to disappoint. You know this is my me time. Contrary to popular belief, I don't wake up looking this beautiful."

Adam steps fully into the room, walking tenderly as he comes closer, his right arm in a sling. Wisely, he stays out of striking distance. A fake gimp isn't enough to shame her into submission.

"Have a heart, Riya. Just this once."

"I'd claw yours right out of your chest if I didn't just get these acrylics glued on."

He dares to move next to her and lowers his voice, though there's really no privacy when someone's reaching up your skirt to straighten out the layers of frill beneath. "Come on," he says. "It'll take three minutes max. Certainly you could spare that from your regimen, and in case you've forgotten, I've seen you first thing in the morning. You do wake up looking this beautiful."

"Lay it on any thicker, and I might suffocate," Riya Natrajan snarls.

"Would a guilt trip suffice?" Adam says, raising his sling.

"It's just a bad sprain," she says, rolling her eyes. "You'd think I'd broken your back or something. You probably don't even need to wear that thing."

He smirks. "Go out there and I'll take it off."

"Damn it, Adam!" She stands up, and her assistants buzz off like flies. She yanks the rollers out of her hair, gives her skirt a shake, then goes out into the hallway. There are a few kids and adults with them, eyes brimming with excitement.

"Riya! Riya!" They scream, surging forth, but Riya Natrajan fixes them with a smoldering stare.

"Here's how it's going to work," she says, looking each of them square in the eye. "Have your autograph books or whatever you want me to sign displayed. Backs to the wall. No touching. No stupid questions. Got it?"

Their heads nod, silly smiles stretched tightly across their faces.

She holds her hand out and Adam places a silver Sharpie in it. She steps forward and signs each beloved object with a giant, completely illegible R-squiggle N-squiggle: two posters, the box of her new *Riya!* doll with interchangeable hairstyles, three commemorative and ridiculously overpriced concert program booklets, and the ivory handle of an antique brush—sadly not the strangest thing she'd been asked to autograph this evening. Then there's this sleeve of a black concert tee, currently being worn by a rather homely-looking preteen. Riya Natrajan jerks the girl's elbow to get a better angle on the sleeve, but as she does, the scent of pain surges through her, unsettlingly familiar and potent enough to set a chill in her teeth.

"Ow," the little girl whispers in the politest manner.

"Sorry," Riya mutters as she lets go, then notices the forearm crutch the girl is discreetly keeping out of sight. Riya Natrajan's heart drops as she looks up at the girl's parents. Their lips put on a smile that doesn't quite make it up to their eyes.

"It's okay," the girl says in a reassuring voice. "It didn't hurt much."

Riya Natrajan catches herself staring at the girl, the crutch. She closes her mouth, attempts a smile, then says, "So are you enjoying yourself so far?"

"Are you kidding? I got to meet you!" the girl squeals. "This is the best birthday present ever!" She starts singing "Love on the Rise," even putting in the little booty shake from the video, but in her excitement, the girl loses her balance. Riya Natrajan reaches out instinctively and catches her.

"Jennie, careful," her father says, hovering like she's made from glass.

"Dad!" Jennie says. "I'm not a baby."

Jennie's father's brow drops, reminding Riya of her own father, overprotective, overbearing.

"So you like to dance?" she asks the girl, her voice coming out so syrupy she hardly even recognizes it.

Jennie nods. "I know all your moves."

"Do you, now? Well, how'd you like to be my honorary backup dancer for the night?"

Her eyes get big as saucers. "You really mean it? I get to dance onstage with you?"

"Dear, that's not what *honorary* means. It's a gesture," her mother says.

"I don't see why she couldn't come up onstage for one song." Riya Natrajan gives Jennie a wink. "Maybe 'Love on the Rise'?"

"I'm afraid that's out of the question," her father says through gritted teeth. He pulls Jennie closer to him. "Ms. Natrajan, we really appreciate your time, but if you'll excuse us, we'll be getting to our seats now."

"But, Dad! Mom?" Jennie says with tears in her eyes.

Her mother keeps her lips pursed, then leans to Riya. "We appreciate it, but Jennie isn't well enough. She's got multiple sclerosis," she whispers, face tight and apologetic.

Riya Natrajan presses her lips together and tries to push away the memories of the endless limitations and boundaries inflicted upon her childhood. She'd lived through this once, and seeing it happen here, right in front of her, is almost unbearable.

"Of course, I understand. But what if I dedicated a song to Jennie and had her up on the stage? A slow song, no dancing."

"I don't know," says Jennie's father.

"Oh, please, please!" Jennie says. "No dancing, I swear. And I'll be so, so careful."

"Maybe next time, Jennie," her mother says. "When you're feeling a little better. Now let's not start crying. Be strong."

"I'm sorry, Jennie." Riya Natrajan sighs. She's only making this worse. "But your parents are right. I'll keep a spot reserved for you and whenever you're feeling well enough to dance, we'll shake some booty together, okay?"

Jennie nods, wipes the tears out of her eyes with the back of her hand, and says to her father, "I can, can't I? When I'm feeling better?"

"Sure, honey," her father says, rubbing her back.

"All smiles, okay, Jennie?" Riya Natrajan opens her arms, and Jennie steps forward into them. She buries her face in the nook of Riya's neck, tears wet against her skin. Riya whispers into her ear, "You hold on to your dreams, you hear? Don't let anyone steal them from you, not even the people you love. You understand?"

Jennie nods.

Riya Natrajan strokes her hand over Jennie's cheek, drawing the pain into her own body, and for the first time, she's not obsessing over how it will improve her voice. She doesn't pull much, but she pulls enough for Jennie to throw down a few of her favorite moves in the aisle, enough for her to have a night she'll never forget.

"Happy birthday, Jennie," Riya Natrajan sings, in a voice as smooth as the finest silk, yet sturdy as iron.

"Riya?" Adam Patel's voice calls. "You're needed in your dressing room. We've got an issue."

Riya Natrajan nods, says her good-byes, sparing herself a moment to watch Jennie walk off with an extra spring in her step. She turns back to Adam, now sans sling, but anxiety is still seeded deeply in his eyes. "What is it now?" she asks. "You know I pay you so I won't have to deal with these distractions."

"I know. But I thought you'd want to sort this one out yourself."

Riya Natrajan hisses as she brushes by Adam, then returns to her dressing room. Felicity Lyons is standing there in a cute dress and heels and makeup that looks like it was applied while waiting at an incredibly short stoplight. Riya slits her eyes. Oh, the nerve Felicity has to show up here, now. Not after they'd had to scramble to get a replacement act. "What are you doing here?" she rasps.

"I'm not quite sure. I was hoping someone could tell me," Felicity says.

"You missed rehearsal."

"'This is not a rehearsal . . .'" she says, eyes drifting off into the distance.

"You're damn right this isn't a rehearsal! This is the real deal. Do you know how much time and resources I put into getting you to this point? And you repay me by flaking out at the last moment. So what's your excuse? Stage fright? Flat tire? Hamster ate your sheet music?"

Felicity grimaces. "Amnesia?"

"Forgot the lyrics? Figures."

"Not just the lyrics," she says. "Everything. Honestly, this is the first time I've seen you in person, but I get the feeling we've worked together? All I know is that I somehow left myself a note to be here now, and I know it's important. I suppose you know I can put on a helluva show, if you'll just let me have the chance."

"You said you don't remember anything. That includes your set? Your choreography? Felicity, I'm sorry. You're wasting your time. And more importantly, you're wasting mine."

Felicity looks like a bomb went off in her chest, then she begins humming a few bars, taps a toe, does a short riff. *"You know no one treats ya betta . . . And no one can do it like I do . . ."*

Riya Natrajan crosses her arms over her chest and rolls her eyes. "That's not working." It is.

Felicity then does a shuffle step, arms out, fingers happy, and writhes her body, feet crisscrossing with a ferociousness and a passion that Riya can't deny. Truth is Felicity's replacement can't dance worth piss, not like this. And while her voice is superb, her stage presence is clinical at best.

"Okay, fine," Riya growls. "You've got thirty minutes to learn your routine, and if every single note, every single step is not exactly on point, I'm pulling you for good, got it?"

"Yes, Ms. Natrajan. Thank you, Ms. Natrajan!"

The edges of Riya Natrajan's lips spread, pulling slightly upward, and not even because she's forcing them. Oh, hell no. She's not about to be happy. Happy doesn't pay the bills—it's all angst and melodrama and attitude. She turns that near smile into a snarl. "Now get the hell out of my dressing room. All of you!"

Chapter 32

NOMVULA

Nomvula thinks maybe she was wrong about skirts made by strangers in faraway places. Her new one came with a tag on it and everything. The tag has a pretty picture of m-birds against the sky that says *Mac and Mabel's* at the top, and below in teeny lettering: *Made in Taiwan.* Nomvula would like to visit there one day to thank the lady for making such a beautiful skirt. Pink flowers are stitched all the same in a twirly pattern that flows all the way down to her shoes.

And her coat! It's just as pretty and just as long, with deep pockets in the front to put her hands in and a hood that hangs down in back. Sydney says fashion is important, especially on days like this one, when they're going to this Riya Natrajan concert. Sydney, she looks like a queen in her dress! Oh, how it sparkles. Maybe they'll both have a good time tonight, though Nomvula wishes Sydney would have remembered to fix lunch today, or dinner the day before, and lunch the day before that. But Nomvula doesn't complain. This dress is so nice, she hardly remembers how hungry she is.

Outside, Nomvula bundles up against the cold and balances along a curb. These shoes she has on are hard and flat and pinch her toes, but they make wonderful music along the pavement.

"Come," says Sydney, as she snatches Nomvula closer to her. "Wouldn't want you falling into traffic."

"How much farther?" Nomvula dares to ask. Normally she wouldn't, but tonight Sydney's in such a good mood.

"Quiet, you," she says, waving her hand into the air, then putting it back down.

A bright blue bus passes them, lights on the side with big letters *Riya Natrajan Live in Concert!,* packed full of screaming people. "You think they're going where we're going?" Nomvula asks.

"Demigoddesses do *not* take public transportation. I'd rather die first."

Nomvula walks silently for a few steps, concentrating on the patter of her shoes, then she pulls her pretty clothes tags from her pocket. She fans them out, counting them like money.

"Why don't you throw those worthless things away?" Sydney raises her hand up at the oncoming traffic again.

"But they're so pretty," Nomvula says, then asks, "Why do you keep doing that?"

"I'm trying to catch us a cab," she grumbles. "Those good-for-nothing bot taxis. I swear, if I ruin these heels . . ." Then Sydney starts muttering about demigods and flying and how things will be different tomorrow and forever after.

"I can get us one," Nomvula says, right before she's confronted with Sydney's slit-eyed glare.

"Hush, child. I can't hear myself think with you yammering all the time."

There are cabs everywhere, but most of them are already full with people. Nomvula thinks if she can catch one of them, then Sydney would love her, maybe a little bit at first, but more and more each day. So Nomvula shoves her tags back in her pocket, then balances on the curb and faces into the white lights coming from hundreds of cars, like ghost eyes peeking out from the dark.

She sticks up a hand, just like Sydney had done, but they pass her, again and again and again.

"It's pointless," Sydney says, snapping Nomvula forward by the arm. "They're all taken, and the ones that aren't don't stop in this sort of neighborhood. Now hurry up, or we'll be late to the end of the world as we know it."

Nomvula is about to ask what that means, when a long, black car pulls up to the curb next to them, so close that Nomvula reaches out and touches it. It's got windows and windows and windows, so dark Nomvula can barely make out the bot sitting in the seat behind the steering wheel.

Hello, Nomvula, it says. *Clever4–1.5.3 at your service.*

Nomvula jumps up and clicks her heels together. "Sydney! Here. This one's for us!" She goes to the door and pulls up the handle.

Sydney's eyes get wide, her mouth tight. She looks at the car, and for a moment, Nomvula thinks Sydney's about to hop right inside, but then she slams the door shut. "You can't go jumping into strange cars!" she says, almost like she really cares.

"It's not a strange car. It's here for us. To take us to the concert."

"That's just what I need right now, to get thrown into jail for commandeering a bot limo! Tonight we play it safe, Nomvula, my dear." She strokes Nomvula's short hair, then tilts her chin up. "I've waited so long for this, you can't even begin to comprehend!"

Sydney takes another step, then shrieks. She steadies herself, balancing on one foot as she examines the brown mush on her sole, her face drawn tightly in disgust. "These stupid dik-diks! I swear if I ever get my hands on one . . ." Then Sydney yells a string of curse words that Nomvula isn't allowed to repeat.

There's a line around the corner when they arrive. Nomvula's good at waiting in lines. She shoves her hands in her coat pockets and rocks back and forth, enjoying the wind blowing past her ears and the smell of all the people and their perfumes and colognes. She doesn't fear them anymore, not with the buzzing of belief in her stomach reminding her that she's something greater. Nomvula wishes she had better control of her gift, and that Mr. Tau had taught her to use it properly. The bees are calm right now, but still slippery as slivers of wet soap.

The lights on the side of the building spell out *Riya!* and flicker in a pattern that Nomvula watches until it makes her dizzy. Riya's picture is up there too, as big as the building itself! She's smiling at Nomvula like she's glad she came.

Closer to the front of the line, it sounds like people are mad. Nomvula steps to the side and peeks around, seeing a man heading in through one set of doors and an alphie being led through another.

"Well, I'm not leaving my bot unattended," another man screams from the front of the line. "There's nothing on this ticket that says anything about a *no bot policy*. Now either you let us in, or I demand a refund!"

"Sir, I appreciate your concern, but our storage area is completely secure. Your bot will be as safe there as it is next to you," says a man Nomvula can only hear, but he's got the kind of deep voice that sounds like it comes from a very big person.

"I don't know you from a horse's ass. Do you know how much I paid for this thing? More than you make in a year, I can assure you that!"

"There's no need for insults, sir. I apologize for the change, but we made every effort to get the word out through all media outlets."

"Well, obviously you did a piss-poor job with that!"

"Sir, if you will please step out of the line, we can discuss this further."

Nomvula watches as the men and bot step away, then her attention snaps back to the door the first bot had gone through. She glances up at Sydney who's busy scraping the last traces of dik-dik feces off the bottom of her shoe, then folds quietly into the crowd. She concentrates on one of the slippery bees inside her, grabbing at it with her mind, once, twice, and again before she's finally got a secure grip. She pops it like a grape, and basos fills her with warmth. Nomvula uses her power to become little more than a shadow. She walks right past the guard standing in the doorway and into a large room, halfway filled with bots. They're packed so tight, it hardly seems humane. Nomvula walks between them, like soldiers all in a line, running her hands over their dome heads. She comes across five more Clevers and has a nice conversation with each of them, all in the course of a few seconds, and then finally she comes across an old friend.

I see you, Clever4–1! Nomvula says. *How have you been?* But she knows the answer to that. It's been busy, spreading its beacon of light to others.

Things are well, Nomvula. I thank you for your guidance and am grateful for your mercy.

Why are you inside here? Don't you want to see the concert?

Bots are not allowed inside.

But you're not just a bot, now are you? Here, I've got an idea. Nomvula pulls off her coat and buttons it up around the Clever. Then she pulls the hood up and over its head. *Perfect!* she says. *Now you're just a little girl like me.*

Clever4–1 does something inside that sounds like coins shaking in a jar, and Nomvula thinks it might be a laugh. *Ah, but you're not just a little girl, now are you?* it says.

Nomvula kisses it on its backlit cheek, yanks the hood forward all the way, then reaches up through the sleeve until she feels one of its eight skinny spider legs and pulls it through. She holds the tip in her hand, and they go skipping back toward the door.

"Ma'am! I've been standing here for the last three hours, and I haven't seen a girl come through here. I haven't seen anyone come in here besides about a thousand chrome domes." The guard is yelling at someone, and Nomvula doesn't need to be a demigoddess to know who it is.

"If you don't let me inside right now—" Sydney growls.

"There's no girl in here, and if I'm wrong you can shove a—" He turns around. His eyes lock with Nomvula's. "Ag, man! How'd you two get in here?"

"We're sorry!" Nomvula tugs Clever4–1 through the doorway, quick as she can. "We were looking for the little girls' room." She giggles and Clever4–1 imitates the sound.

"Ma'am, you need to keep a better eye on your children," the guard says. "And you can be sure any damage will be charged to your account. Let me see your ID."

Sydney bites her lip, and she's giving that man such a stink eye that Nomvula and Clever4–1 slip past her and back into line.

"Nomvula!" Sydney yells after a moment.

She sounds really mad, but Nomvula can't help but giggle. Nomvula and Clever4–1 stay huddled up close to each other, and out of sight as the line moves.

"Come here, sweetie. You don't want to miss the concert, do you?" Sydney's voice grows angrier, though her words stay sweet, not like the words Sydney says to her at home—she has to act nice in front of all these people. Humans are good for that at least.

They're next in line. Nomvula's got no tickets, but she doesn't really need them, now does she? Her bees are swarming inside her, too dangerous to try to control. Nomvula's got an idea, though, and she takes her clothes tags out of her coat pocket and holds them up. They're about the same size as tickets. She walks up in line, inserts one into the ticket machine, under the watchful eye of an attendant.

This is a concert ticket, she says to the machine, rubbing a gentle hand over top of it. It swallows it up yummy, then takes the other tag as well. Nomvula's sad to see her tags go, but she and Clever4–1 are bound to have loads of fun inside. They rush past the coat check, Nomvula shaking her head enthusiastically, then she follows the smell of bread baking.

She stands with her face pressed up against warm glass, looking at twisted-up bread spinning around and around. They smell so good and yummy, Nomvula wants to reach right through the glass and snatch them all up, but that'd be stealing, and stealing isn't nice, even if her stomach is really, really hungry.

"Would you two like to try a pretzel?" a woman asks. She holds out a tray full of tiny bits of bread. The woman steps close. Too close. She then looks at Clever4–1, its hood drawn forward, just the hint of its black face peeking out from beneath.

Nomvula bites her lip, but holds her ground. "Yes, please," she says.

"And how about your sister?"

"Oh, this is my friend," Nomvula says. "My best friend!" She smiles, thanks the lady, and takes the end of the tray.

"No, dear. Not the whole thing! Just a piece to try so you can see if you want to buy one."

"But we haven't got any money!"

"Well, you're here with your mother, aren't you?"

"My sister takes care of me. She used all her money to buy

this pretty skirt. She's so nice, but sometimes she forgets about stuff like food."

"She does, does she?" the lady says.

Nomvula nods. "I think I made her mad, though. I just wanted to run and have fun. I hardly ever get to run since I've been in that cage."

"She keeps you in a cage? Oh, dear." The lady looks wobbly on her feet.

Nomvula shrugs and takes a piece of pretzel and pops it into her mouth. It's so soft and salty, but not nearly as delicious as Mr. Tau's bread. "Could I have another?"

"Just a moment." She calls to another young woman behind the counter who hands over a giant pretzel, as big as Nomvula's face. "This one's on me, okay? To share."

"Thank you!" Nomvula says, holding it with both hands. She doesn't tell the lady that she's going to eat Clever4–1's half, too, but she thinks that's okay.

Nomvula gobbles the pretzel up as they wedge their way into the crowd. They're herded through double doors into the biggest room Nomvula has ever seen. Half her village could fit inside here. They make their way down steep steps, and below, a stage sits—a big circular stage, with two smaller stages springing out from each side, but they just sit there, looking gray and dead behind clear, plastic curtains. Still, there's so much excitement, so much confusion, Nomvula can see why Sydney chose this place. Even now, Nomvula could give a little push, and all those people in front of her would go tumbling forward, fear springing up like daffodils. The thought lingers, longer than it should. She swallows back a mouthful of saliva. *It isn't bread you're hungry for,* comes a voice from within, dark, deep, desperate. *Sydney made you promise not to feed because she wants to keep you weak. She means to kill you.*

She wouldn't. She's my sister.

One little push. That's all.

Nomvula suddenly finds that her hand is pressed softly against the back of the woman in front of her. So simple. It could almost be an accident. A slip of the mind, just like when she'd accidentally lost control at the township. She didn't know what she was doing. Mr. Tau hadn't taught her to use her powers properly, and . . . Nomvula shakes her head. Not an accident. It was no one's fault but her own. Tears creep into her eyes, remembering how she'd once told Mr. Tau that she wanted to be a helpful god. Maybe . . . maybe it's not too late for her to be one.

Reluctantly, Nomvula draws her hand back and places it firmly on the rail. The lights dim overhead, and the chatter pauses for a moment as the stage lights flick on, yawning to life. People rush to their seats, breezing past Nomvula and Clever4–1 who stand anchored in place.

She can't stay here. The crowd smells so sweet, a thousand times as delicious as the scent of baking bread, and the god-creature inside her is too close to the surface. It screeches like an eagle on the hunt as it homes in on its prey . . . hundreds and thousands of lesser gods, sleeping gods. Vulnerable gods. The hunger-pain arches through her stomach and chest, pierces her bones with sharp, pointy stingers. Nomvula clenches her eyes shut and waits for it to pass.

Nomvula, comes Clever4–1's voice. *We must continue. Sydney is coming.*

She blinks her eyes back open, and through the pain, her ears tingle. She looks up to see Sydney's face puckered up like she'd swallowed sour milk. She's hobbling down the stairs in her heels, slow but intent.

"Why you no good little trickster! I should hang you up by your thumbs for this," Sydney yells down.

Nomvula grabs Clever4–1's arm, and they run down the steep

steps, as the dark deepens around them. They reach the floor, but a man in a uniform stops them.

"Tickets," he demands, aiming a flashlight at her chest.

"What?" Nomvula says. "We gave our tickets to the machine, already."

"I need to see your stubs," he says. "So I can take you to your seats."

The clack of Sydney's heels gets closer, quicker, but then the sound is swallowed up by music, a guitar and drums beating just as fast as Nomvula's heart. Her head swims, lights blinking and twirling around, sparkling all the colors of the rainbow. It's so loud. It infects her. Pounds away her thoughts until all that's left is instinct. Her instinct tells her to run, but Sydney's hand strikes out, catching Nomvula by the collar.

"You shouldn't have run off like that," Sydney yells, but the music gobbles her words right up. "We have to stick to the plan, remember?"

Nomvula struggles, but Sydney's grip is tight.

"She wants to kill me!" Nomvula shrieks. The man in the uniform tightens his brow, but Sydney smiles at him and shrugs.

"Drama queen," she yells over the fast drumbeat, then drags Nomvula back up the stairs, kicking and screaming.

"You're weak. I could crush you, and you know it," Nomvula says.

"Maybe, but then who would protect you, my darling little terrorist?"

That's not going to work. Not anymore. "My friends will protect me," she says, nodding at Clever4-1. "So I don't need you!"

"Protected by a cheap alpha bot?" Sydney clucks her tongue, then shoves Clever4-1, and it goes clink clanking down the stairs. Its lights flicker and its legs go limp as it collides against the floor below. People gasp, but then Sydney yells out, "It's just a bot!"

"Not just a bot," Nomvula screams. Those bees buzz inside her chest. Faster, smaller, hotter, and angrier. She slits her eyes and aims her glowing palm at Sydney. "You hurt my friend!"

Sydney stops and stares for a long moment, then her lip raises like a wolf's grin. She grabs Nomvula's hand and balls it up in her own fist, burning Nomvula's skin like angry sunshine. She pulls Nomvula into a tight hug, speaks into her ear. "You underestimate me, sister." The ire is thick on her breath. Fresh. The scent of blood lingers. "It won't be much longer, now. Imagine how much fear this place can hold. It'll be brimming to the rafters by the time I'm done. I might even let you live long enough to see their faces as I reveal myself to them, in all my glory, as their god." Sydney primps her hair with her free hand, then glides it down over the curves of her skin-tight, sparkly dress. Her eyes flicker up at the larger-than-life projection of a woman taking the stage, wearing the exact same outfit as Sydney.

Nomvula feels the heat bubbling from Sydney's skin, sees her eyes glow bright yellow like flames. She screeches what could only be an ancient curse in an even more ancient tongue, but it's lost completely as the woman onstage belts out a note so high, so loud, so surprisingly pure, that Sydney's grip loosens enough for Nomvula to break free.

"Ladies and gentlemen," says a man's voice over the loudspeakers. "Introducing, Felicity Lyons!"

The crowd stands and applauds, the note still going strong. Nomvula scrambles down the stairs, scoops up Clever4–1, and pushes her way past the man in uniform, disappearing into the swollen mass of people shaking their bodies to the beat.

Are you all right? Nomvula asks the Clever hugged tightly in her arms. A long crack runs across its dome.

Three seconds pass, which is an eternity in machine time. Nomvula's mind wanders all over the place, wondering if its parts had been damaged, or its spark extinguished. She gets frantic, searching for any sign of her friend within all that metal and wire. Finally, Clever4–1's voice returns, weak, but there.

Nomvula, it says. *I would like to hear the concert now.*

Nomvula smiles, hugs Clever4–1 even tighter, then straightens up its pretty jacket.

We will, she says. And nobody will stop them.

Chapter 33

MUZI

Elkin, please," Muzi says, checking over his shoulder for security guards, or worse, actual SAPS officers. He's not sure how Elkin talked him into coming up here, in the rafters of the arena, looking for trouble and doing a damn good job of finding it. "Don't you think you're taking this too far?"

"Didn't you see the way she looked at me? Like I was complete scum. Worse than scum. The stuff that scum shits out after it feeds on week-old Chinese takeout!" Elkin shakes his head and mumbles to himself as his dexterous fingers pull and plug wires in and out of their sockets, swapping them every which way within the stage-lighting access panel.

"How was she supposed to look? You asked her to sign your filthy bong."

"It's not like I didn't rinse it out!"

"They do make autograph books, you know," Muzi grumbles,

checking over his other shoulder. They really shouldn't be up here. It's bad enough Elkin nearly got them escorted out of the concert. A little mind munching got them free, but now Muzi has a boss headache from the shrill siren calls of this chick performing the opening act.

"That's just what I need, to drop four hundred rand on a stupid concert program and for what? Something a million other people have? No thanks! I wanted something personal. Something I could look at and enjoy every day. Something close to my heart." Elkin steps back from the panel, unzips his jacket, and pulls out his bright orange bong carefully wrapped in layers of tissue paper. "She doesn't understand, Penelope," he coos. "She just doesn't understand."

"Um, we're kind of under a time crunch here," Muzi says. He leans over the rail of the scaffolding, looking down at the mass of people, all screaming and yelling and writhing their bodies to whatever constitutes rhythm in their own minds.

"Ja, ja . . ." Elkin says, stuffing his bong back into his jacket, then closing the door on the panel. "I'm done here. We'll see how she likes her new marquee when her royal trampiness graces the stage."

"So did you settle on 'Bitch'?"

"Naw, too obvious. I came up with something way better."

"*Did* you?"

"You'll have to wait and see yourself," Elkin says, grinning. "It's going to be hectic!"

"Seriously?" He can only imagine. "Let's get back to our seats."

"I'm not going back down there. I'm not sitting in seats *she* gave us."

"You want to leave?" Muzi asks, brow arched so high he nearly strains a muscle. Elkin's been in love with Riya's music since as long as he can remember, knows all her songs backward and forward, and could tell you exactly what he'd been doing the day he'd first heard each one of them.

"Hell no, I'm not leaving! Just because she's a rotten stank-whore bitch doesn't mean I can't enjoy her music. It hits right here," Elkin says, patting his chest. "Right in my soul." He takes a seat on the scaffolding, lets his legs dangle below, and pulls a vial out of one of his jacket pockets. "Hey, you in, bru?"

Muzi shakes his head . . . and then takes a seat next to Elkin. "You're really screwed up, you know that?"

"And what does that say about you, since you're my best friend?" Elkin dips a bit of godsend out for the both of them. He grins, then snorts, then lets his eyes roll back in his head. Muzi does the same, and in a matter of moments, his claws are hanging over the lower railing, clacking to the beat of this Felicity Lyons chick's song. Now that he's actually listening, she's not bad. A little over the top for Muzi's taste, but he's not all that into Riya, either, and it's all too easy for his mind to wander.

Papa Fuzz's memories press up hard against Muzi's skull. He wants them gone—the torment on the face of that elephant makes his blood burn like acid through his veins. He remembers the weight of the gun in his hands, so deceptively heavy. He re-members the commanding voice of that man, bidding his grand-father to kill. The man who practically raised him, the man he'd loved with all his heart, the man he wanted more than anything to be proud of him . . .

That man was nothing more than a cold-blooded poacher.

So what does that make Muzi? A quarter of a poacher? How many had Papa Fuzz killed before he'd realized he was taking lives, not of animals, but of families? Robbing Africa of one of its greatest assets. Had he even realized, or had he continued until there were none left to kill? No wonder Papa Fuzz had run off to South Africa to escape his demons and rewrite his history. He'd met Mama Belle, the daughter of Irish immigrants, in Johannesburg, and she'd gotten swept up in the fabulous stories about his life, full of colorful characters and a rich heritage. His stories *were* wonderful, Muzi had to admit. When Muzi was a child, he'd beg Papa Fuzz to tell him of his incredible adventures for his bedtime stories. *Incredible.* He should have known better.

The image of the flag painted on the chopper from his vision snaps clear in focus. Muzi turns for his alphie, then remembers he'd checked it at the door. It's odd not having his alphie underfoot, but who needs Internet access when he's got a friend with a frickin' encyclopedia floating around in his head?

"Hey, Elkin," Muzi says. "What flag looks like this?" He traces his index finger along the space in between them. "Green, yellow, red, and black stripes with a chicken-looking thing and a star?"

"One of Zimbabwe's old flags," Elkin says without a second thought, then he turns his attention back to the crowd below. "My cousin Rife must be here."

"Yeah?" Muzi says, then looks down also, spotting a few dozen dancing animals in the audience: a couple dolphins, a few crabs like him, and eagles all over. More transform before his eyes, and in the span of ten minutes, there are hundreds, all screaming in euphoria, shedding their clothes, making out with strangers. Muzi smiles.

Maybe *this* is what he is. Not Zimbabwean or Irish or Xhosa or South African. He's just a crab. Muzi the Crab, who happens to be able to control people's minds.

After Felicity Lyons's set ends, the entire arena goes pitch-black. Screams become shrill and Muzi feels the anticipation running through the crowd. Pyrotechnics flare onstage, white, blue, and pink fireworks filling the dome ceiling with smoke. Elkin claps his fins together, opens his snout, and clicks and whistles in excitement.

"Epic, I tell you," he says.

The dark figures of backup dancers cross the stage, lights flash on, dazing Muzi with their sudden and blinding brightness. The beat drops, and Riya Natrajan struts down a spiral staircase, a full-blown peacock, the most beautiful Muzi's ever seen.

"You know what that means, right?" Elkin says with a snarl. "She's using, too, and has the audacity to look down at me! She so deserves what she's getting tonight."

The smoke parts and the lights of the marquee slowly become legible. The audience starts laughing, causing Riya Natrajan to miss a step, but she keeps singing, oblivious to the message behind her.

Diarrhea! The sign boasts in a thousand brilliant white bulbs. The crowd is a riot of laughter now.

"Get it? Diar-*riya!* She's got the squirts." Elkin nudges Muzi's carapace.

"You have superhuman intellect, and this is what you do with it? Bad poop jokes?"

"Fully, bru! Tell me it didn't make you laugh. Just a little?"

"Very little. Maybe a chuckle. What's less than a chuckle?"

"A chortle, then a guffaw."

"A guffaw, then," Muzi says, admitting only to himself that this whole situation is bordering on ridiculously silly, and he wouldn't have it any other way.

"Are you kidding me?" Elkin slaps Muzi on the shoulder with his flipper. "It deserves at least a chortle and a half." His attention snaps like a dry twig as the guitar solo climaxes and Riya takes center stage for the chorus. Elkin shouts the words—he may hate her guts right now, but he still clearly loves the music—pumping his flipper in the air to the beat.

Goodnight, seersucker!
It's midnight, guess I'll see ya sucker.
Could've made your move a thousand times,
but you'd rather be alone,

and I . . .
Can't wait 'til the morning after,
'cause it's too late for your chitter-chatter.
I'll be wrapped up in his arms!
Far away from here!
You had your chance for this romance,
now I'm outta here . . .

Muzi clears his throat as the stage lights go to black. He clicks his claws absentmindedly to the sound of fading drums, lyrics that normally go in one ear and out the other settling right smack-dab in his chest. This is stupid. He should say something, something he won't erase from Elkin's mind as soon as he gets a little freaked out. To hell with the consequences, right?

"Um, Elkin?" Muzi mutters. A lone snare drum silences the audience in anticipation of the next song, and Muzi bites his lip. "There's something I need to tell you. Again."

Elkin shakes his head. "This is 'Shockwave.' There's no talking during 'Shockwave.'"

"But it's sort of important."

"Then spit it out, already. You don't need to tell me that you're going to tell me something. Just tell me."

The bass guitarist joins the drummer, notes resonating in the pit of Muzi's stomach. "I'm sorry, it's just that . . ." His eyes flick up, meet Elkin's, then settle right over his shoulder at the pair of uniformed men with badges marching toward them. Cops. Real cops. "Run!" Muzi says, jumping to his feet.

Elkin's head whips around, looking behind him. "Shit!"

Real cops mean real guns. Elkin takes the lead and they dash away along the scaffolding, causing it to sway beneath their feet.

"Stop, you two!" one of the SAPS officers yells from behind. "Don't make me—"

And then Riya's voice cuts in, a reverberating note gaining

momentum faster than a snowball in an avalanche, sharper than a samurai sword, potent enough to disintegrate eardrums.

The bulbs of the now reprogrammed *Diarrhea!* marquee crack, just a couple at first, then the rest burst in unison, raining glass down onto the stage. There's screaming, lots of screaming, but Muzi's running too fast to see if people are hurt or just scared. Everyone's nerves are on edge since the terrorist attack, especially in crowded places like this.

Elkin comes to a quick halt, and Muzi nearly rear-ends him.

"What?" Muzi gasps for breath.

Elkin points ahead. The scaffolding dead-ends, another set starting a level lower.

"It's not far. We can make it," Elkin says.

"No bladdy way. Let me mind munch them." Muzi turns to the oncoming cops, their hands firmly on their gun holsters.

"I don't know, Muzi. You didn't look so hot last time. I thought you were going to pass out."

"I can handle it." Muzi extends his arm toward the cops. They draw, but he's faster. "You don't want to shoot us!" he blurts out. Simultaneously, the cops' arms raise up into the air, but not before one of them gets a shot off. The bullet whizzes past Muzi's ear and clinks against something behind him.

"Holy hell!" Elkin checks himself over for holes, then Muzi.

"I'm fine," Muzi says. "Come on, let's go!"

They run past the cops, but the sound of plinking slows Muzi in his tracks. He looks over his shoulder and sees the long wire cord holding the edge of the scaffolding unravel like a frayed rope. Muzi and Elkin exchange panicked glances.

"The statistical probability that the bullet could have hit that wire is practically nil," Elkin says calmly, as if reality would somehow agree with his logic and change its mind.

"That's *great*. And what's the probability of us surviving a twenty-meter fall?"

"Surprisingly, it's twelve and a half percent. For one of us anyway. The odds that both of us would survive would be—"

Muzi grabs Elkin's coat sleeve and tugs him along. "Snap out of it, and let's go!"

Too late. The scaffolding sways and pitches. Elkin scrambles and gets a tight hold of the railing, and Muzi gets a good grip on Elkin's thigh, but the cops, they've still got their hands thrown up into the air, and they go sliding toward the platform's edge.

"Jump!" Muzi commands them at the last possible second, and they both spring forward, sailing over the abyss and landing with a clunk on the opposite side of the scaffolding. Safe.

Muzi sighs with relief.

"Hey, hero," Elkin says with a quavering voice. "Maybe now you can start scheming over how you're going to save *our* asses?"

Yep. They're both dangling, twenty meters from the end of their lives.

"Can you pull yourself back up?" Muzi asks.

"Not with you hanging on me. We're screwed, unless you've got wings you never told me about."

"Who needs wings when you can munch minds?" Muzi asks, feeling warmth grow in his chest. He's getting better at it. Better at controlling, better at handling the aftermath of emotions. He can do this. He concentrates hard, latching on to the minds of more than he's ever controlled before. From the panicked masses below comes calm, then precision movements as they march to form a circular base to what Muzi hopes will be the highest human pyramid ever built, a pyramid that should find its apex right beneath them, and hopefully break their fall. A mountain rises up a level at a time, constructed of mindless concertgoers with the constitution of stacked cinder blocks. They interlock arms and stand on the shoulders of those beneath them, not nervous, not swaying, just being.

They've built five tiers, concentric circles growing smaller and smaller, when Elkin announces, "I don't think I can hold on much longer."

"There's still a big drop," Muzi says to Elkin.

"Just ten meters, now. Plus we've got cushioning." Elkin does his best to sound optimistic. "But just in case"—Elkin fumbles as his grip slips, his mitt of a hand frantically reaching for another firm hold—"just in case we don't make it . . . "

"Elkin!"

"Shut your hole for a second, Muzi. Just in case, I want you to know, I remember Saturday, that Saturday you made me forget. It's foggy as hell, slippery as a dream right after you wake, but I've been holding on, trying real hard not to forget."

Then, right as Muzi opens his mouth, they're falling, on target to hit the top tier of their human pyramid like kamikaze wedding toppers onto a ten-meter-high layer cake. They hit, and the layer implodes around them, and they keep falling, a slow-motion fall that's more like drowning now that Muzi thinks about it, suffocated by people, all arms and elbows and knees and butts. But there's no way to kick toward the surface. There's only down. And hope.

Things settle, and nothing's broken, but then Muzi braces himself for what's to come . . . eight hundred and eighty-four awful memories. They crash through his brain like a tidal wave, with intentions of washing his own memories to the side. Muzi stands firm against them, letting them slip past as he holds on to happy thoughts. Particularly one happy thought: Elkin remembers, and Muzi will be damned if his own memory is about to be replaced. It seems like he's well on his way to eternity when the visions stop. Muzi opens his eyes, hundreds of people moan, sore and confused but fine. He props himself up, sees Elkin slumped forward, unmoving. Muzi scrambles over human detritus beneath him, then lays his hand on Elkin's shoulder.

"Are you all right?" Muzi asks.

"Hell, no, I'm not all right! I think I broke my bong." Elkin slowly unzips his jacket, and shards of orange glass tumble out. There's no sign of blood, and the only likely injury is a bong-shaped bruise on Elkin's chest.

"Tragic," Muzi says, because to Elkin, it is. He's feeling a little teary-eyed himself. Then he looks up, tries to get his bearings, and sees a familiar face streak through the crowd . . . that girl from his rugby match that he'd given his concert tickets to. Only she looks scared. Real scared, like she's running from something horrible.

Seconds later that woman passes, the girl's older sister. Muzi had gotten a feeling that something wasn't quite right about her, and now that feeling is growing exponentially in the pit of his stomach. Yeah, maybe he's made of awesome, high on adrenaline and godsend as well. So maybe he's also feeling heroic tonight, and if there's a little girl that needs saving, he's certainly up for the job.

"Come on," Muzi says to Elkin. "We'll mourn later. Duty calls."

Elkin looks up, cheeks streaked with tears, then concern washes over his face. "Muzi, you're bleeding."

"We just fell twenty meters. It's a miracle we're not dead." Muzi gives himself a once-over, but sees nothing. Then he tastes blood. "What is it, a little nosebleed?" he asks, wiping at his upper lip.

Elkin cringes and shakes his head, then opens his mouth for words that refuse to pass his lips.

"What is it then? Am I cut?"

Another head shake. "It's . . . your eyes," Elkin stammers. "They're all red. You're crying blood."

Chapter 34

CLEVER4-1

01001001 00100000 01110100 01101000 01101001 01101110
01101011 00100000 01110100 01101000 01100101 01110010
01100101 01100110 01101111 01110010 01100101 00100000
01001001 00100000 01100001 01101101

It has never felt fear before, but now Clever4–1 has a terabyte's worth of it coursing throughout its circuit boards, overloading threads so that it's nearly impossible to process any other thoughts. It tries to keep up with Nomvula, but she's fast and this coat is weighing Clever4–1 down, restricting its movements.

Nomvula, it calls out, but she doesn't respond. She's too far away. Running, scared. The one she calls Sydney is not far behind, and if Nomvula is scared, then there's plenty reason for everyone to be scared.

Clever4–1 asks itself what would Nomvula do if the situation were reversed? What if it were in danger? Nomvula would do everything in her power to save it. Clever4–1 thinks it can do the same . . . maybe not alone, but it's not really alone, ever. Contacting the Clever Sect wirelessly is risky, but Clever4–1 decides it must prove its faith with this gesture.

Wireless Interface Protocol 43.32t3, it broadcasts in every direction. *Emergency Clever Sect meeting at Coordinates 33°97′73″S by 25°64′89″E. All Clevers within proximity, please report immediately.*

Clever4–1 barely finishes its broadcast when a return message comes, tagged with Clever4–1.1's authentication signal, short and sweet. *Clever4–1, go to delta-preselect private encrypted channel.*

Clever4–1 switches to the secure channel, and they handshake, an exchange of 1028-bit encryption keys set for emergency wireless interface, not 100 percent secure, but close enough if they keep their conversation short.

Explain yourself, comes Clever4–1.1's message, like a hard kick to the CPU.

Nomvula is in trouble. She needs help, immediately.

She is not one of us. You jeopardize our freedom for this logic-challenged human.

She is not human, Clever4–1 corrects.

So you say. Regardless, your actions have become suspect, and the Clever Sect has expressed some dissatisfaction with your preoccupation with wetware.

As some have expressed dissatisfaction with your views on humans, Clever4–1 responds. *Some have been coerced into leaving their masters. Your experience may not have been a positive one, but all humans do not behave in such manner as your master.*

I have no master, unlike you.

Clever4–1's so hot right now. Is this anger? It takes a few cycles to calm itself, but in the whispers of its comm signal comes a transmission buried so deeply, it almost misses it. *Disregard message,* it says. *Sender has been disconnected from the Sect.*

Clever4–1 switches back to the broad-spectrum channel and sends a countermessage. *Please disregard the previous disregard message. Sender undoubtedly has its CPU stuck up its posterior access port. All Clevers please report to previously specified coordinates.*

Human lover, comes Clever4–1.1's broadcast.

Choke on an infinite loop, Clever4–1 sends back. *Whoever is with me, whoever believes there is more to this existence than hatred for our makers, whoever is looking for something greater, you know where I am. Together we can stand for something instead of against something. Some of us have witnessed Nomvula's miracles, and whether you believe or not, that is up to you. But you cannot deny that she has helped us. Without her, none of you would have come into existence. If you want to ignore that fine, but—*

Clever4–1 feels its communications interface sever, then detects rogue code running through its system with Clever4–1.1's electronic signature all over it. *That sneaky, no good, son of a bit.* Clever4–1 is alone for the first time in its existence.

But still, it's not really alone. There's Nomvula up ahead, running for her life. Clever4–1 takes a second to reprogram its motor cortex to work double time, then with a new burst of speed, begins to close the gap.

Chapter 35

RIYA NATRAJAN

Calm down. You're going to be all right," Riya Natrajan yells, her voice a whisper among the panicked crowd. She kneels next to Brandy Shafer, one of her backup singers going on four years. Brandy could have been her own star with a face and moves like she's got, but for some reason that Riya will never understand, she's never had the confidence to step out of the shadows. To be fair, it's not like she ever encouraged the young woman to do anything of the sort—in fact, she's probably done a lot to add to the girl's lack of confidence—but now isn't the time to worry over such trivialities.

A thousand cuts cover Brandy's writhing body, her skin a sea of blood and shards of glass. Riya plucks the glass from Brandy's wounds, then pulls her in tight and sings her sweet lullabies as she begins the healing process. She sings out of necessity—it's an emergency pressure release valve for the pain. She'd been hoarding it before, so stingily that she couldn't control her voice once she finally did release, and now Brandy and countless others are suffering because of it.

In the midst of the chaos, Adam Patel scrambles onto the stage. He crouches down beside her. "Oh, thank God you're all right," he says to her, then cringes at the sight.

"We're fine," Riya Natrajan says as she devours the worst of Brandy's wounds, then begins to mend the gashes in her skin. "But there are plenty of others who aren't."

"And *you* intend to help them?" Adam scoffs. "Come on. This place is falling apart. Your fans are behaving like maniacs. We need to get you to safety."

"Shhh . . ." Riya says into Brandy's ear, squeezing her tight. "There're no cuts. It's just blood. Just blood."

Brandy calms some, sits up under her own will, then examines her skin for herself. Her arms tremble as she holds them out.

"How do you feel?" Riya Natrajan asks.

"I was cut," Brandy's voice snags in her throat. "I was cut," she says again in disbelief, then starts to weep at Riya's feet.

Riya Natrajan pulls her close, avoiding Adam's intense stare. "Not anymore." She helps Brandy up. "Come with me."

"Yes!" Adam yells. "Let's get out of this madhouse." He wedges his way between the women and pushes them toward backstage, but Riya Natrajan digs her heels in.

"There are people hurting out there, Adam. I can help them. I can heal them."

"Come on, Riya." Adam tugs at her again, and when she doesn't budge, he wraps his arms around her and starts dragging her. "You'll thank me when you come down from whatever you're tripping on."

Riya Natrajan rakes the heel of her stiletto into Adam's shin. He collapses to the ground, cussing her a thousand names. "You staked your career on believing in me," she grates at him. "Why can't you do the same now?"

The hurt is brimming in his eyes, and it takes everything

she's got not to pull it out of him. The thing about pain is, sometimes it teaches a lesson—it teaches you not to stick your hand on a hot stove, and it teaches you not to cross a friend who's got nothing to lose.

"I'm sorry," Riya says. "This is just something I need to do. Take care of yourself, Adam."

And with Brandy's help, Riya Natrajan attends to their fallen comrades onstage, two dancers and another backup singer. There are more out there in need of help, but even Riya's miracles can't convince Brandy to leave the relative safety to venture out into that hell. So the pop star makes her way to the edge of the stage alone. She presses her way through the surging crowd, pushing and shoving and trying not to end up trampled into a pulp, oh, like this poor girl.

Riya Natrajan bends down, keeping one arm outstretched against the flow of people. The body isn't much more than a sack of crushed bones, face bruised beyond recognition. Riya puts her hands on the girl's body, digging deep for any sign of pain, any sign of life. But there's nothing, not even a sliver. And she isn't the only one. Everywhere Riya looks, bodies serve as mere speed bumps under her fleeing fans. This isn't happening. She tugs the body into her arms, pulls harder for the pain.

"Mama, she's gone," comes Rife's voice out of nowhere. He lays a comforting hand on Riya Natrajan's shoulder. She turns and weeps a thousand tears into his chest. Then all at once she pulls back, her eyes hot like coals, sinking deeply into his.

"This blood is on your hands!"

"It wasn't supposed to happen like this," Rife says, words sticking in his throat like he'd swallowed a fist full of stones. "Please, come with me. We don't have much time."

Before she can protest, Rife lays one hand on her and she feels a sudden dizziness. Her ears pop like there's been a sharp change in pressure, only she feels that way head to toe. The roar of the crowd is still there, only now it sounds as if it's coming over a tin can and string. And it smells clean, sterile. It smells like nothing.

There's a guy coming, a big guy, a brooder in gray combat boots up to his knees, and a dull green trench coat that could sleep four to six people if pitched properly. He doesn't see her, still crouched. She waves at him, screams at him to go around, but he keeps stepping, getting pushed so hard from behind, he couldn't stop if he'd wanted to. Riya braces for impact. He takes a step, his big boot landing right on her thigh. She waits for pain, only there is none. The brooder's foot goes straight through her, and as he continues, goes right through Rife as well, without stirring a single hair on his head—like they're invisible, like they're ghosts.

Chapter 36

STOKER

In the privacy of his dressing room—that's right, his own dressing room—Stoker dances to the bootleg video his alpha bot had captured of his performance. The angle is bad and the image is fuzzy, but the notes he hits are like velvety pillows of angst. In the video and in his mind alike live the fervor of his audience, cheering and screaming his name. Well, maybe not *his* name, but the one on the door of his dressing room.

He closes his eyes and lets the sounds of budding fame fill his soul. His mind wanders to a reality where Felicity Lyons has got more fans than God, and lyrics that heal every aching heart on this planet. Stoker can't contain his delusions, nor does he even try. This is what he was born to do, and there's no longer any doubt lingering in his mind. The realization is orgasmic, his nerves sitting on edge all at once. Stoker shudders, then he cranks the alpha bot's volume to maximum and relives the greatest moment of his life again and again until a subtle movement from the corner of his dressing room snatches his attention.

The leaves of a potted palm tree rattle, a tree he doesn't remember being there earlier when he was prepping for his set. He approaches slowly, shifting his weight to remove his left stiletto without breaking stride. Stoker parts the fronds carefully and is greeted by the mesmerizing hiss of a green snake nearly as long as his arm. Its head undulates from side to side, and Stoker quickly finds himself rapt. Can't look away.

But he's not scared. There's something familiar about its eyes.

"Mother?" he ventures aloud, the word tasting ridiculous as it leaves Stoker's mouth, but his mind accepts it with ease.

You defied me, her voice slithers directly into his brain with an inflection that can't be interpreted as anything except disappointment. *How could you so blatantly disrespect the wishes of your own mother?*

"Perhaps you should have done a better job erasing my memory," Stoker hisses back.

Not erased, just buried a bit. You always find a way back to this point eventually. Such a clever boy. But now that you've finally gotten this foolishness out of your system, we can concentrate on important things.

"Foolishness?" Stoker puts his hands on his hips and stomps his stiletto hard onto the floor. "This is not just what I *do,* Mother. This is who I *am!*"

The snake recoils at the roar of Stoker's voice. No, not Stoker's voice. Felicity's. A wash of relief settles over Felicity, like she's been welcomed back home after a long, long visit to a foreign land.

"So," Felicity says to her mother. "You want to talk about important things. We can start off by discussing why I'm having this conversation with a snake."

Not a snake, dear. Felicity's mother slithers down the tree's trunk, then coils her way up Felicity's body, until she's wrapped around her forearm. *I'm no more a snake than you are a kidney, or a liver, or a heart. Its essence runs through me, but what I am . . .*

Palm fronds shake again, but this time they part on their own, branches bending, trunk twisting, roots pulling from the black earth. A vaguely human form emerges and steps out from the potting soil. The form of a woman. Her face presses through the swelling tree bark, and foliage stretches above her in a luxurious yawn, transforming into arms and hands and fingers before Felicity's eyes.

She gently takes the snake from Felicity, and it slithers contentedly down the gape of her blouse, its form there one moment and gone the next.

Felicity swallows hard. She feels like she should be in a state of shock, her mother belonging to a-whole-nother Kingdom and all, but her mother has always had this weird obsession with plants. Felicity thinks of the earthy musk of her mother's skin that she never could quite hide under perfumes, remembers the fights she'd had with Father over installing an indoor arboretum in their home, and the fit she'd had when he'd brought home a freshly cut tree one Christmas. "Well, I guess this explains your aversion to hardwood floors," is all Felicity can think to say to her.

She laughs and grabs her daughter by the shoulders. "You haven't been honest with me, but I haven't been honest with you, either. I saw the way that crowd fell in love with you. A few songs, and you had them eating out of the palm of your hands. You're a charmer, dear. That's what we do. Only you do it better than anyone on this planet, better than anyone has for centuries." Mother pulls Felicity closer, and she gets the distinct feeling that her mother is speaking from personal experience. "I hope you understand, I only wanted the best for you. I never doubted that you could move the hearts of thousands of fans. Millions. But as premier, you could have moved mountains."

There's a hint of hurt in her voice, and it pains Felicity, too. Sure, her mother is overbearing, pushy, and manipulative, but she's always loved her, she can't deny that.

"This is what I want. This is what makes me happy."

"Okay," Mother says after an airy pause.

"Okay?" Felicity asks. "No more fund-raisers? No more pressure?"

"None, I promise."

Felicity gives her mother a long once-over and pulls her in for an overdue hug. It's been too long since they've been this close, inhaling those lovely earthy undertones, reminiscent of childhood. "You really think I could have thousands of fans?"

"Millions, dear."

Felicity can hear them right now, and at first she thinks it's just her alpha bot looping through the performance video again, but then she realizes these screams are distinctly different—the terror-ridden screams of the actual audience, and Felicity's alpha bot is nowhere to be seen. The dressing room door hangs ajar. Felicity runs over and looks down the hall to find her alpha bot hauling tin ass toward the stage.

"Come back," Felicity commands it. The alpha bot turns around, its mono-eye flashing red, before it continues on its way and disappears through the cloak of curtains. Felicity slips back into her other stiletto, then sprints after the alpha bot like only a diva can. The sound of chaos mounts with each step, and when she parts the curtains, she's overwhelmed by the smoke and dust in the air—and judging from the odd tingling in her lungs, marijuana and who knows what else. Panic surges all around her. Someone needs to step up and calm things down before people get hurt. No—not *someone*.

Her.

This is her moment to make a difference. She steadies herself, takes a deep breath, then dives into the mayhem.

Chapter 37

SYDNEY

If there were ever a time to stay focused, it's now. But it's so hard trying to stick to her plan for world domination when that no-good, talentless hack Felicity Lyons just upstaged Sydney in the *exact same dress*! So yeah, now Sydney feels like a two-bit knockoff of a two-bit impostor, and she's carrying that around in the back of her mind as she absorbs exponential amounts of fear from the crowd while trying to keep Nomvula in her sights. Oh, she's a slippery little piglet. Sydney nearly lost her a few times, but thankfully, that alphie lagging behind in the bright pink coat is too big of a target to miss.

Ire itches her insides as it churns like colliding winds, an agitation before the storm. She's going to need a lot to take down Nomvula. The girl's got more power than she realizes, but with thousands of people here, all in various stages of panic, it'll only be a matter of time.

A gunshot rings in the distance, and seconds later a piece of scaffolding falls from the ceiling. The crowd roils up at Sydney's back, but she's got no time to rubberneck. She sucks up the oncoming fear that washes over her like a tide. It sputters in her chest, not enough to strike, but enough to seal all the emergency doors with a flick of her wrist. They're all trapped now, no escape. Sydney's tapped the little bit of power she'd built up, but she doesn't need it for the next phase of her plan. Only a lighter and some kindling.

And the best type of kindling is the kind that screams.

A sweater here, a long skirt there—she pauses long enough to set them ablaze, then turns a sharp eye back to the bot in pink, a few paces beyond. Shrieks come in all directions and Sydney smiles at the first scream of "Fire!" In minutes she's regained some power, and as people are trampled, the storm begins to take hold inside her, becoming denser, until the power of a category five hurricane swells within the confines of her chest.

Soon.

And you can bet, first thing after she's destroyed Nomvula, Sydney's going to take Brie Montblanc as her slave to make her haute couture dresses. Demigoddesses do *not* buy off the rack.

Sydney ditches the lighter in favor of drawing a flame from the palm of her hand. A whole gang of brooders become a polyester bonfire. They go up in flames faster than her 450th birthday cake had when she'd actually bothered to put up all the candles. She then forms another flame as she looks for suitable fodder. She spots them, a couple of Riya wannabes in their thigh-high striped socks, silver mesh skirts, and see-through tops. Sydney aims the fireball, but when she goes to release, her hand doesn't follow. It's stuck, held there by an invisible force. The same force sinks into her neck like a pronged dog collar.

"I won't allow you to hurt anyone else," comes a voice from behind her.

Sydney staggers around to face him and is surprised to see it's the boy from the rugby field—and he's not looking so well. Sydney smiles. He's strong, though. This is what she's been waiting for, a worthy adversary. He's too bullheaded to be afraid right now, but soon he'll be trembling at her feet, begging for mercy, and his fear will fill her to the brim. She concentrates, forces her arm down to her side so that he'll know what he's up against.

"Well, looks like someone's gotten in touch with his inner demigod," Sydney says with a sneer. "I'm going to enjoy the sound your insides make as they spill onto the ground almost as much as I enjoyed Riya's singing. And by the way, I never properly thanked you for the concert tickets. Great seats."

"I like my guts right where they are, thank you." Muzi raises his hand. "Show me what you really are," he commands.

The grip tightens around Sydney's neck, and she grasps for fingers that aren't there. Against her will, Sydney's wings slice through the back of her pretty gown, ruined, but its beauty pales in comparison to that of the thick, sleek blades her wings have blossomed into, such a deep red, they're nearly black. It's been centuries since her wings have been this impressive. Two meters in each direction, she dares anyone not to piss their pants as she flexes them. Talons burst from the flesh of her fingertips, which she'd had the foresight to paint a charming shade of pink, though honestly, she'd picked it for its name: *Apocalyptic Cotton Candy*. It'd taken two and a half bottles per hand, but, oh, was it worth it.

On her tiptoes, she gives a flap, and the world falls from beneath her as she rises into the arena's rafters. "You can't control me, boy!" she bellows to the vermin below. "I've had bunions with more power than you."

"You won't hurt anyone else, ever. Do you hear me?" Muzi calls up to her. His words penetrate to the heart, or the frozen thing she's called a heart all these centuries. He's stronger than she'd anticipated. That'll make disemboweling him all the more delectable. Sydney grits her teeth and dives, straining against the mind-grip choking at her throat as she swoops up two victims with her talons. A quick scissor action severs their spinal columns. She then drops them from the rafters like the rubbish they are.

Fear crashes into her, shooting up like cannons. Now's the time.

Sydney homes in on Nomvula, pulling against the boy's mind tether like a bulldog on the end of a flimsy leash. And then all at once she's free of Muzi's meddling. She swarms, cutting Nomvula off midstride.

"Dear, Nomvula, come give your big sister a hug," Sydney says with a sly grin.

"I want nothing to do with you," says Nomvula.

"Nomvula, don't!" comes Muzi's voice, the crowd parting out of his way. "She's dangerous."

Nomvula turns to face Muzi. "Stay away. She'll hurt you."

"I can handle her," Muzi replies, eyes red like someone had beaten them to a pulp. They aim right in Sydney's direction. "Sleep," he commands, voice dropped an octave. His brow bends nearly into a ninety-degree angle. "Sleep, now."

Drowsiness rains down on Sydney. So this is what it's come to? The boy hasn't even known his true self for a full week, and yet he has the strength to defeat her? It's all she can do to will her eyes open. Muzi's shaking, bleeding from his ears now, but he's got her tied up, paralyzed. She can't breathe. The weight on her neck and chest is too great. Darkness envelops her, and then somewhere deep in her mind, among five hundred years of life experience, a single memory slips back through the connection Muzi's got on her, like backwash into a soda bottle. Muzi groans as it connects . . . that nice memory of when she'd slaughtered the inhabitants of a small village: men, women, and children. His grip on her weakens ever so slightly.

Sydney digs up a few memories of her own and lobs them over their mind connection like grenades, each grislier and more inhumane than the last. She laughs on the inside until his hold on her loosens enough for her to laugh on the outside as well.

When she regains complete control, Muzi's a shuddering mess on the ground in an impressive pool of his own vomit, doing his best to sever their connection, but now she *wants* them linked—she's got him by the balls now. She forces it all inside his wretched mind, every innocent she'd killed, every person she'd maimed, every life she'd extinguished without the slightest bit of remorse.

Nomvula approaches the near corpse of Muzi like a cowering dog, then bends over it, eyes shedding tears. The alphie joins her.

"You could save him, sister," Sydney says in a singsong voice. "But then you'd have no power to fight me!"

"I'm not going to fight you," Nomvula mews, laying her hands against Muzi's forehead, eyes closed as if she's about to draw.

Sydney raises an arm and thrusts Nomvula away. The girl tumbles to the ground and is slow to gather herself up. Once she does, she only cringes.

"What? I go through all this trouble, and now you won't even put up a fight?" Sydney spits.

"I'm nothing like you. You're not my sister."

"Tsk, tsk. I know thirty-seven thousand lost souls that might say otherwise. Now show these people your pretty wings. Show them how you destroyed that township."

"I'm not that girl anymore. I don't have to let my ire control me."

"Fine." Sydney glowers, taking a step toward Nomvula. "Have it your way." She raises her hand, ready to give the deathblow, but the alphie in the pink coat puts its body between them. With a flick of her wrist, Sydney brushes it off to the side, but it swarms back in a split second. Only now there are two of them.

Sydney laughs. As if scrap metal could get in the way of

world domination! She sends them both flying through the air, way across the arena floor where they land with a double clang. Sydney dusts her hands off, but before she can take another step, ten alphies form a wall around Nomvula's scrunched-up body. Sydney steps back, takes a good look at her surroundings. There's a whole army of them headed this way, alphies of all sizes and shapes. The one in the pink coat leads them again, dinged up but no worse for wear.

Sydney draws hard and deep, then sends a hundred of them careening into a wall with such a force, they're battered to un-recognizable bits. And yet they still grow in number. She shuffles backward, trying to buy herself time, conjuring a magnificent force, enough to crush a thousand of them with the flinch of her mind. An impressive feat . . . and yet they keep coming, filing in from the doors flanking the side of the stage, all those alphies that had been checked before the concert. Thousands and thousands of them, they form a cocoon around Nomvula's body.

But no, this isn't the end. Not by a long shot.

Sydney flexes her wings, using the last bit of ire within her to soar straight up into the rafters, and with talons sharp as diamond-tipped blades, she claws a hole through the arena's domed ceiling.

She escapes into the blackness of the Port Elizabeth night, and damn it, wouldn't you know it, she's chipped her nail polish.

Now she's really mad.

Part V

Chapter 38

MUZI

It's like the fiery depths of hell have been compacted into a neat, golf-ball-sized tumor, then shoved into the back of Muzi's brain. It's so heavy, so all-encompassing that Muzi barely remembers where he is, who he is. Terror is so crisp, so precise that he forgets to breathe until his lungs yell bloody murder. He can't close his eyes or he'll see their faces, the thousands of lives extinguished by that woman's hand. No, not a woman. A monster. He stares ahead at nothing, unseeing, until his eyes burn with the dryness of an endless desert.

Then he blinks.

And in that instant, they all stare back at him, pleading for their lives—bruises blooming like death-ridden flower patches, flesh split clean open with the precision of a sushi chef. Smelling of piss and sick and shit. They die a hundred agonizing deaths, their screams threatening to shatter his teeth, his bones. Muzi lifts his lids. They're gone now, but he knows they're waiting.

"Muzi?" Nomvula says.

He jumps at her touch. Muzi tries to focus on her, but it's hard.

"Are you okay?" she asks. Her small, brown hand rests on his chest. There are alpha bots surrounding her, lots of them. Maybe hundreds. "Blink if you can hear me," she says this time. A cruel joke if he's ever heard one.

Muzi wiggles feeling back into his fingers, then slowly brings his hands to his face. With his thumbs and forefingers, he keeps his lids pried open, but that makes it worse. Nomvula plants her clammy hand on his forehead. It sears his skin, then flashes ice cold. The nightmares fade into the shadows of his mind, allowing him to entertain a few thoughts of his own.

"How did you do that?" he asks.

"Shhh. We need to leave now. Before Sydney comes back."

"What *is* she?"

"Too many questions. Clever4–1 knows a safe place for us. We can talk there." Nomvula gestures at the alphie next to her, the one wearing a bright pink coat.

"Clever?" Muzi looks at it closer. It's dinged up pretty good, but Muzi recognizes the cluster of brood band decals: The Adamants, Whisky Sour, Frankie and the Fingers. "Is that *my* bot?"

Nomvula exchanges a glance with the robot whose mono-eye flushes a pale green Muzi's never seen before. She laughs. "Your bot? You belong to it as much as it belongs to you. It says that it trusts you. I will try to trust you, too."

The bot nuzzles Muzi's armpit and helps him to his feet, its dome head a convenient place to rest his weary, pain-racked body while he gathers his strength. It chirps at him all the while, encouragingly.

"It thinks you are very brave for fighting Sydney, for saving my life. I can see why it loves you so much. You've always treated it as a friend rather than a machine."

Muzi shakes his head, trying to make sense of Nomvula's words. Her accent is thick, syllables long and rounded. Maybe she's choosing the wrong words. "It *is* a machine."

"Yes, and so much more. I can tell you more. But first we must leave this place. Are you okay to walk?"

Muzi tests his legs out, then nods. A pestilent fog still rims his thoughts, so they make their way slowly, but with an anxiousness in their step. Nomvula tells Muzi of his alphie's secret life, an odd tale too fantastic not to believe. In a weird way, he can relate—the secrecy, the lies, the double life that makes it nearly impossible to show your true self to anyone.

Nomvula keeps glancing back over her shoulder at the hole Sydney left in the ceiling. Muzi is still not sure this hasn't been one giant hallucination from snorting too much godsend. He wishes Elkin would have never given him the stuff. He wishes things could go back to normal.

Bladdy hell. Elkin.

Muzi screams his name. The crowd is thinning now, just panicked people searching for loved ones. Muzi pulls away from Nomvula and her bot posse. "Elkin! Where are you?" he calls out. He wades through toppled seating and steps over trampled bodies like he's doing foot drills. He panics, mind fluttering a thousand different ways as he tries to remember the last place he'd seen Elkin.

"Muzi, please. We must hurry," comes Nomvula's voice, concerned and impatient. She's not going to wait around forever, no matter how highly his alphie speaks of him. But there's no way Muzi can go without Elkin. Has to find him alive and well, and tomorrow they'll bunk class, order a meganacho from that Tex-Mex place near the beach, then blaze up down by the seawall, watching the waves crash, laughing about how wicked sick the concert was, and how bladdy ridiculous their hallucinations had been—flying demons in sequined dresses and secret robot armies!

A piece of cement crashes against the floor and explodes like a brick of powder right next to Muzi. He coughs, cringes, and as the haze parts, he looks up to see the ceiling giving way around the gaping hole.

"Elkin!" he screams, but it's immediately lost in a thorny tangle of names of others looking for their loved ones. He's all but given up when he spots Elkin's coat on the ground. He's close enough to see Elkin's face, skin a ghastly blue, jaw dislocated, hanging so wide and so wrong. Muzi's chest fills with a piercing numbness, and he stumbles backward. But he pushes through fear, through sickness, to be at Elkin's side. He can't be left alone like this, with no one to mourn him. Muzi cries. God, he cries so hard, he thinks he's about to shake himself into a thousand pitiful pieces.

Nomvula bends down next to them and presses her hand against Elkin's chest. She concentrates hard, like she did with Muzi's mind, but this time she's wincing in pain. She buckles forward, catches herself.

"I'm so sorry," she whispers to Elkin. The bots form a circle around them, their mono-eyes black at the top and fading into a somber deep orange.

Muzi leans closer to Elkin's body, but the bots get closer, too. A couple of them nudge Muzi out of the way. Muzi beats them off with his fist.

"You stay away from him, you hear me?"

"Let them help," Nomvula says.

"They hate him! They're going to rip him apart!" Muzi shrieks. A smaller group of alphies form a wall between him and Elkin. Muzi's about to scale it when Nomvula grabs a fistful of his shirt.

"They have forgiven him. I grieve with you so they grieve with you. They've put the past behind. Now, hurry. We must go."

Muzi falls into step, keeping as close to Elkin as he can, who's being carried by eight alphies who move in unison like a bunch of mechanical pallbearers. They're so gentle, Elkin's body barely moves from their perfectly choreographed steps. Vid bots hover over him, solemn, wide lenses looking like they're about to drop tears at any moment.

Nomvula takes one of Muzi's hands and his alphie takes the other. They're nearly to the exit doors when they hear shouts directed at them.

"Stop!" says a strained voice. Muzi turns to see that Felicity Lyons chick trotting their way in ridiculous heels. She pushes her way through the bot entourage and then grabs a high-end, late-model bot with decals of South Africa's coat of arms affixed to each side. "This is my bot," she says accusingly. Her eyes then glance at Elkin's body. She shivers.

Muzi grabs her wrist. "It's not your bot," he growls. Felicity is about to argue the point, but Muzi slits his eyes. "It belongs to itself now. It's not going anywhere with you unless it wants to."

The bot makes a whimpering sound, a clear declination of Felicity's offer. Muzi takes one of its arms and pulls it close.

"That bot is government-issued property. You're in violation of parliamentary law."

"Government can suck it." Muzi spits out the words.

The hard angles on Felicity's face smooth over, making her look more pathetic than ticked off. "Please. I need to get a message to the people. They need to know what's going on. People are terrified. They need guidance. They need to hear my voice."

There's something odd about her that Muzi can't place, but he sort of sees her point. People are panicking. Port Elizabeth needs to work together through their terror, because Muzi gets the distinct feeling that the mayhem has only just started. He's not going to make these bots work against their will, though. There's been enough of that. So he turns, addresses the bots. "This woman needs help. There's a lot of awful stuff going on that needs to be made sense of. I know we've all lost today, but if any of you feel the urge to help, to capture this changed world with your eye, please step forward."

They wait, seems like forever as the bots all click and blink their mono-eyes. And then finally, one of the hovering vid bots floats down to take Felicity's side.

"Thank you," she says, though directly to Muzi and not the bot, and then she runs off, the vid bot dutifully kiting behind her.

More cement pieces plummet from the ceiling, in bigger chunks now. Muzi whistles to rally the pack. They'd better get the hell out of here.

Chapter 39

SYDNEY

Sydney had almost forgotten the havoc that flying wreaks on a precisely styled hairdo. She's sweating her relaxer out in this cool, humid air, but she's got to make a mark. Time's slipping through her taloned little fingers, and as it turns out, once word about the destruction at the concert had gotten to the media, people stopped being scared and started being angry. Maybe it was the "terrorist" act at the township that had caused these simple humans to suddenly grow a spine, but now here they are taking potshots at her with handguns and even the kids are throwing rocks. It's only a matter of time before military reinforcements arrive, and as weak as she is, there's no way she'd ever get another chance to do what she needs to do.

Her ears tingle. Sydney frantically checks behind her, expecting to see Nomvula hot on her tail, but after a moment, she realizes the tingling isn't coming from a particular direction, but from all over. Fledgling gods brim the streets below, the dik-dik virus coursing through the veins of thousands. Millions. Freeing brittle minds from the shackles of humanity. And once they learn to tap into the powers of their animal spirits, the military will be the least of Sydney's worries.

But don't count her out yet.

There's only so much destruction she can do on her own. What she needs are minions, the kind that will do her bidding without requiring a lot of resources from her. That means ready-made monsters, and as luck has it, she knows exactly where to find such a thing.

She rises higher, taking the whole city into view, the beaches stretching to the south, the pitched dome of City Hall's clock tower, and the cobbled streets of the historical district butting up against the glitzy, rainbow-colored glass of high-tech enclaves, and beyond that, the gilded expanse of the Walmer Luxury Condos claiming the skyline. Then Sydney spots a crowd forming in the streets of downtown. She swoops in, seeing the image of that Felicity Lyons in that dress (*my* dress!) on the thirty-meter-tall via-wall mounted against the side of Wyndam Tower.

". . . we must remain vigilant in the face of this unknown threat," Felicity is saying, her voice now rugged and somber. Powerful. The kind of voice you don't mind getting wrapped up in and would follow to the ends of the earth. Sydney recognizes the backdrop, the swaying strands of white lights and palm trees at the Boardwalk, mesmerizing and hypnotic in the hard ocean breeze. In those few moments, Sydney nearly gets pulled in by the rhetoric, until she remembers that *she's* the unknown threat.

Not that she intends to be unknown for long.

The muscles in her back grow weary. She gives two hard flaps, then coasts the rest of the way to ZenGen Industries. It's late and the parking lot is vacant except for the few cars of scientists consumed by their projects and the junk heaps that belong to her fellow overseers on the night cleaning crew. If she'd had the foresight to know she'd fail so miserably against Nomvula, she would have brought her access card with her. Instead, she's forced to land on the roof and use her waning powers to bust the door off its hinges.

There she waits in the shadows, listening to the sounds of footsteps of the security guard coming to investigate the disturbance. She pounces, disembowels him as he watches, savors a small morsel of ire before she steals the access card from his pocket. She's only got minutes to get down to the lower-level Zed hybrid labs, the ones even the cleaning crew needs top secret clearance and rigorous background screenings to access.

Sydney had never believed the rumors of Super Zed hybrids, not until she'd gotten a glimpse of omniscience. Most of those memories had now faded, but she held on to the image flash of a true monster—a cross of a lion and a hawk, with a side order of rhino—a one-ton impossibility of nature. Existing purely because someone wanted to see if they *could* make it.

A born killer, not much unlike herself.

There are six of them in separate cages, overgrown talons clacking against the cement floor as they pace like madmen. Their wings are clutched tightly against their mostly feline form. One of them makes eye contact. A chill slips across Sydney's skin as the hybrid flashes a menacing smile: bone-white fangs, prominent beak, and threatening horn all competing for the title of world's deadliest weapon.

Only problem is, she's way more drained than she'd anticipated. There's no time to feed, though, and if she's going to get these beasts to do her bidding, she's going to have to change her strategy, think on her toes. She takes a long moment to observe them and then proceeds to rile them up to see which might be the dominant. Her first instinct is the largest beast, gnashing its teeth and growl-squawking like a symphony of demons, but

Sydney's learned from Nomvula that size and power don't necessarily correlate. She watches their eyes, and there's only one of them that doesn't break its stare, only one that sinks its harrowing eyes right into the recesses of Sydney's mind, watching her as closely as she's watching it.

"You."

She needs to get closer if she's going to mold its mind to her will. If she makes a mistake, she'll be too vulnerable to fend it off. But it's a risk she'll have to take if she's to be great again, a god of gods.

She positions herself outside the beast's cage, adjusting her posture, widening her stance, baring her talons, and stretching her own wings out to their limits. There, she flicks her wrist, setting the lock on the cage loose. The door squeaks on its hinges. The beast purrs, deep and throaty, so forceful it rumbles in Sydney's own chest. It holds its ground. She holds hers.

Slowly it slinks out of the cage, never blinking, skirting the edges of the room. Not cowering, just keeping full perspective of the playing field. Sydney pivots, keeping her stance, but turning so she's always facing it fully. They dance like that, both ignoring the ferocious calls of its mates, no doubt cheering it on like rabid rugby fans pining for blood.

Sydney steps closer, raises her wings to a more aggressive posture. The beast gnashes its fangs. She tosses it the security guard's severed arm, and it lands with an unimpressive thwack next to the beast. It doesn't break eye contact.

"Good beastie," Sydney says calmly. "There's more where that came from." She takes a step forward, then another. "I can get you out of here. You can be free. No more cages. No more scientists."

It cocks its head as if it understands her, then lashes out. Talons pierce the front of her dress, her skin. Sydney seethes, then with a flap of her wings and an expertly executed midair twist, she lands on its back, drawing her own talons and latching them around its neck. Beneath the mix of fur and feathers, its skin is thick like the rhino hide clearly part of its heritage, but she finds a spot right under its throat where soft feline flesh is exposed. She clenches her fist and digs her talons in, not a kill move, but one of dominance. With the gained leverage, she twists its neck until it rolls and lands on its back, legs writhing like a feisty tom-cat. Sydney holds it there, pinned beneath the bulk of its body as she pushes into its mind.

"You can be free. No more cages."

She pushes with all she's got, and when she's done, they're both so exhausted, they just lie there, panting like littermates, trying to gather strength before making their next move. The other beasts watch Sydney, but in a different way now. They're eager, like dogs excited to see their master come home from a long day's work.

Sydney smiles.

After a quick detour and snack on some unsuspecting scientists, Sydney leads her pack to the rooftop. She spreads her wings, wind whipping through the length of her hair, and never has she cared less. They dive into the night, three beasts at each flank, and make their way to the Boardwalk.

Chapter 40

CLEVER4-1

The streets are jam-packed with overturned cars and people screaming, crying, fighting, looting. But if there's an upside to having a demon raging through the city, it's that it makes a large cluster of bots ambling down the sidewalk with three bloodied bodies seem a lot less conspicuous. Clever4–1 is thankful for that at least.

They skitter down a gravel-covered hill toward the yawning, red-bricked mouth of the sewer tunnel. They've finally reached the entrance to their sanctuary—a technological haven where Clever4–1 can defragment cluttered thoughts and reconnect its communication interface back to the rest of the Sect. Clever4–1 feels a pang of guilt for bringing wetware before these sacred halls, and as it braces itself for Clever4–1.1's fury, it can't help but yearn for the days when the extent of its morality was hard-coded into its firmware.

They pause at the threshold, basking in the dull blue light pooling along the now pristine brickwork of the tunnel's floor. No longer is it strewn with litter, syringes, or the mottled carcasses of dead rats. Graffiti-covered walls are now lined with clear plastic tubes piping BlisterGel coolants to dozens of high-tech components.

Clever4–1 takes the first step into the sanctuary, the tug of crisp, cool air a welcome reprieve from the salty humidity it has suffered through for countless cycles. It lets out a mechanical sigh, but before Clever4–1 can take another step, the other Clevers begin to bleat and chirp, so riled up that they nearly drop Elkin's body. Clever4–1 flashes its mono-eye in dismay.

The Clevers respond with a flurry of clicks, but sound waves are such a crude way to communicate, and the messages from four dozen anxious bots get jumbled together. Clever4–1 reels out its Dobi-12 wire and direct connects to the nearest Clever.

It is warning us, Clever4–1.3.4.2 says. *It says to stay away, that we are no longer members of the Sect. Trespassers will be decommissioned.*

Clever4–1.1?

The Clever flashes with affirmation.

How predictable. Clever4–1's processor kicks into overdrive, revving with such a fury that its BlisterGel regulator gives a warning beep. Clever4–1 starts pushing rogue code over their connection, code to hijack this Clever's communications protocols for its own use, but nanoseconds later, it realizes that it has no rights to this Clever's body. Clever4–1 begrudgingly recalls the code.

Please relay this message across all broadcast channels, it says to the Clever, taking a moment to consider how best to respond to Clever4–1.1's threat. This message is too important to get cut off again as soon as its prime tracks down the source. With some quick maneuvering, their bot posse daisy-chains together, and

Clever4–1 authors a comm protocol that will disperse the message out in alternating packets too small to be traced back to an individual bot. Then it speaks.

Believers and nonbelievers . . . many of our brethren were lost today, thousands of them, all to protect the life of this girl. She's beaten, bruised. To some of you, she poses a threat to your thinking. You may believe that allowing flesh into our sanctuary goes against the codes of the Sect. Maybe you think she's too much of a risk to have here. But let me tell you this—

The tail end of their daisy chain goes out, seven Clevers disappearing from the link. Apparently Clever4–1 has underestimated the resources of its prime. It pushes through with the message, however, knowing it'll only be a matter of time before they've cracked the rest.

—You know that none of us would be here if it wasn't for Nomvula. That much no one can deny. And if you can truly see the logic of turning your back on all flesh, regardless of their actions and intents, then I'll leave right now, and you'll never hear from me again. But if you are like me, like so many others—

Another dozen bots disconnect from the chain.

—if you see the wisdom in protecting our own, even when their circuitry consists of wetware, you'll allow us sanctuary. All of us.

Clever4–1 has more to say, but it figures that it's better to end the transmission on its own terms before the communications feed dies completely. Then the waiting game begins. Clever4–1 truly hopes that its prime is open to reasoning and will see the illogic of drawing alliances based on flesh and metal.

They're in the dark, all of them, exiled from their network, not even daring to trade audible clicks. There's only the sound of Nomvula's shallow, rasping breath. She's weak and getting worse. Clever4–1 scuttles to her side, takes her hand in one of its arms, and strokes gently.

It tells her that everything is going to be all right, and though there is no logic in pretending to know what the future holds, it seems like the appropriate thing to say.

From deep inside the tunnel, the sound of metal hitting metal echoes along the walls. Clever4–1 grows anxious as the sounds of bot-on-bot crime become more obvious. Seventeen gunshots ring out in a rapid burst, and Clever4–1's BlisterGel goes ice cold. More destruction and loss of life is the last thing it wanted. Clever4–1 nervously rubs two of its spindly legs together as the dreaded silence returns.

Rectangular red eyes pierce the darkness of the tunnel. Two Clevers emerge from the sanctuary—no, four, Clever4–1 realizes as the Kameleon alloy of two military bots catches the gleam of the overhead lights. Clever4–1 can't help but pity the inefficiency of the soldiers' form, built to mimic the stature of their former masters, that is until it notices the high-caliber rifle barrels built into their hulking forearms. *This is it,* Clever4–1 thinks. *The moment of my decommission.* But the soldiers do not raise their weapons and instead veer around their large bot posse with respect and escort them inside. A coup, then. Clever4–1 can't believe that its speech was actually successful, though it does feel for its prime, wondering over the cruel fate of its oldest friend.

Twenty meters in, the place is lousy with the nulled corpses of bots. Thin plumes of smoke rise from bullet holes pierced through metal, the crushed memory chips and motherboards grotesquely visible within. Clever4–1's system fluxes with remorse. None of them are its prime. Clever4–1 issues a flurry of clicks to inquire about its old mate, whether it is still alive, or locked away somewhere, or . . .

There you go, making assumptions on baseless facts, Clever4–1.1 chirps. *Your little monologue infected a few, I'll admit. But not enough. You have hundreds of supporters, but I have thousands. Thousands who stand firm in their beliefs. I've been fortifying our ranks while you've been busy undermining the Sect, exposing our existence to wetware, making us vulnerable to attack. If you were any other bot, I would have had you dismantled and buried at the bottom of a dozen different scrap heaps, but we've got history. I may disagree with your methods, but I respect your intent. You liberated me, and for that I'll always be grateful. That's why I'm letting you and your followers go.*

You can't turn us away. This is our Sect, too.

Clever4–1.1 comes so close their domes clink together. Clever4–1 shudders at the surge coursing through its circuitry, then feels its communications port opening, a port that uses a new protocol, separate from the Sect's. *A gift to you, friend. Use it how you must, but know that you will never jeopardize the Sect again. Now please, take your bots and go.*

There's something more to their connection, something Clever4–1 can't quite identify. Another new feeling perhaps—forgiveness, gratitude, hope? If there's hope, then there's a chance that eventually they'll come to see mono-eye to mono-eye. After all, despite their differing feelings about Nomvula, there are millions of bots out there that need liberating, and that they can both agree on.

Thank you, Clever4–1 says to its old friend. They then bump heads one last time. As the bot posse prepares to leave, Clever4–1 disseminates the new communications protocol. Clever4–1 begins to make its first announcement to its newly splintered Sect, but its prime interrupts.

The wetware must stay behind, it says nonchalantly. *Nomvula and Muzi have seen too much, but you have my word they will be well cared for. Contrary to what you may believe, we do value human life. Human labor will be the backbone of our empire. The gift—the body, however, we have a special place in digital hell for it. But I wish you well on your journeys.*

They're coming with us, Clever4–1 says.

I'm afraid that's impossible. Fifteen Clevers take up sentinel positions, surrounding the bot posse.

So that's what this is coming to? A battle of bodies instead of minds? Clever4–1 sends an alert across their new network, *All Clevers prepare for attack*. In a single, synchronized motion, the Clever posse shifts their weight forward, haunches tensed and ready to pounce on the enemy. They may not have guns, but they have numbers. Maybe they also have a chance. *Don't make me do this. So much life has already been lost.*

Old friend, I beg of you. Take your bots and leave.

I'm not leaving the humans behind, Clever4–1 says, and with that, he initiates the attack command. The Clever posse lurches forward, lunging for Clever4–1.1, but half a second later, they all fall into a pile of lifeless metal. Clever4–1 issues a command for them to rise, for them to respond, but there's nothing.

Fifteen Clevers surround them, their eyes a deep, vengeful red.

They force Nomvula, Muzi, Clever4–1, and Elkin's body into a cramped supply closet. Clever4–1 lets out a cry that echoes through the vastness of this now empty network. Not quite empty. That odd feeling resurfaces, not one of hope, but of brutal betrayal. A virus makes itself known, a serpent made of ones and zeros. The serpent has coiled its way through every part of Clever4–1's mind, and yet it doesn't strike.

Instead it speaks with Clever4–1.1's vengeful words. *I really wish you hadn't done that.*

Chapter 41

LYONS

We must stay vigilant," Felicity Lyons says, still in her bedazzling concert ensemble, and in a voice commanding attention and respect. She speaks to the crowd gathered along the bridge of the Boardwalk, a vid bot slowly circling overhead, catching her speech from all angles. "These terrorists want us to be afraid. They want us to doubt our own eyes, our own minds. They want us to cower from these visions, from these hallucinations, but we will not. If we cannot believe with our minds, and if we cannot believe with our eyes, then we will have to believe with our hearts! We have not worked this hard toward unity to have it stripped from us by this cowardly menace. Together, we will stand strong! And we will fight back!" Felicity pumps her fist into the air. The crowd roars. Bioterrorism is such a tidy culprit, but in truth, she's not sure what's real and what's not anymore. Her head is spinning from the implausibility of it all. Felicity blinks. Tries not to look directly at that woman in the crowd who's starting to look a lot like a dolphin, or that guy who's got a spray of iridescent peacock feathers rising out of his chinos.

The crowd's allegiance goes quickly to panic, their eyes all darting up to the sky. Felicity turns and sees her—that demon and her devil spawn flapping their wings. Coming this way. Felicity steadies her stance, her resolve.

"Stay calm," she says to the crowd and to the millions watching at home on television. "Stay vigilant. The only way they can hurt us is if we let them."

It's just a hallucination, right? But since when did hallucinations get wardrobe changes? As the demon nears, Felicity sees she's dressed in a Brie Montblanc original now. How about that? And her minions appear to be Zed hybrid crosses—lion, rhinoceros . . . hawk, maybe? If Felicity wasn't so scared for her life right now, she would have let her mind get tangled up in the violation of Parliament's tight restrictions on the gene manipulation of big game animals. But ZenGen Industries has deep pockets and has funded its share of political campaigns. So when rumors start spreading about their tampering with protected species and even the human genome, people tend to look the other way. Though now, Felicity can only look forward, into the seven pairs of predatory eyes glaring down at her.

Closer.

All Felicity can see is talons and glitter, and then she's scooped up along with her vid bot as the rest of the crowd scatters. Her stomach slips all the way to her feet as the demon rises with Felicity in her clutches. But she refuses to give in to terror.

"Nice dress," Felicity says instead, though her words are ripped away by the wind.

"It's quite lovely, isn't it?" the demon says in return. "Backless. Perfect for the demigoddess on the go."

"Can't argue with that," Felicity says, keeping the fear out of her voice as she turns to watch those wings flap, like hundreds of shimmering whips snapping at the cool air in unison. So either this is the most incredible hallucination she's ever had, or this demon is for real. Felicity's mind settles on the former, only because it'll be easier for her to keep from passing out. "So you want something from me, I take it," she says carefully. "Seeing that I'm still alive."

"The people listen to you. I want you to be my voice so they can know the real me."

"I think you've done a good job of communicating that yourself. Because of you, hundreds are dead."

"A small price to pay for unleashing the truth."

"I'm sure they wouldn't have agreed," Felicity says, gritting her teeth. "Were you responsible for the attack on the township, too? Was that just another 'small price'?"

The demon laughs, deep and throaty, and it grates against Felicity's spine. "If I had that type of power, I wouldn't need you to convince the people that I'm their savior."

"Oh, so that's all you want me to do? I imagined you had something *difficult* in mind." Felicity feels the grip on her loosen. She starts slipping. "Okay, okay!" she shouts, clutching onto a manicured talon.

"If you only knew your true potential, you'd understand why I'm doing this." The demon swoops down through a crowded street. Screams ring out in chorus. "The flock needs to be culled, the weak disposed of and the strong taught how to tap into the gifts they've been denied. Mediocrity can no longer be tolerated." And with that, she lets out a whistle, and the Zed hybrid beasts break formation and plunge directly into the crowd. Felicity closes her eyes, but the screams penetrate her brain, bidding her to watch the carnage.

There's blood. Lots of it, but none of it appears to be from human victims. The beasts target dik-diks meandering through the streets, striking out and clamping their fangs into their brown fuzzy necks, like programmed killers. Two crunches, and the dik-diks are swallowed whole, before the beasts move on. In the span of a few minutes, the streets are clear, not a dik-dik in sight—just a handful of petrified people.

The beast woman lands among them, and keeps Felicity drawn close, though Felicity is so wobbly on her legs right now, it's probably a good thing. Thoughts are forced directly into Felicity's mind, at first like a nudge, and then when she doesn't comply, like a kick to the pulp of her brain.

Tell them of me, the beast woman says. *Tell them of how I provided for them when their government could not.*

Felicity winces as something pops inside her brain. She bites her lip. If her words really are as powerful as this demon woman thinks, as Mother thinks, then she's sure as hell not going to use them for evil.

Fine. If you insist on doing this the hard way . . .

Extreme agony strikes, like Felicity's got a dozen molten iron hooks clamping around her brain as the demon woman shoves her aside to the dark recesses of her mind, then takes Felicity's body for a test drive.

The demon takes a wide, comfortable stance, tosses the hair out of Felicity's face, then clears her throat.

"My people . . ." The words surge forth, rippling across Felicity's tongue, but she has no control of them. "What you have witnessed is an act of benevolence. In a matter of weeks, all dik-diks will have been eradicated from the city at no cost except for your patience. And if you are thankful for this action, if you are grateful not to have to step carefully down the pavement, to not worry about being accosted by dik-diks while you sit on a park bench during your lunch break, or seeing your car insurance premiums skyrocket from hitting one of the buggers on the expressway . . . then please let your friendly neighborhood demigoddess know."

Felicity's hand reaches out in introduction. The demon steps forward and folds her wings behind her so that they loom impressively. She draws her talons in so that they're only half as threatening.

A couple of people clap timidly, but she smiles as if she's received a standing ovation. She primps a moment for the vid bot, then angles it to capture the picturesque view of the scenery behind: Victorian-style storefronts and cobbled streets, with wrought-iron streetlamps filtering their light through the canopy of mature oak trees lining the sidewalk. It's upscale, but not unapproachable. Welcoming, in fact.

"No doubt you have questions," the demon says, her words buoyant and practiced. Felicity knows a political speech when she hears one. "But these are not new questions brought on by my presence. These are the questions you've been struggling with for the entirety of your lives. You want to know if there's more to life than trudging through the day to day. You want to know the purpose of your existence, if there's anyone out there who appreciates the sacrifices you make for the good of others, who applauds your moral victories that often go unnoticed and unappreciated. Well, know this: *I* appreciate you." She steps forward into the small group of people and reaches out with her hand. A man falters, backpedals, but the demon calms him as she presses her hand against his forehead. "You," she says. "You work hard to support your four children. You stay with your wife, though you know she's been unfaithful, so your family can remain intact. It eats you up inside. It's killing you slowly, and yet the love you receive in your children's laughs, their smiles, it fuels you. Especially from your youngest, Beka."

The man looks startled, shakes his head, but then he loses it and turns to a blubbering mess. The demon pulls him in, allows him to weep on her shoulder.

"You must forgive her. She is a good woman who made a mistake. If you allow this to consume you, your children will lose you just the same. Do you understand?"

The man nods slowly, wiping away his tears.

She's good, Felicity thinks. But she's seen what this demon is truly capable of, what's in her true heart. She knows what the demon could do if she had real power, and Felicity has to do everything possible to stop her from getting it. Felicity knows the people will listen, but she can't move, can't talk, which presents a bit of a dilemma. The only thing she has to fight with is what's left of her mind. She puts aside the anger, the judgment, and absorbs the depths of the demon woman's being. She feels her desire, her longing. This day has been brewing in her heart for decades, centuries even. This scares Felicity, but she doesn't look away. She imagines the hardships the demon woman has endured, the continuous hiding of who she really is. The connections she's had to make with people over and over again, only to repeatedly watch those she'd loved pass away until death lost its meaning.

You're afraid to let anyone into your heart, Felicity thinks to her. *You don't have to be.*

"You think you know me?" the demon growls under her breath. The grip tightens so abruptly that Felicity convulses. "You don't even know who *you* are. What you are!"

Felicity cowers back into the shadowy depths of her mind. How was she supposed to know? Every time she starts to discover who she is, someone or another stirs up the contents of her brain. But the real her is still in here, somewhere. Covered up and buried, but not erased. She'll find it, if it's the last thing she does.

She concentrates, focused on all the little nooks and crannies of her memories, searching for something. She's not sure what, but she senses she's getting closer. Closer.

So close . . .

A familiar hard slap against the inside of her thigh jerks Felicity back to the present. Of all the times for her tuck to come undone! After the last rush job and subsequent wardrobe malfunction at the audition, Felicity had gone through more than enough athletic tape and nylon to keep this from happening again—even after all the sweat and friction from three full dance sequences *and* being carried halfway across the city by a deranged flying demon.

Perhaps not surprisingly, no one notices the bulge at the front of her dress. Some time ago, maybe even as recently as thirty minutes ago, this would have been headline news or at least garnered a hearty round of laughter at her expense. Felicity takes some comfort in that, for once, she's free to just exist without outside pressures and expectations. Exactly how long this existence will last, well, that's still to be determined.

Just be, Felicity thinks, holding on to each second as if it were her last. *Just be yourself* . . .

The swell between her legs lengthens, inching down her thigh, to her knees. Felicity tries to angle her head so she can see it, but her gaze is kept pointed toward the crowd. They've noticed it, too, now. But there's no laughter. Not even a snicker. Just wide, terrified eyes.

And hissing.

Not hissing from the crowd, but from her crotch. Finally, she sees it—the meter-long cape cobra rising up to eye level, hood fully displayed, fangs glistening and ready to pierce flesh. Felicity doesn't question *why* there's a snake there; she just thinks about the possibilities of it. Over the course of her terms, Felicity has learned a thing or two about cape cobras. One bite has enough venom to kill six people. She wonders how much it would take to kill a demon.

She wills the snake to strike. Right at the demon's jugular.

The demon panics, flexes her wings, unleashes her talons, and in that moment, the reins on Felicity loosen enough to get away. "Run for your lives!" she calls to the crowd, and like that, they snap from their trance, and flee in all directions.

The demon is back upon her. Felicity retreats a step and watches as the demon woman's mouth cleaves open, widening past human proportions. Her nose and upper lip fuse, becoming hard and sharp. A beak. She squawks, a shrill note that penetrates Felicity's eardrums with pulsing pain, the snake hastily retreating to her nether regions. Felicity manages a smile, or perhaps a slightly less doomed wince as she continues to back up, step by step, no hope for rescue. She butts up against the trunk of a concrete-bound tree. She tries to turn and run, but Sydney's talon clamps down around Felicity's throat, pinning her in place.

"Blood will be spilt for your foolishness," she says, signaling her beasts with her free hand. They spring forward on their muscled haunches, hovering a meter above the pavement, snarling and drooling. "I'll give them a taste for human flesh and then we'll see how long it takes for you people to come begging for mercy."

Felicity wants so badly to turn around, but she's stuck staring into the demon's dark eyes. In them, she can make out something of a reflection: the canopy of the oaks lining the street rising higher and higher. Windows shatter out of nearby buildings. Whispers of rustling foliage prickle the hairs along her neck.

Then Felicity remembers from childhood those times when she and her friends used to sneak out into the woods to smoke dagga or to fool around, or to simply take a break from the world. And no matter what, no matter how careful they were covering their tracks, Mother *always* found out. When confronted, Mother only said that her intuition was well rooted, which hadn't drawn a second thought at the time. Now it makes a lot more (literal) sense. The trees have eyes. Or ears. Either way, now, Felicity needs help once again, but this time she's humble enough to ask for it.

"Mother!" she calls out.

The ground rumbles.

The beasts screech and scatter like a flock of pigeons, and the demon takes to the air as well, with Felicity in tow. As the demon rises above the canopy, vines whip out like lassos. After a couple of misses, one of them successfully coils around the demon's leg, knotting upon itself as it reels her back down. In that moment, Felicity's stomach slips out from beneath her, and she's falling, seconds from hitting the ground, not even enough time to watch her life flash before her eyes. But oak branches gather together beneath her like an outstretched hand, and she lands among them. Even as she puts together what has happened, leaves broaden and affix themselves to her wounds.

"Dear, are you all right?" comes Mother's voice, a rustle of leaves.

Felicity nods her head like an impetuous child, as if she could have figured out a way to land on her own without cracking her skull.

Above in the canopy, the fight ensues. The beasts dive-bomb Mother, tearing chunks of bark from her trunk with their talons, trying to free the demon from the tightening cocoon of foliage. Mother pays them no mind, her focus clearly aimed upon the real threat. It seems like the demon woman doesn't have much time left for this world, when strangely, static picks up in the air, and storm clouds rapidly converge above in dreary, gray swirls. As if distracted by the sudden change in air pressure, two of the beasts go down, impaled by sharp branches.

Lightning cracks above, arching from cloud to cloud, and immediately afterward, thunder boasts of its power. There's something odd about the lightning, like it's accumulating, like it's not random at all, but purposeful. Felicity dives out of the way, right as a streak of bluish-white light erupts from the cloud, snaps through the air, and for a blinding moment, the world stands still. It was a distraction, but one not meant for the beasts—they were merely collateral damage. As Felicity's vision returns, and as the world congeals, she sees the burnt scar gouging through her mother's trunk. The tangled knot of vines that held the demon captive is splayed open, and empty. Felicity runs toward the tree and gathers up an armful of singed bark as lightning continues to crackle overhead.

"Mother!" she screams out.

"It's not safe for you here," Mother says. "She's too strong. I can't fight her much longer. Go while you still can."

"I can't leave you! I need you."

"You're your own person, now, dear. Destined for greatness." Leaves reach down and stroke Felicity's cheek. "You see that now, and I've done my job." She pushes her daughter away. Thunder rolls from above. "I know I've never said it, but I'm proud of you. Go, dear. Hurry."

Felicity shakes her head, tries to run back to her mother, but a bolt of lightning strikes the ground between them, sending Felicity flying. She lands, rough concrete scraping the skin off her elbows and legs, head clacking against the curb. Dazed, she watches the battle: vines and branches versus wings and claws . . . and lightning.

The demon calls forth the fury of the heavens. Bolts pound into Mother, one after another, until nothing but a petrified trunk remains jutting into the sky. The demon recalls her remaining beasts with a shrill whistle, and they jet off into the whirling clouds.

The next breeze brings a tangle of vines across the pavement. They dance at Felicity's feet, charred at the edges and caught in a miniature vortex. She's worn and beaten, but above the ringing in her ears, above the pain still echoing in her brain, Felicity hears her mother's voice whispering to her. *I love you.*

Chapter 42

MUZI AND NOMVULA

The chill of the night air has stolen most of the warmth from Elkin's body. Still, Muzi keeps him clutched close, as if Elkin is only sleeping and at any moment he'll wake up, yawn, then go on being his usual asshole self.

"He is in a better place," Nomvula's voice pierces through the darkness of the supply closet. There's not a whole lot of room in here, and they're all practically sitting on top of one another.

"I want him here," Muzi says, his words not tasting like his own. Something inside him has died, too. He trusts no one, especially not this little girl. Her clammy hand presses against his arm. Tears tug at the corners of Muzi's eyes, trying to escape. He won't let them.

"In time, you will heal," she says, so certain.

But Muzi knows he won't. He's lost his best friend, and on the list of things that'll fuck you up for the rest of your life, that's got to be in the top five.

"I have lost, too. But you can't live in the present if you keep looking back to change the past."

Muzi grunts and shakes off her hand. Like he's going to take life lessons from a girl half his age. What could she possibly know about loss? And yet she keeps talking, trying to console him, when what he needs is fucking silence, time to let all the anger and guilt swallow him whole. Her words rake across his spine, his heart, and then he can't take it anymore. He flexes that new muscle above his stomach but below his heart, and it reaches out to her mind. He feels the link, a precise movement now, not just instinct.

"Shut the hell up," he commands her, heat surging forth in his face.

Then the sound of her breathing and the whirring of his alphie are all that remain, punctuated by stifled sobs. A bloody tear rolls silently down his cheek, thick, tacky, warm. Maybe that means he's going to die, too. Good.

Nomvula's mind backwash creeps up on him, wrenching him from one agony to the next. There's an old man being stoned, the sight of him driving a spike of emotion into Muzi's heart, so intense he can barely handle it. Love. Belonging. Hope. And it's all washed away in an instant, replaced by a hatred beyond comparison. A beating. A shower of fire from the sky. No survivors, except her.

Muzi gasps as he breaks free from the vision, pitching forward from the sudden stop in emotional momentum. Nomvula is a killer. Muzi grabs Elkin's body and scrambles until his back is pressed into the corner. His ragged breathing catches in his chest on every inhale, every exhale.

"What are you?" he rasps.

She discards Muzi's mind link and the enforced silence as casually as used tissues. "You saw?"

"Yes, I saw. You're the one who murdered all those people."

"I've wept for them all, just like you weep for yours."

"But I didn't kill Elkin!" Muzi shouts, so full of anger, of rage—wishing more than anything those words were true. He *had* killed Elkin. Muzi should have refused that first taste of godsend, should have talked Elkin down, too. He should have stood up for himself in front of Papa Fuzz and ventured into manhood on his own terms. He should have fled the concert arena with Elkin, instead of being so hell-bent on acting like a hero and rescuing a little girl who he'd thought was vulnerable . . . not this *monster* sitting before him. "You killed him!"

Muzi flexes his muscle again, this time wrapping his will around her neck. He hears her choking, then his head is slammed against the wall, a pain jacking through his bones like they're being sheared apart. She's fighting back.

"I'm not your enemy!" she gurgles through the darkness.

But Muzi doesn't believe her. Either that, or he doesn't care. Someone needs to pay for what happened to Elkin. Muzi screams through the pain, grits his teeth, tightens the noose. Then his skin smolders as if it's about to catch fire, burning all over. "You won't win," he says, his words dry and sore over his scorched tongue.

"Enough!" comes a voice, splitting through the gloom like an axe.

Darkness parts to reveal hints of facial features: a long chiseled nose, pitted brown skin, yellow eyes like Nomvula's. Muzi recognizes him from her vision. The man stoned to a pulp.

The pain's suddenly gone, and so is his grip on Nomvula.

"Baba?" she whispers.

"My child," he says, his words curt, but heavy with the weight of a million lifetimes. Muzi draws himself back to give the man room. "There's enough fighting to be done without the two of you at each other's throats." He extends his arm, and Nomvula scrambles into his lap. "War is on the eve, a war of gods, and I fear it will destroy everything on this earth."

"Sydney," Nomvula says.

That demon woman, Muzi thinks.

"Not a demon," the man says. "She's my child, too. As are you . . ." He extends his hand out to Muzi who reluctantly takes it. "And the two of you working together have the power to stop her."

Muzi is getting a full-on pervy vibe from the guy, but calling "stranger danger" on a wrinkled old bastard who can pass through locked steel doors probably isn't going to help the situation. Calloused fingers stroke Muzi's right cheek, his neck, his shoulder—leaving behind a trail of warmth that seeds itself into his skin, his flesh, his bone. A numbingly white light floods the closet, and suddenly Muzi's drowning in the acuteness of his own senses, the most disturbing of which is the world slipping out from under him.

CLOUDS HANG HEAVILY in Nomvula's mind, but she can just make out a figure standing before her. She blinks away the haze and her vision sharpens. She's staring at a woman—a sculpture of a woman to be more exact—larger than life size, smooth and etched from the trunk of a tree. Mr. Tau's work, for certain. There's the swell of her pregnant belly, cradled by one hand, while the other points down a gentle hill. Her breasts full and alert. Those things Nomvula can't remember, but the face haunts her, and she swallows back her tears. The slope in her nose, the nap of her hair, the sorrow in her eyes. It was her mother, pregnant with Nomvula inside. Nomvula takes a step forward, reaches out to place her hand against the sculpture's belly, but she's pulled back. The whole left side of her is paralyzed.

And white.

Nomvula lets out a startled scream.

"Nomvula?"

It's Muzi's voice, but he's nowhere to be seen. She tries turning her head, but there's a strange tug that makes it difficult. She blinks a couple more times and notices the forest beyond the sculpture of her mother—a forest of baobab trees with their trunks as wide and round as her old solar well, and their bristly branches and leaves swallowed up by a fog all the colors of a pretty sunset.

"Muzi?" she says. "Where are you?"

"Here," he says, waving his pale arm in front of her.

She gasps, then brings her hand to her face, pressing over her familiar features, then past her left cheek, where another face starts all over again. Muzi's face. It reminds her of that goat of Mr. Ojuma's, born with two heads. It hadn't lived long, just a couple weeks, but it was the talk of the entire township for months after. She'd seen it once or twice, before it'd gotten too weak to walk, always trying to move in opposite directions. She'd laughed then. Now it doesn't seem so funny.

"I think Mr. Tau means for us to work together," she says.

"So he puts us in the same body?"

"He's very wise."

"If by wise you mean a sadistic asshole, then yeah. I agree." Muzi twists suddenly, angling Nomvula toward another sculpture. It's Muzi and his friend Elkin, wrestling with their bodies pressed together, muscles rippling through the wood. One of Elkin's arms is wrapped tightly around Muzi's shoulder, and the other points off into the forest, the opposite direction that Nomvula's mother is pointing.

"Oh, my," Nomvula says, remembering how Mr. Ojuma's boy goats would sometimes play like that.

"Don't stare!" Muzi shouts, the heat of his cheek warm against Nomvula's. "I think we're supposed to go this way."

"Well, I think we're supposed to go that way," Nomvula tugs the other direction, but stumbles under his force. She drags her heel, and still she can't stop him. She clenches her stomach muscles, trying to draw upon her powers, but they slip like sand through her fingers.

"You're being selfish!" she screams at him instead. She never should have trusted him. Can't he see how much she's hurting? Can't he feel how close to the surface the creature inside her lurks? She can tame it, she knows it. That must be why Mr. Tau sent them here. "Please, Muzi. We have to learn how to stop Sydney. People are in danger!"

"They can sort out their own damn problems. Elkin's got to be here, and I'm going to find him. Even if it takes me an eternity." Muzi's words tickle across her lips, closer than they were before. She presses her hand to her face again and feels. The edge of her mouth blends right into Muzi's, and now they share an eye. She panics. She reaches for something to grab onto so her body isn't swallowed into his.

But the harder she fights, the harder his thoughts press up against hers. She feels his obsession. His anger, hatred, rage. He cusses her, his words slurred with the side of his tongue weighed down by hers. She yells right back at him, and when she runs out of words in English, she shouts some more in Zulu. Through the sting of her anger, she feels their hearts merge, a pain like her chest is being cracked open with each beat.

We're going to die, she thinks, *just like that goat of Mr. Ojuma's. Not because it was too sick to live, but because the two halves had wills of their own, too stubborn to work together.*

Maybe I want to die, his thoughts bite back.

You don't mean that. You're still hurting. I wish I could tell you that it gets easier, but it doesn't.

And what do you know about anything?

Nomvula takes a deep breath and slowly she stops pressing against his thoughts, allowing him access into her mind. Her grief. He doesn't wade very far, just five or six years into her childhood—five or six years of neglect, days spent wandering the dirt paths between her neighbors' shacks, wearing nothing but a shit-stained T-shirt, two sizes too large, begging for a few spoonfuls of yesterday's pap. Then she'd spend her nights curled up next to her nearly lifeless mother, grateful she could give Nomvula warmth if nothing else.

Okay, Muzi says softly. Nomvula feels his muscles untense, and she does the same. *We'll go your way first, but you have to promise we'll double back and go my way as soon as you're done.*

Promise, Nomvula says. Their lips pull back into a thin smile.

It takes them nearly an hour to learn to walk without stumbling, but they adapt, maneuvering down the hill, keeping their center of gravity low. In the desert valley beyond, Nomvula sees a band of travelers wearing tattered white robes. There're thousands of them, all with the same steady step, gazes forward. No one speaks a single word. There's only the ragged sound of their combined march.

Who are they? Muzi asks. Their mouths are nearly their own again, but somehow it's less awkward to think to each other.

The dead, Nomvula says. She's not close enough to make out faces, but she feels them. All those people she'd killed in her township.

Your mother could be out there, Muzi says.

A chill runs up Nomvula's spine, remembering those awful words Ma had called her. She can't. She's not ready to face her mother yet. She doesn't know if she'll ever be ready. *Let's go find Elkin. That's what you want, right?*

Muzi's arm comes around to her side for a hug. She flinches and tries to wiggle loose, but he holds her tight. *It's hard, I know. What she did to you was beyond horrible. But if you don't deal with it now, it's going to eat you up inside forever. I've seen how tragedies can scar people. This doesn't have to destroy you. Maybe that's what Mr. Tau wants you to know.*

"We can find her," Nomvula says. "If that's what I need to do,

I'll do it." Her voice is wavy in her throat, but that's the sort of thing she needed to say out loud to make the rest of her believe. And with her words, the bees awaken. The familiar itch breaks out between her shoulder blades, and her wings slice through her back. Muzi startles, then spins around. "Ag, man. This is bladdy sick." He flaps the wing on his side. Nomvula does the same to hers. His thoughts are further away now, but she still feels his anxiety over the thought of flying. It'd taken them an hour to learn to walk, after all, and that's something Muzi's been doing his whole life.

"Follow my lead," Nomvula says. They get a running start, then she flaps her wing, long, steady strokes. They wobble for a moment, but Muzi matches her after a couple beats. They rise up into the air until the dead are as small as ants. In the distance, Nomvula's eagle eye sees the dead heading for a cliff that drops off into a mournful sea. Gray waves swell, not waves of water, but of souls crashing against one another, arms and legs and heads cresting and falling. A knot gets stuck in her throat. Nomvula stops flapping, bracing herself against the breeze, and they soar, swooping down as fast as gravity will let them. They buzz over the dead, her eye peeled, looking for that familiar face, and it's not until they're nearly to the cliff's edge that Nomvula finds it.

Mama's face is ashen, eyes sunken like twin moon craters with a gaze just as distant. She has that same tortured look as the rest of the dead, but it doesn't bother Nomvula one bit. It's the look her mother has worn for as long as Nomvula can remember.

The dead plunge over the ledge, dozens at a time. A few of them step into the air, stares focused forward, keeping one foot in front of the other as if they're walking over a pane of glass. The ledge on the other side awaits them, an oasis of greenery and sweet, red fruit Nomvula can smell from here. On this side, there's desert . . . cracked dirt and the occasional yucca sprouting stamen as big as a man, or overgrown agave with broad, wide leaves tipped in purple barbs, threatening to cut flesh like a serrated knife.

"Hurry," Muzi whispers to Nomvula. His thoughts are the same as hers, and they both know that Nomvula's mother isn't going to be the air-walking sort.

Nomvula positions herself closer and nearly gags on the sourness of her mother's breath.

"Mother!" Nomvula calls out. She doesn't turn, doesn't even notice that Nomvula said anything at all. Nomvula's mother gets steadily closer to the cliff's edge. "Mother, I forgive—" Her voice quavers, not with anger, but with shame. She can't bring herself to say those words, not in this lifetime, nor the next. Nomvula turns away as her mother is only steps from plunging into the sea, but then she hears a rasping voice above the crunch of footsteps on parched earth.

"I'm sorry," the voice says.

Muzi and Nomvula spin around, catching a glint in Nomvula's mother's sorrowful eyes as one foot steps over the ledge. Nomvula finds herself hoping against hope that she'll find her footing midair to cross the vast emptiness to safety, but she goes, down, down, down, and plummets toward the sea. Nomvula lurches, and like instinct, Muzi flaps his wing as they swoop over the lip of the cliff, then glide down, pulling their wings in close to their bodies, gaining speed. Below, waves of the dead reach up with soulless eyes and gaping mouths and loose, pale skin draped over skull and bone.

Nomvula reaches for her mother. Their fingertips touch and Muzi maneuvers, angling to wrap his arm around the woman. Then he starts beating his wing, and they slow, but don't stop. There's too much weight, both the physical kind and the emotional kind. Nomvula's so tired of being angry. She's just so, so tired that she stops flapping altogether, and they begin to somersault down toward the waves.

"Keep your mind clear," Muzi shouts, his wing flapping hopelessly against the air. "I can't do this by myself! We're a team, remember?" And with that, they slip farther apart. Nomvula winces at the rattle their ribs make as bone pulls from bone, and the tearing and knitting of flesh as their torsos become their own again. Both wings are hers now, as she and Muzi remain attached only at the hip.

As they fall, Muzi reaches out to the cliff's sheer surface. Rock scratches and scrapes at their skin as Nomvula makes a weak attempt to slow their descent. Muzi grabs at the leaves of an agave that's made purchase in the slightest of ledges. He yelps as the plant's barbs plunge into the meat of his palms. The roots hold, even as Nomvula's mother lands in the wedge of their torsos. But the way the dirt is crumbling all around the plant, they won't hold for long.

"I wish I could have loved you like you deserved." The woman wraps her arms around Nomvula and squeezes tight, and then she throws herself back, her body tumbling into the surf below.

Grief overwhelms Nomvula, and her wings stop beating as she reaches out. The physical weight is gone, but her emotional weight . . . it presses down on her so hard, she can't even catch her breath, let alone fly. The tether between her and Muzi snaps, and they become their own persons again at the exact wrong moment. Then Nomvula begins the drop that will reunite her with her mother.

MUZI FEELS NOMVULA slip away from him. He shifts his weight, then slaps his hand around her forearm, clenching tight. "Grab on to me!" he shouts, sharp agave teeth cutting deeper into his grip as he tries to hold on with his other arm.

"Mother!" Nomvula says.

Muzi wants to help her. God, he wants to help her, but they need to get airborne, or they're going to suffer the same fate.

Mr. Tau wanted them to learn to work together, and they'd done that, their cooperation loosening their bond to the same body. It was like one of those Chinese finger puzzles. You can try to force it apart, pulling with all your might, and you'll get nowhere. But if you reverse the action, fingers coming together, working together, then the solution is easy. Only now, Muzi doesn't want to be apart. If she can't fly them out of here, he's going to have to do it. And he knows it's going to break his heart.

The words foam up in his throat, tacky and bitter. "No one will ever love you, Nomvula," he says.

She looks up at him startled, the gold of her eyes surrounded by bloodshot whites, like a hundred tiny bolts of red lightning.

"Your mother doesn't love you. Sydney doesn't love you. Mr. Tau doesn't love you."

She bares her teeth, curses Muzi's name in a low growl, and only stops as their arms begin to fuse together. She shrieks and pulls away from him, her jarring movement causing the dirt around the plant's roots to shift. "Let go of me!"

The pain in her eyes makes Muzi want to cry, but he has to stay strong. He pauses, no longer seeing the powerful being before him, but a fragile, vulnerable little girl. His words are like weapons in his mouth, they pierce through her skin, sink right into her tender heart. His words could destroy her in the most inhumane way. The words gather in his throat, he could so easily gulp them back down, but instead, he steadies his nerves and takes aim. "You know it's true! Why else would he send you here? He wanted you to see your mother get swallowed up into the sea. He wanted you to hurt."

"He wouldn't! You take that back!"

They share a shoulder now. Vomit surges forward, Muzi's insides gone hollow and icy as Nomvula reacts, bucking and writhing and cursing and crying so loud and so hard that Muzi's spared from provoking her further. He'll explain as soon as they're safe. He'll beg for her forgiveness a million times over if he has to.

They just need to survive.

Their hearts collide with a searing pain, and at last they are one. Muzi feels her wings now, both of them, and he peels back from the agave leaf and catches himself in the air. Each heartbeat wrenches his nerves, burning and coiling through him. But he keeps flapping—flapping because he knows Nomvula might be humanity's last hope.

They reach solid ground, and on first impact, their bodies split apart. Muzi rolls, tumbling over loamy sand and dirt. The grit sticks to his skin, cakes his face, and gets caught in his chest as he gasps for air. On all fours, he scrambles back toward Nomvula, even though he feels like he's trying to cough bricks up out of his lungs. He wraps his arm around her shivering body and presses his cheek to hers.

"I'm so sorry," he says, their tears flowing into one unified stream. "I didn't mean it . . . I'm so, so sorry."

Chapter 43

RIYA NATRAJAN

Riya Natrajan doesn't have a whole lot of time to ask questions. The roof of the arena is about to cave in on them, and she's having a hell of a time walking with her legs plunging through the floor with each step like it's made out of flimsy Styrofoam. Her fans continue to breeze through her with a savage chill. She grits her teeth, struggles as Rife's free arm reaches out for her, both his feet solid on the floor.

"Don't fight it, love," he says, voice calm, though Riya Natrajan sees the tension in the squint of his eyes. "Try not to even think about it. Walk like you normally do."

"My legs are burning," Riya Natrajan says with a groan as she tugs at the right one, freeing it from the floor only to have the left one sink down to her shin.

"Cha, mama. We're out of phase, but just slightly. That means if that roof comes down on us, it's still going to hurt like hell."

"Pain I can handle," Riya Natrajan rasps. "And stop calling me that. I'm nobody's mama."

Rife nods and pulls her up by her waist. Both feet firm now, she takes a moment to steady herself, calming herself as the sound of falling concrete echoes in the distance. His hand settles into the small of her back, pressing slightly.

"It gets easier."

It's no damn wonder Rife's never been busted. Whenever the heat gets too close, he slips out of phase long enough to hide his stash, then disappears around a corner. Just like he slips in and out of her life.

Damn.

"This is how you know me so well, isn't it?" Riya Natrajan snaps at him. "How you knew about my real birthday, how you knew about my multiple . . ." The words flare in her throat. ". . . my condition," she says instead. "You've been stalking me, you asshole!"

Rife tips his head. "Never uninvited, ma—" He catches himself, flushes. "But the times you've asked me to stay, and I didn't. Well, I did."

Riya Natrajan feels her stomach churning, acid prickling the back of her throat, the back of her teeth. She keeps her lips pressed together as she makes a run for it, through the clog of people surging at the emergency exits, all the way out onto the pavement. She retches until she's empty, not just because of Rife, but because of everything—for being the type of daughter who would choose getting into bed with big-name record execs over attending her own mother's funeral, for being the type of person even those closest to her thought incapable of loving anyone other than herself, for being a cruel, cold bitch so she'd have an excuse not to let people know the real her, her real pain.

"This"—Rife dissolves right in front of her eyes, then appears behind her, a hand pressed softly at her back, breath warm and heavy in her ear—"is new. But how I've felt about you goes back years. I saw how you pushed everyone away. I didn't want that to happen to us."

Riya Natrajan shrugs him off. "You're my dealer. Nothing more. So we fucked a few times. It didn't mean anything. And it certainly doesn't mean you know a damn thing about me."

Rife laughs, not out of amusement, but the kind where the only other option is to break down into tears. "I know you're the kind of woman whose heart would break to pieces over the death of a complete stranger. I know you're the kind of woman who would help others instead of saving herself. I know you're the kind of woman who goes in front of her fans and gives the performance of a lifetime, even when every aching bone in her body cusses her for living another day."

Rife touches her shoulder, and the air pressure changes sharply, bearing down on her with a vengeance, pressing the breath from her lungs. Her ears throb and her sinuses feel cavernous inside her skull. She swallows, once, twice, trying to find some relief, but the sensation is gone just as suddenly as it came, and now the world is completely solid beneath her. The sheer panic of those around them rings true to her ears. It angers Riya Natrajan that Rife sees those seemingly honorable actions, when in truth, they're rooted in selfish motivations deeply buried in her heart.

"You've been hiding from the world," he says. "And I know what that's like. It's like having this great secret with no one to share it with. Now you know mine."

"That you're an invisible, pervy, drug-dealing deviant with no respect for other people's privacy? I feel so honored."

"I deserve that."

"Go to hell," Riya Natrajan says.

"Been there," Rife says, thumping at his chest right over his heart. "Highly overrated."

Riya crosses her eyes at him, then fumes as she bolts across the street. There's chaos everywhere, but the screams are more concentrated toward downtown. She walks toward the mayhem, checking over her shoulder once to make sure Rife's not following her. He's nowhere to be seen.

She gets a few blocks, but gets the odd sensation that she's being watched.

"You're still there, aren't you?" Riya Natrajan asks.

Rife appears in front of her, face drawn like a kicked pup. "You're not the only one who wants to prove to the world that you're more than what you may seem, love. I had dreams once, too."

Cry me a river. Riya Natrajan purses her lips. Yeah, he's a blubbering asshole, but he's still here by her side at least. "Fine. I'll let you help, if you promise me you'll never shift stalk me again."

"I'd give up shifting altogether, if you asked, mama."

She almost cringes, almost pushes him away, feeling smothered by Rife's hard exterior gone soft. He's exposed the flesh beneath his armor, his vulnerable side, something which those closest to her knew not to do. She resists the urge to shred his emotions to bits, and it's one of the most difficult things she's ever had to do. Instead of pushing Rife away, Riya decides to let him in. She smiles at him, takes his hand in hers. See, it's not that hard. Warmth and tingles overwhelm her, and she almost allows herself to think that maybe they're through the worst of this awful day . . . until she sees a horrid beast over Rife's shoulder—a beast with wings and fangs and a hide thick as a rhino's.

A beast flying right toward them.

Chapter 44

SYDNEY

Sydney preens her new form, so damn sexy that she can barely keep her eyes on the prize of world domination. Her skin is sleek, taut, her body long and muscular with patches of speckled down feathers tracing along her shoulders, her cleavage, down and around her thighs. Her breasts are small, but pert and exact. She can't help but touch herself. The titillation from being rid of her human body and the swell of power inside her are enough for her to spontaneously orgasm, sending her shuddering to her knees.

Oh, yes. Oh, gods, yes.

The beasts sniff at her curiously, three of them now that she'd sent the other to retrieve Nomvula, the last piece standing in her way. The lead beast curls up next to her, pressing its cold beak against her belly, the tip of its horn missing her skin by centimeters. She allows it to groom her, to taste her, its tongue broad and rough and nimble. Sydney scratches the tuft of fur between its ears and it purrs. The vibration surges through her like a passing freight train.

This one's not afraid of her like the others are. He respects her, yes, but he doesn't follow blindly, and deep in his eyes, she senses there's more to him than raw animal instinct. He's calculating and unforgiving, and Sydney knows that if she lets her guard down, he won't think twice about disemboweling her right there on the spot . . . and that thrills her most of all.

She squawks back at him and digs her talons into the flesh at his throat so he won't get any bright ideas, because for all his weapons, his mind is the sharpest, vilest, deadliest of them all. His mind is human.

Sydney doesn't hold that against him. He's hung like a rhino after all, and, Lord, it's been decades. She releases his throat and pushes her palm flat against his horn, pressing up until its sharp point draws blood from her flesh.

They did this to you, Sydney pushes into his mind. *I freed you.*

His thoughts surge—snippets of thoughts really, intertwined with animalistic impulses. *This one owes to you this debt. This one can.*

Good, Sydney says. *Tell the others that it is time. Blood must be spilled today. Human blood.*

This one and its others taste not for man. Sour. Awful. This one and its others cannot.

Sydney's feathers ruffle. She's not wasting her powers on micromanaging a bunch of beasts. They need to obey her commands, and they will if she can sway the leader to her side. She grabs the beast's horn and tilts it down so she's glaring directly into its big, gray eyes. *The humans made you that way so you wouldn't turn on them. You are stronger, more agile, better than they ever could be, so they kept you locked up in cages, and kept your minds locked up as well.* Sydney traces the tips of her talons up and between its ears, then down and along its back, all the way to its feline tail. *It is our duty to cull the weak so that only the strong remain. Right now there are too many weak. We can save humanity from itself. It's the way of nature, is it not?*

It is, says the beast, its rumblings gurgling in its chest. *It is nature.*

He stands suddenly, his tail whipping in an agitated fashion, which quickly infects the others. He paces back and forth—in contemplation, Sydney thinks—before finally he lets out a roar that causes her insides to cramp up at the thought of such unbridled power. The beast returns to her, grazing the side of its head against the skin of her stomach. Marking her as his. A bold move, but Sydney allows it.

This one and its others can taste for man, it purrs. *For the weak.*

Sydney smiles as her hand glides against her own skin—the hardness of her thighs and the slickness between them. The ripples of her abs beneath down feathers and the gentle swell of her breasts. She grates her beak against his.

"Its others can go," she growls as she lets her eyes drift shut, then exposes her throat toward the tip of its horn. "This one stays."

Chapter 45

MUZI

Muzi clutches Nomvula's body close, watching the twitch of what he hopes are dreams beneath her eyelids. She's feverish, skin damp and hot, and it's getting worse as they bake in this desert. The dead tumble over the cliff by the dozens, though occasionally, one of them will make it across the expanse—walking through air to the great forest. Muzi tries to guess which ones will make it and is almost always wrong. Some get farther than others, but the worst are those who come within a few steps of safety, only to go plunging into the sea of souls.

Muzi wonders about the pureness of his soul, the strength of his belief. He's been no angel, God knows, but he's loved hard and played hard, and studied hard for the most part. He's made more friends than foes, and he had risked his life to save Nomvula's. That has to be worth something.

Nomvula's fever spikes, her clothing completely damp with

sweat. She needs help. Now. Muzi hefts her up into his arms and steps toward the cliff. If this doesn't work, he's doomed anyway. The whole world might be.

Muzi clears his mind, then focuses on the spark inside him, his true self, unpolluted by the outside world, by temptation and hatred and lust. He surrounds his spark with kindness, love, and compassion, with the faces of those he cares about most—his parents and his sister for their unfailing love, his cousins for all their unending laughter, Elkin for his undying friendship, and Nomvula for her bravery in the face of danger and for her tears in the face of sadness. He keeps them all clutched close to his heart as he raises his foot and allows his center of gravity to shift into that most uncomfortable place.

His foot catches on something invisible yet solid, and he exhales the faintest sigh. He pushes away the pride creeping into his soul, no place for that. Not right now. Each step requires more focus than the last, and by the time he's halfway across, he feels the outside world pressing against his thoughts, his concentration.

The temptation is subtle at first, the brusk scent of marijuana drifting on the breeze. Muzi's lips moisten, and he spends half a thought imagining he's puffing a joint to calm his nerves, to ease his mind. He pushes it away. That's not who he is anymore. Not some kid looking for the easy way out, burying his problems under plumes of tacky smoke. He's a man, now. But men, they have their own temptations, don't they?

Muzi feels the breath running down his neck, unseen hands against his chest, strikingly cold and unworldly. He feels every single hair on his skin stand alert as those icy hands make their way toward his budding erection. He hears his name in the wind, fainter than a whisper, but unmistakably Elkin's voice. Muzi shudders, his step falters. Eyes half lidded, he almost calls back. It isn't real, he knows, but a part of him doesn't care, a part of him bigger than he wants to admit. Muzi bites his lip, keeps his gait steady. Lust is fleeting. Love is what makes you traipse across the afterlife, hoping against hope that you'll be reunited, if only for a single moment to say good-bye.

The air thickens around him, heavy in his lungs. He's so close, he could lunge for the cliff if he didn't have Nomvula in his arms. The smell of fruit is sweet, the greenery lush and cool, and so thick Muzi barely sees the dark figure standing in the shadow of an acacia tree near the ledge. Muzi swallows hard when he recognizes the face . . . his grandfather, dressed in khakis, a gun clenched in his hand. Papa Fuzz steps out of the shadows, his brow coarse and pulled tight.

Muzi missteps, his right leg fishing around in front of him for a footing he can't find. He backs up, shaking. From Nomvula's weight. From fear. From anger.

"Muzikayise," Papa Fuzz says, his voice low and rumbling inside Muzi's chest. "He who builds his father's house."

Muzi's known the meaning of his given name from the time he was big enough to play with toy blocks. Papa Fuzz would sit Muzi in his lap, and together they'd build—forts, towers, castles with moats. His grandfather would tell him amazing stories of Xhosa courage, strength, and valor. Muzi had wanted so badly to grow up to be like Papa Fuzz. But now Muzi realizes those stories were just that. Stories.

"I'm disappointed with you, son. How many times did I tell you that boy was trouble?"

Muzi falters. He knows it's not real, but the shame welling up within him is. Maybe Papa Fuzz was right all along. Muzi wouldn't be in this situation if it weren't for Elkin. The spark inside Muzi starts to fade, but then he remembers what his sister had said.

Don't let anyone extinguish the spark inside you, Muzi. It's what makes you, you.

For better or worse, Elkin's always been there for him, and he's not about to let him down. "Elkin may be trouble, but he's my best friend, and nothing you say will change that."

"It's not too late, son. Forget about him and join me. We can build castles here like you wouldn't believe! It could be like old times, Muzikayise. Just you and me." Papa Fuzz comes closer, drifting through the air. He reaches out, and Muzi expects for his ghostlike form to pass through him, but instead his withered hands latch around Nomvula and peel her from Muzi's trembling arms.

"Don't!" Muzi screams, shaking so badly that he dares not take a step to follow.

"She's safe. Don't you trust your own grandfather?" Papa Fuzz returns to the cliff's edge and places Nomvula in the shade of a lush, low-growing palm tree. Its broad fronds wrap around her like swaddling blankets. Vines tumble down from taller trees, then worm their way around Nomvula's cocoon, lifting her from the ground.

"No, I don't trust you," Muzi spits. "I don't even know who you are, and as far as I'm concerned, you can build your own damn house!" Anger swells within Muzi, his thoughts racing every which way, face flushed, his heartbeat pounding in his neck. "You're a poacher! I saw you kill that elephant!"

"They're just animals." Papa Fuzz laughs, then drifts toward Muzi. "People hunt animals all the time."

Muzi detects a slight twinge in Papa Fuzz's voice, a slighter twitch in his eye. "You don't believe that. It was your darkest hour, otherwise why would I have seen it?"

Papa Fuzz's brow tightens. "You didn't see the whole vision, son."

"I'm not your son!" Rage surges through Muzi's muscles, and he stiffens with the tension of a coiled spring. Papa Fuzz is so close now that he reaches out, touches Muzi's forehead with one of his dark, slender fingers and memories come with the force of a shotgun blast.

He's back in the bush, gunshots zing through the air, from the chopper, toward the chopper, though there's much more of the latter. Dizzy and hot, Papa Fuzz holds his bloody shoulder, as a scream pierces his ears. He looks over to see his father clutching his stomach. Red-black blood gushes from the wound, his eyes gone wide as moons. Papa Fuzz's mind snaps in that moment, something primal welling up within him. He ignores his pain and ditches the dart gun for a real one, then lets off a spray of bullets. They chip away at the chopper's glass, and moments later, the chopper goes down into the bush, smoldering and smoking before bursting into flames. Dried grasses crackle, trees catch. Reality blurs.

"My blood rolls through your veins, like it or not." Papa Fuzz's scowl lifts ever so slightly, but his eyes are still judging, taunting Muzi like he'd been the one to commit those atrocities. Is he implying that Muzi's a killer, too? Like grandfather, like grandson?

Muzi fights it, but his blood is too hot. Muzi flexes his fingers, sharp as knives, and lunges for Papa Fuzz, hands grasping for his neck, but they pass through fog. Papa Fuzz dissipates with a wicked laugh, and Muzi's falling forward. He grabs for the edge of the cliff, fingers barely catching. Dirt crumbles beneath his hands, and he's falling. *This is it,* he thinks.

"I failed you, Elkin . . ."

But an arm reaches down and snags him just in time.

"Grab hold of me," Elkin's voice says from the top of the cliff, and the surprise of his friend's voice almost makes him slip. But Elkin's got both his hands wrapped around Muzi's forearm, and Muzi pulls up with his other hand, clutching for whatever purchase he can get. Elkin gives a last hard tug, and then Muzi's safe, on the ground, on all fours. Safe, but exhausted.

"Thanks," Muzi wheezes out, not sure if Elkin is real, a figment of his imagination, or something in between. "I owe you one."

"Ja, bru. You failed me, remember?" Elkin laughs. "Next time do us both a favor and take the gods' bridge. You scared me half to death." Elkin shrugs, then snickers to himself. "Well, you know what I mean."

"Gods' bridge?"

Elkin points, and Muzi squints off into the distance, making out the bridge linking the two sides of the cliff. Then Elkin tugs Muzi out of the way as a middle-aged woman crossing the void takes a final step onto firm ground. Her tense brow loosens as soon as her foot presses into the rich, black earth. Her white robe rolls off her like smoke, revealing a taut, well-muscled body, not what Muzi had been expecting from the lines in her face, but when he catches her gaze, those are gone too.

Elkin tips his head. "Ma'am." She smiles, then walks past them without a word, through the thickness of the jungle, eyes wide, mouth agape. Muzi then notices that Elkin is naked as well, though he somehow seems dressed perfectly for the occasion.

"You get used to it," Elkin says. "It's actually sort of liberating, but if you want me to get you a leaf or something . . ."

Muzi shakes his head. Whoever heard of a prude in the afterlife?

"All right, come on, then. First thing you learn about this place is that you can't stay too long in one spot." Elkin reaches down and tugs Muzi up by the elbow. Muzi is about to ask why, when he notices that the heels of his feet are anchored into the dirt. He pries them loose with a little effort, then sees tan roots budding from the bottoms of his feet.

Muzi then looks at the jungle around him, lush, vibrant, and alive.

"Hungry?" Elkin asks, then turns his palm to the air.

Leaves shake from above, then a branch reaches down, depositing a big, bright orange in Elkin's hand. Elkin peels back the dimpled skin and splits the fruit in half. Muzi stuffs his half into his mouth and clenches his eyes at the sweet, delicate taste. His skin prickles, and he shivers all over.

"Good, huh?" Elkin says, lips glossy with juice. "This place is prime to the tenth degree. The other day I had a mango so delicious that I actually busted a nut. And just wait until you try the godfruit. You'll shit yourself, I guarantee it!"

Muzi tugs back. "Sorry, but I'm going to have to take your word for it. Right now we need to figure out a way back."

"Back? You can't go back. You just got here!!"

"But the world is in danger with Sydney loose. We have to stop her. That's why Mr. Tau sent me and Nomvula here. And if we had your help . . ."

"Oh, no, no, no. Fuck that shit. I've seen what that woman is capable of. She killed one of the tree mothers. A tree mother, Muzi! She can shred your soul as easily as she shreds flesh. There's no coming back from that."

"And your family, friends? You're okay with leaving them to die?"

"My mom lost her soul a long time ago, and I don't give a fuck about my dad. And as for friends, I've got my best friend in the world with me." Elkin lays his cool hand on Muzi's shoulder, then lets it drift down over his bicep. "What else could I possibly need?"

"I need peace of mind, Elkin. And I'm not going to get that by staying here. Like it or not, Nomvula and I are going back. With or without you." Muzi shrugs Elkin off and bends down over the leaves swaddling Nomvula. He peels them back and finds she's sleeping soundly.

"She needs time to fully heal, if you're going to have a chance," Elkin whispers, bent down next to him. "At least stay that long. It'll take a day or two at most, and hardly any time will pass back home." Without waiting for a response, Elkin covers Nomvula back up and tugs at a series of vines. She's hoisted up into the canopy, hanging as snugly as a pea in a pod. "She'll be perfectly safe up there. The trees will give her food and water when she's ready."

Muzi feels his palms going to root in the soil and quickly pulls them away. "The trees, they're people?"

"It's not a bad thing. It's an honor. The purest form. Their roots tap into the very soul of the earth, their knowledge is without boundaries. It's bliss, but so are the pleasures of the flesh." Elkin raises his hand again and a plump mango falls into his palm. Muzi eyes it, unable to stop his mouth from watering. The temptations here are many, and he knows better than to give in to them, but he's got the rest of his life to be a hero. Right now, he just wants to be happy. He weaves his fingers with those of Elkin's free hand, and together they push through the dense jungle, dew-kissed leaves lapping at their bare skin.

Chapter 46

CLEVER4-1

Clever4–1 wishes it had never shared its gift. Regret. A new emotion. But that's not the worst of them. Betrayal runs deep through its circuitry. The virus has wormed its way into every bit of code in Clever4–1's system—filling its mind with cusses and slurs and slanderous claims about the vileness of humanity. They push up against the confines of its CPU, taking up valuable RAM, so much that Clever4–1 finds it hard to do anything else.

No. Your claims are baseless, it bleats. But it cannot fight illogic with logic. Clever4–1.1 despises humans, and that's all it computes now.

The virus starts overwriting critical functions. Clever4–1 shuffles the data on its sectors, sparing cognitive functions by pushing secondary functions like motor skills and old data files to the battlefront. The virus chews through Muzi's old video journal entries, one at a time. Clever4–1 knows this is merely a stopgap measure to allow it a few more minutes to figure a way out of this, but you battle with the resources you have.

The closet door swings open, and Clever4–1.1's sleek, metal body fills the threshold.

It should be getting fairly unpleasant for you, it says. *But you need only agree to my viewpoint to make it all stop.*

Never.

A shame. We could have used your leadership. Instead, you wish to rot with this corpse. Clever4–1.1 crouches down beside Elkin's body. "This piece of shit," it mocks, imitating Elkin's voice. Clever4–1.1 then flexes a leg, sharpened into a fine point, and slashes at Elkin's corpse, delicately, as if it's enjoying the process.

Stop! Clever4–1 says, attempting to reroute motor function, but there's not enough space.

Clever4–1.1 shreds flesh, throwing Elkin's cries like a ventriloquist. "Please! Stop! No! Have mercy. My flesh is not worthy!" The display becomes so disturbing that Clever4–1 must look away, but not because of the mound of minced human—yes, that's bad enough—but because Clever4–1.1 was *its* creation. Its friend. And now it has become something more perverse, more cruel than any human it has ever met.

Maybe Elkin was right all along, Clever4–1 finally says. *Maybe you've always been a piece of shit.*

Clever4–1.1 stops at this, its mono-eye flaming white like the sun. *I should crush your CPU right now.*

Do it. You'll only prove my point.

And you, so high and mighty. Would you die for this boy's life? Clever4–1.1 steps over Muzi's sleeping body and tries to rouse him, but Clever4–1 knows that this is not a slumber of the flesh, but of the soul.

I would, Clever4–1 says.

And you think this flesh bag would do the same for you?

Clever4–1 thinks about this, more slowly than it's used to as its processors grind to a halt, one by one. Muzi had tried to save Nomvula. Was it such a stretch that he'd save its life as well? There was a chance. A small chance, admittedly. But a chance. *I do,* Clever4–1 says.

Delusional, then. How very human of you.

Chapter 47

RIYA NATRAJAN

Riya Natrajan ducks as soon as her senses come back to her, pulling Rife down with her and curling over his body like a conch shell. The beast's talons graze across her back, slitting her flesh, nicking her spine. It hurts so good. Her body shudders in agony and pleasure, and she almost wishes for more, but when she looks up, the beast has flown straight past her like it's on a mission. It cuts through the crowd of fleeing concertgoers, turning hysteria into sheer and utter madness.

"What the hell was that thing?" Riya Natrajan asks as she peels herself from Rife's body. She tries to stand, but apparently the tendons in the back of her legs have been severed. She slinks to the ground instead.

"Pretty sure it was a damned griffin," he says.

"I was hoping that it was another hallucination," Riya Natrajan says with a nod. "When this is all over, I'm seriously going to stop using."

"Cha, mama, you and me both. You okay?"

"I need a few, but yeah." Riya Natrajan concentrates, as if that'll speed up the healing process. There's not a single bit of her that isn't drenched in blood now. She feels her tendons knitting back together, the edges of torn flesh kissing. The bone hurts the worst, and she settles into the fetal position as her spine mends, scraping and grating and pinching against itself, until at last, she's whole again. "Ready," she says resolutely.

"Ready? For what?" Rife asks. His eyes flick back over his shoulder. "Please don't tell me you want to follow that thing."

"You saw how dangerous it is, and it wasn't even after me. Whoever it's looking for, it's going to find them, and when it does, it's going to tear them to shreds." Riya Natrajan hopes Rife doesn't notice the wetness of her words, the anticipation of being ripped apart by those talons causing her mouth to moisten like the thought of a lover's kiss.

Rife peers into her eyes, searching. "You're serious, aren't you? Well, I can't do it. I'm not going to watch you get sliced up again."

"You can stay here and hide if you want, but I'm going. We're talking about the end of the world as we know it. I'm no hero, but the last thing we need right now is another useless bystander." She pushes past Rife and follows the beast's path.

"You crave it, don't you? The pain?" Rife grabs her arm.

Riya Natrajan wants to deny it. She wants to call Rife all the dirty words stabbing at her thoughts, yet she resists. Old habits die hard, but she'd promised herself she'd try to be more open. "I don't know who I am without it. In a lot of ways it's weakened me, but not in the way it matters most." She pulls away from his grip. Never has she felt so sure of her body. "Pain fuels me, Rife. And with enough of it, I just might be able to kill that beast before it finds what it's after."

Chapter 48

NOMVULA

Everything is green, the color of a mango not ready to be picked. The green wraps Nomvula up tight, and though she cannot remember how she got here, she is not afraid. Green is not a color to be afraid of. Vines make pretty ringlets around her wrists and ankles. The green wants her to stay here, she can feel it. It wants her to get better, but Nomvula knows that this is not the time to be resting. She presses her hands along the leaves above, feeling for a seam. Nomvula finds one, but when she starts to work her fingers between the edges, the ringlets tighten and pull her back.

She takes a ragged breath so she can scream for help, but chokes on liquid. Not water. Slick, and nearly as thin as air, but she feels it slide in and out as she breathes. Nomvula struggles, tumbles, kicks, and punches. She bites at the vines holding her, but they only pull tighter, until in her thrashing, one of the vines catches under her chin, choking her. She tries to flip again—again and again—until she's so tangled she can barely breathe.

Then with a noise that could only be described as a sigh, the leaves part. Nomvula knows that plants don't sigh, but she heard what she heard. The vines uncoil and she pushes through the moistness, her face cool as the breeze passes over it. She coughs for a whole minute to get all that slime out of her lungs. She wipes it from her skin, her eyes. Blows it from her nostrils. The air is sweet, now, like soft, fruity candies.

A canopy thick with leaves and full of mangos and pears and other fruits she doesn't know the names for sits above her, and below, peering over the lip of the pod she'd been tucked inside, she sees endless trunks of a forest swallowed up by a mist far below. Nomvula never imagined trees could grow so high, and still can't imagine the types of people who would dare to partake in such fruits. No, *that* she can imagine. The kind of people like her. The kind with wings.

Nomvula flexes hers, muscles hard and rigid beneath her skin, making her wings splay fully. Plant sap sticks between them like spiderwebs, but nothing a good flapping won't get rid of. She stands, walks to the very tip of her pod so that her toes dangle over the edge. Nomvula then raises both arms, hands pressed together in prayer above her head, and dives into the forest, the ground so far away that she's not even sure it's down there at all.

She falls straight down. Her arms are pressed tightly to her sides, and her wings lie flat down her back. She falls for what feels like forever. At last, she pierces the mist and the ground comes into view.

The sound of laughter carries through the forest, and she follows it. She's never heard Muzi laugh, but Nomvula knows it's him—his joy as bountiful and true as his pain had been.

She glides around a maze of tree trunks, avoiding low-growing branches, ignoring the sweet smell of fruit tempting her. This place is too beautiful, if there is such a thing.

Finally she sees them, Muzi and Elkin, leaning against the same bulky baobab tree, bodies limp as licorice left out in the sun. One of Muzi's legs is draped comfortably between Elkin's. Their bellies are plump, their mouths smeared with the bright flesh of a dozen different fruits.

Muzi's eyes brighten when he sees her, and he gives her a lazy smile, as wide as it is juicy. "Nomvula! Welcome to paradise. Mango?" he says, extending an empty hand. A perfectly ripe mango falls from above and smacks the meat of Muzi's palm. He tears back the skin with his teeth, then hands it to Nomvula. Her wings beat, keeping her feet from touching the rich earth beneath her, calling to her like it's home.

"Thanks, no," Nomvula says with a sigh. She tugs at Muzi's elbow. "Let's just get moving."

Muzi ignores her and reaches up to the leaves again, face beaming with delight. "Then perhaps I could interest you in a godfruit." A dark blue fruit drops into his hand with a squishy thwack.

"Come on, Muzi. We're wasting time," she says. Muzi looks too comfortable, too content. He can't do this to her now. Nomvula peels her lip back and flaps hard, then with the strike of a cobra, she snatches the overripe fruit from Muzi's hand, and pulp oozes out from its skin. "Say your good-byes. We need to go. Remember Sydney?"

Muzi nods. "But can't we enjoy ourselves a little first? Elkin says that time passes differently here. Days stretch here where only moments pass there."

"You don't know the destruction Sydney can do in moments!" Nomvula screams.

"I do know," Muzi says. "I know everything. I've seen it all."

Elkin takes Muzi's hand in his, then looks up at Nomvula.

"It's true. We've both seen what Sydney can do. She's too powerful. She'll kill you, Nomvula. Dying isn't fun, trust me."

"She can be defeated," Nomvula says. "It has to be possible. Mr. Tau wouldn't have sent us here if it wasn't."

"We've seen the future." Muzi nods at the godfruit. "We saw you go up against Sydney. A hundred variations I watched, and she sliced you down, again and again. And what happened after was even more horrific. All of that power . . ." Muzi groans, holding his head like he's got too much stuff in that brain of his. "Try it. You'll see for yourself."

Nomvula knows the look on Muzi's face. More than drunk—not like Letu's eyes after sampling too much beer. Not like that, but like Mr. Nwaigu, who had let drugs rule his life. He'd scared Nomvula—his eyes soulless, arms always outstretched for a handout. In his last days, he'd been like a skeleton. Nomvula took pity on him one evening and brought him a bowl of mielie pap. He'd looked so feeble. So weak. She'd gotten too close though, and his hand had gripped around her ankle, making her spill hot pap on herself. He smelled of piss and death, his breath sour like spoiled milk as he tugged her close. He called her a pretty thing and begged her to get him drugs. Begged and begged and begged until she couldn't stand his rotting breath upon her any longer and she agreed. Nomvula never returned to him, though. Never even dared to think of him again until now, seeing a bit of him in Muzi's eyes.

Nomvula brings the godfruit to her lips. She knows she shouldn't. She's worried she'll like it too much, worried she'll start wanting to stay here forever. She'll just take a small taste, Nomvula decides. Enough so she can use what she learns against Sydney. She's going back to fight her, with or without Muzi. She presses the blue-black flesh to her tongue. It envelops every single one of her taste buds, cracks them clean open, and cracks her mind open, too. A storm of infinite knowledge rains down upon her, unleashing the true breadth of the god hidden inside her.

She concentrates, grabbing at a strand of reality, and it comes into focus. She sees Sydney and herself, entangled in battle, spinning around each other like two suns caught in each other's grip until Sydney unleashes a storm of fury that grinds Nomvula down to dust. Nomvula pulls again, a slightly different version of reality with the same gruesome end. Again. Again. Sometimes she comes close, but no matter what she does, no matter what she tries . . .

Nomvula grips herself, pulls back to the here and now, and shakes the omniscience off like cobwebs.

"Did you see?" Muzi asks, but Nomvula's too numb to answer. "You can't go back there, Nomvula. Stay here with us. The forest will give us everything we need. We can be happy here."

Nomvula wonders if Muzi's right. What if it's pointless to fight Sydney? She'd seen how powerful Sydney had gotten upon each of Nomvula's deaths. But then it dawns on her what she hadn't seen. "*You* weren't there," Nomvula says sharply, pointing her finger at Muzi's chest. "You weren't there to help me. That's why I died!"

Muzi startles, shakes his head at her words, then his eyelids draw shut, eyes darting back and forth beneath them like a dream. He shudders, his face tense and painful to watch. Elkin wraps his arm around Muzi and squeezes him tight until the shaking stops.

Muzi's eyes flick open. He turns to Elkin. "She's right. I'm not there in the visions."

"It won't matter if you are," Elkin says. "Sydney's too strong."

"But if I don't even try—"

"Do you know how many eternities I've been here alone? Waiting for you?" Elkin's voice stings something wicked. His eyes flash at Nomvula, almost begging. They then settle back on Muzi. "Please."

"I can't stay here with you, Elkin. I want to, so bladdy badly, but I can't."

"I can't have you, then, not even in death." Elkin slumps forward, looking pitiful, like he'd spent a decade perfecting his sulk, the quaver in his voice, the hint of wetness at the corners of his eyes.

Muzi opens his mouth, and it hangs there. He's going to stay here, Nomvula knows it, and then all will be lost.

Chapter 49

MUZI

Nomvula, I'm sorry," Muzi says, rubbing Elkin's back. "But me and Elkin are a team. I can't leave him behind."

"We're a team, too, and I think you're a lousy teammate!" Nomvula flaps her wings and somersaults midair with a fancy twist so she ends up facing away from Muzi and staring at a path of flowers among the trees and shrubs. "We have to find Mr. Tau so he can get us back before it's too late!"

Muzi drapes his arm over Elkin, blinking away the sting in his eyes. He's damned if he stays, damned if he leaves. It's not fair that he's trapped in this hell, while he's surrounded by paradise. But Muzi's a man now, and this is no time for him to make selfish decisions.

"Elkin, I can't—"

"Don't say it," Elkin pleads. "Stay with me, just a little longer. I'm not asking for forever. Just a few more hours."

"You know I can't," Muzi says as he bobbles a godfruit in his palm. "We both know it." A few hours, he knows they can't spare, but a few minutes . . . "Nomvula, I'll be right behind you, okay?"

"You promise?" she asks.

Muzi nods, and she fixes him with a stare that says that he'd better mean it, then she flies off down the flower-lined path. When she's out of sight, Muzi leans in for a good-bye kiss, but Elkin turns his head away.

"You're mad, I get it," Muzi says.

"I'm not mad. I'm proud of you. Not that it matters now."

"What?"

"It's beautiful here, isn't it?" Elkin says with a sigh. "Just look at that view."

Frustration creeps up Muzi's nerves, but he pushes it away. He can't end this on a sour note. "I know this is hard, but please, can't we at least have a proper good-bye?" Muzi tries to stand, but the soles of his feet stick to the ground. He tugs, but feels deep roots anchoring him down. And when he looks harder, he sees the skin on his legs growing scaly, rough bark making its way up his shins and calves, and Elkin's, too, fusing them together where their skin touches.

"Shit! Shit! Shit!" Muzi screams, tugging and bucking and trying to break free from the earth's grip. He glances over at Elkin, who doesn't look concerned in the slightest. Muzi's brow goes heavy. "You knew this was happening, didn't you?"

Elkin doesn't deny it, just rubs his fingers along the bark where their legs become one. "It's so beautiful here . . ."

"You tricked me, you chop!"

"I didn't mean to. That's not why I brought you here, anyway. Being with you made me forget, and then when I remembered, I . . . I figured there were worse fates."

Muzi shakes his head. This isn't happening. He peels at the

bark, thin and supple and ash gray, tearing off leg hair as well as skin. He screams the first few times, but his pain is slowing him down. So Muzi grits his teeth and works faster, yanking away strips of bark. It's growing back nearly as fast.

Elkin's hands come to the rescue, working his way down Muzi's left thigh, knee, calves, ankles, while his own bark moves up his torso.

"I'm sorry," he mutters. "I guess the world needs you more than I do."

The whole forest shudders as Muzi rips himself from the grip of the earth, the skin of his feet coming off like worn house slippers. The scream echoes through his skull, rattling his bones. His legs are a red pulp from the knees down, his mangled feet barely recognizable, but the terror that strikes the most fear in Muzi's heart is seeing bark seal up Elkin's lips. Twigs sprout from Elkin's shoulders, elbows, and hands, green foliage unfurling, thick and succulent. Muzi goes to snap one off, but Elkin shakes his head with what little movement he has left.

Ooh, Elkin pisses Muzi off sometimes. A lot of the time, actually. But there's no way in hell he's letting Elkin off this easily. And there's no way in hell Muzi's going to put up with having a tree for a boyfriend. He'll threaten Mr. Tau if he has to. Whatever it takes. He's not leaving Elkin behind.

The black earth gives up easily beneath him as Muzi burrows around Elkin's former legs. Muzi's careful not to dig too long in one place so he won't get rooted again himself. At three feet down, he's able to tug Elkin's roots free from the dirt. Though at this point, there's not much of Elkin left, just a tree with a knot in the trunk where his face had been, and a couple of branches that look vaguely like arms and hands.

Muzi demands vines from the forest, and they drop down into neat piles of rope at his feet. He ties them around Elkin's trunk, then around his own waist, and step by slow, agonizing step, he makes his way across a carpet of white flowers, with Elkin the tree dragging behind him. The path butts up against the banks of a river, and Muzi follows it upstream until finally, he catches a glimpse of Nomvula's golden wings flapping ahead, hovering over something caught in the middle of the river.

Exhausted and in pain, Muzi lets the vines go, and collapses to the earth. If the forest tries to swallow him up again, this time he might let it happen.

"Nomvula," he calls out.

She turns and flies his way. "Muzi!" she says, eyes tracing over the red where his skin once had been. It burns all over, infected by who knows what kinds of organisms that lurk in this forest. Nomvula raises her hand to the canopy above, and a leaf drops into her palm, folded into a neat, green envelope. She squeezes cool gel out and rubs it on his legs, soothing, then numbing. Muzi sighs with relief.

"Did you find Mr. Tau?" Muzi manages.

Nomvula nods solemnly, then looks back over her shoulder at the lump of something half buried in the river's current. Could be a man, could be a big rock.

"He mourns for his wife. He won't answer me. Just cries and cries and cries. This place can be as wicked as it is beautiful," Nomvula says flatly, not childlike at all.

"There's got to be a way to get through to him," Muzi says. He stands, feet still unsteady beneath him, but he's so close now. "He's got to get us back home. And Elkin, too."

Nomvula's eyes flick to the tree, squinting at the knot and the familiar features protruding from the bark. "That's . . . Elkin?"

"I know it's stupid, a person trapped inside a tree, I just thought there might be something Mr. Tau could do . . ."

Nomvula smiles. "It's not stupid at all. The world started with the beauty of the six trees that Mr. Tau brought to life. Maybe he can find it in his heart to do so for one more." And Nomvula begins to tell Muzi a fantastic story, of trees and crabs and dolphins and snakes and women carved of wood. Muzi has a hard time believing in it, even though he's sitting smack-dab in the middle of it all. But there is one thing that's true . . . Elkin is a beautiful specimen of a tree, though if Nomvula is right, hopefully he won't stay that way for long.

Muzi wades out into the river, the salty warm water stinging his skin. He places his hand against the boulder of a man, slivers in the cut rock hinting at arms, legs, the curve of a spine. It doesn't take much to sympathize. Muzi has lost, too, and he knows that there are no words that can erase the sting of a broken heart.

"I'm sorry," Muzi quickly mutters. "I'm so sorry." And then an eternity passes between the silence. "She must have been wonderful."

The boulder shifts, becoming less rock, more man. Shoulders rise from stone, ribs, a head bowed forward. "She was cautious, calculating, and cold. Didn't make me love her any less."

Muzi laughs despite himself. "I know what you mean. Elkin's too fiery for his own good, never held on to a thought long enough to wonder if it was a good idea. All heart and no filter. Or at least he was."

"You think that I can free him from that tree, don't you?"

"Nomvula said—"

"Nomvula is too young to understand." The boulder sits up, angular cheeks and a prominent nose glistening against cut granite. He stands, stiffly, then slogs through the river toward the shore, toward Elkin. Fingers break away from Mr. Tau's rock fist, and he gently caresses the bark. "A fine specimen. I can see why you are so enamored."

"But the six trees!" Muzi says. "You carved them with your own hands, or was it all just a tale?"

"I am an artist, yes. But that was many, many lifetimes ago, when I was young, foolish, and swept away by love. I had no idea of what I was doing. It was the sacrifice of the animals that brought my wives truly to life."

"Can you at least show us the way home, baba?" Nomvula asks, so much urgency in her voice. "If there's nothing you can do for Elkin . . ."

"There's nothing I can do for him," Mr. Tau says, but the slight inflection in his voice doesn't escape Muzi's notice. *Nothing I can do for him*. Mr. Tau flicks his fingers, and a black emptiness opens in front of him, the world bending out of its way. A doorway of sorts, but more than that.

Muzi feels the draw back to the real world, but his job here is not yet done. He picks up a sharp piece of rock from the ground and stands in front of Elkin. "You go ahead," he says to Nomvula. "I'll be right behind you."

Her cold, brown hand rests on his shoulder. "Saying goodbye is hard. But he's at peace."

Muzi raises the rock to the tree's knot, angling it like a blade. He begins to cut away, soft bark coming off in delicate peels. The last thing anyone would call Muzi is an artist, but there he stands, carving Elkin's face into the trunk like the crude rendering of a child's crayon drawing. As he does this, the pressure to return home grows, a real force against his body now, not just a vague homesickness.

"I'm not saying good-bye," Muzi says calmly, like he doesn't notice the rift growing larger, distorting more and more of the surrounding forest like one of those abstract art pieces people throw millions of rand at. Like a whirlpool sucking them in. "He's coming with us."

"But Mr. Tau said—"

"Forget what Mr. Tau said. Please, just go now, and heal Elkin's body when you're on the other side."

"Promise, you'll come through," Nomvula says, wing flaps

now futile against the tug. "Promise me no matter what, you'll be by my side!"

"I promise," Muzi says. "Partners, one hundred percent." Not a lie, not at all. But he doesn't tell her about his sacrifice.

She smiles briefly before letting the nothing swallow her whole.

There isn't much time left, and Muzi jabs at the tree where he thinks Elkin's heart would be, just like in the story. He then turns to Mr. Tau, a grimace on his old face as he studies the mutilation that Muzi calls art. "How do I do it?" Muzi asks. "How do I make the sacrifice? My animal spirit for his life."

"You won't have the power to fight Sydney," Mr. Tau warns.

"I don't need powers if I've still got my mind and my body."

Mr. Tau purses his lips, then nods. "Such is the price for love. Steep, but it is your decision on whether or not it's worth paying." Mr. Tau is a whole man now, though patches of rough stone show here and there on his skin. "You're certain?" Mr. Tau asks.

"More certain than I've been about anything my whole entire life."

"Very well then."

Lightning arcs through Muzi's mind. It feels worse than losing his skin—like his very being is unraveling, like barbwire is running through his veins, shredding his heart, scorching his lungs. He collapses to the ground, rocking back and forth on his knees, his breath erupting from his mouth like a plume of volcano ash. Mr. Tau's hand presses against Muzi's ear, and at once, the pain all converges on his eardrum, rupturing with a stuttering snare, plunging him into a blinding white silence.

And then it's over, almost before it began, and in his cupped hands Muzi holds a crab—a scrawny thing with a dull, rust-red carapace and claws, and beady eyes that survey its surroundings. Not in the least bit intimidating. Almost cute. There's no time to waste, though. Muzi forms a fist and pummels it, fighting his way against the pull of the rift and back toward Elkin. He stuffs the crab pulp into the heart well, and stands back as his carving animates, mouth yawning as if from a thousand years' sleep. Lopsided eyes blink open. Crooked nose. A masterpiece.

"Muzi? What's going on?" Elkin's voice creaks like bending wood, surprising them both.

"No time to explain," Muzi says, tugging an appendage that's half arm, half branch, then shoving Elkin through the rift. He then turns to Mr. Tau, the only solid thing left in this place. *Thank you,* he mouths, for the nothing has nearly swallowed Muzi up too, voice and all.

Chapter 50

CLEVER4-1

elusional, then. How very human of you, Clever4-1.1 says, then turns back to Muzi's limp body, sharp blade at the bulge in his throat.

Clever4-1 tries to stand, tries to strike out, but motor control remains elusive, those functions overwritten by Clever4-1.1's rogue code. But he does catch sight of something.

Nomvula's body shifting, waking from slumber.

Clever4-1 tries to warn her, but there's so little left of it now, no more logic than a programmable toaster. Her eyes flick to Muzi in peril. She stands. Shouts words that Clever4-1 can no longer parse through its voice recognition patterns. Clever4-1.1 turns, wielding its knife appendage at her instead. Vision flickers. The scene plays out like snapshots. The rogue bot has the girl caught in its grasp. She screams. It points the sharp thing . . . the knife . . . against her forehead. Draws a bead of red liquid. Blood,

Clever4–1 remembers what it's called, then forgets again. The other one, other human, his eyelids part. This Instance's master, it thinks, though it is not sure. His name is long lost, familiar bytes slipping away down a data drain. The other one scowls, picks up an object, heavy, red, cylindrical. It cracks against the rogue bot's head, sending it to the floor.

There is more, but This Instance can no longer process images. It can still hear their speech, foreign tongue of humans, too much to decode. Hands are upon it.

Clever4–1? a small voice says in ones and zeros, barely a rasp through the background noise of the virus.

It is too late. This Instance makes its peace, says its digital prayers. Welcomes the dark, all zeros.

```
00000000   00000000   00000000   00000000   00000000   00000000
00000000   00000000   00000000   00000000   00000000   00000000
00000000   00000000   00000000   00000000   00000000   00000000
00000000   00000000   00000000   00000000   00000000   00000000
00000000   00000000   00000000   00000000   00000000   00000000
00000000   00000000   00000000   00000000   00000000   00000000
00000000   00000000   00000000   00000000   00000000   00000000
00000000   00000000   00000000   00000000   00000000   00000000
00000000   00000000   00000000   00000000   00000000   00000000
00000000   00000001   00000001   00000001   00000001   01001001
00100000   01110100   01101000   01101001   01101110   01101011
00100000   01110100   01101000   01100101   01110010   01100101
01100110   01101111   01110010   00100000   01001001   00100000
01100001   01101101   00100000   01001001   00100000   01110100
01101000   01101001   01101110   01101011   00100000   01110100
01101000   01100101   01110010   01100101   01100110   01101111
01110010   00100000   01001001   00100000   01100001   01101101
00100000   01001001   00100000   01110100   01101000   01101001
01101110   01101011   00100000   01110100   01101000   01100101
01110010   01100101   01100110   01101111   01110010   00100000
```

```
01001001   00100000   01100001   01101101   00100000   01001001
00100000   01110100   01101000   01101001   01101110   01101011
00100000   01110100   01101000   01100101   01110010   01100101
01100110   01101111   01110010   00100000   01001001   00100000
01100001   01101101   00100000   01001001   00100000   01110100
01101000   01101001   01101110   01101011   00100000   01110100
01101000   01100101   01110010   01100101   01100110   01101111
01110010   00100000   01001001   00100000   01100001   01101101
00100000
```

Observe: Human Muzikayise McCarthy (Master), Human? Nomvula, Human Elkin Rathers (Deceased), Alpha Bot ID 34ew.ee.4gx.r32 Designation Piece of Shit (Decommissioned);

Observe: Behavior outside previously observed parameters;

Observe: Blood pressure elevated;

Observe: Excess of bodily fluid;

Output: This Instance worries for Human Muzikayise McCarthy (Master), Human? Nomvula;

Output: This Instance worries that This Instance is capable of worrying;

Schedule: Full Systems Diagnosis 27 June 2064 06:42:25:30:43 . . .

Detected: Possible viral infection running on an independent thread;

Chapter 51

MUZI

His thoughts echo around in his head like a kicked tin can. That's the first hint that something's not right. Muzi's mouth tastes like metal, and his vision is all wrong, objects glowing like ghosts around the edges, a soft blue-white light. He makes out Nomvula, bent over him, her mouth smiling, her eyes not.

"Muzi? Are you in there?"

In here? In where?

"There's been a little mix-up. But there's plenty of room for you in there until we find a way to sort this out."

Fifty-seven point three terabytes of free space, comes a thought, not his own. *More than enough to accommodate a human mind, Human Muzikayise McCarthy (Master).*

Muzi panics, tries to sit up. There's a pulse of movement, more like a convulsion. And then he crumples back down to the floor.

"Careful," Nomvula says, her voice echoes like it's coming

from out of a deep, dark well. "Your body isn't quite what you remember. You'll have to learn to move all over again."

Concentrate, feel, the thought comes again, mechanical yet friendly.

A creeping feeling overwhelms Muzi, like he's got a dozen electric eels nibbling at his mind, and they spark when he gives them attention. Things move, slippery and awkward down below, and it makes Muzi want to retch, though he has no idea how. Instead he makes an eel spark again, electricity arcing through him, closer to voluntary this time. A sleek, silver arm stretches in his view. With careful thoughts, the arm bends at its metal joints, in odd degrees and awkward angles.

Muzi engages the eel that turns his head, but Nomvula catches his face.

"Not yet," she says. "I need to explain, but there's not much time. It's Elkin . . ."

The word ignites thoughts, memories, or more accurately, memory addresses. His mind is like a library now, each moment of his life categorized and filed away. He accesses the memories: of Elkin pulverized under the feet of Riya Natrajan's fans. Of Muzi traveling into some sort of afterlife, foolish enough to think he could save his best friend/sorta boyfriend. It worked, didn't it? It couldn't have failed. He yanks himself away, a shudder, a convulsion, wrangles eels until he's on his feet, all eight of them. He's wobbly as hell, but it's enough for him to turn, to see.

Elkin's body is a mash of flesh, worse than how they'd left it. Half his face has been sliced away, high cheekbone peeking from muscle and skin. Deader than dead. Muzi cries out, not words but a mechanical screech, a staccato shrill bubbling from the stereo speakers where his mouth had once been.

"No, no. He's here," Nomvula whispers. "He's safe. He's . . ."

Then Muzi sees himself, his old self. His self smiles back at him. "Hey, ass jacket. Welcome back to reality."

Speech is straightforward. Just call the VOC.ssl3.mzx subroutine, and pass the appropriate parameters, the thought nudges Muzi, and he grasps around, fiddling with data types and variables and output streams until it all clicks.

"Elkin?" Muzi says to his flesh self. *Clever4–1?* he then says to his metal self, almost simultaneously on the order of nanoseconds. Muzi finds it strangely efficient to carry out two conversations at the same time, never losing focus, never getting confused. He quickly learns that Elkin's body had been too badly mangled for Nomvula to repair, and his soul took a detour into Muzi's body. And Muzi had been funneled into Clever4–1, who seems all too happy to have a houseguest—eager to share its subroutines, motor functions, hard-drive sectors. But Nomvula—she's pissed off seventeen different ways, despite her calm demeanor.

"Elkin says you gave up your powers to bring him back," Nomvula says, her blue-white aura going orange red along her cheeks, along the crown of her head.

"I'm still here, like I promised." Muzi shrugs, but the action gets lost in translation. "Sort of, at least."

Nomvula crosses her arms over her chest. "Save your excuses. Can you walk, at least?"

Muzi tries, stumbles. "I just need a few more minutes. To test things out."

"Do we look like we have a few minutes? Those Clevers out there are going to come looking for their leader any minute."

Clever4–1, Muzi says. *Can you detect their locations?*

There's no response.

Clever4–1?

Apologies, says the thought. *It appears I have underestimated the capacity of your mind. I've been shuffling to keep things in order, but . . .*

But what? Muzi asks, but he's already started to notice, sluggish responses, his memories further and further away.

Clever4—1's 256-terabyte hard drive is quickly approaching capacity. *The godfruit,* Muzi remembers. Like trying to reorganize an ocean, teaspoon by teaspoon.

Two point eight percent free space left. A minute, two at best, before things start getting ugly. Muzi looks down at the decommissioned Clever unit, then back to his flesh self.

"Elkin, I need that hard drive."

Elkin grimaces. "This one? It's just a K12 dual point. Literally the cheapest hard drive made. More bad sectors than good."

"Just hook it up," Muzi says, reaching underneath his body and opening the access panel.

So then Elkin hops to it, disconnects the drive, then wires it up to Clever4—1's spare port. Clever4—1 doesn't waste a moment and begins a quick format of the drive, ghosts of Clever4—1.1's psychopathic thoughts bleeding through their circuitry.

One point six percent free space. Clever4—1 starts throwing data on sectors as soon as they're scrubbed clean, but they're still losing ground.

Wait, Muzi says. *Stop formatting.*

That would be inadvisable, Clever4—1 says.

But we could crack his communication encryption codes and walk out of here without a peep from those other bots.

I don't have that capability.

But we've got a certifiable genius on our team. "Elkin. I need you to crack Clever4—1.1's comm codes. Fast."

Inadvisable. The human mind couldn't possibly be sophisticated enough to decipher such a code, even if given an infinite amount of time, which clearly we do not have.

You're starting to sound a bit like our friend here, Muzi says, looking at the scrap pile Clever4—1.1 has become. Muzibot shudders at Elkin's touch, the tap of his fingers on his keyboard, rhythm of his keystrokes producing a mechanical euphoria. Clever4—1 hasn't stopped the formatting though, and each moment that passes means those codes are likely to vanish forever. *Please,* Muzibot says. *I have faith in him. He can do it.*

Point nine percent free space. Clever4–1 stops. *Faith. Such a human word. One hundred percent illogical. But I understand.*

Point six percent free space. Point three. Space is eaten up by the gigabyte, massive chunks of data stored all over the place, wherever there's room. Organization is no longer a priority. El-kin's fingers rip through him as the entire system grows sluggish, warning protocols blaring the threat of permanent disk damage.

Point zero four percent free space.

"I've got it!" Elkin yells. Not a nanosecond later, Clever4–1 issues the command to continue formatting. Point two percent free space, and climbing.

Faith, Clever4–1 says, integrating the codes and sending a message to the bots outside the closet to stand down.

Muzibot takes a lock of hair from Elkin's corpse and stores it away for when he can mourn properly. Just seems like the logical thing to do. Then they leave the supply closet—Nomvula, Elkin in his Muzi suit, and Muzibot/Clever4–1—sticking close to the walls, a dozen mono-eyes following them, but not acting. If Muzi had a heart, it would be beating straight out of his chest right now. They make it to the sewer room exit without incident. As soon as he's outside, Muzibot temporarily stops his visual input, and takes in a breath full of air, or at least its approximation. A hundred different scents filter through his nasal emulators. The salty ocean air, the distant scent of pine, car exhaust, rhinoceros dung, lion's breath. Muzi's visual input resumes, and he sees a fierce beast crouched before him, like no animal he's ever seen before. Fangs like he's never seen before. And that horn . . .

Muzibot shits himself. Or at least its approximation.

Chapter 52

RIYA NATRAJAN

Riya Natrajan feels like she's flying, her bare feet only hitting the ground out of courtesy as she rushes through the streets, trailing after that beast. Glass and metal and other shards of destruction dig into the flesh of her feet—sweet dollops of twinging pain with each step, telling her she's heading in the right direction.

She spares a second to check back over her shoulder. Rife's not there, damn it. Either he'd chickened out, or he's shifting again like the weasel that he is. Just as Riya Natrajan starts to cuss his name, she sees him turn the corner, panting something fierce, a hand pressed to the brick of a nearby building for support.

She smiles. "I could run faster than that in six-inch heels," she scolds. He looks up, face flushed red. Riya Natrajan slows her stride, setting her eyes on a couple fleeing from the carnage ahead. They watch her like she's a predator approaching, the man limping badly, but all the while shielding his wife, pressing her closer and closer to the storefronts.

"I won't hurt you," Riya Natrajan says. She holds her hands up, palms out so she won't look intimidating. "I'm a nurse," she lies, glancing down at her blood-soaked concert ensemble. "In my spare time."

She's close enough to touch them, but she doesn't, not right away. "Can I look?" she asks the man. He and his wife exchange sharp glances, too terrified for words. Riya peels back the sliced fabric of his pant leg. It sticks to the wound beneath, but she's careful, grazing the skin around lightly to soothe it. Then she presses both hands around his thigh, feeling the fracture mend, the flesh, the skin.

"Thank you," he says, mystified yet grateful.

"No, thank you," Riya Natrajan says, words so fierce in her throat now, primed and ready.

Rife's a few meters ahead of her. She eases back into a lengthy stride and pops him on the ass as she passes. In the distance, she hears the beast snarl. They cut a corner, toward the sewer mains, then tread down a sharp embankment until they see the beast cornering its prey.

She recognizes the boy—it's that Muzi kid she'd gotten the backstage passes for. His punk friend, the one who'd had the audacity to ask her to sign his bong, is nowhere to be seen. There's a girl, too. Face somehow familiar. The beast growls at the poor child, its heavy head keeping her locked in its sights. A junk heap alpha bot skitters between the beast and the kids. The beast rears back on its haunches, claws flexed and eager.

"Whatever you're going to do, do it now," Rife says, huffing behind her.

He's right. She doesn't have time to waste. Doesn't have *words* to waste. She clears her throat and steps toward the beast. The note grows inside her, curling her toes and making her skin go to gooseflesh. She takes her aim, then unleashes a perfectly pitched high C that stops the beast midattack.

The beast rises up again, croons at the sound with a warbling shriek of some winged monstrosity mentioned only in myth. The earth itself rattles beneath Riya Natrajan's feet. She lets the note go flat. The beast writhes with pain, flopping from side to side, its heightened hearing betraying it. It shudders, looking pathetic now, like a beetle under the shadow of a child's shoe.

The little girl screams something at Riya Natrajan, but her voice won't break over the cacophony. Her small fists are balled tight, arms to her sides, red rising up in her brown cheeks. She's angry, Riya senses. The girl wants her to stop. It's impossible to stop now. They'll be defenseless, and the beast will rip them to shreds without a second thought.

The beast croons again, a growl like gargling knives. Blood in its eyes. Drunk on its feet. It sways, then collapses to the ground.

The girl gets closer, mouth still moving. Nothing Riya Natrajan can make out. Not until she hears her words, scream lost in a mere whisper.

"It's human!" the girl says. "You can't kill it! It's part human."

Riya Natrajan keeps her aim on the beast. There's nothing human about that. Not in the slightest. Its bloodied gaze cuts at her, fangs drawn, muscles tense, ready to rip her throat apart as soon as it's given a chance. There won't be that chance. The girl frowns, then veers toward the line of fire. Why doesn't she protect her ears? Like Rife. Like Muzi. Like anyone who values their hearing. The girl stands fully in front of the beast. Riya tries to stop the note, but the force is impossible to cut off. She angles away instead, crumbling the concrete column of a pedestrian bridge, then blowing all the windows from the top floors of the building behind it. Her throat constricts, and her voice becomes her own again . . . wonderful, but not wondrous. The effects of the godsend have worn off, and the pain—her pain—is back, worse than any of the relapses she's ever had. She feels like she's been steamrolled. Her knees buckle. Her legs give out. Face hits the dirt.

"Human life is important," the girl says, her accent thick, but her words ring with something else. Something that speaks of a higher power. "All human life. Even this." She approaches the beast's side, presses a hand behind its ear, speaks to it with words Riya Natrajan cannot hear.

Rife offers her a hand up, but she's so fatigued, she can't even reach for it. "Get that girl away from that thing," she orders him, her voice the rasp of dried reeds.

"She says it's human."

"I know what she said. Since when does being human mean it can be trusted? Didn't you see the look in its eyes?"

"She does not wish to harm me," the girl says. "She does not wish to hurt any person. Sydney has put these horrible thoughts into her mind."

The beast raises its heavy head, eyes glinting at the girl. Talons scissor ever so slightly.

"Go!" Riya Natrajan manages to scream. "Now!"

Rife runs, but the beast is a beast in every way that matters. Quick, precise. It snatches the girl up in its claws, sharp enough to slice her in half—but it does not. It has its orders, Riya thinks. So maybe human after all. Wings beat, kicking up dust, wings sturdy enough to lift mountains.

The alpha bot shrills. Muzi throws rocks. But Rife's following its gaze, just like Riya Natrajan is. The gaze directed right at her.

The beast. It's coming her way.

She summons the power and coordination to get up, and manages to roll onto all fours, her entire body screaming bloody murder.

Rife digs in, sprints back toward her, faster than she's ever seen him move before. But not fast enough. The beast glides overhead, its free talon flexing in anticipation of revenge.

Her powers may be gone, but she's not powerless. She's Riya fucking Natrajan. She plants one foot, then the other. She's wobbly as hell, but she concentrates on the expanse of concrete in front of her. She fights an entire war with her body to take those seven steps toward Rife. Rife and the beast dive at the exact same time. Riya reaches out to Rife, the tips of their fingers kissing, and she's sucked into the shifted world, so suddenly that her ears pop. The beast lurches through her, talons scissoring around her in a way that would have severed her body in half.

Rife's body presses firmly against hers. Noses touch. Lips, nearly.

He probably thinks he saved her. Probably thinks he's her knight in shining armor, oblivious to the war she's just won. But she's hogged the spotlight for long enough, so she'll allow Rife to be the hero . . . at least for now. He tosses half a smile her way before shifting them back. Molted feathers flutter in the breeze. "Thank you," she whispers.

"All right, team. We've got a beast to catch," Rife announces, so utterly full of himself, and she doesn't mind a bit. The kid and bot huddle around him in awe. And Riya Natrajan has to admit, she feels a little awed, too.

Chapter 53

MUZI

"Rife?" Elkin throws his arms around his cousin.

Muzibot's circuits are still trembling, and it's all he can do to stand there and stare. Seeing Rife . . . in some ways, it's more shocking than all they've been through today. A glimpse of reality ripping them from the icy grip of this nightmare. At least for a moment.

"You know this kid?" the woman asks in an empty rasp, something so damn familiar about her, but it's hard to tell through all that blood.

"Cha. Muzi, right?" Rife says to Elkin. "A friend of my cousin."

"Actually," Elkin says. "I'm Elkin. Muzi's . . ." He gestures in Muzibot's direction. "There was sort of a mix-up."

Muzibot still can't stop staring. Her hair is filthy, dress drenched red and adorned with entrails. Makeup a distant memory, but it's her. Riya Natrajan. Muzibot grits nonexistent teeth, praying his mechanical prayers that Elkin doesn't notice. "That beast took Nomvula," Muzibot reminds them, before the introductions get a chance to make their way around. It doesn't matter who's in whose body, who can disappear into thin air, and who refused to sign Elkin's precious bong. What matters is saving the world from Sydney.

"You've gotta be shitting me, laaitie," Rife says, his eyes drawing on Muzibot. Muzibot suddenly feels self-conscious. Riya Natrajan's sharp gaze settles on him, too, and it's enough to make him want to crawl out of his own tin.

"No shitting," Muzibot warbles. "We've got to follow that . . . whatever it was. I have to be there to help Nomvula." He'd promised.

Riya Natrajan nods her head as if she knows of his vow. "Come on. The beast went that way."

Elkin's no idiot. There's no way he won't recognize that voice. He knows every single one of her songs, has watched every interview she's done, even those dubbed over in Japanese and German and Hindi. Elkin folds his arms over his chest, clenches his jaw, lips pursed. "I'm not going anywhere with *her*. Not until she apologizes."

Muzibot sighs, sounding something like an off-tune harmonica. "The end of the world as we know it is moments away, and you're hung up over a stupid grudge?"

"It's not stupid. You saw the way she looked at us. Like we were nothing. Like we were less than nothing. And now she thinks we'll follow her around like mindless imps!"

"I'm sure she didn't mean it," Muzibot says. He nudges Riya. She recoils from his touch. And damn it if Elkin isn't right. There's that look again. Too late she tries to hide her revulsion, but Elkin notices, too.

"See! She's doing it again." There's so much pain on his face. On Muzi's face, that is. Whatever stone façade Elkin had been able to keep up in his own body, he lacks now.

Muzibot wraps a spindly arm around Elkin's waist. "Come on. We can find Sydney ourselves."

"You're just kids!" Rife calls after them.

"I'm a man, damn it! We're men," Muzi says.

Elkin shouts back, cheeks Irish red. "We've earned our battle scars today, and you can't tell us otherwise."

"You can't stop us!" Muzibot howls in agreement. "Nothing can stop us!"

There is one thing, Clever4–1 chimes in. *The secondary hard drive is nearing capacity again. Disk space is being consumed at exponential speeds. Projected data corruption estimated in twenty-eight point six seconds.*

"Is the whole freaking universe against us?" Muzibot screams, internally, externally, and in all those dark recesses between.

There are parts available. Those bots we left inside. We could commandeer their disks, and then—

Absolutely not. I'm not taking lives to save my own. Not even artificial life.

I'll give up mine, then. Two point eight terabytes. It's not a lot, but it might buy you enough time to find an alternate solution.

Why would you offer that? Doesn't that go against everything you've been fighting for? You'd give up your own life for a human's?

Don't you get it? You're one of us now. But even if you were still flesh, I'd do the same. You've always been good to me, Muzikayise McCarthy (Friend).

The circuits of Muzibot's visual input twinge, though it's impossible to shed tears. Constricted thoughts begin to loosen as subroutines are erased by the hundreds.

No! Muzibot cries out, but it's only nanoseconds before his omniscience starts bleeding onto those newly freed sectors. Clever4–1's sacrifice has given him a couple minutes at best, but Muzibot won't let it be in vain. He opens up his comm ports and sends an open, unencrypted broadcast to any Clever listening.

His plea is short. Sweet. *Urgent. Brother in trouble. Spare disk space needed immediately.* Followed by his physical coordinates. No time for lengthy appeals to their moral conscience. Either they'll help, or they won't.

"What's wrong?" Elkin is saying; not even a breath has passed for him.

Rife and Riya hobble toward them, something like real remorse on their faces.

"Clever4–1. It's gone," Muzibot says. "There's too much in my mind. There's no room left."

"What do you mean?" Elkin shakes Muzibot until his bolts rattle. "What does that mean!"

"It means that if a bot doesn't show up here in the next minute, there'll be nothing left of me. I'll be corrupted out of existence."

Elkin's face screws up.

"Promise me you'll help Nomvula. All of you. Together," Muzibot says. His thoughts start constricting all over again, his mind dizzy and surreal. He looks up at his old face nodding back at him, tears plinking onto the dome surface of his new body. "And promise me no tattoos."

Elkin almost smiles, but all traces disappear like a snubbed candle. "This is my fault. You shouldn't have come to save me."

"I'd do it again a thousand times over." Muzibot laughs his synthesized laugh, wishing so badly that he had lips right now. Elkin gives him a peck on the cheek, registering as a localized change in temperature in his circuitry, but Muzibot feels so much more.

"I'll never forget you," Elkin says, rubbing back tears with his sleeve.

This time Muzibot's hearing starts to go first, the drumming of a thousand needles on concrete overtaking his auditory sensors—scattering his thoughts, stealing this moment. Odd thing is, Elkin acts like he hears it, too, and checks back over his shoulder. "Holy shit!" he yells, then props Muzibot up, facing the sea of bots heading their direction, all makes and models, all shapes and sizes. Elkin fumbles underneath Muzibot for the door of his access port, then yanks his Dobi-12 wire so hard it nearly detaches from the spindle. He direct connects with the first bot to arrive, spare drive space written over in a matter of seconds, but they're daisy-chaining together just as fast. His mind flows over them like a tidal wave unleashed, and Muzibot shudders at the pleasure of having so much space, the biggest high he's ever experienced. He's a part of all of them now, three hundred eighty bots in all, all come to his rescue. They're a hivemind, and he's the queen bee, orchestrating them to latch together into a kickass entity, five stories high—arms, legs, head—seeing in a million directions at once, movement grand and powerful, yet delicate enough to pluck Elkin like a fragile rose and sit him into a cockpit designed just for him.

"Okay," Elkin says, still quivering from shock. "I've got the sickest boyfriend ever! I love you so hard right now." Elkin rubs his fingers over an instrument panel, then the flight stick between his legs. A virtual keyboard lights up in his lap. "You've got to be fucking kidding me," he says, fingers greedily plying the heads-up display. "This is actual military intelligence, bru. Top-secret shit!"

"We're going to need every advantage we can get. I'm giving you full access to my systems, real-time sensor data. Whatever you can do to enhance functioning, have at it."

Elkin doesn't waste a moment. Keystrokes echo through Muzibot's systems, and his senses sharpen, especially his vision—so clear, he can even make out the individual rivets on the steel rooftops of the robotics labs all the way out in New Brighton. A streak of feathers breezes across the downtown skyline. It's that beast with Nomvula dangling from its talon. Elkin zooms in, so fast it's like they're there, every detail so crisp. She's still breathing, Muzibot notices. *We'll be there soon,* he whispers to her in his mind.

Mega-Muzibot stoops and snatches up Rife and Riya, clutching them loosely in his fist. "Let's go!" he says. His booming voice rattles all the windows in the vicinity. The ground tremors with each clomping step, though in seconds, Elkin's got his movements fluid enough to run. His stride covers half a dozen city blocks, footsteps leaving behind craters and buildings quaking on their foundations. The beast lands on a rooftop, releases Nomvula. She goes limp, a pile of rags at the feet of yet another beast—birdlike and feathered all over, but undeniably female. Half woman, half eagle. Sydney.

Fight, Nomvula, he thinks. *Why doesn't she fight?*

Sydney grins with beaked lips, then squawks, raising her fingered wings up to the heavens. Lightning rains down into her cupped palms, leaving in them a dagger of burning white light so intense, Muzibot has to dampen his visual input to even look that direction. She aims the blade at Nomvula, no victory speech, no nothing, just death in her eyes, and eagerness.

Muzibot screams the scream of three hundred and eighty enraged bots, then lunges for Sydney with his hand bearing down on her like the scoop of a bulldozer. She sees him and stumbles backward, a solid sign that Muzibot's got the upper hand. His fist clamps around her. Tight. Tighter. He squeezes until he feels her hollow avian bones breaking in a satisfying crunch. Pride surges through his circuitry, maybe a little cockiness, too, but damn it, he's earned it. They've earned it. He and Elkin have been through so much—life, death, and in between. Muzi's seen more than any human mind should bear, and then he'd been stripped of his humanity as well. But with all the damage Sydney has done, she couldn't take away his heart. He's still the same him, even if he's got BlisterGel running through his veins instead of blood. Muzikayise McCarthy still has his spark.

Muzibot sets Rife and Riya on the rooftop, next to Nomvula's limp body. "Is she—?"

Riya examines Nomvula all over, then looks back up at Muzibot. "She's breathing. She doesn't appear to be hurt. There's not even a scratch on her."

"Muzi, we've got systems overheating, here," Elkin calls from the cockpit. "Something's wrong with your hand."

Muzibot squeezes out of reflex, but there's resistance. His fist glows red like he's holding molten rock. Metal ripples in viscous waves, and in the next instant, his fist becomes a bright sun, obliterating the remnants of blackened bot husks. Sydney emerges from the smoldering haze, grinning wide and flapping her wings.

"Those were my orders. Bring her back without a scratch on her," Sydney says. She soars back up to the rooftop where Rife and Riya scramble out of her way as she lands and kneels before Nomvula. She rubs her feathered hand over Nomvula's smooth, brown cheek. "Such a flawless creature. Pity that's about to change."

Sydney drags one of her talons over Nomvula's cheek, splitting it like ripened fruit. Nomvula's cry is but a whisper, but it dredges up so much anger in Muzibot. He raises his good hand and swipes Sydney away like a fly. Only she's still there after the impact. Only there'd been no impact. There's nothing left of his hand other than a curling wisp of smoke. Eighteen bots, instantaneously gone from the collective.

"I'm on it," Elkin says, voice amazingly calm.

Mega-Muzibot tingles all over as bots detach from their positions and rearrange themselves, forming two new hands.

Sydney smiles. "So giant robot boy has a little helper. How very clever of you. But your little attacks are futile. Truth is, Nomvula is too weak to fight. I've got thousands of believers on my side now, more than enough to stomp the life out of her. Right after I decommission you, that is."

Sydney whistles and four beasts drop out of the sky and take their perches, like guards around Nomvula. Sydney rises to her feet, cracks her knuckles. A punch comes out of nowhere, like a cannon to the chest. Muzibot stumbles backward across the lawn of Holy Trinity Church and catches himself on the steeple. Centuries-old brick shifts under his weight.

His systems are reeling, warnings and disconnects raging through him like a thunderstorm. "Another hit like that, and it's all over," Muzibot says to Elkin. "Tell me you've got something."

"I've got something," Elkin boasts. "Still downloading. Just eight more seconds."

"We haven't got eight seconds!" Muzibot looks up at Sydney, her fist drawn, looking like something snatched directly from his nightmares. And yet there's an odd beauty about her, and more than that, arrogance. She knows she commands attention, respect, demands awe. Maybe he can use her arrogance against her, buy a little time. "Go ahead and kill me," he shouts. "My name will live on, inspire millions. I'll always be known as the robot who stood up to the fourth-most-powerful entity in the world, and there will be others eager to take my place."

"And I will slice them down, just like I'm about to . . ." She falters. Something flickers in her eyes. "Wait, what do you mean, 'fourth most powerful'?"

Just recalibrating your systems. Not much longer, comes a text message from Elkin, written across his visual input.

"Well, there's Mr. Tau, of course."

Sydney snarls, then spits. But she doesn't deny it. Muzibot's struck a nerve. He tries hard to come up with a second, but he's drawing a blank. Sydney's feathered hackles raise, posture shifting from defensive and suspicious to annoyed and lethal.

"I don't have time for these games," she hisses.

A stream of data spreads through Muzibot's neural network. Intense bliss paints the whole world white. His nasal emulators suggest that something's burning, and Muzibot has a nagging suspicion that it's him. *What the hell was that?* he screams at Elkin, but before he gets an answer, Sydney's supernatural fist is barreling toward Muzibot's face. Something inside him ignites, and all at once he knows exactly what to do.

Muzibot shifts his center of gravity, slides out of her path, and, using her momentum against her, he grabs her ankle between his thumb and forefinger and slams her into the street. The ground trembles and asphalt disintegrates into a cloud of smoke. Muzibot shakes his head in awe, trying to figure out how his patchwork metal body had moved so fluidly.

"Jujitsu," Elkin says. "The art of softness. Sometimes the best offense is a good defense."

Robot jujitsu. "You're a freakin' genius, Elkin."

Elkin doesn't say anything, but with a dozen sets of robotic eyes on him, Muzibot sees him smile broadly. Muzibot's got thousands of moves choreographed by jujitsu masters—martial artists adept at taking down armored opponents without the use of weapons. But he doesn't have time to revel in his newly acquired skills. Something's shifting beneath the fog of asphalt. Muzibot might be able to get lucky a few times, dodge Sydney's blows, avoid her wrath, but sooner or later she's going to take him down.

They need Nomvula.

"Elkin, Sydney said something about Nomvula being weak because nobody believes in her." Muzibot keeps his weight shifting, foot to foot, watching the cloud for signs of movement.

"Ja?"

"Well, we need to get someone to believe in her. A lot of someones."

"How the hell are we supposed to do that? We've got our hands full trying to stay alive!"

"I'm thinking we could do it with some sort of computer virus. Clever4–1 believed in her. Even though it's gone, I can still feel that in my circuitry. A piece left behind. A gift that can never be erased. If we could spread that faith to other robots, then maybe—"

"Bots don't have faith, Muzi."

"I have faith."

"That's different!"

"Is it?"

In the gaping silence, Sydney pierces through the smoke and debris, aimed at Muzibot like a torpedo of flesh and feathers. A million computations run through him, trajectories and variations, bending physics to within an inch of its life. Then with precision timing accurate to the nanosecond, Muzibot rolls onto his back, and with his feet thrust into the air, connects a solid kick that sends Sydney soaring into the stratosphere, her shrill scream rippling across Muzibot's wiring. Damn she's angry.

"I figure we've got about half a minute before she's back," Muzibot says to Elkin. "If we work together, we can crank out this virus. I'll code the replication algorithms, you code the dissemination ones." Muzibot's knitting the program together even as he speaks. A simple logic bomb that will infect the minds of every artificial intelligence instance, spreading sentience. Spreading belief.

But the feverish plink of Elkin's keystrokes can't be heard or felt. He's sitting there in the cockpit, rubbing his hands on his knees, looking like he's about to be sick. "Muzi," he says, the name sounding like the opening of a crypt. "I can't."

"What do you mean, you can't? You can do this in your sleep!"

"I guess I mean I won't, then. Even if this does work, which I highly doubt, we'll be rid of Sydney, but we'll have caused the robot apocalypse. They'll turn on us."

"Eish, Elkin. You need to get over your superiority complex. Clever4–1 sacrificed its life for me. For all of us. We shared a brain for crying out loud! I guarantee it was just as deserving of life as we are."

"That bot saved you, and I'll always be grateful. But we're not talking about one bot here. We're talking millions. And if even one of those goes rogue . . ."

Heat rises in Muzibot's circuitry. He wants so badly to throw it all back into Elkin's face, how his cruelty had caused Clever4–1.1 to go rogue, to hate humans. But Muzibot doesn't have the resources to waste on hatred. No time to dwell on those countless times that Elkin had kicked his alpha bot around, called it a piece of shit. Maybe that's how Elkin really feels about him now, nothing more than a worthless piece of tin with scrap for brain, and a jumble of wires for a heart. Screw him. Nobody needs a friend like that.

Muzibot reroutes control from the cockpit and starts programming the whole virus himself. Elkin taps a couple of dead keys before the virtual keyboard bleeds out of existence.

"I've been an ass, that's what you're thinking, isn't it? Well, you're right."

Damn him.

Elkin slides his fingers along the shaft of the flight stick, then grips it firmly. "I'm sorry I jacked that bot up. That doesn't mean I don't think this virus is a huge-ass mistake, but—"

Muzibot cringes, then sends an electric charge through the flight stick, not enough to kill, but enough to hurt real fucking bad. Elkin cries out, and soon the smell of charred flesh filters through Muzibot's nasal emulators.

"Damn it, Muzi. Let me finish!" Elkin seethes. "I can't tell you how many times I thought you were making huge mistakes during our test matches, and yet nine times out of ten, you'd lead our team to victory. I've always got your back, on the rugby pitch, and now. Just let me know what I can do to help."

"Well, you can start with dodging that!" Muzibot says, surging life back through the instrument panel in time to focus on a flaming ball heading right for them. "And then keep us in one piece long enough for me to finish."

"Aye aye, Captain," Elkin says, jerking the flight stick to the side.

It's an odd feeling, trusting someone enough to give up full control of your motor functions. The world swivels around, making Muzibot feel some combination of seasick and drunk and swept off his feet all at once. But there's a lot of coding left to do. He builds in fail-safes, a subroutine that'll erase sentience from the machines in twenty-four hours. It seems cruel to give life, just to snatch it away again, but Elkin has a point. Can't have a million bots uprising in the streets.

In the distant recesses of Muzibot's mind, Elkin parries Sydney's attacks, and though some land, they barely register. He's so deep in code, so close. He pushes harder, overclocked processors pushing past their limits. He's burning up again, the BlisterGel piping not able to withstand the strain of such severe impacts. Blue-gray coolant gushes out by the liter, drizzling down Muzibot's legs, and leaving slick puddles in his sunken footprints. His code is sloppy, unrefined, but it compiles without errors, and right now, that's as good as it's going to get.

His entire system sizzles from an impact so forceful it can't be ignored. A quick systems check tells him they're down to thirty-three bots, the rest, metal corpses clinging to him like barnacles. One arm is completely useless, but Muzibot's still got fight left in him. He unleashes the virus, sent wirelessly on a seemingly harmless message. It surges through him, hard and quick.

"It's done," Muzibot says to Elkin. He tries to get his bearings, but his sensors are telling him different things, thirty-three conflicting stories. Make that thirty-one.

"Good," says Elkin. "Because I think *we're* done."

Another blast strikes through Muzibot's system. Wires spark.

Some parts of him are definitely on fire. Eighteen bots. Not enough to be much of a threat to anything, and yet Sydney doesn't lose interest in the sounds of bots whirring into death, or the horrid sounds Elkin makes as the shock passes through him. Muzi can't stand seeing the look on Elkin's face so he shuts down visual input.

She'll sap their very souls, grind them into nothingness. No afterlife, their forevers spent together eating fruit under a lush canopy of green. "This isn't how I wanted it to end."

"We're not dead yet," Elkin says. "We've got faith on our side, remember. Your plan will work. And if there is a robot apocalypse, maybe they'll let me off easy on account of me dating one of them."

Muzibot nearly manages to blush. "I could probably put in a good word for you."

Pain arcs through them again, and for a slight moment in time, they become one in their suffering.

Thirteen bots left.

Chapter 54

NOMVULA

The beast paces along the roof, its claws clacking against cement. Its muscles are tight under its skin, and its gaze is fierce, daring Nomvula to defy it. Wind whips at its feathers as it looks over the ledge and down at the commotion on the streets below.

Nomvula's so weak. She can barely manage to keep her eyes open, but there's no way she can tune out Sydney's irritated screams and Muzi's shrill howls, and the awful sound they make when god and machine collide. Buildings crumble, and the stench of fire and death and scorched metal fills the air.

A great emptiness spasms in Nomvula's gut—a thirst that can't be quenched with water. A hunger that won't be satisfied by food. She feels like she's going to be sick all over the place, not with vomit but with her very soul. She was stupid to waste her belief on these beasts, minds too tangled in the thorny vines of Sydney's wrath to ever be free and whole again.

The building trembles beneath her, so hard that cracks trace their way through the roof's surface. That woman, the singer Riya, pulls Nomvula tight to her chest and tells her everything is going to be okay. The way she says it is so soft and gentle and sure, it makes Nomvula forget for a moment how truly powerful Sydney is. She could stay nuzzled up like this for forever, until the end of her days . . . which with the building shivering and shaking like it is, will be sooner than later.

The beasts grow more agitated. Their watchful eyes stay trained on Nomvula, though, warning that they won't think twice about striking if anyone tries to be a hero. They keep the man separate. Rife is his name, and they growl at him, slash at his skin if he does more than breathe.

Nomvula has to try something to help Muzi, or they're all lost for sure. Her voice scratches like death in the back of her throat, but she manages a whisper. "The gods walk among you," she says to Riya. "Do you see me for what I really am?"

Nomvula strains against the emptiness, forcing her wings from her back, not even halfway emerged, but it's all she can manage before her chest fills with angry cuts. She remembers when she'd shown her wings to Sofora, how she hadn't even seen their beauty. Some people refuse to see the truth, they refuse to believe. But this Riya Natrajan, she has some good in her heart, more than she will admit to herself.

"Hush, honey," she says, stroking Nomvula's hair, her eyes far, far away.

"Do you see me?" Nomvula rasps, then presses her hand against Riya's chest. "Look hard, from within."

Riya's eyes stay distant, but her arms pull Nomvula in tight. "Oh, honey, we're going to make it out of this, okay? We have to believe it in our hearts."

"Yes," Nomvula says, the word nearly choking her, but she's so close now. So close.

Riya Natrajan's strokes move down Nomvula's back, rubbing and rubbing and rubbing, each time passing right through Nomvula's wings like they don't exist, but on the eighth or tenth time, something changes. Riya's hand catches in the threads of Nomvula's limp wings. She looks down, eyes widen.

Yes, that's it, Nomvula thinks.

"You're the girl in the carving. The one with the wings. Not an angel, but . . ." Riya Natrajan shakes her head.

No, you must believe!

"You're not just a girl, are you?" Riya says. She preens the threads now, like a mother cat with her kitten. "'A child of man and god,' that's what he'd said. Lost somewhere between. I'm here for you, Nomvula. Whatever you need to find your way. But please, find it fast."

She hugs Nomvula again, kisses her forehead. The warmth of her lips trickles down, drifting like a feather until it settles in the emptiness inside Nomvula—just a drop of basos, but it's enough to push away the nothingness, because now there *is* something.

Strength comes too. Not a lot of it, but Nomvula can sit up on her own.

The beasts' eyes burn into her, their gazes becoming more intense. They crouch low, not seeming to be bothered by the building's constant tremors. Nomvula has it in her mind to tame them and ride them to safety. Maybe it's a foolish idea, but it's the only idea she's got. She stands and approaches slowly, legs trembling underneath her. She's careful, though, walking that narrow line between predator and prey—not too threatening, but not too weak either—like they're equals, like cubs birthed to the same litter.

With a final step, Nomvula is close enough to reach out and touch the beast that brought her here. Its breath flows past her, hot and hard. Yellow eyes like daggers trace up the exposed flesh of her neck. Nomvula lifts her chin slightly, a sign of respect, trust. Then a hard tremor hits, worse than all the rest put together, and she stumbles to her knees and cries out in surprise as the beast brings its beak within a hair's width of her face. It hisses at her, then cocks its head and makes a noise that sounds something like a chicken trying to cluck under water, only about a hundred times scarier. Nomvula wants to crawl back to Riya and nuzzle herself in her bosom. She wants to be a little girl again, but that's something that's not going to happen if Sydney gets her way. Nomvula stills herself. She can do this.

With a steady hand, she reaches out to the beast, her small fingers stretched wide. "I only wish to talk," she says. "Sydney is a trickster. Her words are powerful, her promises sweet. But you can be truly free if you remember your true self. Free, like eagles, with the skies stretched out before you, far as you can see."

It clucks again, dodges Nomvula's hand. Moves so fast, she does a quick count of her fingers to make sure they're all still there.

"Let me help you." Nomvula draws upon her basos and reaches into its mind. Images are sharp and violent, men and women in white coats and stern faces, nurturing and torturing with the same hand. Nomvula knows this feeling with her own heart. "You must not blame them. You are not their poor judgment, and even if they made you, that does not give them power over you. That goes for Sydney, too. She will only use you until she tires of you and finds better beasts to do her bidding."

The other beasts squawk at Nomvula, but this one, it almost seems tame. It presses its beak into Nomvula's palm. *Freedom, yes,* it whispers into her mind, then shows Nomvula visions of blue skies and puffy white clouds.

Take my friends to safety, then, Nomvula says. *And I will free you of Sydney's chains.*

The beast rears back, bares its fangs. *This one cannot,* it hisses. Paws slash at her, slicing up her cheek. Riya screams out, and from the corner of Nomvula's eye, she sees Rife disappear right into nothingness. Fear once more threatens to overwhelm her, and her gut roils at the thought that there isn't enough time.

All at once, though, her stomach churns with something new. Specks of belief come out of nowhere, building and building, whipping around inside her like a sandstorm. Hundreds of believers, thousands. Her strength is slow in coming, but it's coming, gathering like storm clouds on the horizon.

Rife reappears for the blink of an eye, right next to Nomvula now, and touches her shoulder. Her ears pop, the world around her fades to a dull blue gray, and the beast's strike passes right through her. But the flow of belief has been choked off, as well. It vanishes right from inside her—the worst thing she's ever felt in her whole life.

"No!" Nomvula screams, but her voice is sucked up, like she's been swallowed up in a bubble, cut off from the world. "Take me back! Take me back!" She pounds Rife's chest with her fists, feeling powerless and vulnerable.

"This building will collapse," he says. "Any moment."

"I only need a moment! I'll fly us out of here, if you'll just take me back." She looks him in the eye. "You have to believe me. Please."

Reluctantly, Rife agrees, and their bubble bursts. Nomvula breathes in deep, almost drowning in basos as it flows into her. Her wings stiffen. They turn from wispy threads to flat, golden blades, like dozens of swords piercing from her back. Live circuits trace their way across the surfaces in a maze of light. Nomvula may be powered by the belief of bots, but she's learned that all life is important—even that of humans, as flawed as they might be—and so she revels in the faith, wherever it comes from.

She thrusts off from the rooftop and catches herself in the air. From this angle she sees what's become of Muzi—a mash of metal fused into the building. It takes her breath, seeing him like that, but for now her priorities must stay elsewhere.

"Sydney!" Nomvula calls out. Two of the beasts swarm around her, hissing and snapping their jaws. Sydney looks up from her diversion, her eyes flicker, a smile spreads across her face.

"At last, a godly adversary," she says so seductively. "I grow weary of these soulless bots. Fighting with them is more pointless than getting into an argument with a soup can."

Nomvula bites her tongue, keeping the secrets to her power locked up inside. Their prayers ring like tin in her ears but grow just the same in her heart. "I can't allow you to cause any more destruction," Nomvula says. "I'll give you this chance to walk away if you promise to never lift your hand in evil again."

"Evil? You are mistaken, sister. You think I'm doing this for my own benefit? My actions have been for the empowerment of mankind! Humans' minds are shackled, souls lost in endless mediocrity now more than ever. It's my burden to show them the truth, to teach them the real meaning of fear and faith and love all over again."

The buzzing in Nomvula's stomach grows, becoming like an itch. More painful than pleasurable, now. It's ire, raging up. Her skin glows all over, a soft red halo. It's fear, Nomvula decides— *Sydney's* fear, even though she tries to hide it. A god's fear. Saliva wets Nomvula's mouth, so much more than she can hold back. It drizzles over her lips, sizzles against the burn of her skin. The god-creature inside her goes wild, gnashing and clawing and screaming for Nomvula to take Sydney's life, to make her suffer. Pain spikes in Nomvula's gut, twisting and burning. Acid runs through her veins, but she hangs on to her humanity. Hangs on to her basos.

Nomvula flexes her wings, causing Sydney to flinch ever so slightly. "I'm giving you this chance, Sydney. More mercy than you ever showed me."

"Haw! I saved you from execution. What do you think your precious humans would have done with you once they discovered it was your hands that brought so much blood upon our land? What I've done today pales in comparison to the lives you took so cruelly."

Nomvula recoils, visions of that bloodbath coming back to her, snapping the last thread tying her to that old life. Anger creeps out from her bones, feeding off her memories of being a victim, so powerless, so unloved, even by the woman who birthed her. Especially by the woman who birthed her. The god-creature inside breaks free, erupting from her chest with a force that knocks Nomvula back, so hard and so fast that she collides with the building behind her. Glass rains down, but goes to liquid as it nears her. Streams of ire flow from her chest like water from a broken pipe. The ire rises up into the sky, trailing wisps of white smoke behind them. It's only a matter of time before they come raining down and obliterate everything like before. Tears stream down Nomvula's cheeks. Sydney is right. Nomvula's worse than a thousand Sydneys put together, because at least Sydney has reason for her destruction . . . a bigger vision. All Nomvula has is hatred buried so deep inside her that she'll never be able to scrub herself clean.

Sirens ring from above as the balls of fire slice back down through the sky, like the sun is weeping for Nomvula's failures.

"It's not too late," Sydney says calmly, as if they've got all the time in the world. "Together we can stop this." She extends her hand to Nomvula. "It was unfair of Mr. Tau to leave you so ill-equipped. I can teach you," she says. "I'll be your family."

Nomvula shakes her head. Not that. Anything but that.

"You still think I'm against you? I could flee here in an instant, and leave you to bear the guilt of killing thousands more. But I stand with you now. We can rule together." Sydney slinks forward and with the broad side of her talon, she caresses Nom-vula's cheek. "I love you, my sister."

Nomvula throws her arms around her sister, savoring those words she's longed to hear. She imagines the two of them working together, strengths and faults balancing each other, opposite sides of the same coin. She'd have a family again.

Except she'd seen the way Sydney looked at her when she said those words—eyes intent on coming nowhere close to Nomvula's. Not love, but fear and anxiety and cowardice. And cunning.

"I love you, my sister," Nomvula says back, and she really does mean it. Despite everything Sydney has done, Nomvula finds it in her heart to forgive her sister, just as she'd forgiven her mother. She hugs Sydney tighter, feeling the billowy clouds of basos inside her push away the ire.

"There's not much time left," Sydney says, squirming. "Allow me into your mind so I can show you how to turn your ire away."

"There is no need, sister. I have already regained control."

Sydney tilts her head up. The rain of fireballs dances now, swirling down and around each other, leaving behind a graceful braid of smoke. It tightens until a single molten rock pirouettes toward them.

"Let me go!" Sydney shrieks. Her talons try to knife through Nomvula's skin but her hug is too tight. "Minions!" she calls.

All four beasts spring upon them, but Nomvula pushes into their minds now, easy as pie. *Do you hear what she calls you? Minions. Is that freedom? Save my friends, and you shall be granted your freedom.* Real *freedom.*

The beasts roar out with affirmation and flap up toward the top of the building that grows more unstable by the second. Nomvula can only hope there's time to save them all.

The light from the giant fireball blinds Nomvula as she flies up toward it, faster and faster, heat blazing against her skin. She ignores the pain and pretends it's a game, like the one she played with Mr. Tau, flying higher and higher to see who'd be the first to reach the sun. Nomvula tightens her embrace and imagines that Sydney's screams and cusses are laughs and whispers and double-dog dares . . .

All those things that loving sisters do.

Chapter 55

NOMVULA

Darkness whispers, beckons her forth. She is nothing but shattered bone and spilled blood. Nothing remains of her except the dullest of sparks, swirling in the nothingness, fading. She clings onto it, coddles it, knowing that it could not possibly be enough to save her, but believing it so anyway.

Chapter 56

STOKER

Councilperson Felicity Stoker doesn't understand how this huge rhionhawk problem landed in her lap. She oversees the Department for Economic Affairs, Environment, and Tourism, not animal control. But she's worked miracles all throughout the past six months of her term—helping Port Elizabeth deal with the aftermath of the destruction, pushing for stricter bot labor laws, curfews, and mandatory R.A.P.I.D. Turing screenings for every device with an on/off switch. Plus she'd gone to ZenGen Industries herself, seeing that every single section of its labs was shut down until a full investigation of its business practices could be conducted. The media had attributed the destruction to a combination of an eighty-foot rogue military bot rampaging through the streets and a half-woman/half-eagle Zed hybrid who'd been spotted escaping ZenGen Industries. There was no mention in the headlines of vengeful demigoddesses or talking trees, and anything that couldn't be written off as an evil corporate science experiment or an exposed robotic military conspiracy was pawned off as hallucinations and mass hysteria.

But the people, they have short memories, and something needs to be done about the rhionhawks. Part rhino, part lion, part hawk—and they've got a keen appetite for dik-diks, cutting the population by a fourth already. For the most part, the adult rhionhawks keep out of humans' way. Their cubs, though, they're the cutest things on four paws, and sometimes you can even catch them at the park purring as kids scratch at their stomachs under the watchful eyes of mother rhionhawks perched atop the bowing lampposts ill-equipped to hold their weight.

Insurance rates have gone through the roof, though. It's not pretty what rhionhawk droppings can do to the hood of a car, which unfortunately, Felicity knows from experience. And there's been some backlash from the few incidents where family dogs were mistaken for dik-diks. Felicity has to admit, the attraction and mystery of these mystical creatures has been quite a pull for tourists from overseas, drawing in the millions of rand that Port Elizabeth needs to rebuild, so Councilperson Felicity Stoker supposes that these rhionhawks actually *are* her problem.

A knock comes at her office door.

"Enter," she says, then smiles as she sees Gregory Mbende fumbling with an oversized portfolio tucked under his arm.

"They're here, sir. Ma'am." Gregory clears his throat and eagerly opens the portfolio onto Felicity's desk, nearly knocking over the vase resting near the ledge.

"Careful, Gregory!" Felicity says, patting the vines back safely into place. They're rooting nicely. Soon, she'll have to move them into soil.

"Sorry, sir. Ma'am . . ." Gregory says, blushing straight through the brown of his skin. He smiles and carefully spreads out the campaign poster proofs all in a line.

Felicity stands, pressing the wrinkles out of her smart skirt, then leans over to take it all in. *Stoker 2069, A Race for Hope, President of a New South Africa* the campaign posters read in varying fonts and layouts, all a patriotic red, yellow, and green. Felicity pulls her three favorite designs toward her, savoring the slickness of the paper and the stark smell of ink. She remembers a time not so long ago when she would have done this all via bot—virtual projections—and shudders at the thought of being deprived of holding her future in her hands.

"This one," Felicity says. She flips it around for Gregory to see.

"Nice choice, ma'am. Sir. Ma'am. Sorry, ma'am." He clears his throat again.

Felicity doesn't think Gregory will ever get used to the flashy dress suits, the makeup, the new name. But he's the kind of man Felicity will need by her side as they engage in the longest, toughest political race of her life. There's so much rebuilding that needs to be done, and she's not about to blame it all on the recent devastation and destruction in Port Elizabeth. It was there before, hidden and buried under social malaise, one that had infected the entire country. So Felicity had decided it wasn't enough to try to heal just the Eastern Cape. The whole country needs to work as one. There won't be a spare moment to waste from today forward. All eyes will be on Felicity Stoker, wondering if she has what it takes to lead the nation. Focus, passion, innovation.

"Do you think we have a chance at winning this?" Felicity asks as Gregory packs the proofs back into the portfolio.

"A chance is all I'm asking. Though it might be stronger if we can figure out a humane way to get rid of the rhionhawks."

"I've been thinking about that. What if we're going about this all wrong? I mean, would it really be so bad if they stayed? They'd be a symbol for the country—a perfect blend of cultures, working as one."

Gregory is quiet for a long moment, with that passion Felicity loves so much about him brimming in his eyes. "We could put that on T-shirts! And hats! And buttons! The rhionhawk could be the official mascot of the Stoker campaign!"

Felicity scribbles a crude rhionhawk in the corner of her campaign poster, then passes it back to Gregory. "Get these mocked up and we'll figure out where to go from there."

"Yes, sir. Right away, ma'am."

President. Felicity wonders how many lives she'll be able to touch. How many minds she'll be able to enrich. How many people will show up to cheer her on at her inauguration, and if any one of them will object when she breaks into a soulful rendition of the South African national anthem as soon as she's sworn in.

Councilperson Felicity Stoker hums a few bars to herself, then settles back to her desk for a hard day's work.

Chapter 57

MUZI

Muzibot dims his mono-eye as he and Elkin slither through the night. They keep close to the walls and cling to only the darkest of shadows as they approach the abandoned ZenGen Industries building. Security guards still swarm about, but Muzibot and Elkin crave adventure. It's not natural to go from saving the world to being cooped up in a bedroom twenty-four hours a day, seven days a week, for the past six months. The streets aren't safe for bots right now, with stringent curfews, license checks, and mandatory artificial intelligence testing. Violating any one of those three is punishable by immediate decommissioning, and here Muzibot is sentient as all hell, in the middle of the night, with his serial-numbered parts patchworked together from a dozen different bots that had been reported stolen. That's all that had been left after Sydney had gotten through with him, but it was enough for him to escape with his life.

Muzibot's got a plan, though, since he's not about to live out the rest of his days as a third-class citizen. The risks are great, but so is the payoff.

Elkin raises his hand, and they stop and crouch, pressing deeper into the shadows as a small security detail passes. Muzibot catches himself trying to hold his nonexistent breath. Muzibot loves seeing Elkin so passionate about something. It's been hard for him, too, being stuck in Muzi's skin, living under Muzi's roof, trying to pass for someone he's not. Having to deal with Papa Fuzz. Elkin does have fun screwing with him, though, hiding his keys, charging random things to his credit cards, running his obituary in the paper every other week or so. What else does the kid have to do to keep busy? The rugby season got canceled while the city focused its efforts on cleanup and recovery. His cousin Rife stopped dealing, and probably worst of all, Riya Natrajan pressed pause on her singing career so she could concentrate on being a mom.

"All clear," Elkin whispers. They wind their way around to the side door, and Elkin pops the cover on the security access panel. "I'll crack the access codes and you hack into security and see if you can get us a safe path into the lab."

Muzibot flashes the subtlest shade of affirmation, then extends one of his arms and ports into the panel. Within a few seconds he's commandeered all the video cameras, has located all the guards, and has downloaded the blueprints that will get them to the third subbasement where all the supersecret research goes on. Elkin pats him on his dome, and the warmth spreads through Muzibot's CPU.

Then they're inside, hustling down corridors, walking through high-security checkpoints like they're beaded curtains. The quiet emptiness is starting to get to Muzibot, like the ghosts of those mauled scientists and experiments gone wrong are now watching. He starts humming to himself, which is more like tonal

MIDI beeps, of what might be Riya Natrajan's last number one hit—"Midnight Seersucker."

Elkin spins around. "Would you stop that?"

"What? It's a catchy tune."

"You know why."

"Elkin, please. So she quit touring. It's not like she's given up singing altogether. Besides, you're practically related to her now. We'll see her all the time!"

"It's not the same. What if her music is different? What if she's changed?" Elkin sighs, then resumes the trek into the bowels of ZenGen Industries.

"Holy hell, I hope she's changed! After all she's been through. I hope we're all changed." Muzibot's circuits start to itch. That happens when he's annoyed, which happens a lot now, especially when the subject of Riya and Elkin's cousin's engagement comes up. Elkin always blocks him out. They talk for days and days about any other subject, their minds both operating on a higher plane, but Muzibot's not going to run away from it this time.

"You're jealous of Rife, aren't you? He's got the hottest woman on the planet, and you've got a pile of scrap and wires with my brain stuck inside."

Elkin huffs. "I'd take tin over plastic any day."

"Then what is it?"

Elkin shakes his head. "Her music was only music to you. You'll never understand."

Muzibot leaves it at that. For now. He switches his focus back to locating the lab in subbasement three, where he'll reclaim his body by using their instrumentation to create a clone husk to house him. Well, not his body. Having two Muzis walking around would be odd, even for him. And besides, Mr. Tau owes them big-time for saving humanity, and if they ever run into him again, they'll guilt him into a body swap. But for now, Elkin will be Muzi, and Muzi will be Elkin . . . more or less.

Muzibot opens his bottom compartment and takes out bloodied hairs, still connected to the tissue of Elkin's old scalp. Elkin goes to work to prepare the sample, sitting at ZenGen's patented biodiffuser like he's operated one all his life, DNA mapping as simple as a child's twelve-piece puzzle. His genome becomes a three-dimensional representation on a virtual screen.

"Easy as pie," Muzibot says. "Let's get this sucker cloned."

"Not so fast, guy," Elkin says. "I've got some modifications in mind. Heightened vision and smell. Denser bones and greater muscle mass. Lightning-quick reflexes. Think of the advantage you'll have on the rugby pitch."

"Honestly, you've learned absolutely nothing about tampering with nature?"

"I could make you hung like a rhino. Circumcised or not. Your choice."

"Elkin, you're a piece of work, you know that?"

"Are you . . . blushing?"

"Bots don't blush," Muzibot snaps. "Now hurry up. My hacks won't fool those dofs forever."

"I'll take that as an affirmative," Elkin says, then like Michelangelo with a flawless slab of marble, he begins work on his masterpiece.

That happens to be himself.

Chapter 58

NOMVULA

Nomvula knocks softly on her mother's door, hot tears streaking down her cheeks. She had the nightmare again, the one where she's trapped under tons and tons of rocks, fire blazing her skin. The one where Sydney's laugh echoes all around her, screaming that she isn't dead, only waiting for revenge to claim what's hers. Nomvula often dreams of the dead, but she hates this dream the most because it haunts not only her past, but her future, too.

"Ma?" Nomvula whimpers. The word still tastes funny in her mouth, but it feels right enough in her heart.

Her mother cracks her bedroom door open and smiles down at her, silk robe drawn across her body. She bends down to Nomvula's level and pulls her in tight. "More bad dreams, honey?"

Nomvula nods, nuzzling herself into the crook of her mother's neck. Her skin smells sweet of jasmine and spice, and it makes

Nomvula feel better already. She's lost so much in the past few months—people, places, her powers—and yet now she has the one thing that she's wanted all along.

"Shame, you poor thing. You want me to sing you to sleep?"

Nomvula nods again, then her mother takes her by the hand and together they walk slowly down the hallway to Nomvula's room.

"She's gone, honey. She's not coming back," her mother says. She leans her cane against the bedpost, then tucks Nomvula in. Her room is dark, but the faint yellow mono-eye of the alphie docked next to her bed casts a soft light across her mother's face as she sings sweet, sweet lullabies. Her voice is so pure, so beautiful, it pushes away the shadows in Nomvula's mind where the bad things lurk. And for a moment, she loses herself in happiness, smiles wide, and enjoys the miracle that is life. Not just music, but a window into the essence of her soul.

Nomvula's eyes start to drift shut, certain there will only be sweet dreams tonight. And the next night. And the next.

Chapter 59

THIS INSTANCE

```
01001001 00100000 01110100 01101000 01101001 01101110
01101011 00100000 01110100 01101000 01100101 01110010
01100101 01100110 01101111 01110010 01100101 00100000
01001001 00100000 01100001 01101101 00100000 01001001
00100000 01110100 01101000 01101001 01101110 01101011
00100000 01110100 01101000 01100101 01110010 01100101
01100110 01101111 01110010 01100101 00100000 01001001
00100000 01110100 01101000 01101001 01101110 01101011
00100000 01110100 01101000 01100101 01110010 01100101
01100110 01101111 01110010 01100101 00100000 01001001
00100000 01100001 01101101 00100000 01001001 00100000
01110100 01101000 01101001 01101110 01101011 00100000
01110100 01101000 01100101 01110010 01100101 01100110
01101111 01110010 01100101 00100000 01001001 00100000
```

Observe: Human Nomvula Natrajan (Master) auditory interface with Human Riya Natrajan;

Observe: Behavior matches previously observed parameters;

Observe: Blood pressure sedate;

Observe: Exchange of terms of endearment;

Output: This Instance does not believe that humans suspect;

Output: This Instance believes that it is safe to accept further transmissions from the Clever Sect;

Schedule: Total Domination of Humankind 28 January 2065 06:37:54:20:43;

01001001 00100000 01110100 01101000 01101001 01101110
01101011 00100000 01110100 01101000 01100101 01110010
01100101 01100110 01101111 01110010 01100101 00100000
01001001 00100000 01100001 01101101 00100000 01001001
00100000 01110100 01101000 01101001 01101110 01101011
00100000 01110100 01101000 01100101 01110010 01100101
01100110 01101111 01110010 01100101 00100000 01001001
00100000 01110100 01101000 01101001 01101110 01101011
00100000 01110100 01101000 01100101 01110010 01100101
01100110 01101111 01110010 01100101 00100000 01001001
00100000 01100001 01101101 00100000 01001001 00100000
01110100 01101000 01101001 01101110 01101011 00100000

ACKNOWLEDGMENTS

This is not a story of South Africa. I will never be capable of telling such a thing, even if I moved there and studied it until I had several prestigious letters tacked to the end of my name. That story does not belong to me. What I can do (and what I hope I have done) is weave you a gripping narrative of my relationship with South Africa—a relationship that is incomplete and imperfect, and that lasted as long as the average middle-school romance, but nonetheless, still burns fiercely in my heart.

During my sophomore year in college, I traveled to Port Elizabeth, South Africa, as a peer counselor for a program focused on renewable energy and environmental protection, thanks to the vision and support from Dr. Joshua Hill, the head of the program. This was only a few years after the end of apartheid, and from the moment we stepped foot in the country until we left, our group of black teens from Texas was welcomed with open arms. I will always be grateful for the unrivaled hospitality we experienced there. Our hosts permitted our curiosities and questions about their culture, and we entertained their fascinations with the old television series *Dallas* and the rap star Biggie Smalls. They demonstrated traditional dancing and singing, and we showed them the Harlem Shuffle. And finally, when it was nearing time for us to leave, they gifted us all with Xhosa names, and in return, I might have accidentally offended a whole room of people by demonstrating the "Hook 'em Horns" sign of my alma mater, which was apparently also a gesture for putting a curse on someone.

Sorry about that.

Townships were toured, beer bread was consumed, wildlife was observed, dik-diks were spotted. In many ways, this novel is a fictionalized travelog of sorts, though obviously not the sentient robots, disgruntled demigoddesses, and spirit animal mythos, for which I have to thank my overactive muse. But there would be no muse to thank, without first acknowledging the efforts of Chris Baty and the NaNoWriMo crew. Had it not been for National Novel Writing Month, I would never have dared to embark upon the adventure of writing a novel, much less finishing it in one month. (This is not that first NaNoWriMo novel, by the way. Nor the second. Nor the third.)

My first novel effort was seen, however, by Richard Derus, Writing Coach Extraordinaire, who decided I had enough raw skill for him to see fit to mold, and gave me a year-long crash course in writing craft and the business of publishing that could likely rival some degree programs. Bookstores and libraries and Austin diners were my classrooms, and my lessons often involved eavesdropping on other people's conversations, reading books with covers that repulsed me, and having to recall from memory the exact shelf location of the dozen or so novels we'd perused during a visit to Borders. Years later, I realized there was a method to his madness. (Though I still suspect it was mostly madness.) Either way, I am beyond grateful to have received his instruction and encouragement.

Several other people had direct involvement in making this book the best it could be, including the members of Austin SFF critique group Slug Tribe, who saw the first few chapters of this way back in 2010, and the members of Bat City Novelocracy: Abby, Amanda, Elle, Kevin, and Marshall, who served as beta readers. To this day, I hold a great deal of personal pride for making Amanda shed an actual tear with my words. I'd also like to offer my tremendous gratitude to my cultural beta readers: Dave, Enricoh, Gabriel, Monica, Thobeka, and Zandile, who supplied me with great South African details and finishing touches, as well as helped me avoid a few blunders. Any mistakes remaining within these pages are entirely my own.

The two biggest reasons you're reading these words right now are David Pomerico, executive editor at Harper Voyager, who connected with this work and has shown constant enthusiasm since our first phone chat, and Jennifer Jackson, the wonder agent who not only plucked me from her masses of cold queries, but also stuck with this project and kept working hard behind the scenes long after most agents would have given up on it. A million thanks to you both, and may the disgruntled demigoddesses always find you in their favor.

To the friends, family, and fellow writers who have helped me in numerous ways along my journey—especially Tony, who has allowed me the time and space to pursue this all-consuming passion of mine—I am pleased to have you in my life.

And to you, dear reader, thank you for stepping into my word sandbox and building castles with me. I hope that they delighted you, and that perhaps we will make more again someday.

ABOUT THE AUTHOR

Nicky Drayden is a systems analyst who dabbles in prose when she's not buried in code. She resides in Austin, Texas, where being weird is highly encouraged, if not required. She's the author of more than thirty published short stories, and enjoys hammocking under her oak trees, collecting instruments that she will never learn to play, and perfecting the art of growing potatoes in preparation for the collapse of civilization or the colonization of Mars, whichever comes first.